"Let's start our work together with our first rule."

"What's that?" Abby asked.

"Honesty. If I don't understand something you say, I'll ask you. You do the same with me."

"I like that rule."

"Good. Now, what should be our next rule?"

"We make this fun for the teens and for ourselves. If we act as if this is drudgery, the kids will sense it, and we'll lose our chance to help them."

"Fun?" David arched his brows as if responding to something he'd heard in his head, then sighed. "That may be harder for me to follow than the first rule. Nobody's ever described me as fun. In fact, the opposite."

"Well, then we'll have to see how we can change that, ain't so?"

He gave her the faintest grin, but she took it as a victory. As they continued to talk about possible activities for the youngsters, she couldn't doubt he cared about his daughter and her friends. He was a man of strong emotions, though he tried to hide that fact. She couldn't help wondering why.

LOVE INSPIRED®
INSPIRATIONAL ROMANCE

Recycling programs
for this product may
not exist in your area.

ISBN-13: 978-1-335-62187-0

Easter in Amish Country

Copyright © 2023 by Harlequin Enterprises ULC

An Amish Easter Wish
First published in 2020. This edition published in 2023.
Copyright © 2020 by Jo Ann Ferguson

Anna's Forgotten Fiancé
First published in 2018. This edition published in 2023.
Copyright © 2018 by Carrie Lighte

For questions and comments about the quality of this book, please contact us at CustomerService@Harlequin.com.

Love Inspired
22 Adelaide St. West, 41st Floor
Toronto, Ontario M5H 4E3, Canada
www.LoveInspired.com

Printed in U.S.A.

Easter in
Amish Country

Jo Ann Brown

&

Carrie Lighte

2 Uplifting Stories

An Amish Easter Wish and *Anna's Forgotten Fiancé*

LOVE INSPIRED
INSPIRATIONAL ROMANCE

CONTENTS

Jo Ann Brown loves stories with happily-ever-after endings. A former military officer, she is thrilled to write about finding that forever love all over again with her characters. She and her husband (her real hero who knows how to fix computer problems quickly when she's on deadline) divide their time between western Massachusetts and Amish country in Pennsylvania. She loves hearing from readers, so drop her a note at joannbrownbooks.com.

Books by Jo Ann Brown

Love Inspired

Amish of Prince Edward Island

Building Her Amish Dream
Snowbound Amish Christmas

Green Mountain Blessings

An Amish Christmas Promise
An Amish Easter Wish
An Amish Mother's Secret Past
An Amish Holiday Family

Amish Spinster Club

The Amish Suitor
The Amish Christmas Cowboy
The Amish Bachelor's Baby
The Amish Widower's Twins

Visit the Author Profile page at LoveInspired.com for more titles.

AN AMISH EASTER WISH

Jo Ann Brown

Let your light so shine before men,
that they may see your good works,
and glorify your Father which is in heaven.
—*Matthew* 5:16

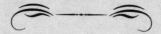

For Justin and Mikayla,
who are writing a beautiful love story of their own.

Chapter One

Evergreen Corners, Vermont

"Is he here yet?" Abby Kauffman called.

The freezer couldn't have picked a worse time to stop working. Supper must be served in three hours, and nothing was started. Worse, tonight was supposed to be a festive gathering for the local teen volunteers and their families, as well as those from Amish Helping Hands who'd come to help rebuild the small town.

Abby scanned the list of food stored in the freezer and sighed. It might not be an accurate list because she and the other volunteers working in the community center's kitchen had made it from memory. Nobody wanted to lift the top of the chest freezer and peer inside to count the boxes of meat and frozen vegetables and tomato sauce. A specific inventory wasn't necessary. With hundreds of dollars of donated food inside the freezer, every minute counted.

She went to the wide pass-through window from the kitchen to the main room of the community center. A trio of young people were lounging among the collection of mismatched tables and chairs where the volunteers had their meals. She'd lost count of the number of breakfasts, lunches and suppers they'd served since the October flood five months ago had washed away houses and businesses along Washboard Brook and damaged more buildings farther from its banks.

So tonight, in addition to the ten to fifteen volunteers who needed to be fed at each meal, there would be almost twice that number joining them for a roast beef dinner with the fixings. The meat had been thawed, but the volunteers' favorite part of the meal—the pies—were in the freezer. Digging through the containers inside to find the unbaked pies would mean allowing precious cold air to escape, threatening the rest of the food stored in the chest freezer.

Where was the repairman? She'd found his name on a list in the community center office and called. He'd said he'd be there as soon as he could, and that had been almost two hours ago.

She put her hands on the counter and looked toward the door. When she hit her head on the pass-through, she grimaced and rubbed her heart-shaped white *kapp*. She was only a few inches over five feet tall, so she wasn't used to having to duck. One of these days, she was going to remember how low the top of the window was and stop bumping her head on it.

How she wished she could be more like her older brother! Isaac never overlooked a single detail about anything. She'd heard one of the residents of their small Vermont town, far to the north of Evergreen Corners, describe her brother as having a laser focus. She couldn't agree more. When Isaac was involved, nobody had to worry about the smallest item being forgotten.

Isaac was at home on the family farm, and she was working in the community center kitchen in Evergreen Corners for at least the next six weeks. If needed, she would stay on, though that might not make her family happy. She couldn't walk away when people needed her here. Since her *daed* had recently remarried, she no longer had to take care of the household as she'd done since her *mamm*'s death almost twenty years ago. Her stepmother, Lovina, was a skilled cook and housekeeper who could handle everything on her own.

And, more important, in Evergreen Corners, Abby could avoid anyone who reminded her of the worst days of her life, days after her selfishness almost caused a young man's death. Busying herself with work allowed her to pay forward to others the blessing she'd been given, a blessed reprieve when the young man recovered. She kept on working, day after day, because she couldn't forget her guilt about how her foolish decision had nearly led to tragedy.

"Is he here yet?" Abby called again as she came out into the main room.

As if on cue, the outside door opened. A man she didn't know stepped in. Seeing he carried a battered metal toolbox, she opened her mouth to tell him to hurry to the kitchen and check the freezer before the food began to defrost, but no sound emerged as she stared.

He moved with the ease of a man who was comfortable with his long limbs. His shoulders were muscular beneath his unzipped coat. Black hair was ruffled by the cap he'd removed as he'd entered, and a single curl dropped across his forehead toward his full eyebrows. His eyes, as brilliant blue as a spring sky, looked around the room.

"Are you the repairman?" Abby managed to ask before his gaze reached her. She scolded herself for reacting like a hormonal teenager at the sight of a *gut*-looking man.

And an *Englischer* at that!

Isaac would be more than annoyed if he heard she was gawking at an *Englischer* with her mouth open like a fish pulled from a pond.

The man glanced her way. He took note of her plain clothes and *kapp*, and his assertive brows lowered in a frown. However, his voice, as he spoke, was a pleasant baritone. "I'm David Riehl." He crossed the room and held out a business card with words and logo to match the ones embroidered on his coat. "Riehl's Appliance Repair."

Startled how her fingers trembled as she reached for the card, Abby nodded. Again, she didn't trust her voice. She stored the card in the pocket of the black apron covering her dark green dress and motioned toward the kitchen. She walked in that direction, aware with every molecule how David followed a few paces behind her.

As they entered the kitchen, voices burst out behind her. Had the teenagers waiting to hear where they were working today gone silent when David entered, or had she been so focused on the handsome man that her other senses had stopped working?

Abby gave her thoughts a *gut* shake. She should be thinking of one thing: getting the freezer fixed. She stepped aside as he put his toolbox on the floor and walked around the freezer that sat in ominous silence. When he asked about the brand and model number, she answered, glad he hadn't yanked up the top to look.

Her shoulders eased from their taut line. David Riehl of Riehl's Appliance Repair knew what he was doing. Sending up a quick prayer of thanks, she watched as he put his hand on the freezer. She guessed he was searching for any vibration to give him a clue why the freezer wasn't working.

"When did you notice a problem?" he asked, not looking at her.

"It was running this morning. Then the compressor stopped, and it didn't start again."

"That could be caused by a few things, but let's look at the obvious ones first." He pulled a small flashlight from beneath his coat and switched it on. "I'll check the evaporator coils first. Dust and dirt get on them. It's almost like you're suffocating the unit because moisture can't evaporate. That may keep the compressor from starting."

"Our kitchen is clean."

He arched his brows before squatting to peer behind the freezer. "Even the best housekeepers forget to keep the coils clean."

"Or sweep under the refrigerator."

"Exactly." He tilted his head and glanced at her with a cool smile. "I don't mean to insult you or any of the volunteers. We appreciate you coming here to help." He shifted the flashlight to examine the freezer from another angle. "Looks pretty dust-free."

Straightening, he moved around to the other side and reached to pull the plug out of its outlet.

"Must you unplug it?" Abby asked.

"If I don't want to get zapped, yes." When he smiled this time, it wasn't as icy as the interior of the freezer should have been. She wouldn't describe his expression as warm, but at least it seemed genuine. "Don't worry. It won't take long to do a diagnostic on the freezer, and you said when you called the shop the contents are tightly packed. That should keep them cold far longer than you expect."

"I hope so."

When David didn't answer but bent to unscrew an access panel on the side of the freezer, Abby knew she was in the way. He didn't need her standing behind him, watching everything he did.

She went to the two stoves and turned the ovens to 325 degrees. The beef roasts cooked in aluminum foil at a low temperature, giving the juices time to mix with onion soup mix and mushrooms to flavor the roast. On the table, four pans she'd lined with foil waited. Putting meat in each pan, she began to slice the mushrooms she'd washed before she realized the freezer was silent. She'd taken packets of onion soup mix from the pantry and was opening them when David spoke.

"Looks like you've got a bad thermostat." He put an electronic tester in his toolbox. Standing, he added, "I brought one along because that's a pretty common problem with older chest freezers."

"Is it quick to fix?" She sprinkled the mix over the meat and mushrooms.

He nodded. "Your freezer should be working in about fifteen minutes. I'll be right back."

"Thank the *gut* Lord," she breathed with relief as he left. When was the last time she'd taken a complete breath? Since the freezer had stopped working? Since David had walked through the door?

She was startled by that thought. He was an *Englischer* and terse almost to the point of being rude. Because he was easy on the eyes didn't mean she should see him as anyone other than skilled hands to get the freezer working again. She was glad she wasn't watching the door when it opened and his strong, assertive footsteps crossed the tiled floor.

He didn't say anything as he went to the freezer and knelt beside it. His broad hands navigated the small space afforded by the access panel as he removed the useless thermostat.

Abby averted her gaze again. She shouldn't be studying each of his motions, though she was fascinated by his knowledge of how the wires should be handled. Now wasn't the time to ask her usual questions about the way things worked.

The front door opened again and a cacophony of footsteps burst into the community room.

She smiled, knowing more of the teenage volunteers had arrived. On any day, about a half dozen boys and girls offered their time to assist the adult volunteers. She knew they wished they could climb on rafters to raise roofs or use the excavation machinery. However, the policies of Amish Helping Hands and the Mennonite Disaster Service and other organizations limited the teens to working on the ground. They could climb a ladder to paint a ceiling, but nothing more dangerous.

"Hey, what's going on?" asked Jack Gundersen as he stretched through the pass-through window to peer into the kitchen. The teen, who'd been one of the first to ask to help with rebuilding houses swept away by the flood, hadn't lost his enthusiasm in spite of weeks of hard work. He and his best friend, Reece Maddox, put in several hours of work each day after school and on Saturdays.

Abby smiled at the boys. Anyone looking at them might dismiss them as trouble because of their tattoos and cropped hair, but she'd come to see they had generous hearts. She didn't understand why anyone would ink their arms with identical verses from Proverbs 17, as the boys had done. Yet she admired their faith and friendship that had led them to put the words *A friend loveth at all times, and a brother is born for adversity* on the insides of their forearms.

"Something went wrong with the freezer," she said in answer to Jack's question. "The thermostat. It's getting fixed by—"

"Hi, Mr. Riehl!" called Reece, leaning next to his friend on the counter. "Anything we can do to help?"

"Just finishing," David said without looking at them. "But thanks."

"Are you and Mikayla coming tonight?" Jack asked.

Abby looked from the boys to the man kneeling by the freezer. She knew only one girl by that name. Mikayla St. Pierre was the newest teen volunteer, a pretty, quiet girl who liked to work alone. Someone had told Abby the thirteen-year-old was an orphan after her sole surviving parent, her *daed*, had died in a car accident and she now lived with a guardian. Was David Riehl the one who'd taken her in? Maybe there was more to him than the curt man who looked at her as if she'd come from another planet.

David reached into the freezer, his face turned away. "Tonight? What's tonight?"

"The volunteer supper." Jack grinned. "Roast beef and the fixings."

"And desserts." Reece's smile was broader than his

friend's. "Lots and lots of yummy desserts. Isn't that right, Abby?"

She heard an odd sound behind her. Turning, she discovered David regarding her with a strange expression. She wasn't sure if he was upset or surprised or something else.

"Is everything okay?" she asked.

Instead of answering her, he asked a question of his own, *"You* are Abby?"

"Ja." When he continued to stare with indecipherable emotion glowing in his eyes, she hurried to add, *"Es dutt mir leed."* She flushed anew, not wanting to admit his presence had unsettled her enough to forget to speak in English. "I mean, I'm sorry. I should have introduced myself when you arrived. I was in a hurry to get the freezer fixed. Is it all right now?"

Again, he acted as if he hadn't heard a word she'd spoken. *"You* are Abby? Abby Kauffman?"

Concerned by his odd behavior, she wasn't sure what might be wrong with him. Moments ago he'd acted curt but polite, as she'd expected a busy repairman to act. Now he was gawking at her as if she'd grown a second head. What had she said to cause him to react as he was?

She couldn't halt herself from asking, "Are *you* all right, David?"

No, I'm not.

David Riehl was glad the woman standing between him and the door into the main room couldn't read his mind. Or maybe it didn't matter because his thoughts were so jumbled he didn't know how to sort them out.

Abby Kauffman—the Abby Kauffman whom Mikayla had mentioned over and over—was Amish? He'd assumed… He wasn't sure what he'd assumed, but he'd never guessed the name belonged to an Amish woman.

There was no doubt she lived a plain life. Her shimmering blond hair was pulled into a tight coil beneath a heart-shaped organdy head covering.

A *kapp*, whispered a memory from the depths of his mind. He couldn't remember what the pinafore-type apron was called. The color of her dress reminded him of pine needles, and her eyes were the color of a tree-covered mountain on a foggy day. Not quite green and not quite gray.

He shouldn't be staring at her, but he couldn't pull his gaze away. There was something undefinable about her that drew his eyes. Something more than her pretty features or her plain dress. He couldn't figure out what it was and, for a man who spent his life getting to the bottom of problems, not being able to put his finger on what intrigued him was unsettling.

David mumbled under his breath, hoping she'd think he was impatient to install the new thermostat. His fingers were clumsy because knowing Mikayla's Abby was Amish bothered him more than he'd guessed. He tried to concentrate on his task. It was almost impossible because his thoughts flew in every possible direction.

As they had too often since the night ten months ago when he'd gotten the call that Boyd St. Pierre, his best friend since they'd gone to Evergreen Corners High School together and a single parent after his wife died in childbirth, was dead. A slick mountain road, a careless driver and a ten-car pileup left four people dead and twice that many injured. Mikayla hadn't been hurt other than bruises and blackened eyes from the airbag.

David had had the air knocked out of him almost as

hard by the shock of discovering Boyd had named him Mikayla's guardian. What did a bachelor who was an only child know about raising a thirteen-year-old girl?

At first, the necessary flurry of a funeral and settling his friend's estate and handling insurance claims had kept him too busy to think, but in the past couple of months, the pace had slowed to something similar to normal. He'd come to realize, though, he had no idea how to be a parent to a teenager.

Mikayla didn't talk much, but on the few occasions she did, almost every comment contained Abby's name. When she'd joined the other young people from their community church in volunteering, he'd been glad to see her spending time with people her age. However, he couldn't remember more than a handful of times when she'd mentioned any of the teens by name.

Just Abby.

Always Abby.

"Are you okay?" Abby asked again, ripping him away from his uneasy reverie.

"Fine, fine." It wasn't a lie. He was doing as fine as he could in this odd situation.

Why, among everything else Mikayla had said about Abby being so welcoming and fun and funny, had she failed to mention Abby was Amish?

As he finished affixing the thermostat and reached for the access panel cover to screw it into place, he knew the answer to his question. Mikayla hadn't said anything because being Amish didn't mean anything to her other than it was part of Abby's identity.

It did to him. He could hear his father's voice, low and filled with anger, deriding the ultraconservative Pennsylvania Amish community where their family had lived for generations. David's parents had left when he was about to start school, so his memories of what had happened were fuzzy and contradictory.

"We were chased away by closed minds and open mouths," his father had said so often the words were imprinted on David's brain. Neither of his parents had spoken about why they'd abandoned family and friends and moved to Vermont, but they'd never taken any pains to hide their disgust with the Amish.

"Hey, Mikayla!" Jack pushed away from the window. "Did you take a bath in Pepto-Bismol?"

Mikayla appeared in the doorway to the kitchen. The stylish glasses perched on the end of her nose were pocked with bright pink as were her worn T-shirt and jeans. She was a slender girl of medium height who looked like her mother. A mass of brown curls surrounded her face that was dotted with enough freckles to be cute.

"Hi, Abby," she said with the shy smile he'd seldom seen. It vanished as she noticed him by the freezer. "Oh, David."

He waited for her to say more. She didn't. Instead she wrapped her arms around herself and stayed in the doorway. The boys by the pass-through window seemed as much at a loss for what to do or say as he was.

Abby, however, walked over to Mikayla and put an arm around her shoulders. "I was so hoping you'd drop in today. Have you enjoyed painting Kaylee Holst's bedroom? Every five-year-old wants a candy-pink room, ain't so?"

"It's been fun, but I don't know if I ever want to see pink again." Mikayla didn't push her hair back from her face, hiding her expression.

From him or from everyone?

David watched as Abby steered the girl he called his daughter, for lack of a better word, across the kitchen to the table where she was preparing the roasts. She chattered with Mikayla as if they'd been friends for years.

His fingers curled, his nails cutting into his palms. He should have been aware that Mikayla had become friends with an Amish woman. He prided himself on knowing the facts, so he could plan ahead. That skill served him well as a repairman and in life...until Mikayla had become part of it. He'd made it clear he was available whenever she wanted to talk. He'd changed his life insurance and made a will to provide for the girl in case something happened to him. He'd started a college fund for her, though she didn't want to talk about going.

He'd never considered she'd choose an Amish woman to turn to. He had to find out more about Abby Kauffman. The last thing he needed now was to have the fragile girl being judged as cruelly by the Amish as his parents had been.

Chapter Two

David gathered the tools he'd used and stored them in the toolbox. He tossed the old thermostat in a nearby trash can. The freezer was humming, a sure sign the problem had been solved. Usually he felt a sense of satisfaction when he confronted a problem, evaluated the situation, considered the facts and found a solution.

Not this afternoon. He felt nothing but utter confusion, which was growing by the minute like dandelions would in a few months across his lawn.

He watched as Mikayla chopped garlic and sprinkled it on the roasts while Abby closed the foil over them. He hadn't guessed Mikayla knew how to do that.

He didn't know because he hadn't asked her. He'd gotten used to the silence in his house broken only by the television. Before Mikayla had moved in, he hadn't watched it much, but he'd assumed she, as a teen, would have a variety of shows she followed. If she did, she must be watching them another way, because she spent most evenings in her room with her headphones on.

His daughter wasn't wordy with Abby, but she was

giving the Amish woman more than the yes or no answers he got.

"Are you okay?"

At Abby's question, David flinched. He hadn't noticed the roasts had been put into the ovens and the preparation table cleaned. Mikayla was in the other room and he hadn't seen her leave the kitchen. He wasn't cut out to be a parent if he couldn't keep an eye on one teenage girl when she was standing right in front of him.

"David?" Abby prompted him.

"I think I'm done here," he replied, knowing she couldn't guess how he meant those trite words. He berated himself. Self-pity wouldn't get him—or Mikayla—anywhere. Boyd must have expected David to give her a family, but after ten months, the girl was still pretty much a guest in his house.

"How much do we owe you?" Abby asked as she opened the fridge and pulled out two dozen eggs.

"Don't worry about it."

She set the cartons on the table. "But you provided the part as well as your time."

"I'm glad to be able to help you. You're doing so much for my neighbors."

When her eyes widened and then warmed with gratitude, an answering smile tugged at his lips. He halted it. Because he wanted to do his part in helping with the flood recovery efforts didn't mean he should toss aside a lifetime of listening to his parents' stories about how they'd been banished by their Amish kin and friends from the only world they'd known.

Abby smiled as she wiped her hands on her black apron and he knew she had no idea what he was thinking. That was for the best. She hadn't done anything out of line.

Yet.

"That's kind of you, David," she said before bending to get a deep bowl from a cupboard near the table. "*Danki* for sharing your knowledge and your time."

"You're welcome." He couldn't help being flustered by the brilliance of her smile and the way her face glowed with a sincerity he couldn't doubt. Someone had told him the various Amish volunteers in town had come from different places and groups, and each of the church districts had their own unique customs. Maybe hers wasn't like the one his parents had belonged to.

Don't let a pretty smile persuade you to throw away your common sense, warned the most cautious portion of his mind. The part he took pains to listen to whenever possible. He'd learned the hard way disregarding its warnings could lead to trouble. It had whispered Chelsea Shipley was the wrong woman for him and he hadn't listened…until she'd dumped him.

"Is there something we should do to make sure the freezer keeps working?" Abby asked.

"Keep the coils cleaned and clear away any layers of ice inside the chest." He was glad to return to neutral territory where he could talk about work and not be assaulted by uncomfortable memories of what had happened fifteen years ago with Chelsea. "Don't leave the door open. Grab what you need and close it fast."

"*Gut.* Those are things we can do. *Danki* again, David, for coming today."

"It would have been a shame for the donated food to go to waste."

She laughed. "I worried, too, but realized I could

have farmed out the meats to every oven in town and roasted them before they spoiled. Somehow, we would have found a way to store the meat in the refrigerators. You saved me from going door-to-door and asking to borrow an oven."

"That would have been quite the feast."

"Wouldn't it?" Her smile brightened more. "We're having a feast tonight to give thanks for how God has brought us together in Evergreen Corners. Are you and Mikayla planning to join the other teens and their parents for supper here? We'll be eating around six thirty."

How he wanted to believe the kindness in her expression! He could say yes without hesitation. Right now, Mikayla needed good people around her as she faced life without her father. It had to be devastating for her. It was for him because he'd lost his best friend, and the void left after the accident was greater than he could have imagined.

Before he could answer, Mikayla stated from the doorway, "I'm coming." She didn't put her hands on her hips as she faced him, but she might as well have.

"All right," he replied. "I'll come, too."

"You don't have to."

He translated her words to mean "I don't want you to." Not that it mattered. He wasn't going to leave her on her own with strangers.

But they weren't strangers to Mikayla. She'd been spending lots of time volunteering. He'd agreed when she'd said she wanted to help. Last night, she'd actually spoken a few words during their supper and each had been about painting inside the new houses.

That explained why her clothing was spotted bright pink. He wondered if the paint was water soluble and would wash out. He flinched. Maybe Mikayla hadn't changed much in the last ten months, but he had. Before, laundry hadn't been anything he'd thought about until he ran out of clean clothes.

Satisfied he'd agreed to attend the supper, Mikayla hurried to catch up with the two boys who were already out the door.

"Hey! Where are you going?" David called, but she didn't look at him.

Abby said, "Don't worry. They're headed to house sites to assist."

"I thought she was painting today."

"The kids pitch in wherever they're needed. They're a *gut* group of kids." She smiled again and he felt that twitch of reaction deep within him. "Mikayla has been a true blessing for us."

"I'm glad to hear that."

"In spite of what she's been through this past year, she's always ready to help others. I enjoy working with her in the kitchen." A hint of a chuckle came into her voice. "And, for a girl her age, she's an accomplished cook. You must appreciate having her be able to put a delicious meal on the table."

He was stumped on how to answer. He didn't want to admit he'd never asked Mikayla to make a meal, having promised himself she must never think he considered her a burden or a servant.

Abby's enthusiasm overwhelmed him. He wasn't accustomed to someone being so blatant with their emotions and their opinions, and he found it disconcerting. He was glad to hear Mikayla was fitting in, but to say that might reveal how little he knew about the girl.

"Six thirty for supper?" he asked to change the subject.

"*Ja*, but we'll be setting up about an hour ahead of that."

Was that an invitation or an order? David decided it would be wiser not to ask. He told her that he and Mikayla would be back later. Not waiting for her answer, he darted out of the community center so fast he didn't realize he'd left a screwdriver behind until he needed it at the shop he'd set up in an old garage next to his house.

He'd get it later, he told himself. For now, he had to get his thoughts sorted. He didn't want to be drawn into the plain world and end up wounded as his parents had been.

We were chased away by closed minds and open mouths. As his father's words rang through his head, he had to wonder—as he hadn't before—if any of those closed minds and open mouths had been wearing a lovely smile like Abby's.

The community center looked *wunderbaar*. Even her big brother, Isaac, would have to admit Abby had taken care of every detail. Outside, snow huddled in the shadowy corners beneath trees, though it was early April, and remained in ugly gray piles on the sides of the roads. Abby had been able to convince several local volunteers to share late snowdrops and bunches of crocuses, so the tables inside were brightened by small vases filled with purple and white flowers. They offered a positive sign that spring would fill yards with daffodils, forsythias and lilacs.

A half dozen women, both plain and *Englisch*, worked in the kitchen. They dished out the vegetables, mashed potatoes and sliced meats and breads. Jenna, who was the local librarian, carried bowls of applesauce and chowchow from the kitchen. The young woman had worked long hours to salvage materials at the library, where both the basement and ground floor had flooded. She flashed Abby a smile and a thumbs-up before turning to the refrigerator to collect more relishes to put on the tables.

The door to the street opened, allowing in cold air and an explosion of voices as teenagers and their parents arrived. Abby searched the faces. She breathed a sigh of relief when she saw Mikayla's among them.

Not only Mikayla, but David Riehl had returned. Abby hadn't been certain he would. Making sure her surprise was well hidden, she waved to the newcomers with one hand as she poured water into glasses with the other. Mikayla hung up her coat before rushing to the kitchen to help.

"No, no," Abby said with a chuckle as she put up her arm to keep the girl from going into the kitchen. "You and the other teens are *our* guests of honor tonight. Let us serve you."

"I want to help." The girl glanced at David, who was talking to one of the other *daeds*. "Please."

"Is everything all right?" Abby asked, her smile falling away.

"Everything's as it always is."

The girl's tone sent a pulse of sorrow through Abby. Mikayla seldom spoke of the car accident that had left her an orphan and had never said a word about David. Yet, the teen's grief was bubbling right beneath her too composed exterior, a volcano ready to erupt at any moment.

Abby wished she knew a way to help Mikayla to be honest with her and with her guardian. There must be some way to reach the girl.

How?

The question plagued Abby while she finished setting the tables. Her half-formed hope she could sit with the girl and David vanished when they found the last two seats at a small table with Jack and his parents. The question continued to dog her during grace, which was led by Pastor Hershey. The Mennonite minister preached at the church attached to the community center.

She ate the food that had smelled so delicious, but it had no flavor for her as ideas for helping Mikayla burst into her mind and were discarded. When the meal concluded with thick slabs of *snitz* pie, she was no closer to a solution.

Then everyone was leaving. She sought out David and Mikayla.

"*Danki* for joining us tonight," Abby said. "I'm glad you both could come. And *danki* again for your help this afternoon, David. I hope you don't have too much homework tonight, Mikayla, because you must be exhausted after helping so much this afternoon."

"Just French and English." The girl shrugged. "I speak both already, so they're easy."

Had she made a joke? If so, it was the first Abby had ever heard from her. She clamped her hands to her sides before she could fling her arms around the girl and say how delighted she was to hear humor in Mikayla's words. Glancing at David, she saw he was astonished as she was. Before she could find the right thing to say that wouldn't embarrass the teenager, they'd thanked her again and left.

Abby sighed. There had to be something she could do. *What, God?*

Knowing she must be patient because God answered prayers in His time, she turned to head into the kitchen. She was told there were enough hands to help and she'd done more than her share that day. She would have argued most days that she didn't want to leave the cleanup to others, but she was weighted with her concern for Mikayla and David. Going home to seek God's guidance might be the best thing she could do.

Reece held the door open for her after she'd put on her black coat and tied her black bonnet over her *kapp*. The teenager fell into step with her as they walked up the hill along the village green.

"My folks needed to head over the mountain to pick up my sister," he said when Abby asked why he was walking home instead of going with his parents. "They had to slip out before dessert because her math tutor gets annoyed if they're late picking her up."

"There was extra pie. You could have—"

He held up a grocery bag she hadn't noticed and grinned in the thin glow from the streetlight. "Already taken care of. Enough for them and for my sister."

"And for you?"

"Yep." He chuckled. "I didn't want them to eat alone."

"You're a *gut* son."

"It's good pie."

Abby laughed along with him. It'd taken some of the teens a little time to get accustomed to being around plain volunteers, but, once they'd realized the Amish weren't going to chide them for every action or expect them to be serious every minute, they'd relaxed and treated her and the others like the rest of the adult volunteers. With respect and the assumption their elders were out of touch. She remembered feeling the same way when she'd turned thirteen and known she'd be finished with school in a little over a year.

They were a block from where she lived in an apartment over the mayor's garage when a dark-colored car raced over the top of the hill and squealed to a stop not far from them. Reece tensed beside her as both windows on the driver's side rolled down. Seeing several teens, at least one of them a girl, in the car, she wondered what they wanted.

"Hey, Maddox, going for an older woman now?" Laughter burst from the car. "You going to grow one of those beards to impress your Ay-mish girlfriend?" They pronounced the word with a long *a*. More rude laughter was followed by smacking sounds as if they were trying to kiss something as huge as an elephant.

When a teen made a comment about his sister, Reece put down the bag with the pie and took a step toward the car.

Abby grabbed his arm, halting him. She hid her grip from the kids who rained taunts on him. They mustn't guess she was keeping him from stepping into their snare. There were at least four kids in the vehicle and they'd let Reece take the first swing before they pummeled him.

"*Danki* for your comments," she said as she picked up the bag and handed it to Reece.

He looked from it to her, but she said nothing. Instead she continued along the steep sidewalk at a slow pace that would look as if she didn't have a care in the world. As she passed the car, the teens exchanged glances as if they couldn't believe what they were hearing. *Gut!* Giving them pause might allow them time to realize they were acting like *dummkopfs*.

Suddenly the car peeled out as another vehicle came up the hill. She guessed they didn't want to be seen. They went down the street too fast and skidded with a squeal around the corner.

Beside her, Reece let out his breath in a sigh. She patted his arm in silent commiseration, but tensed when the red truck came to a stop beside them. What now?

She got the answer when the driver stepped out and called, "Were those kids bothering you?" David's voice was laced with anger.

"We're fine." Abby pointed at the bag Reece carried. "The pie is fine."

"Abby?" Both David and Mikayla, who'd stepped out of the passenger's side, gasped her name at the same time.

Mikayla rushed to Reece, who was shaking with residual emotion. He nodded to her, but spoke to Abby. "I thought I'd make sure you got home okay." He knocked his work boot against the pile of refrozen snow mixed with last fall's leaves. "I didn't think I'd have you saving the day for me."

"Will that cause more trouble for you?" she asked.

He shook his head. "Nothing can cause *more* trouble for us with those guys and their girls. They're bullies, and they harass everyone."

"Everyone?" David joined them on the sidewalk.

Reece faltered, then said, "Yeah, everyone."

"And nobody does anything about it?"

"We ignore them. The Bible says not to speak evil of someone else, so we're trying to ignore their words. We know they aren't true." He glanced at Abby. "At least, we try to ignore them."

"And you're doing a *gut* job." She patted his arm. "You'd better get that pie home before your family wonders if we've kept you washing dishes."

He nodded and headed up the street with Mikayla matching his steps. The two teens spoke softly, so Abby couldn't guess what they were saying.

"Are you sure you're okay?" David asked as he watched the two kids moving together from shadow to lamplight.

"I'm fine, and Reece will be. He knows well-aimed cruel words can hurt, but they're words spoken by people he doesn't respect."

"Bullies start with words, Abby. When those don't get them what they want, they turn to other means."

"I know. That's why I'm going to urge the kids to stick together." She hesitated and then asked, "Would you drive Reece home? I don't like to think of those other kids finding him by himself."

"No need. His house is there." He pointed to the top of the hill. "I'll wait and make sure he gets home. I'll give them a few minutes. Then I'll pick up Mikayla."

"That's a *gut* idea. I think Reece needs someone his own age to talk to right now."

"You've got real insight into these kids, don't you?"

"I try. If you see something else I can do better, let me know."

"I will," he replied, but he didn't look at her.

She fought not to frown. David had avoided her eyes several times this afternoon. Now he was doing the same. What was he trying to hide? His life had been turned inside out by becoming the *daed* to a teenager.

Maybe both he and Mikayla needed guidance to ease into their new lives.

She would be glad to help. But how? She hoped God would show her the way.

Chapter Three

"Abby, are you here?"

Looking up from the menu she was preparing for the coming week, Abby glanced at the clock in the community center kitchen. It was nearly 10:00 a.m. Where had the morning gone?

She smiled as Beth Ann Overholt walked into the kitchen. The dark-haired midwife volunteered when she could in Evergreen Corners. With her practice in Lancaster County, Pennsylvania, she had to find times—two weeks each visit—to help with the rebuilding. She was much taller than Abby and wore a brace on her right leg. Like Abby, she dressed plainly, but her *kapp* was pleated as befitted her life as a Mennonite.

For a moment, Abby considered asking Beth Ann's advice on how to help David and Mikayla. She'd been pondering the question for the past week and didn't have an answer. She guessed that because most of Beth Ann's interactions were at births, she wouldn't have much more insight than Abby did into teenagers.

"I'm right where I always am at this time of day,"

Abby replied as she motioned for her friend to come over to the table. "Getting ready for the midday meal and trying to come up with menus based on what we've got in the freezer. It looks as if we'll be having venison burgers a lot in the near future."

"All right by me."

"You'll eat anything put in front of you."

"Hard work makes a girl hungry."

"I can't argue with that." Abby laughed as she put down the paper and pencil. "A cup of *kaffi*?"

"Yes, but I'll have to take it to go. We're supposed to finish the painting at the McGoverns' house today."

"Then let me get you enough cups for the whole crew. How many?"

"Five. Do you have disposable cups?"

"Thanks to the generosity of Spezio's market, we do." The grocery store, situated at the edge of town, had been cut off from many residents for more than three months. Everyone had been pleased when that route out of Evergreen Corners had been opened to traffic again. "I don't know what we'd do if they didn't keep us supplied with paper goods."

Beth Ann chuckled. "You'd figure out some other way to get by." She scanned the kitchen while Abby went to the pantry and lifted out a stack of insulated cups. "Are you alone here today?"

"*Ja.* That nasty cold has half the town in bed and the other half trying to avoid catching it."

"I know. That's why we've only got five on the painting crew today."

Abby poured *kaffi* from the big urn and set packets of creamer and sugar onto one of the trays used to transport drinks to the various building and work sites.

"We need to contact Isaac to see if anyone up north can come down for a few days."

"That's already been done." Beth Ann hefted the tray. "I heard someone over at the high school saying your brother will have more volunteers here by the end of the week."

"I'm glad to hear that."

"Thanks, Abby." She turned to go, then paused. "Oh… I almost forgot the reason I came by. Glen wants to see you."

Glen Landis was the project manager for the rebuilding in Evergreen Corners. He worked for a Mennonite organization but coordinated with Amish Helping Hands and other groups who'd sent volunteers and supplies to help. As well, he kept each project on schedule by making sure building materials were ready when the crews needed them. Handling any disputes was also part of his job, and he did it so well Abby had heard of only one instance where there had been a major disagreement.

He was the busiest man in town. Maybe in the whole state, and Abby knew his time was precious. If he wanted to see her, it must be for something important.

"When?" she asked.

"Now." Beth Ann gave her a guilty grin. "I was supposed to deliver the message an hour ago, but I got waylaid when I was recruited to help unload a truck of donated furniture. I must have carried two dozen lamps into the town barn. People can come and pick out what they want once their houses are repaired." Rolling her eyes as if she were no older than the teen volunteers, she said, "Look! I'm delaying you again, and the coffee is getting cold."

"Sounds like I don't have any time to waste, do I?" Abby followed the other woman to the door. Grabbing her coat and black bonnet, she closed the door.

Beth Ann strode away toward the center of town, but Abby lingered for a moment to draw in a deep breath of the fresh air that was flavored by mud and the aroma of freshly cut lumber. It'd been close to freezing when she'd come to work before dawn. Now the sunshine was making the snow dwindle into puddles.

She smiled when her feet sank into the damp earth as she crossed the village green. The faint color of new grass was visible beneath the brown remnants from last fall. Without snow, the damaged gazebo appeared more rickety. That project must wait until homes and businesses were safe and repaired.

And then she would need to leave Evergreen Corners. She didn't like to think about that. In the small town, she'd found many ways to help. At home, her older brother would have everything under control, as he always did. There wouldn't be anything for her to do, he'd tell her as he had so often, other than to find a husband and set up a household of her own.

Abby didn't realize she'd been stamping her feet with the intensity of her thoughts until the heel of her boot got stuck. She wiggled it free and rushed toward the sidewalk as she forced herself to calm down. Isaac believed the only way she could find happiness was to marry.

She didn't have anything against marriage. In fact, she dreamed of becoming the wife of a man who loved her, but she didn't trust her heart. The last time she'd listened to it, putting her own yearnings first, tragedy had followed. A shiver rushed along her spine when the memories of that night almost nine years ago exploded. Instead of being there for Bert, a troubled young man she'd known needed help, she'd thought of spending time with Wilmer, who'd caught her eye and made her heart beat faster. Her heart had betrayed her, because Bert might not have been injured in an accident when he challenged Wilmer to a buggy race. At the time they'd lined up their buggies, she'd been asleep, never knowing about the drama playing out along the road not far from her family's farm. She hadn't imagined what could happen and how her name and reputation would become synonymous with the accident.

Since that night, when she'd joined others praying Bert wouldn't die, and during the long months of his recovery and Wilmer's trial afterward, she'd promised herself and God she wouldn't let her desires come before anyone else's. She would focus on helping with her family's move to Vermont two years ago as well as volunteering to work with Amish Helping Hands. That had kept her too busy for walking out with a young man, especially the *wrong* young man. Not that she'd ever met anyone who made her think of walking out together.

Except David Riehl.

She silenced that thought as she reached for the door in one wing of the high school. David was an *Englischer* with no time for walking out, either. What did she know about him other than he was struggling to be the *daed* to a teenager?

Not giving herself a chance to answer, Abby went into the school. She stopped at the office to let them know she had a meeting with Glen and then half ran to his office, knowing she was late.

She knocked on the door with its frosted glass and

heard the call for her to come in. As she'd expected, Glen sat behind a cluttered desk in what had been a classroom in the high school. For the past five months, it had served as an office for the project manager who oversaw the volunteers and vendors together with the families who were having their homes rebuilt. Calendars listing when supplies should be ordered and when they'd be delivered vied for space along the walls with house plans. Samples of flooring and cabinet doors were stacked in one corner while cases of light bulbs leaned at a precarious angle against another.

"Come in, Abby!" he said as a greeting when he stood. His kind face was lined with more wrinkles daily. "We've just started."

We?

In astonishment, she saw the man who'd been filling her thoughts rising from a straight chair across the desk from Glen. She almost demanded to know why David was part of the meeting, then bit back the words. She was there to help, not cause friction.

"Danki," she said when David cleared another chair of stacks of paper so she'd have a place to sit.

Folding her hands on her lap, Abby waited for Glen to speak. She didn't have to wait long.

As he sat, pulling his chair in closer to his desk, the project manager said, "You may have heard I wasn't in favor of having youth volunteers when it was first suggested to me."

Abby nodded. Michael Miller, an Amish volunteer who'd decided to remain in Evergreen Corners in the hope of building a church district in the town, had first suggested having the teens help. Once he was baptized, he would marry and share with his family one of the new houses set far enough from the brook that they shouldn't be flooded again. The mayor had hired him to build new shelves in the library, but that project had been put on hold. So, for now, he'd kept working with the house crews, using his skills as a fine carpenter to piece together moldings and window frames.

"You've changed your mind," David said.

"Completely. I've talked with the supervisors at each building site, and they agree with me."

"Agree about what?" Abby asked.

"That we need to make our teens into a cohesive group that works together while enjoying the special fellowship they would experience if they weren't volunteering so many hours. We're developing a program to balance their volunteer hours and their homework hours and allow them time for socializing with each other. We want, as well, to include faith lessons as part of the program." Glen leaned forward and folded his arms on his desk. When papers crunched under his elbows, he grimaced. He moved the offending papers and then refolded his arms on the empty blotter. "We want to give them the tools they need to deal with the challenges they're facing right now."

"So you've heard about the bullying, too?" Abby couldn't see any reason not to be blunt.

He nodded, his expression grim. "We would like to think when someone sees a gathering of brothers and sisters toiling in God's name, that sight should inspire love. Unfortunately, some young people prefer to belittle our volunteers."

"Talking to the bullies' parents—"

"Has obtained us promises they'll speak with their children. Some of the bullies have stopped. A couple have inquired about helping us. However, a core of about five teens have continued to be disruptive."

"What can I do to help?" Abby asked.

David cut his eyes toward her as he corrected, "What can *we* do to help?"

"That's what I meant," she hurried to add.

He looked away, but this time he wasn't hiding anything from her. He was irritated at her choice of words. She hadn't wanted to speak for anyone but herself. He should know that. With a start, she realized—again— she had no idea what he should know because she didn't know him.

"I'm glad to hear both of you are eager to get this program going," Glen said with a broadening smile. "We need two adult coordinators to develop our program and work with the kids on a two-to three-times-a-week basis. Will you be willing to get us started?"

"*Ja*, of course, we will." Abby stiffened. She should have thought before she blurted her answer because she was committing David to something he might not want to do. He had a lot on his plate with Mikayla and his repair business.

However, working with the teens could be the best way for her to help David and Mikayla grow closer. They'd been brought together by tragedy, but they needed to believe God wanted them to have joy and love in their lives. Could David see that? She must not push too hard because she'd already learned both David and Mikayla were stubborn. Being subtle when she could help people wasn't her strong point, but she must try.

"I mean," she added, hoping she hadn't already messed up this opportunity to help David and Mikayla and the other teens, "*I* am willing to help with this program."

"Good." Glen turned to focus on the man sitting beside her. "And what about you, David?"

She gasped. She hadn't intended to put David in the hot seat and she hoped he'd see the needs of his family as she did. If he didn't... No, she didn't want to think her hopes had been dashed before they'd come to life.

David didn't have to look at Abby to know she was sorry for having spoken out of turn again. First, she'd acted as if she didn't want to work with him; next, she was volunteering him without asking if he was interested. He'd heard her quick intake of breath in the silence following the calm question Glen had posed to him.

Every instinct told him to jump to his feet and tell Glen he had the wrong guy. If David agreed to this idea, he—and Mikayla—would be spending more time with the Amish volunteers.

Mikayla already talked about Abby almost every time she opened her mouth. His daughter didn't need to spend *more* time with her. Mikayla would want to be part of the program, and the one way he could be certain she didn't put herself in a position to be hurt as his parents had been was to be there to keep an eye on her.

He wasn't sure how he was going to find the time with the work he had lined up, but he'd vowed at Boyd's funeral to take care of Mikayla as if she were his own flesh and blood. Somehow, he'd figure out what to do. He'd go over his schedule to find pockets of time to spend with the teens.

Knowing what he must do didn't halt him from being

cautious enough to say, "I like this idea, Glen, but I think Abby and I need some time to talk about how we would handle this."

Abby looked at him in astonishment. Did she always jump off a cliff without bothering to see how deep the chasm was?

He couldn't do that. He had to consider each of the alternatives in the hope of seeing a solution instead of getting tangled up in his emotions. That was the way to deal with problems. He looked at his hands spread across his knees. His knuckles were pale from where he'd been gripping his legs.

"I can give you a couple of days," Glen replied. "No more. The bullying seems to be getting worse. I want to, as they used to say in the old movies, head the problem off at the pass. I can't think of anyone better to do the job than you two." He relaxed and smiled. "To tell you the truth, I asked around for recommendations, and your names were the ones I heard over and over. Abby, you've done a tremendous job with the teens and, David, the word around Evergreen Corners is you can fix anything."

David smiled wryly. "I don't know if people meant I could put an end to bullying. It's not like finding the right part and installing it."

"I think it is," Abby said. "We need to figure out what's bothering those youngsters and help them."

"We're not talking about Amish kids here." He tried to keep his annoyance out of his voice. "Your kids may be well behaved but—"

Her laugh halted him. "Our *kinder* can be as badly behaved as *Englisch* ones." She grew serious. "I know *Englischers* like to think we're different because of what we wear and how we try to live our lives as close as we can to Jesus's teachings, but we're human beings. Everyone makes mistakes, and we hope we can learn from those. Most important, we learn to offer forgiveness and accept it."

He wanted to say that wasn't the experience his family had, but talking about the past wouldn't help deal with the future. "Look, we need to talk about this, and I'm sure Glen has other things to do than to listen to us."

The project manager gave them a grin as he patted a stack of papers almost eight inches high. "These have to be handled before I can hit the hay tonight. So talk it over when you have a chance and get back to me in two days. I'd like to be able to give you longer, but I can't. We need to deal with this before it becomes a crisis."

David stood and watched as Abby did, every motion she made graceful. As he turned to leave, Glen called his name.

He turned. "Something else?"

"I wanted to let you know we'll be deciding in the next month whose three houses we're going to build next."

"Good." He was too aware of Abby listening, so he didn't give Glen a chance to say more before he walked out of the room. Aware of Abby following him down the hallway to the office, he waited for her to sign out after he had. He held the outside door open for her.

She paused on the sidewalk and faced him. "Are you going to be working on the next houses?"

"I lend a hand now and then when I can."

The answer seemed to satisfy her because she asked, "Do you have time for a cup of *kaffi*?" A warm flush climbed her cheeks, brightening them until they matched the soft pink shade of her dress. "I mean, coffee."

He smiled. "What you said was close enough to English so I could figure it out. Yes, I think having a chat is a good idea."

"Let's go to the diner." Twin dimples emphasized her smile. "I've been curious what it looks like now, and they should have the windows open on the sunporch so we can enjoy this beautiful day." She must have misread his hesitation because she added, "My treat."

He forced any hints of surprise from his face. He'd heard his father complain that the Amish were so frugal they wouldn't spend a penny unless absolutely necessary. Abby was offering to pay the tab. Though it wasn't for more than a cup of coffee, her easy offer contradicted what he'd assumed was true.

Had he misunderstood his father? He couldn't keep from wondering if she were unique among the plain people or if he, like his daughter, was setting his new family up for trouble.

In either case, the only way he would know for certain was to spend as much time with her as Mikayla did, so his daughter wouldn't be blindsided and hurt.

Chapter Four

Della's Diner was at the center of Evergreen Corners, just west of the bridge crossing Washboard Brook that bisected the village. It faced a huge mill building that had been converted to artists' lofts. Most studios on the lower two floors had been damaged during the flood. The building's foundation had been undermined, so nobody could go inside until the stone was replaced by concrete.

The diner had been half stripped away by the rushing water, but its owners had shored it up as soon as the brook began to recede. It had reopened three weeks ago.

David wondered what had changed inside and was surprised to see not much had. The light green walls glistened with fresh paint. They were covered with new pictures of chickens and roosters as well as knickknacks sitting on open shelving in the place of the old pictures and bric-a-brac that had washed away. Everywhere he looked there was poultry of various colors from traditional to a steampunk rooster set next to the cash register. That rooster was made out of bright purple metal with faucet handles for eyes and webbed feet like a goose. He was amazed the owners had found so many items to replace the lost ones.

A few patrons sat at the counter running along one wall toward a swinging door to the kitchen. Pies topped with generous amounts of meringue were displayed in tiered glass cases set not far from the coffeepots giving off an enticing aroma.

A middle-aged waitress came forward to greet them. Her astonishment when she glanced at Abby was quickly hidden behind her professional smile.

He had thought, by now, the residents of Evergreen Corners would be accustomed to seeing plain people. He almost laughed. Not a ha-ha laugh, but an ironic one. He'd stared the same way himself when he'd realized Mikayla's Abby was Amish.

The waitress held a pair of menus. "Inside or on the sunporch?"

"Sunporch," David said, thinking of how Abby had mentioned sitting by an open window.

Abby had noticed Glen's comments as they were leaving, but seemed to believe that Glen had been asking for his help. Letting her think that meant he didn't have to answer questions—as he had for FEMA personnel and Boyd's private insurance company—about the house where Boyd had raised his daughter. It'd been destroyed in the flood during Hurricane Kevin last fall. If Mikayla hadn't been living with David, she could have been lost in the storm. He hadn't spoken of that to anyone, but it tainted his dreams night after night.

"This way." The waitress aimed another glance, one she must have figured was too surreptitious for anybody to notice, at Abby before leading the way through a broad doorway to the diner's other room.

If Abby noticed the waitress's gawking, she gave no sign. Was she used to people staring? She might be too polite to acknowledge them. Or maybe—and he was astonished how much he wished this was true—she hadn't seen the waitress's looks in her direction.

He was shocked at the sense of protectiveness surging through him. Not because he wanted to make sure his daughter wasn't hurt again. This time, he longed to shield Abby from being wounded by a rude look in her direction. Shocked by his reaction, he pushed it aside and focused on following the two women onto the sunporch.

A row of windows lined one wall and the others were decorated with more chickens. A couple of televisions hung near the ceiling and were on but muted. Both were showing weather maps of the Midwest with areas marked in red for strong storms.

The waitress led them to a table next to a window. As he glanced out, he noticed the brook was much higher than it'd been a few days ago. Snow on the mountains flanking the valley must be thawing fast. The water was a pale brown with mud, and white foam marked the large boulders. Even with the spring melt, the brook remained below its banks.

David took the seat across from where Abby sat and smiled his thanks when the waitress handed them each a menu and hurried away to seat other patrons.

"What's tasty?" Abby asked.

He hesitated, aware she'd offered to pay for their tab. "The coffee's good."

"I saw those pies on the counter. Don't you think we need to try some? A friend of mine makes them, so I'm sure they're delicious."

Though he was curious which of her friends baked the pies, he didn't want to pry. Better to keep his distance on any personal matter when dealing with the plain folk. He'd learned that from his folks, though they'd never used those exact words. Instead he'd listened to what they *hadn't* said about their lives as Amish.

When the waitress returned to the table, Abby ordered a cup of coffee and a piece of strawberry-rhubarb pie. He asked for coffee as well as chocolate-cream pie. He could see that pleased Abby. Now that he'd volunteered to work with her, he should get to know her better, so he could discover what strengths she had to offer as well as any ideas. He wanted to get their project started. The sooner begun, the sooner finished.

Or at least he hoped so.

"So were you born and raised in Evergreen Corners?" Abby asked after two cups were set on the table.

"I moved here before I started school." He stirred sugar into his cup. "I've lived here long enough that everyone accepts me as a native."

"What made you decide to be a repairman?"

"I like using tools and figuring out puzzles, so it seemed an obvious step to fix broken appliances." He waited until plates topped by generous slabs of pie were set between them. After he thanked the waitress, he asked Abby, "Do you always ask people you work with questions?"

Her smile looked far more genuine than his had felt. "I ask everyone questions. How else can I learn about people if I don't ask? I know you're Mikayla's guardian and you're concerned about her and her friends. That's it."

"I know you like to cook and you're Amish." He

didn't add how often his daughter spoke her name… on the few occasions when Mikayla talked.

"I don't enjoy cooking that much. What I love is baking." She took a bite of her pie. "Though I don't think I've ever baked anything as delicious as this."

He didn't respond as he might have with anyone else. His parents had often told him how plain people disdained bragging about themselves or others.

Instead he said the obvious. "Glen wants us to work together with the kids."

"Ja." Faint pink brightened her cheeks. "I'm sorry if I forced you to accept the assignment."

"You didn't force me. I want to help the kids deal with these bullies."

"Has it been going on long?"

"The bullying?" He took a drink of coffee, savoring its flavor while he thought about when he'd first heard rumors of the bullies. "About three to four months, as far as I know."

She leaned back in her chair and looked out the window, offering him a view of her profile. Her chin might be a bit too assertive, but her face was lovely from any angle.

Taking another gulp of coffee, he silenced the thought. He shouldn't be thinking about anything but trying to convince Mikayla that they were family. And he shouldn't be admiring the Amish woman sitting on the other side of the table. What irony that the first woman who'd caught his attention in years lived the life his parents disdained.

"I wonder," she mused, "if the bullying has anything to do with the tragedies inflicting Evergreen Corners."

"I don't see any reason how or why."

"And I can't see any reason how or why not."

He arched his brows. "You're beginning to sound like a true Vermonter."

"Really?"

"Vermonters enjoy being contrary, or so we're told." He folded his arms on top of the checkered tablecloth. "There's one thing we agree on. The weather is and always will be the most important topic."

She laughed. "It is for farmers."

"And everyone else. What the weather was, what it will be, when it'll rain, when it'll snow."

She laughed. "I haven't been in Vermont long, but I know the saying. 'If you don't like the weather—'"

"'Wait a minute and it'll change,'" he said in unison with her.

A hand clapped on his shoulder and David looked up at a thin, rangy man whose blond hair was laced with silver. "Jens, how are you?"

"Doing great. You?" Jens's eyes cut toward Abby.

"Jens, this is Abby Kauffman. Abby, this is Jens Gundersen. You know his son, Jack."

She smiled. "So nice to meet you. You have a *wunderbaar* son. He's always willing to pitch in."

"I'm glad to hear that, Ms. Kauffman."

"Abby, please." She motioned toward an empty chair. "Would you like to join us?"

"Thanks, but I dropped in to get some coffee to go." He gave them a jaunty wave. "If my boy gives you any trouble, Abby, let me know."

"I would if he was a problem, but he isn't. You're raising a *gut* kid."

Jens was grinning with pride as he walked over to where a large cup was waiting for him by the register.

A storm of unexpected sensations rushed through David, too many to identify as each fought for dominance. Except for one.

Confusion.

He was confused by the contrast between what he knew about the Amish and how Abby acted. She was the epitome of kindness and generosity, the complete opposite of how his parents described the plain people. Somehow, he was going to have to figure her out before he—and Mikayla—could be wounded as his father and mother had been by trusting the Amish.

Abby thanked the waitress for refilling her cup. As she stirred more milk into her *kaffi*, she listened as yet another person stopped to speak with David. She'd been sitting with him for almost a half hour and they had yet to discuss any ideas for working with the volunteer teens. People paused by the table for various reasons. Some wanted to say hi. A few had questions about work they wanted him to do. Others were simply curious why he was at the diner with an Amish woman.

She smiled when he introduced her to each person, but was aware of time passing without anything getting done. She couldn't linger too much longer because she needed to get tonight's supper started.

Drawing in a deep breath as David spoke to the mayor's husband, she gazed out the window. She could hear the brook murmur to itself.

"Fascinating, isn't it?" asked David, startling her because she hadn't realized he'd finished his conversation.

"*Ja.* Peaceful and beautiful, though I know it wasn't during the flood." She leaned closer to the cool glass.

"I wonder if the brook feels bad about the damage it's done."

"That's a fanciful thought."

She smiled at him. "And *fanciful* is a fancy word."

"Something you're not allowed to say?" he asked with unexpected heat.

Her brows lowered and her grin fell away. "The only things we're proscribed from saying are listed in the Bible. Not taking the Lord's name in vain, for example."

"I assumed that."

"But you assumed there were other things we aren't allowed to say because we're Amish."

A hint of a flush climbed from beneath his collar. Was he embarrassed by what he'd said? She couldn't help recalling other comments he'd made suggesting he had no use for plain people. That didn't make sense. He'd been nice to her and he hadn't kept Mikayla from working with her and other plain volunteers. *Ja*, he'd hesitated when Glen had asked him to work with Abby, but she didn't think that was because she was Amish.

Could she have been wrong? Did he have an objection to being around Amish people?

If so, she wasn't helping matters by being confrontational. So many verses in the Bible spoke of the importance of gently teaching those who needed to learn.

"Now I need to apologize," she said. "Talking to people is the best way to find out more about them. That's what my *grossdawdi* always said." Heat surged up her own face. "I mean, my grandfather. I need to remember you don't speak our language."

"German, right?"

"*Ja*, but it's not quite the same as the language spoken in Germany. More of a dialect. We call it *Deitsch*." She smiled, hoping her expression would lessen the tension between them. "So what do you say to getting to know each other while we hammer out what we're going to do for the teens?"

"You like to help others, don't you?"

"Ja." She picked up a forkful of pie but didn't taste it as she asked, "What about you? You must be willing to help others if you took Mikayla into your home after the accident."

"I was surprised to find myself appointed as her guardian by Boyd's will." He stared down at his *kaffi* as if he'd never seen it before. "I don't know why he chose me."

"Maybe because he knew you'd give his daughter a *gut* home."

"Maybe. I don't know. I never had a chance to ask. All I know is Boyd depended on me to take care of his daughter."

"And you don't want to let him down?"

"No." He took a drink and shifted his eyes away.

Abby chided herself for bringing up the subject. From what she'd been told by Mikayla's friends, Boyd St. Pierre had died less than a year ago. Her words, though she meant them to be comforting, might be like picking at a barely healed scar.

"Let's talk about the program for the teens," she said.

"You make it sound as if there's something already in place. Don't we have to start this from scratch?"

"Ja, but I don't think Glen expects us to do anything structured. It sounded to me like he wants us to spend time with the kids and help them discover tools to protect them from these bullies. We can combine fun with lessons about living with God."

"Don't take this the wrong way, but some of the parents might not want their kids being taught by someone who's Amish." Again, his eyes didn't meet hers.

Was he one of the parents who'd be upset if a plain person spoke of following God through life? She should ask, but didn't. Putting him into a more unpleasant position wasn't going to help them complete the task Glen had given them.

"Most of our teen volunteers attend services at the Mennonite chapel. Let's speak with Pastor Hershey."

"I can do that."

"Danki."

"You're welcome."

She waited for him to say something else, but silence grew between them. Sounds came from other diners and the traffic passing in front of the building. David looked everywhere but at her. She didn't need a sign on his forehead announcing he'd rather be somewhere else.

"David," she said as she pushed her plate and cup aside, "if you don't want to work on this project, say so. I know you're busy with your job and with Mikayla. I understand, and I'm sure Glen will, too."

"No, I said I'll help, and I don't renege on my promises."

"No one would think less of you if—"

"Thank you, Abby, but I don't need you offering me platitudes and convenient excuses." Her shock at his icy words must have been visible on her face because he apologized.

She waved aside his words. *"Danki."* Again, she felt her cheeks grow warm. "I'm sorry. I mean, thank you."

"I got that. The words sound pretty much the same. Let's start our work together with our first rule."

"What's that?"

"Honesty. If I don't understand something you say, I'll ask you. You do the same with me."

"I like that rule."

"Good. Now, what should be our next rule?"

"We make this fun for the teens and for ourselves. If we act as if this is drudgery, the kids will sense it and we'll lose our chance to help them."

"Fun?" He arched his brows as if responding to something he'd heard in his head, then sighed. "That may be harder for me to follow than the first rule. Nobody's ever described me as fun. In fact, the opposite."

"Well, then, we'll have to see how we can change that, ain't so?"

He gave her the faintest grin, but she took it as a victory. As they continued to talk about possible activities for the youngsters, she couldn't doubt he cared about his daughter and her friends. He was a man of strong emotions, though he tried to hide that fact. She couldn't help wondering why.

Chapter Five

Giving the kitchen floor one last swish with the mop, Abby bent to pick up the bucket of filthy water. She or one of the other volunteers mopped the floor at least once a day, but it never seemed clean.

She couldn't get rid of the dirt and she couldn't get rid of the feeling there was more than David had explained to his assertion last week that he wasn't someone others believed liked to have fun. Who had accused him of that and why?

She flinched. Accusations weren't always based on truth. She knew that too well. When she'd accepted Wilmer's offer to take her home in his buggy, she'd never anticipated she'd be blamed for a horrible accident later that night when he and Bert decided to race their buggies. The whispers that had followed were filled with half-truths, and she'd learned her attempts to correct the rumors added fuel to their speed along the Amish grapevine.

Looking around the kitchen, she sighed. She'd been silly to think she could leave the past behind in Pennsylvania. Maybe David was wiser than she was because he hadn't tried to do the same. Instead he'd remained in Evergreen Corners, making a life for himself and now for Mikayla. He'd accepted himself as he was and moved forward.

As she'd been trying to do.

Abby finished cleaning the kitchen. The other volunteers would be arriving to begin preparations for the evening meal. According to the schedule posted on the refrigerator with a magnet, tonight was supposed to be hamburgers and french fries.

After she'd put the cleaning supplies away, she checked to make sure there were plenty of potatoes. Fries were a favorite, and she'd learned to make extra because no matter how many were prepared, every morsel would be gone by the time the volunteers rose from the tables.

There were enough potatoes for the evening's meal, but the pantry needed to be resupplied. She made a list of the items for next week and set the list on a counter while she tied on her black bonnet and pulled on her wool coat, which was the same color.

A chill clung to the wind, but the sunshine was bright on the purple crocus buds between the sidewalk and the building. They wobbled, top-heavy, as they waited for the perfect moment to burst into welcome bits of color.

A shadow crossed the sidewalk in front of her. Looking up, she grinned.

"Isaac!" She gave her older brother a big hug. His black hat was askew on his light brown hair that the sun bleached with blond streaks every spring. More than ten years her senior, he remained clean-shaved because he'd never wedded.

Her older brother was, like David, not someone who

displayed his feelings. Not that it was necessary. Isaac loved her as much as he did the rest of their family, which were the center of his world. When he wasn't in Evergreen Corners, he spent long hours working on their farm in northeastern Vermont. He would never inherit the farm—it would go to their youngest brother, Herman—but Isaac was the best dairyman in the family and he'd taken on the responsibility of passing along his skills to their other brothers. He'd been scouting farms for when he was ready to marry and start a home and a herd of his own.

Not bothering to hide her grin when she saw the paper bag he used as a suitcase, she asked, "How long can you stay this time?"

He motioned for her to lead the way up the street toward her apartment over the mayor's garage, he replied, "At least a few weeks. I want to be back before the next group of calves is born."

"You've got to learn to trust Herman." She always teased him about his overprotectiveness of their brothers. "One of these days, he'll have to handle a birth on his own."

Isaac grumbled as he stepped around a pile of unmelted snow. "When he's ready, but that's not now."

Knowing by his tone Isaac was worried about the calving, she said, "Your room is just as you left it." She gave him a teasing smile. "Except you've got clean sheets on your bed and no dirty towels in the hamper."

"You didn't need to change the sheets. I'd slept on them only a couple of nights last time I was here."

"You're my brother. Until we find some woman silly enough to marry you, I need to make sure you have a decent meal to eat and fresh linen to sleep on after a long day of work."

He smiled. "Are you saying I should be looking for a wife because you've found yourself a husband?"

"Who's here for me to marry?" She ignored the abrupt image of David's handsome face in her mind. She hardly knew him, and he was *Englisch*. "All the plain men here are married." She grinned. "However, there are several women who aren't."

"No matchmaking, little sister."

"I'll agree to no matchmaking in Evergreen Corners if you will."

He nodded. "You're right. We're here to help others, not to look for spouses."

As they reached a white Colonial with dark green shutters, a woman burst out of the house. Gladys Whittaker was mayor of Evergreen Corners, and she was talking on her cell phone every time Abby saw her. The mayor's neat, bright blue suit reminded Abby how her own dress and apron were covered with stains from making the midday meal. She and Isaac stopped to let the mayor rush past them.

Gladys looked over her shoulder to say, "Good to see you, Isaac." She didn't add more as her phone began beeping and making other odd sounds.

Abby said a quick prayer for Gladys Whittaker. The mayor worked with national and state emergency management agencies on flood recovery. While Glen coordinated the volunteers, she handled everything else with the tiny staff at the village hall. The first floor of the building had been flooded, but as the brook rose, many of the records had been rushed upstairs by the mayor, her husband and the village clerk. They'd spent a perilous night stuck in the village hall, which had struggled to hold against the raging waters. It had given Gladys and the others a bird's-eye view of other buildings being destroyed.

"How are you doing, Gladys?" Isaac asked when the mayor frowned at her phone.

"Looking for my mind, which I lost when I agreed to run for mayor."

Abby smiled. Her brother always asked the mayor about herself, and she always gave him the same answer.

"Did you bring other volunteers with you?" Gladys asked. "I hope so. We aren't blessed with many as dedicated as the Kauffmans."

"I brought four volunteers. They're with Glen getting their assignments for work and where to sleep. All men, though two are sixteen."

"The younger ones should join the group Abby is overseeing with one of our parents."

Isaac gave his sister a curious glance, but she didn't explain. That could wait until he dropped off the few things he'd brought with him. She'd leave the account of how she and David had agreed to help with the teenagers until later.

Abby followed her brother up the outside stairs along the side of the garage. Going into the tiny apartment, she waited in the cramped kitchen while he took his bag into the larger of the two bedrooms. She chuckled her breath. *Larger* was a silly way to describe a bedroom with space for a twin bed and a dresser. Her room didn't have a dresser, but she'd found cardboard boxes to store her things in the tiny closet.

He didn't say anything to her as they walked down the

stairs. She guessed her brother was eager to get to work and wouldn't ask her more about the teen group now.

He confirmed that when he said, "I need to head over to the school. Glen told me before I left to let him know when I returned to Evergreen Corners."

Abby wasn't surprised. Isaac had extraordinary skills as a mason, and he had overseen setting up the forms for each new house's foundation as well as supervising pouring the concrete. There never was any question if his calculations were right or his corners square. He laid out the foundation by hand, using a laser only to confirm what he'd done. Not once had the forms needed adjustment.

"I was heading that way myself," she said. Fishing the slip of paper from her pocket, she smiled. "Could you give Glen this list of the supplies we need for the community center?"

He nodded and took the wrinkled page. Glancing at it, he grimaced. "I'm glad I'm not working in the kitchen. One hundred pounds of onions? I wouldn't want to peel and chop those."

"I hope the weather is warm enough we can open the windows soon. I'm tired of onion tears." She started to add more, then noticed a familiar silhouette coming toward them out of the brilliant sunshine.

David's easy gait made short work of the distance between them. He wore a bright yellow knit hat with green stripes along with his black puffy coat. Thick gloves covered his hands. His eyes narrowed when his gaze alighted on her brother, but his smile didn't waver.

"David, this is my brother Isaac Kauffman," Abby said, hoping she sounded as if she didn't have a care in the world other than tonight's supper. "Isaac, this is

David Riehl. He lives here in Evergreen Corners, and he's been helping, too."

The two men shook hands, sizing each other up. She wasn't sure what they were looking for as they appraised each other.

"So you're one of the volunteers?" Isaac asked.

"I'm working with Abby on a program for the teen volunteers."

Her brother turned to her. "You are?"

"Glen asked us last week to put together a program," she said quietly. "Glen wants to make sure the teenagers understand they can move closer to God at the same time they're offering their help."

Isaac nodded. "Hmm...that's a *gut* idea."

"I thought so," she said.

"*We* thought so," David said.

Why had he used a tone that challenged her older brother? Isaac, in spite of his officious exterior, was eager to get the residents of Evergreen Corners into their homes again.

"Your idea, Abby?" Isaac asked.

"No. It was Glen's." She turned toward the community center. "Excuse me. I need to get to work."

Her hope that would end the discussion failed when Isaac said, "I'm curious why Glen asked you two to work on the program."

"My daughter is one of the teens," David replied. "And the kids are fond of Abby. It may have to do with the cookies she has waiting for them every day after school."

"So that's how you two met?"

Abby shot her brother a frown. Hadn't they just

agreed to no matchmaking? Not that Isaac would consider *Englisch* David a proper match for her.

"We met," she explained, "when David came to fix the freezer at the community center." She laughed, hoping it sounded natural. "As I heard someone once say, not all superheroes wear capes."

Isaac gave her a puzzled frown but she wagged a finger at him. "Don't pretend with me, Isaac Kauffman. I know you used to read comic books and I've heard you say those very words."

"You know about the comic books?"

"If you'd wanted to keep them a secret, you should have found a better place to hide them than in the hayloft, where you kept your radio. I found your stash when I was looking for somewhere to put the bottle of fingernail polish one of the neighbor girls gave me."

"Which one?"

Again she laughed and this time it was an honest one. "Do you think I'm going to tell you? I wouldn't want to get a respectable Amish *mamm* in trouble." She looked at David and smiled. "We've all done things better left in the past, ain't so?"

"If you think I'm going to answer that loaded question, think again. I'm not sure what the statute of limitations is on my teen mistakes."

She wanted to hug him for following her lead in leaving the heavier topics behind. When Isaac announced he'd lingered too long and had to get to the school to meet with Glen, she kept her sigh of relief silent. She and her brother needed to have a talk straightaway before he made things worse with his mistaken assumptions. She glanced at David's taut face as he watched her brother walk away and hoped it wasn't already too late.

* * *

David pushed down his irritation. His fingers curled into fists at his sides. Until he'd met Isaac Kauffman, he'd been wondering if his parents had been mistaken in their negative opinions of the Amish. The plain people he'd met in Evergreen Corners were generous, caring folks eager to walk in the path they believed God had for them. He'd worked several times with Michael Miller, a plain man who'd come to Evergreen Corners to help and then decided to stay to make the village his home. Michael oversaw one of the building sites and he'd asked David to come check some of the mechanicals before they were hooked up in the new houses.

Michael was a good man, hardworking, honest and with a wry sense of humor. David enjoyed chatting with him, often about their kids. Michael's were young, but the challenges of being a father were the same whether a man was Amish or *Englisch*.

Isaac fit the description his parents had given him of the stiff-necked men and women who'd driven them away. David could imagine Isaac banishing those who disagreed with him.

Stop it! Isaac was Abby's brother, a brother she respected and cared about. David had been wrong in his first impressions of people before and he couldn't make that error again.

As if she could sense his uneasy thoughts, she said, "You and Mikayla should come for supper tonight so you can get to know Isaac better."

"At the community center?"

She smiled. "In spite of how it must seem to everyone, I don't spend every hour of every day there. Today,

I'm working on preparations for the evening meal, but not the meal itself."

"So you want to cook for us on your evening off?"

"I'll be cooking for Isaac and myself." Her eyes twinkled like sunshine through a pine forest. "And I've gotten so used to cooking for a crowd I don't think he'll be able to eat it all."

Was she trying to avoid being alone with her overbearing brother?

Whether that was the reason or not, he heard himself accepting the invitation. Mikayla would be thrilled, though he had to wonder what she'd make of Abby's brother.

Abby's smile sent unexpected sensation zinging through him like lightning. Her cheery wave as she rushed along the green made him grin. No matter how much he'd tried to ignore it, her charming warmth was winning him over as it had Mikayla.

To count Abby as a friend would go against everything his parents had taught him. He thought of giving them a call and talking about how she was different from the Amish they'd described. He didn't want to bring up old injuries and open them anew.

The cold splash of reality reminded him that he needed to get to the school cafeteria to fix the dishwasher that refused to pump water out. He would concentrate on his task and try to forget about her sparkling green eyes.

And David almost succeeded, though wisps of Abby's smile kept invading his mind as he worked on the dishwasher. Two hours later, he was finished and the cafeteria workers were filling the dishwasher so they could complete their work and head home to their families. He nodded to the thanks they called out to him.

He walked into the corridor, which was almost silent with school dismissed for the day. He heard bits of conversation from a room across the hall and saw several teachers and students gathered around a table.

Hurrying along, he glanced at his watch. He had just enough time to go home and get cleaned up before he collected Mikayla at the community center. He'd made an effort each day to stop by so she didn't have to walk home alone. Neither of them spoke of the bullies, but he guessed he wasn't the only parent keeping a close eye on the teens. Not once had Mikayla complained about him picking her up, which he took as a sign she was worried about being the next victim.

"Do you have a moment, David?"

His eyes widened when he saw Isaac Kauffman striding toward him.

"Certainly," he replied. "Can I help you with something?"

"*Ja.*" Isaac stopped in front of him. He glanced at an open door leading into a classroom. "We can talk in there. I wish you to know my opinion on an important matter."

Again, David was amazed a vivacious woman like Abby Kauffman could be related to the far too serious Isaac. She seemed to care about everyone, and her brother acted as if he'd be fine if everyone followed his orders.

Memories of his parents talking about the unbending Amish flooded his mind. His mother and father had used the words *the deacon* and *the ordained men* as if they spoke of the worst kind of people. Though they'd never shared any specifics about what the Amish leaders had done, he hadn't been able to mistake their contempt for the men who refused to listen to anyone's opinions but their own.

Now Isaac wanted to air *his* opinions.

Quelling his uneasy thoughts, David walked into the room after Abby's brother. He leaned against the wall and faced the man who was taller than his own six feet.

The other man crossed to look out the window at the playground. For a long moment he stared out the window; then he faced David.

"After my meeting with Glen, I went to the community center. Abby told me more about the program to put an end to the bullying that's been going on. I'm not surprised she jumped in to help." His austere face creased in a smile that came and went swiftly. "And she mentioned you have a teenage daughter, so I guess I can understand why you want to be involved."

"That sums it up." He wasn't going to explain to a stranger his complicated feelings about working with Abby. If he spoke of his discomfort at spending so much time with an Amish woman, he'd insult her brother. If he broached the topic of how he was at his wits' end in his efforts to convince Mikayla to open up to him, he was sure to embarrass himself.

"You are *Englisch*, David, so you may not understand it isn't the Amish way to become engulfed in the problems of nonplain folks."

"I do understand." *And you plain people won't consider the needs of those who count themselves as one of you.*

He was glad he'd halted that from bursting past his lips. It was a petty thought when the plain folks had come to Evergreen Corners to help and never asked for anything in return.

"That's why I think it would be for the best if Abby didn't continue working with *Englisch* teens." Isaac turned back to the window.

"You expect her to stop helping?" A guffaw burst from him. "Abby Kauffman stop helping people? Is that even possible?"

"It needs to be."

David pushed aside his amusement when he saw Isaac had taken his laugh the wrong way. It hadn't been his intention to insult Abby's stuffy brother.

"I think you're fighting an impossible battle," David said. "What do you expect me to say to her when she asks me about plans for the kids?"

Isaac tensed. "I don't expect you to speak to her about this. I wanted to let you know why she won't be working with you any longer."

"You believe she'll stop working with the teens because you tell her to?"

"I am her older brother."

When Isaac didn't add more, David realized the man thought that answer was explanation enough. "Abby may not be willing to accept your authority on this."

"Why wouldn't she?" For the first time since he'd turned away, Isaac looked at him.

David shrugged. "You tell me. She's *your* sister, so you know her better than I do. Since I first met her, I've learned one thing about Abby Kauffman. I don't know how she was before she came here, but she has made her job here the center of her life. I don't think you'll be able to talk her out of that."

For the first time Isaac loosened up enough to sigh

with obvious frustration. "You're not telling me anything I don't know, but she can't think only of helping people here. Nor can I. Abby is my sister, and I need to watch over her." He cared about his sister. "My sister needs to think of her future, as well."

"I can't argue with that." How he longed to tell Abby's brother to stop worrying! Abby's future wasn't with the son of runaway Amish.

Even as he thought of her spending time with some other man, another twinge raced through him. Only this one left a searing pain in its wake as it hit his heart.

Chapter Six

Clattering pans together was a *gut* way to work off frustration, Abby decided as she searched for the exact cookie tray she wanted to put beneath the cherry pies she had ready to go into the second oven. The other was filled with pans of chocolate-chip cookies.

Isaac had refused to tell her where he'd gone this afternoon, and she'd discovered why half an hour ago. She'd happened to overhear a couple of the *Englisch* volunteers talking about whether David would be joining their teams at the new houses. They'd overheard her brother talking with David. That, the *Englischers* were certain, was a sign David would be bringing his skills more often to the new house sites.

She wasn't so sure.

Isaac had rushed out after he'd learned more about the job Glen had given her and David. Knowing her brother as she did, she should have guessed he'd gone to see David so he could remind David an Amish woman shouldn't marry an *Englischer*. She wanted to remind her brother she was a grown woman, but that wouldn't make any difference. Isaac saw it as his job to watch over his only sister until the day she exchanged vows with an Amish man of whom he approved. For Isaac, her future was an unfinished detail, and he hated leaving anything undone.

What could she say to him? *Don't care about me as much as you do?* She appreciated how much he worried about her. To be honest, in spite of teasing him about leaving their younger brother in charge of the farm, she was always shocked when he left long enough to come and help in Evergreen Corners. He was torn between his duty to family and his duty to help others as Jesus urged His disciples to do.

It is more blessed to give than to receive. That was one of the earliest lessons the *kinder* in her family had learned. She and Isaac had taken that verse from Acts to heart.

"Hey, Abby!"

Her grumpy mood vanished at Mikayla's voice. The girl sounded carefree, a *gut* sign she hadn't had a run-in with the bullies after school.

In fact, the bullies hadn't bothered anyone the last few days. It might have been only a reprieve, but Abby prayed they'd given up their hurtful ways and found better venues to expend their energy.

"Hey yourself, Mikayla." Abby bent to take the pans of cookies out of the oven and slid them, one at a time, onto the butcher-block counter next to the stove. With the ease of practice, she used a spatula to lift the cookies from the trays to the aluminum foil where they could cool. "The other kids have stopped by already and headed out to where they're working today. Aren't you joining them?"

"I am, but I came to talk to you first. Do you know Doris Blomgren?" Mikayla came into the kitchen and reached around Abby to snag a chocolate-chip cookie.

"Be careful! Those are hot."

Bouncing the cookie from hand to hand, the girl grimaced. "You could have warned me."

"I would have told you to be careful if I'd known you were going to grab one right after you watched me take them out of the oven. Would that have stopped you?"

"Probably not. Your cookies are the best, Abby." After taking a bite of the soft cookie and melted chocolate, she sighed. "So good." She didn't pause before she asked again. "Do you know Doris Blomgren?"

"*Ja.* I should say I know of her, because we've never met. She's been generous in sending casseroles over to share with the volunteers."

"She's Jack's aunt." Her nose wrinkled. "Maybe his great-aunt. Anyhow, she's a nice old lady."

Abby had to wonder how old "old" was in Mikayla's estimation. It could mean Doris was any age from forty up. Maybe even in her thirties. To a teenager, that was *old*.

"She needs help with something," Mikayla said, "and I thought we might be able to help."

"We? You and me?" Abby asked as she set the cookie sheets aside to reuse with the next batch to put into the oven.

"No, the teen volunteers. I heard David talking on the phone to Glen about the project you two are supposed to be working on with us."

Delighted the girl was interested in a project that would mean spending more time with her guardian, Abby said, "We're hoping to do projects and fun events."

"Fun? David?"

The girl's words echoed what David had said at the diner. Was he averse to having a *gut* time? No, he'd said someone else had told him he wasn't fun.

Abby asked, "Do you think he's fun?"

The girl looked away, lowering her eyes. The motion told Abby everything she needed to confirm her suspicions. *Daed* and daughter were leading parallel lives, residing under the same roof but having little interaction. Sorrow bubbled tears into her eyes because she couldn't imagine anything sadder than two people resisting anything that would make them a family.

"Well," Abby said, trying to sound casual, "if you don't think he's fun, maybe you think he's funny, too."

"Too?" The teenager stared in astonishment. "You think David is funny?"

"He's always saying things that make me laugh. He's got a way with words, I guess you could say."

"Really?"

"It's subtle, ain't so?" She reached for the bottle so she could pour a thin sheen of oil on the cookie sheets. "I find I've got to listen for the jokes he's making. If I wasn't paying attention, they'd probably go right over my head."

She held her breath, watching as the girl digested her words. It was a long shot, Abby knew, but if Mikayla listened more to what David had to say, there was a chance they could become closer.

When Mikayla mumbled a noncommittal answer, Abby let her breath sift through her teeth. Getting the two to see their lives would be enriched by each other was going to be more difficult than she'd thought.

She spooned dough onto the cookie sheet. Once

she finished baking this batch, she would head to the apartment and prepare supper for herself, Isaac and their guests. Maybe she'd have another opportunity then to persuade Mikayla to spend more time with her guardian.

"Abby, what do you say we make our first project helping Doris Blomgren?"

Putting the trays into the oven and setting the timer, Abby asked, "What does Doris need?"

Mikayla snatched another cookie and, as she ate it, explained how she'd known Doris most of her life. "She was my grandmother's best friend. She has an old-fashioned sewing machine that isn't working. Maybe we can help her get it fixed."

"All of us? Fixing an old sewing machine sounds like something David can do on his own."

"It is."

"But?" she asked when the girl again wouldn't meet her eyes.

"Mrs. Blomgren is pretty old-fashioned as well as old." Mikayla rolled her eyes. "She must be close to a hundred."

"Really?"

Lifting her phone, Mikayla tapped it a couple of times and handed it to Abby. "That's Mrs. Blomgren in the photo. See? She's ancient!"

The picture was blurred, but, squinting, Abby could make out the image of a woman. She had pure white hair, and her hands, resting on the arms of an overstuffed chair, were wrinkled. Perhaps her face was as well, but Abby couldn't tell by the photo.

A man stood next to the chair where the woman sat. Like Doris, the man's face wasn't clear. Could that be

Mikayla's *daed*? Was that why she kept such an out-of-focus photo?

Handing the phone to Mikayla, she said, "She looks to be in her seventies or eighties."

"Maybe, but she acts like she was born and raised in Victorian times. She says she doesn't think David should be alone with her in her house for the time it'll take to fix the sewing machine."

"Then why doesn't he take it to his shop to fix it?"

"A good question" came the answer in a deeper voice.

She looked over her shoulder to see David crossing the community center's main room. His coat was unzipped and his bright yellow-and-green winter hat and dark gloves were nowhere to be seen.

Had it warmed up outside? It suddenly felt much hotter inside the kitchen. As if both ovens were set on Broil and each of the dozen burners lit. She realized the warmth came from within her as he entered the kitchen. She was startled by how pleased she was to see him.

She was the only one. Mikayla said something under her breath, grabbed her coat and rushed out of the kitchen.

"Mikayla!" Abby called after her. "Don't you want to tell David about your great idea?"

"You tell him! I've got to go—I should be—" The outer door slammed behind her.

Abby looked at David. He held up a hand before she could speak.

"Don't apologize, Abby," he said in a clipped tone. "You didn't do anything to make her run off."

"Nor did you."

"And that's the problem." He sighed. "How can you

fix something when you don't have any idea what's wrong?"

Abby wished she had an answer for him but, for once, she couldn't see a quick solution to a problem and how she might have been able to help resolve it.

David saw the sorrow on Abby's expressive face and he wanted to kick himself...again. First, his arrival had sent his daughter fleeing. Now he'd upset Abby. Though he didn't want to admit it, maybe her brother was right to worry about David spending so much time with her. Everything he did seemed to distress those around him.

Stop it! he told himself as he had so many times before. He'd made the cafeteria workers happy by fixing the dishwasher. Too bad relationships didn't come with user manuals and a way to repair them with a simple hand tool.

If it'd been easy to mend problems among people, his parents would have discovered how long ago. They would have put to rest the bad memories of their lives among the Amish. Though they'd pretended they had, they hadn't, because anytime he tried to initiate a discussion about his past, they shut him down.

Pushing those thoughts aside, because each day he spent with Abby made him more baffled about his parents' opinions, he asked, "What great idea has Mikayla had?"

He listened while Abby took cookies out of the oven and outlined what his daughter had told her. Not sure why Mikayla wouldn't have wanted to share with him, he said, "I'd be glad to fix Doris's sewing machine for her. I don't know how we would involve the teens."

"I said the same thing. According to Mikayla, Doris

Blomgren believes she needs a chaperone so her neighbors won't gossip about a man being behind her closed doors while her sewing machine is repaired."

When her lips twitched, he felt his do the same. He hadn't thought he'd be able to smile after his conversation with her brother. "I'm not surprised, because Doris has her own view of the world and nobody's going to change her mind at this late date."

"What do you think of it being a project for the teenagers?"

"It would give us the answer to the riddle of how many people it takes to fix a treadle sewing machine."

He heard a soft sound behind him. Shock riveted him when he realized it was Mikayla muffling a laugh. Mikayla? She'd come back? Though he wanted to turn and see for himself that she'd found his weak joke funny, he didn't. Would she stop laughing if she realized he'd heard her?

When Abby looked past him, he rested one elbow on the counter with what he hoped looked like nonchalance. He didn't say anything as Mikayla explained she couldn't show up without cookies. Abby wrapped up almost two dozen of the delicious smelling cookies and handed them to Mikayla.

"Anything else?" Abby asked.

"Not now," his daughter said before rushing for the door.

"Don't be too late. We're having supper at Abby's tonight," David called.

He thought she wasn't going to respond, but she paused and faced them. "Are we really having supper tonight with you, Abby?"

"*Ja*, with me and my brother."

"Okay." Mikayla glared at him before leaving.

He sighed, wondering if he'd ever figure out his daughter.

"At least, she likes the idea of joining us for supper." Abby gave him a sympathetic smile as she put the cookie sheet into the sink to soak. He was no longer amazed she seemed privy to his thoughts, even when they were a jumble in his head. "Our apartment is neutral territory. Maybe she'll open up to you a bit more while you're there."

"I hope so." He did because he was running out of ideas on how to reach the girl.

Chapter Seven

When she heard the knock on the apartment door, Abby emerged from the tiny kitchen into the not much bigger living room. She smiled when her brother opened the door to reveal David and Mikayla on the other side.

"*Komm* in!" she called. "You're right on time."

Her cheery tone seemed to fall on deaf ears because Isaac scowled as he let their guests in. David sidled past her brother, acting as if he anticipated an attack at any moment. Mikayla hurried across the small living room to stand beside Abby, apparently hoping to be out of the way of any angry words.

For a moment, Abby was tempted to tell Mikayla not to worry. Isaac had assured her less than five minutes ago he'd say nothing to David about her participation in the youth group. As she watched the two men eye each other, she wondered if she should have asked her brother to act as if the conversation at the school had never happened.

Isaac saw the whole world in black and white. Trying to convince him to be any other way would have been futile.

"Supper is ready," she said to break the silence. "Mikayla, why don't you and David take off your coats and leave them on the sofa? Then you can join us in the kitchen." She hooked a thumb over her shoulder. "Right through this door." Without pausing, she said, "Isaac, I could use your help in getting the roast on the table."

Her brother looked at her, startled. An Amish kitchen was a woman's domain and a male entered it only to eat.

"I was going to get the extra chairs..." he began.

"That can wait. Lots to do before we're ready to sit down, and I could use your help." She *did* need his cooperation to make the evening pleasant.

She let a soft sigh drift past her lips as her brother went into the kitchen. Isaac was going to try his best to make their guests feel welcome. Again, she should have expected that. Being hospitable—even to outsiders—was an essential tenet of the plain people.

Mikayla asked question after question about the process of making gravy, and Abby answered each one. She guessed Mikayla was wary of letting silence fall again. Abby was, too, which was why she kept up a steady monologue. "Mikayla, will you get the butter out of the fridge? It's on the top shelf of the door. The bread was made today. Not by me. I picked it up at the diner. You know they have a nice selection of breads there. Do you know what chowchow is, Mikayla? It's in the clear bowl with the dark blue top, on the second shelf in the fridge. Will you put it on the table, too? I'll get the mashed potatoes into another bowl and then I'll pour out the gravy, and we'll be set to go. We..."

Her voice trailed away when she saw regret in David's eyes. His gaze was on his daughter. He looked at Abby and quickly away. Sadness sifted through her.

David and Mikayla led overlapping lives but had raised barriers between them. She prayed they'd find a way to break through.

"Where do you want the roast, Abby?" asked Isaac, drawing her attention to him.

She flinched, knowing he'd been aware of that fleeting moment when her eyes and David's had connected.

"On the table anywhere," she answered, the raw heat of tears filling her throat.

Had this been the worst idea she'd had since the night of the buggy race accident? It was unlikely anyone would be injured tonight, but the tension in the room was strangling her.

When Isaac went to get extra chairs from the garage downstairs, David moved closer to the stove.

"Maybe we should go," he said. "Your brother is unhappy about us being here."

"No," she said, not giving herself the opportunity to admit he was right. "We invited you for supper, and I doubt you've got much of anything in the house to make a meal for yourself and Mikayla."

"We can order pizza."

She looked into the living room, where the girl perched on the well-broken-in sofa, paging through the latest copy of the *Budget*. Abby doubted the teenager was pausing to read news from plain communities published in the letters the newspaper's correspondents had submitted from around the world. The girl was hunched into herself.

"Did something happen to her?" Abby asked, not wanting to alert the girl that they were talking about her.

David's mouth hardened. "Those bullies went after

Mikayla and Lily DeMent today on their way home from the site where they've been volunteering."

She gasped. "Are they okay?"

"So far the bullies are using just words."

"Words hurt."

His expression eased. "That sounds like the voice of experience."

"I've seen this happen to others." *And to myself*, she added silently.

"I wish I knew how to halt this. I keep a close eye on her and the other kids, but somehow the bullies find out when I'm not around. Same with the other kids' parents."

"I'll keep praying that a solution will be found."

"Thank you, Abby." He put a hand on her shoulder. "I appreciate that more than I can say. I—"

David pulled back from her as the outer door opened and Isaac walked in. She realized how close they'd been standing. If her brother had seen, nothing she said would persuade him that she and David both understood they could be no more than friends.

Abby ignored her anxiety when Isaac set the chairs by the table. Mikayla came in to join them. When Abby motioned for them to take their seats, she was glad to see David and his daughter sitting side by side. The other side of the table was left for her and Isaac. Her brother hesitated for a long moment, and she knew he was trying to decide what was worse: him sitting across from David or her. When he pulled out the chair opposite Mikayla, she wished she could reassure her brother that he had nothing to worry about.

She couldn't. Not when her heart jumped for joy at something as silly as being able to face David throughout the meal. Silencing that thought, she set the mashed potatoes and a big bowl of dark gravy on the small table before she pulled out her own chair.

"We pray silently," Isaac said after she sat, "but you're welcome to say grace aloud if you wish."

Mikayla leaned forward. "What do you pray?"

"My gratitude for the food on our table and those around it," Isaac said in his most pompous tone.

When the girl quelled, Abby jumped in to say, "*Ja*, but when I was a little girl I used to say the Lord's Prayer as many times as fast as I could before *Daed* gave us the signal to begin eating."

She was amazed when Isaac asked, "You did that?" She didn't want him to scold her in front of their company. Then he grinned. "I did the same thing. I got up to four repetitions completed one time when *Grossdawdi* Kauffman was at the table."

Laughing, she looked across the table at David and Mikayla. "When we were young, we loved our *grossdawdi*. Our grandfather. However, he took the longest time to say grace. If one of us became antsy because we were hungry, he'd take longer because he thought we should be focused on gratitude, not the delicious food *Grossmammi* put on the table." She winked at her brother. "Four, huh? That's got to be a record."

"Haven't heard of anyone who's ever done more." He puffed his chest out in a false pose of pride. That brought laughter from them.

As they bent their heads for grace, the first thing Abby thanked God for was how the conversation had turned so that the glowers and silences had become *gut* humor. The distrust Isaac had for David wasn't gone, but she hoped, for the next few hours, it could be forgotten.

* * *

Abby rose before the sun the next morning to have *kaffi* brewing while she cooked breakfast for Isaac. Though he didn't have to milk while he was in the village, he kept the same hours he did up north.

Isaac said nothing more than a mumbled *gute mariye* as he sat at the table now edged again only by two chairs. He'd waited until she'd put their eggs, bacon and toast on the table along with the pot of *kaffi* and had pulled out her own chair. Bending his head for grace, he remained silent. That silence she understood.

As she did almost every time she prayed, she began by thanking the *gut* Lord for His kindness in bringing her to Evergreen Corners, where she could do His work. She'd asked for healing for her battered heart and He had led her to a place where she was kept so busy she seldom had time to think about the past and the mistakes she'd made.

Isaac cleared his throat, raised his head and reached for his fork. Before he took a single bite, he said, "After hearing you and David Riehl talk about your plans for the youth group last night, it's clear to me you're spending too much time with this *Englischer*."

Her relief at how well the previous night had gone sifted away. "I spend lots of time with lots of *Englischers*. There aren't many plain folk in Evergreen Corners. Even the Mennonites here aren't conservative. They drive cars and have TVs and computers." She knew she was avoiding the conversation about David that she didn't want to have, but she also was aware of the fact her brother wouldn't be put off any longer from saying what was on his mind.

"Abby, you should be more serious."

"I'm serious about helping people get back into their homes and businesses." She picked up a piece of toast and buttered it, though her appetite had vanished. "As you are, Isaac."

"You need to think of your future. You don't want to become an *alt maedel*."

She wasn't bothered by his concerns about her never marrying and being labeled an old maid, but she wouldn't say that to Isaac. If she did, he'd try to find another way to convince her to heed his worries about her future if she didn't wed.

"Of course, I don't," she replied, putting the toast next to the rest of her untouched breakfast, "but for now, I've committed to helping here."

"Someone else can step in to do your job. You must never forget how important it is not to create gossip about yourself."

"Wouldn't I create more gossip if I walked away from what I'd promised to do?" Getting up to put the *kaffi* pot on the stove, she kept him from seeing her grimace.

She could imagine how he'd react if she said the same thing to him. Though with her brother's skills as a mason and being able to lay out a foundation with square corners, he might not be as easy to replace as a cook.

"Isaac, you asked me to come with you and our cousins to Evergreen Corners."

"I did, but I didn't think you would want to stay for months and months. I'm beginning to wonder if you ever intend to come home."

She faced him and saw disconcertment lining his forehead. If she'd needed proof he cared about her, there it was. However, she couldn't let his sense of obligation

for her future persuade her into doing something that
would ruin the rest of her life.

"Of course, I intend to come back to our farm." She
let her own devotion to her family fill her voice. "My
home is with you and the rest of our family, but right
now, helping here is where I can best serve God and
His people. He has led me to guiding a group of teenagers closer to Him. How can I walk away from that?"

"You're changing the subject again."

"I thought what I'm going to do in the future was
the subject." She came to the table and sat beside him.

"David Riehl is the subject. I don't like how much
time you're already spending with him. You should be
enjoying the company of young men who might be willing to marry you."

This time Abby couldn't hide her frown. "*Willing* to
marry me? Do you think I'm such an *alt maedel* that
someone has to settle for me?"

"No, no." Issac had the decency to appear embarrassed and she hoped he'd realized he shouldn't be harp-
ing on the subject. He hadn't announced any plans to
wed, either. "But, Abby, it's an older brother's place to
look after his younger sister."

"If you're worried about anything between David
and me, stop. David is an *Englischer*. I'm plain. We can
be friends but nothing more. We're working together
to help the teens learn to trust God will guide them to
know how to deal with these bullies." She was glad he
couldn't hear her thoughts because a pinch of sadness
warned her that, in spite of her words, she'd thought
about sharing more with David than friendship. No!
She was trying to help him build a better relationship
with his daughter, not with her! Annoyance at her own

thoughts sharpened her tone. "You know I know that, Isaac. Why are you acting so anxious over this?"

"Because I know your heart hasn't given you the best advice before."

She froze, horrified that Isaac would throw the past at her now in an effort to prove his point. Didn't he realize that every day, every decision she made was colored by what had happened the night Bert Fetter was almost killed during the buggy race?

"Es dutt mir leed," he said, breaking the silence.

"I know you're sorry."

"I didn't say that to hurt you, only to..." He sighed. "I want to make sure you don't get hurt again, little sister."

She continued to stare at her plate and her untouched breakfast. The eggs had congealed. No matter, because she doubted she could eat a single bite anyhow. "I understand that, but I also know how hard I work so I won't make the same mistake twice. I've learned my lesson, and listening to my heart is the last thing I'm ever going to do again."

Had that been a knock at the barn door?

David switched off the battery-operated screwdriver he'd been using to open the underside of a toaster. Looking over his shoulder, he saw a silhouette in the doorway of the old barn he'd turned into a repair shop.

Sunlight streamed through the translucent shape of a heart-shaped *kapp* atop a head that was the right height to belong to Abby Kauffman. Of course, it was Abby. Why would any other plain woman be standing by his shop door?

Why was *Abby* there?

He grimaced. What had her brother said to her after

he and Mikayla had left? David doubted Isaac had been as uncommunicative as Mikayla after supper last night. Every attempt he'd made to get his daughter to talk about the incident with Hunter Keyes and the other bullies had been fruitless. She was upset, but she didn't want to tell him what had occurred.

Had Mikayla spoken to Abby about it? Was that why Abby was knocking on his door now?

"David, are you inside?" she called as she rapped her knuckles against the door again.

Knowing he was lost in the shadows because the barn's few windows were draped with dusty spiderwebs, he brushed crumbs from the toaster off his hands. He opened the door and drew in a deep breath when he saw how the spring sunshine shone off her golden hair. She looked the embodiment of spring with her crisp white *kapp* and pale pink dress that was the color of the hearts of the apple blossoms that soon would burst open.

"Come on in," he said once he got both his breath and voice back, though he wanted to ask if she'd talked to Mikayla about the bullies. "How are you today?"

"I'm fine. I wanted to let you know that I spoke with Doris Blomgren. She's agreed for the two of us to come to her house the day after tomorrow. I've got time after lunch. Would that work for you?"

"Let me check." He ignored his disappointment that Abby hadn't come to talk to him about his daughter. He went to a simple plank stretched across two sawhorses. Opening a calendar on top of it, he flipped the page to the new week. "Michael Miller asked me to stop by his building site that afternoon to look at a circular saw that isn't working. It shouldn't take long. How does two work for you?"

"I need to be at the community center by three at the latest."

"We're just looking at her sewing machine, so it won't take long."

"Sounds *gut*." She smiled, and his center melted.

Why did the first woman who'd made him react like that in years have to be Amish? She'd never given him any suggestion she was open to any relationship other than friendship. It was good that at least one of them had their head screwed on right.

To cover up his hesitation, he asked with what he hoped sounded like irony, "Do you think I can make hundred-plus-year-old parts appear when I snap my fingers?"

Abby smiled, and he was delighted to see a dimple on either side of her mouth. How had he missed those before now?

"I've heard you're the best in town," she replied in the same teasing tone, "at repairing anything. Maybe you can make parts appear as you need them."

He laughed and was surprised when his shoulders eased from the taut line they'd assumed the night he'd heard of Boyd's death. They'd grown more rigid when he'd discovered Boyd's house had been washed away by the flood. Had they been so stiff for almost a year?

"I'll do my best," he said, "but I'm not that good."

"I don't think you'll need to. Doris may be stubborn and more than a bit old-fashioned, but she seems kind."

When she started to turn to leave, he heard himself asking, "Would you like a tour of the shop?"

Had he lost the last vestiges of his mind? He should be relieved she wasn't planning to linger. She hadn't flirted or led him on. She was being the friend she wished him to be. He knew she was smart, but, for a moment, he wanted to be foolish.

He almost laughed again. Foolish? His ex would have snorted in derision if he'd described himself that way. Chelsea's favorite words for him had been *dull* and *boring* and *stick-in-the-mud*. And maybe he had been when he was with her, because, in retrospect, he'd come to realize they'd had too little in common. She'd wanted to go barhopping, and he'd liked to spend a quiet evening with a close friends.

"*Danki*, David," Abby said, bringing his attention back to her. "But what I'd really like is a tour of your big barn."

"The big barn?"

"*Ja.* Barns here in Vermont are different from the ones I'm familiar with in Lancaster County."

"I thought you lived in the Northeast Kingdom."

She smiled again when he used the common term for the section of the state that bordered both New Hampshire and Canada. "Our dairy barn is a bank barn like the one we had in Lancaster County. Your barn isn't built into a hillside like those."

"All right. C'mon." He opened the door. The fresh breeze refused to surrender its chill and he zipped his light brown barn coat and closed the snaps along the front.

Walking beside him, Abby wrapped her arms around herself as if she could hold off the cold. Her black coat was made of thick wool, and she wore thick socks beneath her dress that peeked from beneath the hem of her coat. Her bonnet protected her from the wind, but he guessed it became a wind tunnel when they turned into the breeze.

"Whew," she murmured once inside after he'd opened the small door next to the huge sliding one on the front of the barn.

Dust motes danced in a crazy swirl as the wind found every crevice in the barn's walls and around the windows. A miniature tornado twirled, raising remnants of hay and chaff off the concrete floor. Overhead came the sound of swallows disturbed by the eddies of air reaching into their haven in the hayloft.

Abby scanned the space. He watched as she turned around, taking in everything. When she took a deep breath, he did the same. It was flavored with the aromas of a barn, the dry odor of the hay as well as the lush scents of oats and other grains.

"You don't keep any animals in here?" she asked. "I don't smell them."

"I used to have a few chickens, two horses, a donkey and an ornery old goat when I was a kid. When my repair business started to consume my time, it wasn't fair to animals not to be fed and cared for on a regular schedule."

"True." She faced him. "So you grew up on this farm?"

"From the time I began school. My parents sold it to me when they decided they wanted to live somewhere else."

"It's interesting to see how much is the same about this barn and the ones I'm familiar with." She walked to a ladder that was made of thick pegs set into two uprights supporting the roof. Touching them, she said, "I've seen something that looks like this in almost every barn I've been in. Is this ladder the only way to reach the hayloft?"

"No, but the hay had to be pulled up to the hayloft." He gestured for her to follow him over to a nearby window. Wiping the dust off the panes with the elbow of his coat, he pointed upward. "See that small extension sticking out from gable end? It's above a door on the upper floor. It's called a hay hood. A pulley was attached there to lift the hay up to the loft. That door is nailed shut now because I didn't want any kids trying to sneak in. Plenty of the boards in the loft floor are rotted. One of these days, in my spare time, I'll look into replacing them."

"What would you use the space for?" She edged back from the window and looked up again.

"Apartments are always at a premium around here, especially ones for families with lower incomes. There's enough room upstairs for a couple of two-bedroom apartments. I'd add extra windows so the renters could enjoy views of the mountains." He gave her a crooked smile. "Sometimes I think I should talk Mikayla into helping me, so we could work on the project together. But first, I'd have to convince her to say more than two words in a row to me."

"She will."

"I wish I could be as sure of that. The few times I've gotten her to talk to me, she says no to anything I suggest. I know she's grieving, but I don't want heartache to be her life."

"It won't be, David." She wiped dust off the sleeve of his coat. It was a motion he could imagine her doing with the teens, but he was riveted by the craving to pull her closer. He longed to know how she would feel in his arms, how her soft mouth would taste, the sweet scent of her hair.

He was saved from his own thoughts when she said, "Give Mikayla time, David. Each of us mourns differently."

"I wish she'd be more positive about the things I suggest."

"She's a teenager. Give her the benefit of the doubt and stay optimistic that things will work out. She's grateful to you, though she seldom shows it."

Mikayla was grateful? That was news to him, especially after last night when the only thing she'd said had been a grudging good-night before she'd gone upstairs to her room the minute they'd returned home.

He wanted to believe Abby, but everything in his world had turned upside down in the past year. First, he'd become the father of a teenager. Now he'd met a woman who made him question everything his parents had ever told him about the Amish.

After he walked out of the barn with Abby, he told her he'd see her in a couple of days at the Blomgren house. She gave him a quick wave and hurried down the drive between his house and the shop. He wished there was a reason to ask her to stay longer. It didn't have to be a good reason.

But not the truth that he couldn't stop thinking about: how much he wanted to kiss her.

Chapter Eight

"There. That should do it." David straightened and wiped his hands on his trousers. "Remind your workers to clean out the sawdust from around the blade at the end of every day, so it doesn't start building up."

With a chuckle, Michael Miller settled his black wool hat on his head. "I do remind them. They tell me they forget." He shook his head. "I'll keep after them. We can't work if our tools don't."

Closing his toolbox, David said, "I'm amazed you use power tools. I thought electricity was off-limits to you Amish."

"No, it's not off-limits. We *choose* not to connect our homes to the power grid but we use what we have to in order to get a job done."

"I don't understand why one's okay and the other isn't."

His friend leaned against an idle skid steer. Crossing his arms in front of him, he smiled. "That confuses a lot of folks, but it's simple. We want the focus in our homes to be on God and our families. Not television shows or the internet or whatever else is going on. The choices our ancestors made were intended to keep us more involved with each other and less caught up in the concerns of the rest of the world."

He thought of how Mikayla spent each evening in her room, plugged into social media and distancing herself from him. Would it be different if they lived a plain life?

The thought startled him. As he listened to Michael explain the Amish used buggies because it also allowed them more time with family and close neighbors, he wondered if that was the reason his parents had left. They'd often traveled during their careers with the successful construction company his father had built from the ground up, leaving David with sitters when he was too young to be by himself. He'd assumed family was important to them, but he now began to wonder.

As he drove to Doris Blomgren's house later, David couldn't shake the questions from his head. Why *had* his parents abandoned everything they'd known to strike out on their own?

David had no answers and more questions to taunt him as he got out of his well-used red truck in front of Doris's house. He wasn't surprised to see Abby waiting by the front walk. He hoped she hadn't been there long. Checking out the circular saw had taken longer than he'd planned.

"Sorry I'm late," he said.

"You're right on time," she replied when he reached the sidewalk.

He glanced at his watch and saw that she was right. "The clock in the truck must be running fast." He chuckled. "The only thing about that old piece of junk that is."

"Shall we go inside? I've seen Doris peeking out

the windows several times, so I know she's eager to talk to us."

"Lead the way."

He followed her along the sidewalk and up the steps to the small front porch. There was nothing otherwise modest about the old house. Wings wandered in every possible direction and he wondered when each had been added to the original building. Three stories high, it was topped by a widow's walk enclosed in glass.

Abby rang the bell and the door opened. Doris Blomgren was a bright sprite of a woman. Her pure white hair was braided and arranged in a coronet on her head. She wore a light pink shirtwaist dress with a garish print that belonged to a time more than sixty years ago. A Donna Reed type with a pearl necklace to match her earrings. With a smile that rearranged her wrinkles, she motioned for David and Abby to come in.

He kept his nose from wrinkling as the odors of old grease and fresh liniment hung in the air. It was the same smell that had filled the *dawdi haus* where his great-grandparents had lived during the earliest years of his childhood. He hadn't liked it then, but now found himself realizing how much he'd missed it after his parents had taken him far away from their family's home.

Odd how he'd forgotten about that until now. Every time he was with Abby, some aspect of his past seemed to sneak out from behind the walls he'd built around his memories. What bothered him was how many good memories he'd cast away along with the painful ones.

"No need for introductions," Doris said as she ushered them into the hallway that separated the front two rooms. "I've seen you around town since you were knee-high to a grasshopper, David, and Abby and I talked a few days ago. And you know who I am. I'm the only one here older than the mountains." Her laugh was a raspy chortle that invited him to join in.

He did, along with Abby, as they followed Doris into a crowded room that might once have been a dining room. A large table had been placed in the middle. Its legs appeared to be darkly stained maple, but the top was so covered with books and boxes and paper and stacks of other items he couldn't guess if it'd been made from the same type of wood.

The rest of the room was as overloaded. Chairs that must have been used with the table were mixed in with a pair of rockers and two overstuffed recliners. The drapes were pulled, keeping out the sunshine, but he thought he saw photographs or maybe paintings on the wall. One door, propped open with a brick at the bottom, led into the kitchen, which was, he was shocked to see, neat. Other than a canister set and a microwave, nothing was on any of the glistening counters.

"Go ahead," Doris said. "Say what everyone says."

"What's that?" David asked, edging between the table and one of the recliners so he could give Abby enough space to enter, too.

"That I need to have a yard sale and get rid of this junk."

"It doesn't look like junk to me." He lifted a basket from the table. "This is handwoven and it's old. It's got to be worth quite a bit of money."

Doris smiled at him as if he were the most wonderful person on the planet. "That's what I've told folks, but all they see is the mess. They don't realize how long it took me and my husband to find these items." She crooked a finger. "Come over to this corner. It's where the sewing machine is."

Abby stayed back while David followed the old woman toward the farthest corner. It was a tight squeeze between the furniture and the various items stacked everywhere. He put his hand on a pile of records that reached almost to his waist. The top one was the Beatles' first album, and he wondered what other gems might be hiding in that mound.

"Here it is," trilled Doris as she flung out her hand like a ringmaster in a tiny circus.

He peered through the dusk and made out the shape of a shadowed treadle machine. He wasn't sure he would have been able to see it if he hadn't known what he was searching for.

"Do you mind if I open the drapes, so I can get a good look at it?" he asked.

"They don't open." Doris gave him an embarrassed smile. "The gizmo that moves them in the track broke a few years ago."

He smiled. "They come off their tracks pretty easily. I can check it and fix it for you, if you'd like."

"Go ahead and look at it, but I warn you. It's most likely broken. I gave it a big tug and I heard something snap." She looked at Abby. "I'm not the most patient person in the world. You'd have thought years of teaching home ec would have taught me patience, but it seems to have done the opposite."

"What's home ec?" asked Abby.

"Home economics." The elderly woman smiled. "What you Amish, my dear, learn from your mothers and grandmothers as children. How to run a household, how to cook, how to clean and how to sew."

"There are classes for that in *Englisch* schools?"

"There were. I'm afraid the programs aren't what they used to be." Doris looked sad for a moment, but brightened. "What is? I'm not what I used to be, and neither is my old sewing machine. What do you think, young man? Do you think it can be fixed?"

"Anything can be fixed. All it takes is time and money."

"I don't have oodles of either." She winked at him.

David looked at the sewing machine. He guessed Doris had been quite the flirt in her younger years. Then he corrected himself. He'd never heard a whisper of scandal about Doris or her late husband. More likely, as an older woman, she enjoyed the chance to act a bit shocking and watch how people reacted.

"Then we should get started, shouldn't we?" He grabbed a handful of the brown drapes and gave a quick jerk.

A blizzard of dust exploded around him. As he coughed and sneezed almost at the same time, his eyes burned. He squinted and realized the drapes were green beneath the thick layers of dust. Waving the dust away, he started to speak, but kept sneezing.

When a tissue was pressed into his hand, he was thrilled to discover it was damp. He dabbed at his eyes, hoping to ease that discomfort first. As soon as he could open them without pain, he pulled out his own hand-kerchief and blew his nose.

Solicitude filled Abby's voice. "Are you okay, David?"

"I will be." He looked through watery eyes at Doris's dismay. "You should have warned me your draperies were loaded."

His teasing comment eased her distress and Doris

laughed. "Look at him, Abby! That's how *he* is going to look when he's old."

He understood when Abby slid past the piles of assorted items. When she warned him to put his hand up to his forehead, he did, and she reached up to brush dust from his hair. Bits of it drifted onto her *kapp*.

"Be careful. You're just transferring it from me to you," he said, flicking dust off the white organdy.

"Don't worry. Everything is washable."

He was captured anew by her pretty eyes. As the rest of the world vanished, he savored the invisible thread between them. He thought of how they'd stood so close before, and how on each occasion it seemed as if the stolen moment lasted a lifetime and at the same time sped past so fast he didn't have a chance to grasp it.

The bridge between them collapsed when Doris called, "You'd better step out of the way, Abby, before he moves the other drape. There's a bunch of dust on it, too, I'm sure."

Blinking as if awaking from a sweet dream, Abby moved back from him. She bumped into the table and reached out to keep a half dozen metal pails from falling over. In the faint light, he could see how her cheeks had colored when Doris urged her to be careful.

"I'm sorry," Abby said.

"Don't apologize, my girl." The old woman sighed. "I should have emptied this room long ago, but I couldn't bring myself to throw out a single thing Arnie and I collected. This was his room, you know. The room where he displayed his favorite finds. After he retired and began attending auctions and flea markets almost every day, the room began to fill up. When I'm here with his special items, it's almost as if I can believe he's hiding behind one of the piles." She waved her hand at them. "Listen to me. I sound like a silly, old woman."

"No," said Abby as she edged over to Doris. "You sound like a woman who found the love of her life and knows how blessed she was."

"You're wise for such a young woman." She patted Abby's hand before adding, "Now, David, be careful with those drapes, so you don't end up sneezing again."

David heeded her warning. He drew aside the both sides with care and dropped the ends of the drapes over chairs to hold them open. The room brightened as the sunlight flowed through the window for the first time in what he guessed had been years. As he recalled, Arnie Blomgren had died around the time David was in fifth grade.

The sewing machine beside the window was dull with rust. The veneer on its case had been raised in several spots along the top, and one of the hinges on the top had lost two of its three screws, leaving the lid at an angle. The belt that should connect the treadle to the handwheel on the right side of the machine was lying in dusty black pieces on the floor. No needle was in place and the feeding mechanism set above the bobbin was as rusty as the table legs. However, the lettering for the manufacturer's name was bright, not a hint of the paint missing.

"It can be repaired, can't it?" the old woman asked. "It belonged to my grandmother first and then my mother and now me. I want to have it in working condition when I pass it along."

"It needs a lot of work, but we have volunteers who want to help us with it."

"Volunteers?" Doris scowled as she looked from him to Abby. "Exactly how many people are you planning to bring into my house?"

* * *

Abby saw David's shock at the old woman's abrupt, sharp question. When he sneezed again before he could answer, she jumped in. "Our volunteer youth group wants to do more than rebuild houses. They want to help others in town. I thought, after speaking with you, that the sewing machine might be the perfect project. It'll teach them about something they may never have encountered before. However, having them here is up to you."

Doris considered her words. "Will I be able to oversee them?"

"If you want to. It'll be *gut* for them to work with other adults, and I'm sure you have a lot to teach them. Like I said, it's up to you. If you don't want others here, David and I will make sure your treadle machine is fixed. I do hope you'll consider having the youth group involved."

The old woman looked around the room and a slow smile emerged across her face. "This old house has been silent for too long. It might do it—and me—some good to have youthful voices in here." She raised a single gnarled finger, wagging it first at Abby and then at David, who was struggling not to sneeze again. "They've got to be willing to learn what I can teach them."

"Home ec classes?" Abby asked as David dashed tears from his watery eyes and inched away from the sewing machine to join her and Doris at the other end of the table. "Cooking and sewing?"

"You can teach them about cooking, but I don't know many young people who understand how to sew on a button properly."

"A *gut* lesson for you to teach them, ain't so?" She glanced at David, urging him to join the conversation.

He gave her a quick nod. "That's a lesson I could use, too, Doris."

"Well, then, it's settled." The old woman led the way out of the crowded room into the entry hall.

Abby gasped when David stumbled into her. His arms wrapped around her and she fought to keep her knees from buckling. As swiftly as he'd grabbed her, he released her. His cheeks had become an attractive shade of red.

"Sorry," he said as he looked at the rag rug on the floor. "I caught my foot on it."

Doris tsk-tsked. "I thought I had that rug secured better. Wait a minute." She disappeared into the kitchen.

Abby knelt by the rug. It was stuck to the floor on the far side, but was loose enough to catch David's foot. "This is a tripping hazard."

"What do you—" He halted his own question as Doris returned.

"Here." She held out a roll of wide tape.

Abby recognized it as double-sided tape. She took the roll. "This should be only a temporary solution, Doris." She glanced at the wall behind the old woman. "What do you say to hanging the rug on the wall? It's way too pretty to be walked on."

"On the wall? Nonsense! It's an old rag rug I made out of even older rags. People would think I'm crazy if I hang that beat-up old rug on the wall like it was some fancy painting." She waved her hand toward the rug. "Tape it down and it'll stay in place."

"Please think about moving it. If you trip…"

"I didn't. Your young man did."

Wanting to argue further, Abby knew she risked alienating Doris. "You know what? This rug is the perfect size to put beneath the sewing machine while we're working on it. Don't you think so?"

David started to answer but she motioned him to silence. The response had to come from Doris.

Again the elderly woman thought about the question before she nodded. "That makes sense. If oil drips on it while you're getting the rust off, it won't ruin anything important. I can always make another rug if this one gets stained."

David pulled up the rug, leaving stickiness behind on the hardwood floor. He carried it into the overfilled room and lifted each corner of the treadle machine to put it beneath it.

Abby stood and took a step toward the kitchen. Doris halted her by saying, "Don't worry. My cleaning lady will get the excess glue off the floor when she comes tomorrow."

"And we'll be back next week with the teens," David said once he'd rejoined them in the hallway. "Is next Tuesday okay for you, Doris?"

"I should check my social calendar in case I'm entertaining the queen that afternoon." With a guffaw, Doris added, "Next Tuesday is fine."

Smiling as they bade the elderly woman goodbye, Abby went out with David. Neither of them spoke until they reached David's truck, which was covered with dirt and salt stains from driving during the winter.

"It's good to see," David said with a hushed chuckle, "that age hasn't slowed her down."

"She's a *wunderbaar* lady. *Danki* for agreeing to the project for the youth group." She drew her coat around her. Would spring ever get to Evergreen Corners?

"Helping those who need us is a lesson these kids

have already learned, but now they can learn that those older than them have special skills to teach them." He looked past her to the house. "The sewing lessons will have to wait. The first thing the kids are going to have to do is move that stuff out of the dining room so we can get to the sewing machine."

"Wouldn't it be easier to move the sewing machine into the other front room?"

"Easier, maybe, but I don't know if, before it's stabilized, it could endure that journey."

She smiled. "You'll figure out something, David. Challenges don't seem to scare you, and I've got one for you."

"What's that?" He leaned his elbow on his truck.

"I'd like to get the kids involved in a special project before next week. What do you say to taking them on an outing on Saturday?"

"Where?"

"A hike."

He pushed away from the truck, his eyes wide with disbelief. "You want to hike up a mountain *now*?"

"Why not? The snow is gone."

"Here in the valley. There will be plenty of snow up at the top of the higher mountains."

"I wasn't thinking of a big mountain. More like a small one." She pointed to the gap where the road ran east and west through the valley. "Like that one. I asked around and I was told that there was an easy trail that should be passable to the top."

"That's Quarry Mountain." He put his hand up to shield his eyes. "It looks as if most of the snow is gone, but looks can be deceiving when it comes to mountains. The weather changes quickly up there."

She sighed. He had a rebuttal for everything she suggested. "Maybe it's a *dumm* idea. I thought it'd be fun for the kids. They're pretty down after their latest runins with Hunter and his cronies."

"It would be fun...in a few months."

"When the bugs are out?"

He smiled. "Okay, you've got me on that one. The bugs can be nasty once the weather is warm. Even this time of year, we'd need to make sure the kids put on bug repellent. Ticks don't take any time off."

"We want to give the youth group some time away, and what better way is there to do that than to get them up on a mountain where they can spend time with nature and God? It'll also give you a better chance to get to know the kids."

"I know most of them."

"True, but working together toward a common goal helps us see the truth about each other. It could be a lot of fun." The wrong word, she knew, when his smile slipped. She kept her own in place. "It'll also give you a chance to discover which kid has which skills that will be useful in fixing the sewing machine."

And for you and me to be together for a day. She held her breath as she waited for him to reply, hoping he couldn't discern the words she hadn't spoken.

"We'll give it a try...as long as the weather cooperates." He opened the passenger door. "I know you Amish prefer horses and buggies, but can I give you a ride to the community center?"

"Ja," she started to say. But as the image of the night when she hadn't let Bert Fetter take her home in his buggy exploded into her mind, she made some trite ex-

cuse about needing to run an errand on her way to the community center.

It wasn't a lie. She'd planned to stop at Pastor Hershey's house soon to talk to him about other ideas she had for the youth group.

David's eyes became hooded as he nodded. He closed the passenger door and walked around his truck. Getting in, he drove away without a wave.

She watched until the vehicle turned a corner. Then she began to walk toward the community center. A shiver that had nothing to do with the cold slid down her spine. Hadn't God wanted her to avoid following her heart, which brought trouble to her and others? Shouldn't it be second nature now to listen to common sense rather than what her heart yearned for?

It was becoming more obvious when she spent time with David that she hadn't learned a single thing.

Chapter Nine

On Saturday, bright sunshine woke Abby as it peeked around the shade on the window beside her bed. Sitting, she pulled up the shade and peeked out. The day looked beautiful, but she'd learned better than to trust how a day *looked*. Especially on a New England spring day when the weather changed more often than *Englisch* teens altered their hairstyles and colors.

Unlatching the window, she lifted it. A gentle breeze, cool but promising to grow warmer as the sun rose, drifted into her room, sweeping away the winter stuffiness. It made her want to jump to her feet and twirl around as she had when she was a little girl. There was something about the first days of spring, something so fresh, so precious, so fleeting, she could understand why the birds sang and the butterflies danced from flower to flower.

She let the curtains fall into place for privacy as she dressed for the day ahead. This was the day she and David were taking the teens up Quarry Mountain. Since their conversation in front of Doris's house, she hadn't spoken to him other than a quick greeting when he'd come to pick up Mikayla the next day. For the past two afternoons, Mikayla had been biking to and from the community center.

What would it be like when they spent time with the teens today? Anticipation made her clumsy and she spilled the milk and toast on the floor while making breakfast. Though her brother couldn't hide his curiosity about her uncharacteristic clumsiness, Isaac didn't ask what was bothering her. Instead he talked about the next foundation they must finish preparing, so the concrete could be poured on Monday morning.

One of the *Englischers* working with her brother came to the apartment to give them a ride. She'd be dropped off where the hikers would be meeting. He and Isaac then would head out of town to get more wood for the concrete forms. The trailhead wasn't more than a half mile out of their way.

She was the first to arrive at the parking area edged by thick trees. As she shrugged on the backpack with her hiking supplies, she urged the men to go ahead with their tasks. Isaac hesitated then nodded when she told him she'd wait at one of the picnic tables that gave her a view of the footbridge over the brook.

The truck left and she listened to the birds calling to one another. The trill of a cardinal and the more raucous cry of a blue jay both silenced as a hawk soared on the thermals high above the woods.

A few minutes later, another familiar truck pulled into the parking area. She raised her hand to wave to David and Mikayla, but paused when she saw only one person in it. Sliding off the picnic table, she waited while David parked the truck and got out. He slung a pack over one shoulder.

"Good morning," he said as he walked toward her.

She returned the greeting, then asked, "Where's Mikayla? She's coming, isn't she?"

"She is, but she wanted to ride her bike. She's decided she wants to enter a triathlon this summer."

Abby arched her brows. "That's quite a goal."

"If you ask me, her goal is to spend time out of the house."

She started to reply but he waved her to silence.

With a sigh, he said, "Ignore me. We've had a few tough days."

"Is there anything I can do to help?"

"I'd say yes, if I knew what would help."

She put her hand on his arm. When he settled his fingers over hers, she wished she had the words to tell him everything would be fine. God had a plan for David and Mikayla, and only He could see what it was.

When she heard voices, she looked past David. Two people, one pushing a bike and one slowly driving a car, approached the parking lot. She stiffened when she recognized the car. It was the one she'd seen the night the bullies had taunted Reece. Her breath caught over her pounding heart when she realized the person with the bike was Mikayla.

Abby was racing across the parking lot before she'd come up with an idea of what to do or say. Before she could reach them, the car accelerated with the screech of tires. Hands seized her arms, jerking her aside as the car sped past her, so close its passing ruffled her heavy coat. She held her arm up over her face to protect it from the gravel spewing from the tires.

"Stupid kid," David snarled. "Are you okay?"

She nodded, then ran to Mikayla, who'd let her bike

fall to the ground with a clang. Putting her arms around the girl, she held her while Mikayla wept. Abby wanted to offer solace, but any she could think of sounded trite even to her.

"Don't ask," Mikayla whispered as if Abby had spoken the banal phrases. "Please."

"He made you cry."

"Please let it go." She raised her head and dashed away the tears. "There's nothing you can do. Either of you."

Abby wished David would embrace his daughter, but he stood to one side, as unsure as she was about what to say. When she saw his hands were clenched at his sides, she hoped he wouldn't do anything foolish.

More vehicles pulled into the parking area, and Mikayla ran to join her friends.

"Don't worry," David said as he picked up the discarded bike. "I won't punch that kid's lights out, though I'm tempted. I wasn't raised to solve my problems by punching someone."

Relieved, Abby said, "There must be something we could do."

"If you figure out what it is, let me know." He didn't add more as he walked the bike to his truck and lifted it into the back, locking it in place so it wouldn't be stolen while they were hiking.

The kids—mostly *Englisch* except for the two plain teenagers, Dwight and Roy, who'd come to Evergreen Corners with Isaac—spilled out of the vehicles and grabbed their backpacks, flinging them over their shoulders as their parents urged them to have fun. While the other trucks and SUVs backed out of the parking lot, David made sure the hikers had put on bug spray before he checked each teen had brought everything on the supply list they'd been given the day the hike was announced.

Two boys forgot to bring extra bottles of water, and Cindi didn't have a second pair of socks. David pulled four bottles out and handed two to each of the boys while Mikayla found an extra pair of socks that would fit the girl.

Cindi wrinkled her nose when she saw they were simple white crew socks, but didn't say anything but thanks as she tucked them into her pack. Abby wanted to thank Mikayla. She didn't, not wanting to draw more attention to the girl who was acting as if she hadn't been crying minutes ago.

David led the way to the hiking trail. The kids motioned for Abby to follow. She'd planned on bringing up the rear, which would allow her to keep a *gut* eye on them, but she realized she had to trust the teens when she saw how they drew Mikayla into their midst. Her concerns were eased when she realized David's daughter's attempt to hide her tears from her friends had failed.

Abby caught up with him and began the slow, steady walk up Quarry Mountain. It didn't take long before isolated clumps of snow beneath the trees began to connect together like bubbles of mercury condensing into a puddle. Abby discovered what looked like snow was closer to ice. The tops of the snow piles had melted and refrozen over and over into miniature glaciers.

"Watch where you walk," she cautioned, though it wasn't necessary. The kids from Evergreen Corners had been climbing the sides of these mountains their whole lives. The plain teens were already being careful.

The path led them among tall trees and around raw ridges of rock that rose in front of them like ancient walls. Each time they stepped around one, Abby longed to pull her coat closer. The wind seemed to be waiting to ambush them on the far side of each outcropping.

"I think it's getting colder with each step we take," she said.

"Just your imagination." David laughed. "What would your pioneer ancestors say if they saw you now?"

"That I was foolish to leave the indoor comforts they couldn't have envisioned."

His laugh soared at her sour tone, and she smiled. She liked the sound of his laughter, probably because she heard it so seldom.

A tiny waterfall, no wider than her shortest finger, dropped over layers of stone to fall into a pool edged with last fall's leaves. Everything glistened as if covered with a thin sheet of ice, but the plants around the pool were only wet.

"Watch your step." David took her hand and led her around the pool.

When he continued to hold it as they climbed the ever steeper path, she knew she should draw away. She couldn't force her fingers to slip out of his. He withdrew his to pull aside a branch to let them pass, and she wished she could devise a way for him to hold her hand again.

The teens' voices grew quieter as they continued ascending through the thickening woods. She wasn't sure if it was because they were awed by nature's beauty or if the steep path was leaving them short of breath. David walked ahead with a slow, steady pace and called for breaks to hydrate every twenty minutes.

After the second stop among the trees that hid the other mountains and the valley from them, Abby dropped back to walk with Mikayla. The other kids surged to catch up with David, giving them a moment of privacy.

"How are you doing?" Mikayla asked before Abby could speak.

"I'm discovering muscles I never knew I had in flat Lancaster County." She laughed. "I'll have a chance to use my *grossmammi*'s surefire muscle liniment tomorrow."

"Better use it tonight before your muscles cramp up more." A faint smile pulled at Mikayla's lips. "I've learned that the hard way since beginning my training for the race." Pausing as she walked around a boulder that split the path, she said, "I've been thinking about Mrs. Blomgren. Do you think she's going to be alone for Easter?"

"I don't know. I thought you said she was Jack's great-*aenti*. Will his family be going to her house that day?"

Mikayla shrugged. "Maybe, but it would be sad if she's alone."

"It would." She watched the girl's face, which never hid her emotions.

Now Mikayla was wrestling with the problem of making sure Doris had a memorable Easter. Abby didn't say anything, waiting to discover what solution the girl would find.

"Y'know," Mikayla said, looking at the path ahead of them as her thin smile returned, "Dad and I always exchanged decorated eggs on Easter morning. My first one ended up in pieces because I'd tried to paint it with a crayon. Later on, I learned how to dye them and put pictures on the eggs. I cut them out of magazines and catalogs, and I tried to find pictures that would remind him of something fun we'd done in the past year. Mine got to be as fancy as the ones he made." Her smile faded as she said, "I'm going to miss doing that this year."

"You don't have to stop doing it. There must be someone who'd love an egg you decorated."

"You mean David?" She shook her head. "He's too serious. He wouldn't find it as funny as my dad did when I gave him an egg with silly pictures on it."

"Think about it, Mikayla. There must be someone who'd love to get an Easter egg from you."

"Maybe Mrs. Blomgren!"

"That's a *wunderbaar* idea. You could talk to Jack about it and maybe he'd like to make one for her, too."

Mikayla shook her head. "It's *my* family's special tradition. I'm not sure I want to share it."

Abby nodded. Though she knew how much it would mean to David for his daughter to give him a special egg and include him in that precious tradition, she must be careful. Following her heart had wreaked havoc in too many lives already.

More than an hour later, they reached the top of Quarry Mountain. The forest opened and they had a magnificent view of the valley and the twisting path of Washboard Brook through its center.

A cheer rose from the teens when Reece pulled out his cell phone and motioned for the others to gather around a marker at the top. It identified the nearby mountains and villages. The *Englisch* kids rushed to crowd in around it for the selfie.

"Abby? David? Aren't you coming?" Jack shouted.

He waved to the plain teens. "C'mon, guys. Don't you want to be in the picture?"

"Not me." Abby took a half step back. Glancing at Dwight and Roy, she saw their relief that she'd spoken up, saving them from having to do so. "We Amish don't get photographed."

"Why?" asked Lily as she sat on the slanting surface of the marker. The redhead was as close to Jack as possible. Abby guessed her participation in the group was because of her crush on him.

"We're taught it goes against God's commandment to make any graven images."

The *Englisch* kids exchanged uneasy looks, and she realized they'd come to accept her as just another volunteer. Maybe Isaac was right that she was spending too much time with *Englischers*.

Mikayla's soft voice broke the silence. "That's from the ten commandments. The second commandment, so it must have been a big deal to God."

Reece looked at his phone and started to put it in his pocket. "I'm sorry, Abby, Roy, Dwight. We didn't mean to make you uncomfortable."

"You didn't make us uncomfortable," Abby hurried to reassure him. "Go ahead and take your picture." She tapped her bonnet. "I've already put the image of you dancing around the top of the mountain right here. I've learned to keep my memories close so I can enjoy them, and I'm going to have lots of great memories of this hike."

She watched the teens take their photos before finding rocks to sit on as they pulled out their lunches and water bottles. Glad to see that Roy and Dwight settled in for the lunch right along with the teens from Evergreen Corners, she relaxed. Everyone had been honest when they'd said they hadn't meant to make anyone else feel ill at ease.

David walked over. "Is this rock taken?" He pointed to her left.

"I was saving it for you."

"It doesn't look comfortable."

"Beggars can't be choosers, or so I've heard."

Again he chuckled, and again she savored the sound. Like seeing the kids exultant at reaching the top of the mountain, his laugh would be a memory she'd pull out later to enjoy over and over.

"You handled that picture issue well," he said as he opened the bag containing a turkey sandwich.

"Plain people have to walk a fine line between the *Englisch* world and our own. We believe we shouldn't play a large part in worldly matters, but it's impossible not to find ourselves in your world at times like this." She opened her own lunch bag and pulled her feet up on the rock. "In order to help those in need, it's necessary that we live among you."

"Yet tomorrow you and the other Amish volunteers will worship alone."

She grinned as she corrected, "We will worship together while you attend your own services. God listens to each of us when we gather into our congregations."

"You seem so sure of that."

Reaching for a potato chip, she halted as she asked, "Aren't you?"

"I try to be, but I find doubts creeping in sometimes."

"It's okay to have doubts. We're imperfect humans, so our faith is imperfect, too. Only God is perfection." She took a bite of the chip, then said, "I try to remind

Isaac of that when he becomes too focused on getting everything perfectly right and becomes impossible to be around."

David unscrewed the top of his water bottle. "You love your brother, don't you?"

"Sometimes more than others." She laughed. "Isaac wants so much to avoid making mistakes."

"Don't we all?" His gaze crossed the mountaintop to where Mikayla was perched on a flat-topped boulder between Reece and Dwight. "I'd like to know the right way to reach her."

"Let me tell you something my *daed* used to say. Teenagers are like onions."

He gave her a lopsided grin. "Do you mean because they can smell bad?"

"No, I mean they're like onions because they have layers hidden one within another. If you look at them, you see a thin skin, but not inside."

"And if you delve too deeply, you can end up crying." He sighed as he stared off into the trees. "You've cut them, and tears fall."

"Exactly."

His gaze focused on her again. "How did you get to be an expert on teens?"

"Through trial and error." She smiled. "A lot of error."

"Now *that* I understand."

She resisted reaching out to pat his hand. If she touched him again, she wasn't sure if she could persuade her fingers ever to let go. She wanted to help David and Mikayla, but listening to her heart, which urged her to jump in with both feet, might be the very thing that destroyed whatever chances they had to become a family. She couldn't risk heeding her heart.

Not now when the stakes were so high.

David wasn't surprised when Abby changed the subject. Why would she want to be encased in his dreariness? If he'd chosen to prove to her that Chelsea had been right when she'd said he was no fun, then he was doing a great job.

Finishing his lunch, he stood. His leg muscles protested and he winced. He'd considered himself in good shape, but he hadn't been ready for a long hike after a sedentary winter. He heard muttering from the teens as they got up, too.

"Just think," he called out to them as he shoved his lunch bag into his backpack and pulled out an unopened bottle of water. "We'll be using a different set of muscles going down the mountain."

That brought a new round of groans, but the kids were eager to see what awaited them on the far side of the mountain. Not that they'd discover anything new. They'd been up and down the highway that cut across Vermont. The view from the mountain's side should be quite different from what they saw along the road.

The teens regained their good humor as they started on the path to the neighboring valley. Stopping for lunch had revitalized them, and they teased each other in between singing songs that matched their pace down the mountain. David let them take the lead and hung back to walk with Abby.

She didn't speak, and neither did he as he took in the amazing vista in front of them. From up on the mountain, the extent of the damage from the flood was visible, but he didn't focus on that. Instead he watched dark-colored birds gliding through the sky. He squinted, wondering if they might be bald eagles hunting in the lake north of the village. Without binoculars, he couldn't be certain. The kids pointed out the birds, and he guessed they shared his hope that eagles floated above them.

They were halfway down the mountain when he called for a rest. As he opened his water bottle, he asked, "See the steam, Abby? Look to the left of it. Can you see a sugarhouse down there among the trees?"

She squinted. "A sugarhouse? Oh, maple syrup!"

"It's one of the products Vermont is known for. That and snow."

"And ice cream and cheese."

He grinned. "Spoken like a true Vermont dairy farmer."

"That's what my family is now. Vermont dairy farmers."

"Including you?"

"I will be once I return home. Nobody escapes barn chores in my family."

His smile wobbled as she spoke of leaving Evergreen Corners. It was inevitable, and he knew it was for the best. That didn't halt the pain piercing his heart.

He was saved from having to come up with a reply when Jack sprinted over to them and urged, "Let's go visit the sap house! It'll be fun."

"We told your parents we'd have you down the mountain at three. They'll worry if we're late."

"Come on. It'll be fun."

From behind him, he heard Mikayla mutter, "He doesn't ever want to have fun."

Shock riveted him as her words echoed what he'd heard when Chelsea dumped him. The fifteen years collapsed into a single second, and he could recall his soon-to-be ex-girlfriend walking out after she'd told him that she wanted to have fun. Lots of it. Without him.

Was that really how his daughter thought of him, too? Not any longer!

"Anyone got a decent signal on their cell phone?" David asked and saw Abby smile at him.

Cindi and Mikayla each had a couple of bars, so he set them to contacting the parents and Isaac, who was responsible for the plain teens, to let them know the kids would be an hour later than planned. The parents agreed to meet the kids at the sap house.

David wondered if something sweet was the lure that sent the kids at a faster pace down the mountain. They reached the bottom and crossed the road to the sap house in less than half the time he'd expected.

The sap house, set in the shadow of some tall pines, was about the size of a pair of one-car garages set back-to-back. Made of logs covered with bark, it had a door at the front. A couple of windows broke the long expanse on the sides. In front of a second building, which had big front windows, was the parking lot. Signs hanging from the other building identified it as a gift shop.

"Watch where you're walking," he warned. "There's plastic tubing running out to the sugar bush. Take a minute and look. You'll see the sap coming into the sap house."

Squatting as if they were little kids, the teens watched the sap slide through the tubes. When a dead bug slipped past in a tube, there was a combination of laughter and disgust. They were assured no insects went into the syrup, but they kept jesting about maple syrup being a good source of protein.

"I've never seen these tubes up close before," Abby said.

"Syrup is big business in Vermont. The traditional taps, which are metal spigots driven into the maple trunks, are used by private individuals who get sap from a few trees. People producing lots of syrup have changed to this system. The sap is vacuumed out of the tree before being sent to the sap house."

"It doesn't hurt the trees?"

He smiled, not surprised her gentle heart was touched by the possible plight of maple trees. "There are studies going on to find that out, but for now, it doesn't seem to be having an impact on the trees. You can be certain the smart syrup producer wants to protect his sugar bush."

Herding the kids ahead of him toward the gift shop, he watched them go inside to the counter, where they could buy treats. The man behind the counter took orders for what was listed as maple snow.

"It's not snow." He gave them a slow wink. "There's not a lot of clean snow now, so we use shaved ice for our maple cones."

David helped Abby hand small paper cones to the teens. She had such an easy way with them, teasing and laughing along with the kids. They adored her, and it was simple to see why. When she spoke to them, she acted as if each teen was the most important person in the world. They crowded around her.

Not all of them.

Mikayla sat alone by the door.

"Go ahead," Abby murmured without looking at him. "She needs a cone, too."

Did she have eyes in the back of her head, or could she guess what he was thinking? He wasn't sure which possibility was more unsettling. If he went over, would Mikayla welcome him or not? Recalling how Abby had urged him to look on the positive side with his daughter rather than assume the negative, he took the cone she held out to him.

Sitting beside Mikayla, he held out the cone. She took it with a hushed, "Thank you."

He ate his own and hoped she'd say something else. She didn't, so before the silence grew too oppressive, he asked, "Do you like it?"

"Yes."

Instead of letting her terse answer put him off again, he said, "Me, too. I think the shaved ice is a nice contrast to the syrup."

"You do?" She looked at him directly as she seldom did. Surprise filled her eyes, and he guessed she hadn't expected him to say more after she'd tried to put an end to the conversation with her truncated response. Her eyes shifted to her cup as she added in a gentler tone, "I do, too."

"Sweet ending to a nice day. I'm glad you guys suggested we stop here."

A faint smile brushed her lips. "Me, too."

He considered saying something else, but didn't when a couple of the other teens joined them. Listening to them chatter, he scooped the last of the maple syrup from the paper cone. Mikayla listened more than she spoke.

Was she normally shy and quiet?

He searched his memory, as he had so many times, but couldn't pull up a single recollection of any conversations with her while her father was alive. Then, for the first time, he tried to remember how many times he'd witnessed Mikayla gabbing with her father.

Amazement struck him like a bolt of lightning as he couldn't recall a single time Mikayla had ever said more than a few words while he was present. He couldn't remember a single time when Boyd, like many other fathers, complained about his daughter babbling on and on about something that interested her.

Had he built up an image of what he'd assumed his life with a teen would be without considering the specific person involved? He didn't want to think that he'd let his own grief prevent him from seeing the reality right in front of him.

Abby joined them as vehicles pulled into the parking lot outside. The teens' parents had arrived. As the kids thanked him and Abby for the hike, he couldn't stop smiling. It'd gone so much better than he'd hoped, especially the last ten minutes when he'd had an actual conversation with his daughter.

"Didn't it go well?" Abby asked as they paid for the cones.

"Better than I'd hoped."

"I'm glad to hear that. Really glad." She walked beside him outside, where the teens were as loud as the crows cawing in the trees. "*Boppli* steps are unsteady ones, but they take us where we need to go."

"*Boppli?*"

"Sorry. I should have said 'baby steps.' You understand some *Deitsch*, so I forget you don't know the language."

"I now know what I've gotten through osmosis from being around you Amish folks."

"Now?"

He struggled not to scowl at his own unthinking comment. Because he was happy Mikayla hadn't cut him off with a single-word reply wasn't an excuse for revealing too much to Abby. She was suspicious, and he couldn't blame her. His excuse had sounded feeble to his own ears. Would she let the whole matter go?

Unlikely, because her kind heart would urge her to find out what was bothering him so she could offer him help as she did everyone else. He needed to find a way to divert her curiosity without piling a layer of lies on the half-truths he'd lived with since he was a child.

Chapter Ten

After breakfast on Tuesday, Abby took the grease drawer outside. It was kept next to the griddle on the larger stove. Grease and debris were scraped into it each time someone cooked another batch of eggs or bacon or pancakes. Keeping the griddle clean made the food taste better, but the drawer had to be emptied once each meal was over.

Her nose wrinkled as she carried it to the grease barrel behind the kitchen. Though they dumped it twice a day, the used grease reeked. She opened the barrel while balancing the drawer with care. Using a long spatula to slide the grease and food out of the drawer, she made sure the drawer didn't fall into the barrel. She'd done that once and learned her lesson after spending hours washing grease off the stainless-steel drawer.

That was a lesson she didn't need to be taught a second time.

As she closed the grease barrel and made sure it was secure so wandering bears, hungry after their winter hibernation, couldn't force it open and make a mess of the whole parking lot, she paused and looked down the hill. Listening to the birds and smiling when she saw a full-chested robin hunting in the grass, she watched the water in Washboard Brook tumble over the rocks.

A phone rang in the distance, but she ignored it. The men working on the house rebuilding sites wouldn't be ready for their midmorning *kaffi* for another hour. They were the only ones who called the community center. Everyone else contacted the secretary at the chapel.

She took in a deep breath. If she spread her arms, could she take off like the birds and soar through the early-spring morning? Laughing at her folly, she grimaced when she saw the grease staining her hands. She'd better wash it off right away.

When she went inside, Abby propped open the door to let in the fresh breezes, but had to close it after too many bugs decided to come in. What they needed was a screen door. That way the wood door could be left open to let air circulate through the kitchen. She would ask Pastor Hershey if there were screens for the door and windows. Soon they would be roasted as much as the food if they couldn't open up the kitchen and let fresh air in.

Would she be in Evergreen Corners by the time summer arrived?

She sighed. After their worship service on Sunday, she'd heard Dwight and Roy talking about how they'd be finishing their time in the village at month's end. Isaac had hinted she should leave in the hired van with them. She'd told him she couldn't go while she was helping with the youth group. Her brother had said he'd talk to Glen about the program and see what could be done.

Why did Isaac have to be so insistent that he knew best for her? She was taking care to do what needed to be done instead of what her heart longed to do. He couldn't be upset about her relationship with David. She hadn't seen David since he and Mikayla, along with Reece, had stopped to visit Doris yesterday. The old woman had welcomed them like long-lost family and Abby had realized anew how lonely she must be.

She looked up when the door to the street opened. Glen walked in, and her heart clenched. Was he coming to tell her that she should go home as Isaac wanted?

Then she noticed he was with a woman whose head reached as high as his shoulder. On her shiny black hair, she wore a *kapp* pleated in a box shape. Her black apron over a pale blue dress made parts of her disappear into the shadows as they crossed the room.

"I've brought you some new help," Glen announced with his usual smile. "We've got a bunch of new volunteers, so we can start the next three houses soon. By the way, this is Rachel Yoder. Rachel, this is Abby. She can show you around the kitchen and get you started."

Greeting the woman who looked to be in her thirties, Abby waved to Glen as he left to deal with one of the other dozens of issues he had to handle each day. Glad Glen hadn't mentioned a word about Abby giving up the youth group, she gave Rachel a quick tour of the kitchen, interspersing her descriptions of what they did and when with questions about the newcomer.

Abby learned Rachel was from Maine. Rachel was a widow who had come to Evergreen Corners with her young daughters. She'd left them at the day care center that had moved from the community center to a nearby church basement a couple of months ago.

"You'll find folks in Evergreen Corners are welcoming," Abby said with a smile after she'd offered Rachel *kaffi*.

Taking the cup with a shy smile, Rachel said, "I've already seen that. We arrived less than two hours ago, and we already have a place to stay and my *kinder* are being cared for while I work. What do you want me to do first?"

"Why don't you—" Abby flinched when the phone by the back door rang.

It startled Rachel, too, because she stiffened and looked in every direction until her gaze alighted on the phone.

"Wait a sec. I should get that." Glancing at the clock, Abby frowned. Who was calling at this hour? Maybe one of the other volunteers couldn't come in today. She ignored her guilt that she might have ignored the call from an ill person when she was outside earlier.

"Abby?" came the response to her hello.

"David?" she asked, astonished. She blurted out her first thought. "Is Mikayla okay?"

"She's fine, but I need you to come over to Doris's house right away."

"What's happened?"

"Get over here. I'll explain when you get here."

She started to ask another question, then heard other voices in the background. Did they belong to the teen group? No, that was impossible. The kids were in school on a Tuesday morning, so they wouldn't have gone to Doris's house until their classes were over.

The phone went dead. David had hung up. What was going on?

Pausing long enough to tell Rachel that she had to leave and to begin making sandwiches for lunch with the leftover beef in the fridge, Abby pulled on her coat and bonnet. She was glad for her sneakers as she ran down the side of the village green toward the short street where Doris Blomgren lived. Each time her feet struck the sidewalk, fear rammed through her.

God, watch over us. The prayer repeated in her head on an endless loop.

As she hurried along the slate sidewalk on Doris's street, she gasped. Doris's house looked deserted. No motion was visible beyond the sheer curtains crisscrossing the tall windows, not even the flicker from the TV.

She raced up the steps and across the porch. She was reaching for the bell when the door was flung open. David, his coat half-unzipped, motioned for her to come in.

"What's wrong, David? You look pale. Are you sick?"

"I'm fine, and everything is okay now. The rescue squad just left."

The rescue squad was what the locals called their volunteer EMTs. "Why were they here?"

He wiped his hands on the dish towel he'd tucked into the waist of his jeans. "Doris fell sometime during the night."

"Oh, my! How's she doing?" She turned in both directions, hoping for a glimpse of the elderly woman.

"She's at the hospital. The EMTs are transporting her there."

"And you're doing dishes?"

He shook his head. "I've been cleaning up while I waited for you to get here."

"Waiting? You just called."

"I tried calling a few times before, and I didn't get any answer."

"I was outside." She began to explain about emptying the grease drawer.

He interrupted her. "Doris hit her head when she fell." He sighed. "She tried to crawl to the phone before she collapsed. I found her less than a foot from it."

Abby put her hands over her mouth to silence her gasp of dismay at the thought of the kind woman suffering such an injury. When David put his fingers on her arm, she looked up at him and saw her distress mirrored in his eyes.

"You found her?" she whispered.

"Yes." His voice was clipped, as if he feared he would be sick to his stomach at any minute. "I stopped to make sure I had the tools we were going to need for working this afternoon on her sewing machine. I found her in the hallway." He stepped aside and pointed at a rag rug half in and half out of the living room. It wasn't the same one they'd moved last week. "She must have put this one down in place of the rug I slipped under the sewing machine. I think it slid out from beneath her and sent her flying."

Abby started to nod, then gasped again. "You *think*? Didn't she tell you?"

"She wasn't conscious when I got here. By the time the rescue squad team was putting her into the ambulance, she'd opened her eyes, but she wasn't making much sense. She lost quite a bit of blood." He looked down at the floor. "And *that* was what I've been cleaning up."

She didn't hesitate. She flung her arms around his shoulders. "Oh, David! I'm so sorry you had to be the one to find her."

"I thank God I found her when I did. Who knows

what might have happened by the time we arrived this afternoon?" His arm curved around her, keeping her close.

Leaning her head against his chest, she listened to the firm thump of his heart. It escalated when her cheek touched his coat. Warnings filled her head. Warnings that following her heart instead of what she should do would lead to disaster. She would listen to them…in a moment. For now, she savored drawing in the scent of his soap and whatever he'd used as aftershave.

Abby wasn't sure which one of them stepped back first.

David looked into the cluttered dining room. "I'd better head over to the hospital to see how she's doing."

She wasn't fooled by his nonchalant tone. He remained as upset over Doris's fall as she was. She tried to emulate his calm demeanor. "Do you mind if I tag along with you?"

"No. In fact, I was hoping you'd ask." A will-o'-the-wisp of a smile fled across his lips before he became serious again.

The faint change in his face generated an answering warmth deep within her where the coldest core of her fear cramped every breath she took. It wasn't much, but at the moment, it was more than enough.

The regional hospital, a building that looked as if it'd been added onto dozens of time in a hodgepodge of design, was filled with hushed urgency. David had sensed it the moment he and Abby walked through the automatic doors. He gritted his teeth as he waited with her by the elevator. The last time he'd been in this hospital had been the night of Boyd's accident. At least, today, they hadn't had to come through the emergency room, where the fight against death was more dire and immediate.

He and Abby had stopped at the information desk and learned they'd be allowed to visit Doris. It hadn't been the same the night Boyd died. David hadn't had a chance to see him until the funeral because nobody had been allowed into the curtained space where his friend had been taken. It'd taken hours to discover Boyd was dead and more time to convince the staff that the now-orphaned Mikayla shouldn't be left alone in another section of the emergency room.

With effort, he shook those horrible memories from his head as one of the six elevators pinged and the green up arrow over its door lit. He stepped to the side as a man and a couple of women, wearing white coats and talking in hushed tones, emerged. Holding the door while Abby entered, he punched the button for the third floor.

"It must be a *gut* thing that she can have visitors," Abby said over the piped-in music as the elevator began a slow climb.

"You're probably right."

"Stop it!" she ordered, putting her fingers on his arm.

"What?" He was amazed she'd touched him again. Amish women didn't do such things with an *Englischer*. What astonished him more was how the casual touch sent a flood of sweet sensation dancing across his skin. As it had when she'd given him that unexpected hug.

"Stop blaming yourself for what's happened."

"I'm not blaming myself."

"No? You aren't thinking about Doris as well as your friend's death?"

He stared at her. "Do you read minds?"

"No." She gave him a sad smile. "I do read faces, and yours is as easy to read right now as a large-print book. David, you must hand your guilt over to God. He had a reason for choosing you to be where you were both that night and today."

"I wouldn't have minded if He'd selected someone else."

The elevator lurched, and Abby's green eyes became almost perfect circles. Her fingers on his arm tightened when the car stopped and the lights flickered.

He waited a few seconds, then a few more, as the lights kept going on and off. The music jumped around like a record with a skip in it. Hearing the squeal of an emergency bell, he guessed someone in another elevator had pushed the call button.

Deciding he should do the same, he heard a voice through the speaker. "Please stay where you are—"

"As if we have any choice," he whispered to Abby.

When she smiled in the faint glow from the emergency lights, he gave her a grin in return.

"There's been a power surge," continued the voice, "but we're getting the systems back online. You should be moving in a few sec—"

The car bounced once, then a second time, as the lights returned to full strength. It began to move again.

David grinned when Abby sent up a prayer of thanksgiving. He added an *amen* when she finished. He said nothing more when the car stopped and a ding announced they'd reached their floor. The doors slid open. He motioned for her to lead the way out.

She did quickly. As the doors closed again behind

him, she said, "I've got an idea. Let's take the stairs down."

"Sounds like the best idea I've heard all day."

A stop at the nurses' station gave them directions to Doris's room. It was halfway down the hall on the right. The beep of machines and the hushed squeak of sneakers on the tiled floor was topped by quiet voices and the sounds of televisions in the rooms they passed.

David paused in the doorway and looked to the bed on the right side of the curtain. Doris was lying with her eyes closed while a young man put a tray with her lunch on the table beside the bed. He nodded to David and Abby as he slipped by them on his way out the door.

Tiptoeing, David led Abby toward the bed. He didn't want to wake Doris if she was able to get some rest. Other than a pair of small bandages near shaved spots on her head, she looked unchanged.

The old woman's eyes popped open. "Oh, it's you! At least you don't want to drain me of blood or poke something into some part of my body." She raised her bed up into a sitting position.

"How are you feeling?" Abby asked.

"I don't know why they're keeping me here," the feisty woman complained. "I've told them I've been fine in that house for the past sixty-five years."

"You know," David said, "they won't let you go until they're satisfied you won't fall again."

She rolled her eyes as if she were no older than Mikayla. "David Riehl, I don't need you parroting to me what those doctors and nurses say. My knees may be giving out, but my ears and eyes are—praise the good Lord—working fine. I wish I could say the same for the rest of you."

"We want to keep you safe."

"I simply tripped on that stupid rag rug." She glanced at Abby and gave her a wry smile. "I should have listened to you, young lady, instead of worrying about my hardwood floors and the dirt brought in during mud season. If I had, I wouldn't be a prisoner in a hospital gown. I'm glad my Arnie isn't here to see me looking like this." Her smile widened. "I made sure I had makeup on every morning before he came down for breakfast. I wanted him always to see me at my best. You know? He won my heart by telling me I was the most beautiful girl he'd ever met, so I was determined he'd never have a reason to rue saying those words."

"I'm sure he thought you were beautiful, no matter what makeup you wore," David said as tears welled in Doris's eyes.

"I know the truth!" She wagged a finger at him, then pointed to Abby. "I was never as pretty as she is. She might be the most beautiful girl on God's green earth. I know you've got eyes in your head, David Riehl, so you've got to agree."

He glanced at Abby, who was blushing. He had to admit she was lovely, even without a hint of cosmetics to enhance her green-gray eyes. Wisps of honey-blond hair had escaped from her *kapp* to twist like corkscrews along both sides of her face. However, she must marry an Amish man, not David Riehl.

When Doris's eyelids became heavy, he and Abby turned to leave. Doris called them back and demanded they find out when she could get out of the hospital.

"I'm not sure if the staff will tell us anything," Abby said. "We're not your family."

"You're as close as I've got at the moment." She shut her eyes again, clearly believing the matter was settled.

Arching a brow at Abby, David walked with her into the hallway and to the nurses' desk.

A tall woman with a name tag that said Marilyn stood behind the counter. She smiled as they approached. "Can I help you?"

"We're friends of Doris Blomgren," he said. "She asked us to check when she'll be released."

"Your names?"

He gave them to the nurse and added, "I was the one who found her and called the rescue squad."

"Then you know she was unconscious. Until it can be determined whether that was the cause or the result of her fall, we won't release her."

"I agree," David said. "I'm sure Abby agrees, too."

Abby nodded. "Everyone agrees except Doris."

"She has a great-niece who's supposed to be coming later today," Marilyn said. "We'll give her the facts, and she'll need to help Mrs. Blomgren decide where she can live now."

"You mean she won't be able to go home?" asked Abby.

"That's for the family to decide."

David saw Abby's shock, and he understood. Plain people kept their aged relatives near them. He recalled the *dawdi haus* where his great-grandparents had lived. It'd been connected by a breezeway to the main house where his grandparents and his father's unmarried siblings filled its many rooms. How many of them were still in that house? He hadn't thought about his aunts and uncles in years.

He thanked Marilyn for the information and, putting

his hand on Abby's elbow, steered her away from the nursing station. Abby hesitated a moment and looked over her shoulder.

"This may be one time when you can't fix everything, Abby," he said.

"I can pray."

He flashed her a sad smile. "I suspect you've been doing that already."

"*Ja*, of course. My initial prayers were answered when I walked into Doris's room and saw her looking so much like her normal self. *Danki*, David, for caring enough to check at her house today. If you hadn't..."

She didn't finish, and she didn't have to. He'd had similar thoughts while waiting for the ambulance to arrive.

Neither of them said anything more as they went down the stairs and left the hospital. The silence wasn't oppressive, and he knew the near tragedy had drawn them closer together. He couldn't stop thinking of how right she'd felt in his arms.

Somehow he needed to find a way to turn off those thoughts.

Chapter Eleven

Two days later, Abby closed Doris Blomgren's front door behind her and smiled with relief. The elderly woman had been released from the hospital and her great-niece, Barbara, had come to oversee the house during Doris's recovery.

Abby had liked Barbara immediately. She was a younger version of Doris, and her *gut* sense of humor and no-nonsense demeanor would be an asset during the weeks ahead. Though Doris insisted she would be fine in no time, she was far from steady on her feet. Not only could Barbara help her deal with her new walker, but she would also make sure Doris took her pills. As the *doktor* had told them, a single mistake with her heart medicines could lead to another fall, and that fall might be fatal.

Doris had insisted Abby say nothing about the treadle sewing machine and David's plans to oversee the teens repairing it. The elderly woman wanted the working machine to be a surprise—and now a *danki*—for Barbara. It was a *wunderbaar* idea, and Abby had been delighted when Doris had shared her plans while Barbara was out of the room.

Before she'd left, Abby had promised Doris that the youth group would return to begin work as soon as Doris was allowed to have company. She had a project to work on with the teens until then, and she was anxious to discover what they thought of her idea. If it went as she hoped, she could share the story of the teens' efforts with Doris and see the old woman smile.

The sun was shining and Abby's steps were jaunty as she climbed the hill toward the community center. She could hear the staccato beat of nail guns and the shrill whine of power saws closer to the brook. Her steps faltered. In the not too distant future, she wouldn't have any excuse to remain in Evergreen Corners.

No, she wasn't going to think of that today. She had plenty of reasons to be in the village, and they weren't excuses so she could spend time with David and the teens.

Get out of my head, Isaac. Her brother hadn't bugged her again about heading home when he left in a few weeks. Had Glen convinced him that her help was important? Maybe Isaac had finally accepted she could be as stubborn as he was.

Several women, including Rachel, were busy in the kitchen when Abby walked in. She waved to them and then focused on the main room. She had a lot of work to do before the teens arrived after school. Hearing a sliding door on a van open behind the building, she smiled. Today should be an interesting one.

By midafternoon, everything was ready, and she was sure it was going to be fun. Abby watched as the teens arrived and approached the tables where she'd placed sewing machines she'd borrowed from the high school. The kids acted as skittish as if they were slipping into cages filled with wild man-eating tigers.

She hid her smile at the thought. Not giving any sign she'd expected them to be astonished by the activity she'd planned, she led the way to the tables.

"I thought we'd do something different today." She allowed herself a smile. "As you know, we were supposed to go to Doris Blomgren's house today and begin repairing her old sewing machine."

"How is she?" asked Lily, for once not focused on Jack.

"She's, as they say, resting comfortably. She won't be up to having guests for at least a couple of weeks. Until then, I thought we'd work on some projects in her honor."

"Like what?" Cindi frowned at the sewing machines. "Those look older than the hills."

"Not quite that old. They used to be part of the home economics classes Doris taught at the high school. When the program was cut, the machines were put in storage. Glen found them, and David oiled them before they were delivered here, so they're ready to go."

"Go where?" asked Roy, always the most literal one.

Abby laughed. "Go to work. In honor of Doris, I thought I'd give you some of the lessons she used to teach in her home ec classes."

"I thought home ec was cooking." Mikayla hung her coat on a hook and inched toward the closest machine, bending to peer at it with curiosity.

"Not from what Doris has told me." She glanced at each of the teens in turn. "We Amish don't have home ec courses in our schools. We girls learn to cook from our *mamms* and *grossmammis*."

"Not the boys?" Reece asked.

"Nah, they do the dishes," retorted Cindi.

"No, we don't." Dwight stuffed his hands into his pockets. "We do barn chores and work in the fields while the women handle the cooking and cleaning."

Cindi frowned. "Can't girls help with chores?"

"Anytime they want," Abby said, "especially at harvest time. However, we're not talking about chores today. We're talking about sewing. I'm wondering how many of you know how to sew a button on the right way."

The teens exchanged puzzled glances and Mikayla said, "I didn't know there was a right or wrong way."

"Then it's time you learned." Abby went to the closest machine and pulled out the chair in front of it. "If each of you will take a seat by a sewing machine, we can get started."

"Us, too?" The boys looked at each other with expressions that suggested they thought she'd lost her mind.

"Ja." She sat and gestured again at the chairs. "One of these days, you'll move out from under your family's roof, and you'll be on your own. What will you do if you need a button sewn on or a piece of clothing repaired?"

"Get a girlfriend to do it?" asked Jack.

Over enthusiastic boos from the young women, another boy called, "Ask *Mamm* or *Grossmammi*?"

"You shouldn't need to ask someone else," Abby said, waving her arms to get their attention and quiet the hubbub again. She was pleased to hear the two Amish teens jumping into the conversation. Even a week ago, they would have been too shy to speak up.

Isaac would approve of the change in them, too. Once a young man was baptized and became a full-fledged member of the *Leit*, it was important he speak up when his opinion was sought.

When the teens were paying attention again, she repeated, "You shouldn't need to ask someone else. Not if you can handle such a simple task as doing a bit of repair work on your own." She smiled. "It's not as if I'm asking you to learn to make a quilt or embroider a sampler. We're going to focus on basic sewing."

"I don't know…" Jack didn't move as the other boys took a single step toward the tables. They paused, too, looking to him as their leader.

"Jack, I hear you've been helping on some of the power equipment at the work sites."

He grinned with impish delight.

At first, the teens hadn't been allowed to do much beyond running errands for the adult volunteers. The kids had asked over and over to help with the actual building. Glen had relented, insisting they only use hand tools. But, when so many volunteers left and didn't return as jobs demanded their attention, Isaac had taken up the teens' quest. He'd urged Glen to let the project leaders at each of the three house sites teach the older teens how to use the equipment. There had been some pushback, but, as her brother had reminded the project leaders, most of them had begun using power tools when they were the same age as the teens. Making sure none of the youngsters ever worked without supervision, they'd begun to make the change a few days ago.

"Big boy toys," Jack said as his smile broadened.

"Big boy *and* big girl toys." Cindi aimed a challenging tilt of her chin at her friend. "I got to use the skip steer yesterday to move some of the trees that had fallen out of the way."

"Just the branches."

"Big branches."

Abby interjected before their teasing became a real argument. "I'm glad you learned to use those machines because that will help you with these."

"My *mamm* uses one of them," Dwight said. "My *grossmammi*, too. They're no big deal."

"No?" Abby crossed her arms in front of herself. "Do you think you'll say the same thing if you end up with that needle in your finger? It won't cut it off as a saw might, but I can guarantee you that it'll get your attention."

That might have been the wrong thing to say because several of the kids stepped away from the machines. With a sigh, she made a quick change in her plans. Deciding to start with a simple task, she urged the kids to sit.

As she began to outline what she wanted them to do and how, she felt contentment for the first time in longer than she could remember. She was supposed to be in Evergreen Corners now. She was certain of that. What she wasn't certain of was how long she could— or should—remain.

David kneaded his lower back with his knuckles as he got out of his truck in front of the community center. Fixing the pump in Ricky Herndon's dairy barn had taken him a lot longer than he'd expected. At one point, he'd been ready to tell Ricky that patching together the system would be a waste of David's time and Ricky's money. The system, which pumped milk from the milkers to the holding tank, wasn't an antique, but was older than David.

He straightened and stretched as he noticed the sun hadn't disappeared over the mountains. A couple of weeks ago, it would have vanished by this hour of the day. That was a welcome sign that spring was on its way to stay.

Not that it felt that way now. Once the sun was down, the chill would become cold, and he hoped nobody had been foolish enough to believe a couple of warm days in a row meant fragile plants should be put out in the garden.

He opened the door to the community center, entered and halted in midstep. He wanted to rub his eyes to make sure he was seeing what he thought he was. The youth group was sitting around tables, like a quilting circle, each of them with a needle and thread they were using with such concentration they didn't look up to see who'd come in. They were chatting and checking each other's work.

In the kitchen, Abby was busy with three other women. She must not have heard the door because she was talking with a short woman he didn't know, her back to him.

He went to where Mikayla sat at a table with the other girls. They each held a needle and were darting it in and out of shirts, sewing on buttons.

"Hey, Mr. Riehl," said Lily as she raised her head. At her voice, the other girls looked up.

"What are you up to?" he asked, though it was obvious. Each of the teens was doing the same task.

"Before she went to the hospital," Mikayla answered,

"Mrs. Blomgren planned to teach us some basic sewing. Abby decided we should learn now and surprise her."

He hadn't been sure she'd acknowledge him after the sharp words they'd had at breakfast that morning. She'd insisted she would ride her bike to school and refused to give any credence to his argument she was making herself an easy target for the bullies. She'd ridden away without heeding a word he'd said.

"We're doing some on the machines," Lily said when he remained silent, "and the rest by hand."

Cindi laughed as she nudged Mikayla with an elbow. "We're crushing it while the boys haven't gotten one right yet."

"We're taking our time," shot back Jack. "We're going to be experts at sewing on buttons so we won't need you silly girls any longer."

Lily leaned toward him. "You've got to leave more space beneath the button to wind the thread around the base so it can be tilted in and out of the buttonhole. Do it like Abby showed us."

David left the kids debating the proper way to sew on the buttons and walked to the kitchen pass-through window. He rested his arms on the counter while he waited for Abby to have a moment to talk to him.

It didn't take long. One of the women elbowed her and motioned with her head toward where he was standing.

When Abby turned, his breath caught. It'd been a couple of days since he'd held her at Doris's house, but his longing to draw her into his arms again hadn't diminished. That one stolen second had filled his thoughts during the day and delighted his dreams at night.

"Hi!" she called as she walked into the main room.

"I didn't expect to see you now that Mikayla is riding her bike home."

"I wanted to stop by to ask you if you'd had a chance to check on Doris." He didn't want to go into the details of the disagreement he and Mikayla had gotten into that morning. Knowing Abby would have suggestions on how to bridge the chasm between them, he said nothing. This was something *he* had to fix, not Abby. "How's Doris doing?"

"Well. When I visited, her great-niece told me Doris has been listening to the instructions her *doktor* gave her. So far, at least."

"I'm glad to hear that. I'd planned on stopping over this afternoon, but today's project took a lot longer than I'd expected."

"Would you like a cup of *kaffi?*"

"Do you have some fresh?"

"Always." She laughed as she went to where the pot was on the other side of the pass-through. With ease, she stayed out of the other volunteers' way. "People are constantly in and out of here, and most of them want something warm to drink after working outside."

"It's rumored that spring is supposed to arrive one of these days."

"When it does, we'll put the *kaffi* over ice cubes."

While Abby prepared a large cup for him, he watched Mikayla with the other teens. She seemed much more at ease with them than she had a month ago. Instead of staying by herself off to the side, she sat among them and laughed as Cindi tried to help Reece thread a needle. When she said something that made the teens roar with laughter, he couldn't keep from smiling.

"She's doing better every day," he said as Abby

handed him the cup and gestured to the back door. He followed her, knowing that she had something on her mind she didn't want to discuss in front of the others. Doris? Mikayla? Something or someone else?

When Abby sat on a winter-battered bench in the tangle of weeds that was supposed to be a garden, he sat beside her. He waited for her to say whatever was on her mind.

"Mikayla is doing better every day," she said in a somber tone, "but prepare yourself that she'll have bad days as well as *gut* ones. Grief wants to cling to us for as long as it can torment us."

"'And God shall wipe away all tears from their eyes,'" he whispered.

"That's from Revelation."

He faced her. "I know. Someone shared it with me at Boyd's funeral, and I have thought of it often since while listening to Mikayla crying in her room. I wonder why God hasn't wiped the tears from her eyes as He promised."

"You must have faith that a day will come when the tears stop. A heart doesn't heal quickly, even with God's help. It's the price we pay for the ability He gave us to love. With that gift comes the cost of losing someone we love."

"Have you lost someone?"

"*Ja.* My *mamm*, I mean—"

"Your mother. I've heard that word before." He shifted so he could see her face. "I don't think I've ever heard anyone mention that your mother died. I'm sorry about that."

"*Danki.* She died when I was little more than a *boppli.*"

"Is your father alive?"

"He is, and he remarried a *wunderbaar* woman who makes him happy after many years of him struggling with depression. I tell God *danki* every morning and night in my prayers for bringing her into our lives." She put her hand over his, startling him. "Have faith, David. God brought healing to my family when I thought nothing ever would make us happy again. He'll do the same for Mikayla. And for you, because I know you have lost a dear friend."

"My best friend. Boyd and I were friends from the minute we met our first day of school. When we weren't in the same class, we spent every possible second together on the playground or after school. We worked together in our first jobs, and we saved our money and bought our first cars within days of each other. Almost every milestone in the life of a boy and a young man I shared with him, including falling in love. That's where our paths diverged. Chelsea, the girl I thought would be with me forever, dumped me the same night Boyd proposed to Jill, Mikayla's mother."

"Ouch."

"Yeah, ouch. Being happy for Boyd and Jill meant I couldn't waste time feeling sorry for myself."

"Don't you see, David? That's what Mikayla needs. A reason for the two of you to be happy so she isn't imprisoned by her grief. You had your friend and his future wife to help you through the toughest time you'd ever faced. You need to help her."

"I would if I knew how."

"You know how, David. Stop feeling guilty for every little thing that happens. Give that guilt and your pain to God. He's strong enough to shoulder the burden and let you find joy again."

"You make it sound both easy and as if it's a sure thing."

"Isn't it? One of my *grossmammi*'s favorite verses was from Romans. Romans 15, verse 13 to be exact. 'Now the God of hope fill you with all joy and peace in believing, that ye may abound in hope, through the power of the Holy Ghost.' Joy and peace and hope. What *wunderbaar* gifts from God!" She smiled at him. "All you have to do is open your heart to accept them."

He started to reply, but a woman appeared in the doorway and called to Abby in a rather frantic tone. Smoke billowed out the door around her.

Jumping to her feet, Abby ran into the kitchen. He stood to follow, then paused when he heard someone call, "It's out!"

He saw that was true, so he headed toward the street before Abby could return. Their conversation had been wandering into areas of his life he wanted to keep off-limits, even from himself. And if he knew what was good for him and for Abby, he wouldn't let her entice him to go there again.

Not ever.

Chapter Twelve

David decided the mid-April morning was just what the day before Easter should be. Frost clinging to the grass would soon vanish. Bright sunshine poured into the bathroom as he finished shaving. Washing the last of the soap off his chin, he hurried downstairs.

The newspaper was waiting by the porch and he hurried to bring it inside when the cold morning air sliced through his clothes. He made breakfast and waited for Mikayla to come downstairs. During the week, she waited until the last possible minute so she could grab a couple of pieces of toast and a banana, then run out the door to get her bike and head to school without a word spoken to him. The weekends were different. She didn't have the late bell at school as an excuse to avoid spending time with him.

As Abby was?

The thought seemed petty, but he hadn't had a chance to speak with Abby since their conversation behind the community center two days ago. He'd thought he might run into her at Doris's house. Going there twice in the past week, he'd been told that he'd "just missed her" each time. He got the same response when he went to fix a door that wouldn't close properly at the Mennonite chapel. Abby had been working in the kitchen until minutes before he'd shown up.

It would be easy to accuse her of avoiding him. However, he knew that wasn't the case.

"It's got to be coincidental," he said to himself.

"What?" asked Mikayla as she came into the kitchen. She was wearing an old T-shirt and a bathrobe. Though she'd braided her hair, strands had come loose while she'd slept.

"Talking to myself." He put scrambled eggs and bacon on two plates and carried them to the table.

She poured orange juice while he made toast. It was a choreographed performance they'd perfected in the past ten months. The tasks kept them occupied so they didn't have to talk, and they never bumped into each other as they crisscrossed the kitchen.

They sat at the same time, and Mikayla bowed her head over her clasped hands while he said grace. As soon as he was finished, she picked up one section of the newspaper he'd tossed on the table and raised it between them. She might as well have put out a sign that said No Trespassing.

David ate his breakfast in silence. He considered reading another section of the paper, but that didn't appeal to him. When Mikayla had first moved in the day after the car accident, he'd tried to engage her in conversation during breakfast. He'd come to realize it might be a lost cause, but he couldn't give up. She'd lost so much, and she shouldn't be suffering alone.

She's not alone. She has her friends. She has Abby. The voice in his mind refused to be quiescent. Arguing with it would be futile, but how much longer did he need to wait for Mikayla to stop acting as if his house were a temporary home?

Not having an answer to that question—and to so many others, he said, "By the way, Pastor Hershey was hoping you'd help today."

There was a long pause and he wished he could see her expression on the other side of the newspaper. Was she rolling her eyes as she did so often when he made a comment? Or maybe she was listening.

"I know," she said, getting up and putting her dishes in the dishwasher. "I told him I'd be glad to help."

"With what?"

She stared at him as if he'd sprouted an antenna in the middle of his forehead. "The Easter egg hunt." She startled him by grinning. "Didn't you see the flyer at the community center?"

He didn't want to say that when he went in the community center, he usually had eyes only for Abby. "I guess I missed it."

"The flyer is bright lime green and in almost every window in town."

"Maybe I need to borrow your glasses."

That earned him a rare smile. "I should get dressed. I don't want to be late."

"When does it start?"

"Around 11:00 a.m." She went upstairs.

He folded his hands together on the table and bent his head once more. "God, thank You for convincing her to open up to me. Reach into her heart and ease its pain. Give her hope, like it says in that verse Abby's grandmother loved. Hope and joy."

A half hour later, David heard Mikayla come down

the stairs. He pulled on a light coat as he crossed the kitchen and met Mikayla by the door.

She'd rebraided her hair and twisted it behind her head, looking less like a child and more like a young woman. She wore a pale blue coat that reached almost to her knees. When he noticed how short the sleeves were, he made a mental note to talk to her later about getting a new spring coat. She hadn't mentioned anything about clothes in the time she'd been living with him. He'd thought teenage girls loved clothes, but Mikayla seemed to have no interest in them, though he'd seen her at the grocery store paging through teen fashion magazines a couple of times when she hadn't realized he was paying attention.

If she hadn't moved into his house before the flood, she'd have nothing. He'd never forget her blank countenance when they'd gone to see what was left of the house where she'd grown up. There hadn't been more than a crumbling chimney and a few broken boards. Everything else had been swept away.

"I should have said this before. Happy Easter eve," he said with a smile as he held the door for her.

"Happy Easter eve." She didn't meet his eyes, but a hint of a smile pulled at her lips. When she climbed on her bike, she waved before pedaling toward the center of the village.

By the time David reached the village green, families were already gathering. The Easter egg hunt was sponsored by the churches and several merchants in town. Mikayla stood with her friends, who'd gathered beside the bandstand that had been battered by the floodwaters.

Teens needed to be independent. He'd felt that way

when he was younger, too. Yet he kept wishing some part of Mikayla could be a little bit dependent on him. Something to show him she considered him a part of her life.

When he saw Abby carrying a large punch bowl filled with pink liquid topped with a chunk of sherbet, he rushed to her. He did a slalom through the plastic eggs that had been tossed into the grass for the children to collect. He took the bowl and followed her to a table where cups and napkins were already waiting.

"Danki," she said with a smile. "Isn't it a *wunderbaar* day for little ones?"

He couldn't pull his gaze from her pretty face to look at the children, who were eager for the fun to start. "I didn't expect to see you here today."

"Why not? We volunteers are a part of the community while we're here, and we want to help keep Evergreen Corners's traditions alive after the flood."

"No, it's not that. I didn't realize Amish hunted for Easter eggs."

"Our *kinder* love coloring eggs as much as *Englisch kinder* do." Her smile wavered. "You have some odd notions of us. We're people like everyone else."

Except your people chased my family away because of… His thought halted as he wondered anew why his parents hadn't shared why they'd left their Amish community. The plain volunteers he'd met in Evergreen Corners, even Abby's exacting brother, were warmhearted. Were they the best of their kind or were they a true example? If they were…

He stopped that thought. Going around and around when he didn't have enough information was silly. He needed to talk with his parents and get the truth.

"Anything else I can help with?" he asked.

"Later you can help toss out more eggs for the next group to gather. For now, I've got everything covered."

He was sure she did. In that way, she was a lot like her older brother. They both liked to have details tended to before any new project began.

David let out an exultant yell along with the other adults as the youngest children rushed forward to collect eggs. Several of the little ones had been dressed as bunnies and their ears bobbed with their uneven steps. Parents were allowed to help the preschoolers, and he wasn't surprised when Abby offered a hand to a mother who had three little ones who might have been triplets.

He watched as she bent to show a toddler how to pick up the plastic eggs and the chocolate eggs without squashing them between his fingers. The harried mother, who was overseeing her other youngsters, flashed her a grateful smile.

"David, come and help," she called.

For a moment, he hesitated. Most of the fathers were lingering on the sidelines, some keeping their older children from rushing onto the field to grab the eggs. Others were talking together and not watching the scramble on the field. A few, however, were squatting beside their little ones, urging them to pay attention to the candy instead of a bird or a twig or a bug.

He wondered which sort of father he would have been if Mikayla had been as young as these toddlers when she'd come to live with him. Maybe it was time he found out. With a widening grin, he joined the hunt and soon found himself laughing along with Abby and the children. He looked toward the bandstand and saw Mikayla laughing. When his daughter gave him a thumbs-up, he wanted to dance in the middle of the green.

He glanced at Abby. Had she seen Mikayla's reaction? When she smiled, he knew she hadn't missed it. A sense of something he could only describe as joy filled him, astonishing him because he couldn't remember the last time he'd felt this way. He knew he wanted to savor it now and feel it again.

Soon.

What a *wunderbaar* service it had been! To celebrate the Resurrection with friends who'd become as close as family filled Abby's heart with happiness. Everyone had sounded exultant while singing the familiar hymns, and the *kinder* had been less antsy as they'd listened to the message of hope and love and promise. It had been a true coming together of a community of faith on a wondrous day.

As she cleaned the tables after the men had finished their midday meal, which was served outside on the lawn behind the chapel, she chatted with the women who were bringing food from the kitchen for themselves and the *kinder*. She paused when she saw two familiar forms, one of them pushing a bicycle, walking toward them.

Abby wiped her hands on her apron as she went to greet Mikayla and Reece. The two teenagers looked uneasy when they paused by the kitchen door.

"Happy *Oschderdaag!*" she said and then added, "Happy Easter day!"

Mikayla leaned her bike against a tree. "I hope we're not intruding."

"How could you be intruding? Today we're all family

celebrating a glorious day." She looped her arm through Mikayla's and led the girl to the table where the women and *kinder* were beginning the communal meal. "Are you hungry? Would you like a sandwich?"

Reece gazed at the thick ham and turkey sandwiches with obvious yearning, but Mikayla replied, "It's your Easter dinner, not ours."

"Nonsense," said Rachel Yoder as she patted the end of the bench where she and her young daughters sat. "We love to share."

Abby grinned. "And, besides, you don't want these sandwiches to go to waste, ain't so?"

The teens didn't need another invitation. They joined the meal and the conversation that switched from *Deitsch* for their benefit. Mikayla updated Abby on Doris's recovery, because Mikayla and Reece had stopped by the old woman's house.

"So you made your special egg this year for Doris?" Abby hid her sorrow that the girl hadn't given it to David as she used to share it with her *daed*.

"No, I didn't make her an egg." Mikayla took a big bite of her sandwich. "She said she hopes we come to visit soon."

"That old machine of hers isn't that different," Reece added, "than the ones you taught us to use."

Rachel glanced at Abby in a silent question. Abby told her new friend about the teen group and the sewing lessons. When Mikayla and Reece asked the little ones about the egg hunt the previous day, they heard plenty of stories about the treasures in the plastic eggs. Tiny books, rings and more chocolate had been hidden in them by the donors.

After the meal, Reece and Mikayla joined the softball game played in a field that was part of a now-abandoned farm. Abby went inside to help with the cleaning up. She paused when David walked into the community center.

"I've been expecting you," she said as she met him by the door. "I'm assuming you're looking for Mikayla."

"She said she was going for a ride after church, and I thought she'd be home by now."

"She and Reece came to share our Sunday meal. They're playing ball now."

He relaxed. "I should have known she'd end up here."

"Here? Why?"

"Because you're here." He gave her a sad smile as they walked outdoors so he could see his daughter playing with the others. "I've learned that whenever we lock horns, Mikayla will find a way to be with you."

"If *daed* says no, then maybe *mamm*..."

"No, she doesn't think of you as her mother. She sees you as the big sister she wishes she had." He ground the tip of his boot into the muddy ground.

"What she wants is what you're offering her. Somehow, she needs to come to see that."

"I agree, but how?"

"Talk to her."

He gave a mirthless laugh while they continued walking past the chapel and the impromptu ball field and toward a scraggly orchard. "I've talked to her until I'm blue in the face. I ask her opinions. I talk about her friends and what they're doing. I ask her about the latest book the kids are reading or the show they're watching. Yet, most of the time, I feel as if I'm talking to empty air. I can see her. I can hear her, but it's like she's not there."

"Is it different when you're with the teen group?"

"Not much. Most of the time, she uses her friends as a buffer. I think she encourages them to talk to me so she can avoid doing so."

Abby shook her head, not reaching out to him as she wanted to. They were out of sight and out of earshot from the ball players, so she resisted touching him, unsure if she could let him go if she did. "You're wrong, David. I've never seen her do or say anything to them to urge them to talk to you."

"They do, and she doesn't."

She stopped and leaned against the prickly bark of a twisted apple tree's trunk. "They talk to you because they want to, not because she persuades them to."

"That doesn't make sense."

"Why not? Don't lots of people talk to you?"

A smile slid across his face as he reached up and picked a shriveled apple off a branch over her head. In a few weeks, the trees would become white clouds of apple blossoms. "Some of them talk to me far too much."

"That's because they like you."

"I don't know about that."

She frowned at him. "We Amish consider *hochmut*— pride—a sin, but I think false modesty is as much of one. I'm going to be blunt. People talk to you because they like you. I've seen it over and over."

"So Mikayla doesn't like me. Is that what you're saying?"

"David Riehl! If you want a pity party, find someone else to have it with." When he laughed, she looked at him in amazement. "Did I say something wrong?"

"No, you said the right thing. Pity party. I never expected to hear those words come out of the mouth of an Amish woman."

"I've learned a lot from the kids." She laughed. "And I'm not the only one. I've heard Isaac say phrases he's never used before. Not that I'd ever point that out to him because he'd be horrified."

"If you ever decide to do so, let me know. I'd like to see his reaction."

Her laugh became a giggle. "And I thought you believed you weren't any fun, David."

"I'm not, but—"

"You *are* fun, and you are funny, and whoever said otherwise was wrong."

"You believe that?" His voice deepened as he moved a half step toward her.

"Ja." She gazed into his eyes and saw a storm of powerful emotions in them.

When he edged an inch closer to her, his hands rose to take her face between them. He leaned forward to brush her lips with his own.

She raised her hands to push him away, as she should, but his silent persuasion urged her instead to wrap her arms around his shoulders. Delight filled her and exploded as if she were a firework decorating the sky.

Then he raised his mouth away. She murmured a protest but halted herself when she heard the despair in his voice as he said, "Abby... Abby, I'm so—"

"Please," she whispered. "Please don't say you're sorry."

"But I am. Because you are what you are and I'm what I am, I'm sorry I'll never be able to kiss you like this ever again." He clasped her face again and pressed his lips to hers.

He released her so quickly she rocked on her heels. As she gripped the tree behind her, he strode away. Her tears blurred his form as she fought not to give chase.

She'd promised herself and God that she wouldn't make the same mistake again. She wouldn't follow her foolish heart because nothing *gut* ever came of it.

Yet she'd heeded her heart when she'd surrendered to her yearning for his kiss.

And she might have ruined the best friendship she'd ever had.

Chapter Thirteen

What was the name of that old song? "What a Difference a Day Makes"? That was the one, and David wondered if he'd ever been aware of the truth in those few words than he was on during the week after Easter. As he drove south from Ludlow, almost an hour to the north of Evergreen Corners, he wished he could start the day over again.

Not just today, but yesterday and the day before that, too.

"Would it make any difference?" he asked himself as he slowed for a stop sign, eager to get home.

Watching the traffic rush past in both directions while he waited for a chance to turn left, he wished today hadn't been the day he'd agreed to work on the refrigerator at Moo Beans, a coffee shop near the road leading up to the ski resort on Okemo Mountain. He usually didn't travel so far for work, but he'd done other jobs for the owner since the original Moo Beans opened in Evergreen Corners four years ago.

Back before Mikayla became his responsibility. Back before he had to guard every word he said and everything he did in an effort to prevent another quarrel with his daughter. Today's had been because Mikayla didn't want to wear her boots to school. It was the same one they'd had most days since the snow had begun to melt and she'd started riding her bike.

Today, it'd been a battle he'd conceded for two reasons. He'd realized if he persisted in insisting she wear her boots to school and carry her sneakers in her backpack, she would have changed from boots to shoes as soon as she was out of his sight. He didn't want her to feel she had to sneak around, because that would drive them apart rather than open doors for communication.

Now he sounded like Glen, who was always talking about ways to keep ideas flowing among the volunteers.

However, the real reason he'd given in was that Mikayla had spent a good part of the previous evening in her room, upset and crying. Not that she'd shared the reason for her tears with him. He'd asked, and she'd made it clear she didn't want his help.

He could imagine what Abby would say. She would tell him…

Dismay stabbed him. Would she speak to him after he'd kissed her on Easter?

He refused to think of that, but he was no more successful than he'd been for the past forty-eight hours. He'd made a big mistake. Hadn't his parents spent almost of his whole life warning him not to get mixed up with the Amish? If he'd listened, he wouldn't be drowning in guilt because he'd hurt Abby and destroyed any chance of having her help with Mikayla.

David frowned as he pulled into his driveway and saw an unfamiliar car parked by the house. Whose was it? The silver car had Massachusetts plates. Maybe some tourist had gotten lost and decided to turn around in his driveway.

The car was empty. Why would somebody from Massachusetts leave their car in his driveway?

As he opened his truck door, he wondered if the car had broken down. That made no sense. Everyone had a cell phone and, if the driver had called for a repair truck or a tow, wouldn't he or she be waiting by the car?

"There he is!" came a familiar voice from the porch.

David was astonished to see his parents, Ed and Nora Riehl, sitting in rocking chairs he needed to paint. As he approached, they stood. His mother waved as if he were on a ship sailing off into the ocean.

Why hadn't they told him they were visiting?

"David, it's so good to see you!" Mother rushed to enfold him in a hug, but he held up a quick hand to halt her before the dirt on his work clothes got on her pretty navy blue suit. She contented herself with giving him a quick kiss on the cheek.

He saw her faint frown and recalled he'd forgotten to shave that morning after the argument with Mikayla.

His father shook his hand and smiled. "You look surprised. We told you we were coming today."

"No, you didn't. Did you leave a message on my cell or the shop phone?"

"I don't know," his father said with a chuckle. "Ask your mother. She's the one who called."

"I didn't call, Ed." His mother shook her head. "You said you were going to."

"No, Nora, you told me you were going to."

His mother threw her hands up in the air, the charms on her bangles chiming against one another. "Oh, well. I guess we should say, 'Surprise, David!' Here we are!"

Looking at his soiled clothes, he said, "Let me change, and we'll chat."

"Sounds good," Father replied.

David was startled to realize that his father's *good* sounded close to Abby's *gut*. Odd, how he'd never stopped to think the faint accent on their words had come from their plain upbringing. When he was growing up, they'd simply sounded to him like his parents. Now, after spending time with Abby and the other Amish volunteers, he recognized the accent. He must have spoken the same way once, but somewhere along the way, he'd lost that inflection.

"Where's Mikayla?" His mother glanced at her watch as they climbed the porch stairs. "School can't still be in session, can it? It's after four."

"She's working in the village. She's part of a group of teens who have been assisting in repairing houses and businesses after last fall's flood."

"What about her studies?" Mother sat in a rocker again. "She's not going to get into a good college if she doesn't keep her grades up."

"She's doing well." He didn't add that Mikayla avoided any conversations about her future. Or the past, for that matter. Envy cramped his heart. How wonderful would it have been never to think about the past?

Mikayla *did* think about the past, he knew. She might not speak of it, but her father and the life she'd lost must have been on her mind. He'd learned that from Abby as he'd discovered so many other things about his daughter.

Teenagers are like onions. He wanted to smile each time he recalled Abby's words. So simple and yet true. Every day he was discovering something new about

Mikayla. Was he seeing her in a new way or was she revealing more about the girl he'd thought he'd known but hadn't?

He'd been learning more about Abby each day, too, until he'd messed up everything by kissing her. His practiced distrust of anything Amish had disappeared. At least as far as she was concerned. He reserved judgment about the sect as a whole.

Or, more specifically, her brother Isaac, who hadn't relented in his determination to keep Abby from spending any more time than necessary with an *Englischer*.

He had to admit her brother had been right.

Abby wiped the sheen of sweat from her forehead. As the weather continued to warm, they were going to have to figure out something to do to vent the built-up heat in the community center kitchen. Her hope that there were screens for the windows stored somewhere else in the building had come to naught.

Rachel opened the door and wafted her hands to try to keep out the bugs attracted by the aromas from the ovens. "We need to do something about this."

"I know. I was thinking the same."

"We need a screen door," said another volunteer. "Why don't you ask David, Abby? He'd be willing to do that."

She forced herself not to flinch at the mention of David's name. Nobody else knew what had happened in the orchard, and she must keep it that way. If Isaac learned that David had kissed her, her brother would ship her home immediately and insist she not return.

"There's no sense bothering David when we don't have a door," she said.

"He might know where to find one that will fit. You know him best, so do you mind checking with him?"

As every face in the kitchen turned toward her, Abby reminded herself of the promise she'd made to God. She'd do what she could to help and stop listening to her heart.

She ignored her instincts that warned her not to go to David's house. If he wasn't there—and she wasn't sure if she wanted him to be or not—she'd leave him a message about putting a screen door on the kitchen. If she didn't speak to him today, she would have to eventually. She suspected delaying would make that encounter more difficult.

When she walked up the driveway ten minutes later, she was surprised to see strangers sitting with David on the porch. The man and the woman must be related to him because she saw something of each of them in his face. However, they couldn't be more unlike him in how they dressed. She'd never seen him in anything more formal than khakis and a neatly pressed shirt. Most of the time he seemed to prefer jeans and a casual polo shirt or T-shirt.

The man with his neat mustache and dark plastic-rimmed glasses wore a navy jacket over matching trousers. A pale blue tie clipped with a gold clasp accented his pristine white shirt and the handkerchief in his pocket. His shoes shone like sunlight on the brook.

Beside him, the woman was dressed as formally. Her navy suit, made of a fabric Abby guessed might be silk because of its sheen, emphasized her figure. Her eyes were a similar color, astonishing Abby because she'd never seen eyes of such a hue. Jewelry—necklaces, earrings and bracelets—glittered with each motion she made. She appeared as tall as her husband, but then Abby noticed she was wearing shoes with ultrahigh, pencil-thin heels.

The newcomers stared at her and Abby realized they expected her to speak first. She wasn't sure what to say. Searching her mind for something that wouldn't sound forced, she decided on the obvious.

"I didn't realize you had company, David." She glanced at the silver car parked next to his truck. "I should have. *Es dutt mir leed.*" She flinched when her self-consciousness led her to speak *Deitsch* again. "Oops. I meant to say 'I'm sorry.' I didn't intend to interrupt you and your guests."

David's voice was emotionless as he came down the steps and motioned for her to join the others. "Come and meet my parents."

She smiled, but her expression wavered when neither of the newcomers did. In fact, they regarded her with cool, suspicious expressions that reminded her of David's the first time she'd met him when he'd come to fix the freezer. She hadn't understood his antipathy then and she didn't understand his parents' now.

Both Ed and Nora Riehl gave her the faintest of nods while David spoke their names and introduced her. Reminding herself that *Englischers* often felt uncomfortable with plain folk, she made sure her smile was in place again.

"It's nice to meet you," she said. It wasn't a lie. She *wanted* it to be a nice moment, but she hadn't known his parents would look and act as these people did.

How could she have known anything about them? David seldom spoke about his family other than Mikayla. He and Abby had talked about so many other things, but she was startled to discover she didn't know if he had brothers or sisters. He'd never mentioned either.

"We didn't know there were any Amish in Evergreen Corners, did we, Ed?" asked Mrs. Riehl.

"Never heard of any around here. There weren't any during the years we lived here." He looked down his nose at her as if she were a germ about to infect the perfection of the place.

"We're here to help with rebuilding Evergreen Corners after the flood." She kept her voice light, but was careful not to add that one Amish family had already decided to remain in the small town and was hoping others would stay, too.

As she wished she could. *Stop listening to your stupid heart!*

"We didn't realize that," Mr. Riehl said. "David didn't mention anything to us, did he, Nora?"

"Nothing at all."

Abby waited for David to respond. When he remained silent, she said, "Amish Helping Hands is the name of the organization that oversees our volunteers." She tried to smile but halted when she realized she must look like she was grimacing. "We've been working with the Mennonite Disaster Service and other plain groups to help local merchants get their businesses going and to build homes for families who lost everything. If you have some free time while you're visiting, you should pay a visit to the homes that have replaced those washed away."

"We might," Mrs. Riehl said in a tone that made it clear she had no plans to do so.

Growing more desperate to put an end to the uncomfortable conversation, Abby said, "David, I came over to talk to you about getting a screen door for the community center kitchen. I can come back later."

"No, you don't need to do that." He turned to his parents. "If you want to get unpacked, I'll get supper started after I'm done with Abby." Some emotion flickered through his eyes. Regret at his choice of words? Or relief he'd announced to her—and to his parents—he didn't intend to spend more time with her than necessary?

His parents exchanged a worried glance but complied. As soon as the door closed behind them, David took Abby by the arm and steered her to the far side of the truck.

"My mother is an eavesdropper," he said without apology as he moved his hand away.

"I don't know what you're worried about. I gave you my message and I should get back to—"

"Abby, do you know what's bothering Mikayla? She came home a half hour ago, and she barely greeted my parents before heading upstairs."

She closed her eyes. "She came to talk to me this morning before school. She had a run-in with Hunter and his band of hooligans again last night at the wrestling match at school."

"Is that what it was?" He shook his head and sighed. "She wouldn't talk about it last night, and I heard her crying when I went to bed. I knocked on her door. She told me she was fine, that she was reading something sad."

"You didn't believe her?"

"You don't have to make it a question. No, I didn't believe her. She might have been reading something sad, but I didn't—not for an instant—believe she was fine."

"You've got to get her to talk to you."

"I know, but how?"

"I don't know. We both need to pray for an answer." She laced her fingers together behind her, so they wouldn't reach out to console him. If she touched him when her feelings were so raw, so new, so tender, she wasn't sure what might happen next. She almost laughed at the thought. She knew *exactly* what would happen and she knew what the consequences would be. "I should get back to the kitchen."

He stepped around her to keep her from walking away. "Abby, I'm sorry…"

"No, please. I asked you not to say it on Sunday." She didn't want to tell him that her heart would break and might never be repaired if she heard him say he regretted sharing her first kiss.

He nodded. "I won't say I'm sorry about that, but I've got to say I'm sorry for my parents' behavior."

Glad he'd changed the subject away from the precious kiss whose memory she knew she'd treasure for as long as she lived, she asked, "Did I do or say something wrong? I didn't mean to offend them."

"You didn't."

"Are you certain?"

He looked at the door where his parents had gone inside. When she followed his gaze, she saw the curtains on a nearby window being flicked aside. "I'm certain. Sometimes… Well, they're tired from their flight and the drive from Boston."

She wondered what he'd been going to say before he'd interrupted himself. Sometimes his parents did or said what? She couldn't quiz him because she could tell he was upset and she didn't want to add to it. So she thanked him for agreeing to help and left.

As she walked toward the village green, the truth dogged her heels. Something was wrong at the Riehl house. Something was wrong beyond Mikayla being bullied and David struggling to be the *daed* she needed.

Something was wrong, and she had to figure out what it was if she had any chance of helping him.

Standing in his kitchen after supper, David watched their car's lights vanish into the darkness. His parents hadn't been happy about being "tricked" into talking with an Amish woman. His apology, which he hoped would soothe their ruffled feathers, had been as useless. He wondered if they'd return. He could recall wondering the same thing often during his childhood when they'd left on yet another trip without him. He'd known they loved him, and they made sure he was provided for, but he could see—looking back—he was never sure if they were happier when he wasn't around.

He didn't move until he heard light footsteps on the stairs. He looked over his shoulder and saw Mikayla heading for the refrigerator.

"Your parents giving you a hard time?" she asked as she took out a bottle of juice.

He was about to tell her how shortsighted and mistaken his parents were. He was ready to spout off how annoyed he was at them. Every word vanished when the girl turned to face him. How could he complain about his parents when she'd lost both of hers? He was certain that, no matter how upset she'd been with Boyd and how often, she would have forgiven him. He had the chance to make things better. She didn't.

"No more of a hard time than I've given you," he replied, keeping his voice light.

She rolled her eyes before surprising him by leaning against the counter instead of sprinting back up the stairs. She took a deep drink, wiped her mouth with her hand and asked, "So what are you going to do now?"

"Go to bed. There's not anything else I can do," he said, knowing he had to be honest with her—and himself—now. "They said not to wait up."

"They ignored your apology."

He hadn't guessed she'd hear his parents' voices up in her room. "They're angry."

"Then they should have stayed and talked it out. That's what Dad said was the right thing to do."

He fought not to let his gasp escape. It was the first time Mikayla had mentioned Boyd to him in casual conversation since his best friend's death. "Your dad was right."

"He was, and I think not talking things out when you can is wrong. You never know if you'll have another chance." She tilted the bottle again then walked toward the stairs.

"Mikayla?"

She looked over her shoulder but didn't reply.

"You're a pretty smart kid, you know that?"

"Yep."

"I appreciate you giving me your opinion. I appreciate it a lot."

"She said you would." She hurried up the stairs.

She? He didn't need to ask to whom Mikayla was referring. His daughter didn't listen to many people, but she did take Abby's advice to heart.

His shoulders stiffened as he realized he wasn't the only one Abby was trying to fix. He forced them to ease from their taut stance. How could he be irked with

Abby when she'd found a way to reach Mikayla after he'd failed miserably?

Everything came back to Abby.

He sat at the kitchen table. Leaning his head forward to rest on his folded hands, he prayed as he hadn't in longer than he could remember.

"Dear Lord, help me know what to do now."

Chapter Fourteen

Stop beating yourself up about David's parents.

The thought replayed endlessly in Abby's head as she got up, said her morning prayers, dressed and went to the community center. It echoed beneath the clatter of pots and griddles as she worked with other volunteers to make breakfast. When she spoke with the men and women who would be braving the afternoon's spring showers to start another house, the words in her mind repeated as an undercurrent almost as vicious as the flood that had torn through the town.

What had she done to upset them? David had assured her that she hadn't said anything wrong, but his dismay had been displayed on his face. He'd been as tense as the teen volunteers were when they thought Hunter Keyes and his band of bullies were nearby.

She shrugged aside that thought. She shouldn't be comparing Mr. and Mrs. Riehl to teenage troublemakers. They'd raised a *gut* son, and they hadn't been unkind to her. Just cold enough to give her frostbite.

Because they don't like the Amish.

The thought made her stop as she was about to take

her favorite mixing bowl out of the cupboard. Where had that idea come from? Now that it had erupted into her mind, she couldn't ignore it.

"Excuse me," murmured one of the other volunteers who needed to get to the cupboard.

Abby moved aside, not noticing who it was. She was too mired in her conflicting thoughts. She didn't want to believe the Riehls had such negative feelings about the Amish.

Or that David had.

Was prejudice the reason he had acted so oddly the first time they'd met? She pressed her hand over her aching heart. How could it want to belong to a man who'd been raised to dislike the Amish?

No, she couldn't be certain that was the case. After all, why would his parents have such a prejudice against plain folks? It didn't make any sense. Most *Englischers*, if they thought about the Amish, found them pleasantly quaint. She'd heard an *Englisch* tourist in Bird-in-Hand use those exact words.

Pleasantly quaint.

"Abby?" asked Rachel with an urgency that suggested she'd tried to reach past Abby's reverie more than once.

"Sorry. Lost in thought."

"I've got a question nobody else seems to know the answer to. How do you deal with food allergies?"

"We try to have a variety of dishes, but we do ask people when they arrive if they've got allergies or sensitivities." She smiled. "Didn't someone ask you?"

"*Ja*, and I was asked if Loribeth and Eva do." She smiled as she spoke her toddler daughters' names.

"Do they?"

"Not so far, I'm grateful to God. I've seen what families have endured when someone can't eat the food everyone else can. It's like having to run a restaurant."

Abby laughed. "Like we do here. We provide food for vegetarians and for those with salt issues and various allergies. I wish I had more recipes for those who have a problem with gluten."

"I've got a few if you'd like them," Rachel offered.

"I'd love them. Does someone in your family or among your *Leit* need to have gluten-free dishes?"

"They're just recipes I've picked up through the years." She turned away to put the plates on top of the others in the cupboards. "This isn't the first time I've volunteered for a mobilization like this."

"You must have been talking with Glen. He likes to use words like *mobilization* when he talks about his volunteer projects."

Rachel picked up a big pan from the dishwasher and opened cupboard doors, looking for where it belonged. When Abby directed her to the pantry, she said, *"Danki."*

Abby reached for a dishcloth to wipe down a counter, then halted when Glen entered. He looked around the main room, then came toward the kitchen. When she called a *gute mariye*, he smiled.

"Have you seen David Riehl?" he asked.

"No. He hasn't been here."

"Okay, I took a chance. I'll call him at home later." He turned toward the door, then paused. "If you see him, have him give me a call or drop by my office."

"I will." She wanted to ask why Glen was looking for David, but kept her lips buttoned.

As if she'd called the question after him, Glen faced

her. "I need to talk to him right away. We have to decide which families will be getting the next houses rebuilt, and the St. Pierre house came up on our list. I need to know if he wants us to move forward with it now or not."

"St. Pierre house?" She couldn't believe the words as she spoke them. "Are you talking about Mikayla's *daed*'s house?"

"Mikayla's house now."

"It was destroyed in the flood?"

He nodded. "It was set below the covered bridge and dam. When the dam failed, the water destroyed two houses in the curve of the brook. Washed them away as if they'd never been there."

"I didn't know. Nobody ever mentioned it."

"Hmm… I thought I did the day I asked you and David to take over the teen program." His smile returned. "By the way, I'm hearing positive things about what you're doing with the kids. Thanks for your hard work."

Abby managed to mumble something in response. As he left, she sat at one of the tables. Mikayla had lost her home within weeks of her *daed*'s tragic death? Why hadn't David told Abby? He must have, like Glen, assumed she already knew. Thinking of the meeting they'd had in Glen's office weeks ago, she recalled the project manager mentioning how they'd be soon choosing the next houses to be built. Not once had she imagined one of the houses might replace Mikayla's home.

Tears filled her eyes as she bent her head to pray for strength for the girl who'd lost even more than Abby had imagined. She asked God to guide her in helping the girl by being able to listen to Mikayla's needs and fears and doubts.

As she murmured an "Amen," she opened her eyes to see Mikayla crossing the room toward her. "Mikayla, what are you doing here now? You should be at school."

"I know, but I need to talk to you about something." The girl hesitated. "Something important."

"Of course. Anytime." *God, I ask for Your help for this moment. Please be here for both of us.*

Mikayla glanced at the bustling kitchen. "Can we talk somewhere else?"

"How about we talk while I walk to school with you?"

The teen nodded and stepped aside as Abby went to collect her coat and bonnet. Going out into the spring day, Abby admired the crocus blossoms and the spikes of daffodils pushing their way up through the softening ground, but turned her attention to the girl beside her.

Mikayla glanced around again to make sure nobody else stood too close, though the street was empty except for them. She leaned forward to whisper, "I don't like David's parents."

"You've just met them."

The teen grimaced. "Don't tell me to give them a chance to show their true selves. I've already seen them." She folded her arms in front of her and glowered at the sidewalk. "I don't like them, and they don't like me."

Abby resisted saying she understood why Mikayla felt as she did. Abby's own first impressions of David's parents continued to disturb her.

"I won't tell you to give them a chance," Abby said as they crossed the street and stepped onto the green.

"They're going to be a part of your life because they're David's *mamm* and *daed*."

"So I need to grin and bear it when they tell me everything I do and say and how I look is wrong."

"Everything?"

Mikayla's scowl lessened by a few degrees. "Well, maybe not *everything*. I'm not doing anything wrong when I breathe."

Chuckling, Abby put her hand on the girl's stiff shoulder. "Then breathe when you're around them. Don't bristle in frustration. Don't talk back. Don't glare at them. Breathe and be grateful God's given you a chance to see how *wunderbaar* most things are in your life."

"You make it sound easy. To be honest, if I had anywhere else to go, I would." She didn't pause before she blurted, "How can someone like me become someone like you?"

Abby stared at the teen. *Someone like her?* Mikayla didn't want to be like her, living her life in the shadows of events that had happened almost a decade before.

"What do you mean when you say 'someone like you?'" Abby asked.

"Amish, of course."

Abby was shocked speechless. She hadn't expected the girl to say *that*! "Why are you interested in becoming Amish?" She let a hint of levity into her voice. "I know it's not because of the clothes. I've seen you and your friends giggle about what we wear."

Mikayla gave her a shy grin. "I'm sorry about that."

"No need to apologize. God wants us to be honest with one another because that helps us be more honest with Him."

"And *that* is why I want to be Amish!"

"I don't understand."

"Your faith isn't something you talk about on Sundays. It's something you live every minute of every day."

Abby took the girl's hand and led her to a bench by a tree. Sitting, she drew Mikayla down beside her. She swiveled on the bench so she could look at the teen.

"Mikayla," she said, hoping she was striking the right balance between stern and sympathetic, "I can see you're not being honest with me. What's the real reason you're asking about becoming Amish?"

The girl's eyes cut away toward the far side of the village green. "You're a family. You told me your grandparents live in the house with the rest of your family."

"*Ja*, they live with my cousins in Pennsylvania."

"And you've got a new stepmother, but you don't resent her."

"Why would I resent Lovina? She's kind, and she makes *Daed* happy. He was sad and lonely with only his *kinder* around."

Mikayla lifted off her glasses and knuckled her eyes, but tears bubbled at their corners. "I miss being part of a family."

"You *are* part of a family. A small one, but you and David are a family." She leaned forward and put her hand over the girl's. "Have you talked to him about this?"

"Not exactly."

"*Not exactly* means *no*, ain't so?"

The teen nodded.

"You asked me what I think," Abby said, "and I think you and David need to talk. Honestly. David was your *daed*'s best friend for years and years. Your *daed* named David as your guardian."

More tears erupted from the girl, and she hid her face in her hands, pushing her glasses to an odd angle. "I know that, Abby."

Pulling Mikayla's hands away from her face, she looked the tearful *kind* in the eyes as she straightened Mikayla's glasses. "As long as you keep putting up walls between you and David, you won't have the family you long for."

She lowered her head and her long, silken hair pooled on her lap. "I don't want David to be my father."

"Why?" Abby asked, shocked. "He cares for you."

"I can't. Okay? Can't we leave it at that?"

Though Abby knew she should say no, she whispered, "Of course."

"Why can't I become Amish and then everyone will be part of my family? I won't do—" She halted her words and swallowed hard as she wrapped her arms around herself and shuddered. "It'd be easier."

So many things Abby wanted to ask because the girl acted as if some horrible, dark cloud hung over her, but Abby held her tongue. Guiding the girl toward an answer was all she could do. She couldn't make up Mikayla's mind for her. She wondered if she should speak of what Glen had told her about David arranging to have Mikayla's home rebuilt. The project manager wanted to talk to David before Mikayla was informed. There must be a reason for that, and Abby didn't want to make the situation more difficult.

Once Mikayla had pulled herself together, the teen headed to school.

Abby returned to the kitchen. Without a word to anyone, she picked up the phone and called David.

As soon as he said hello, she said, "David, this is Abby."

"Abby! Is something wrong?"

"No. I wasn't sure where you'd be working today, and I wanted to invite you and Mikayla and your parents to join us tonight at the community center for supper."

There was a long pause before he said, "I don't think that's a good idea."

"Maybe not, but you need to come here tonight. That way your parents can meet more of our volunteers, not just the Amish ones."

Again time stretched before he replied, "I'll ask them. I'm not making any promises."

"Of course not, but I'm sure Mikayla would like them to meet her friends. It might create a stronger connection between your parents and her."

This time he didn't hesitate. "Now *that* is a good idea. Thanks, Abby. I'll see you this evening. Around six, right?"

"That'll be *gut. Danki*, David."

She hung up the phone, praying she'd done the right thing.

David half anticipated his parents to balk at the community center door, but when he held it open, they followed Mikayla into the main room. It was bustling with an expanded group of volunteers who'd come to start the next projects. He glanced with guilt at Mikayla. He hadn't said anything to her about Glen's call to let him know the St. Pierre house could be among the next raised out of the mud left by the flood. Glen had said he needed a decision by the end of next week, so David was delaying it until after his parents left in a few days for Old Orchard Beach in Maine.

After putting their coats on one of the many pegs along the wall, his parents hung back as they faced the noisy, jubilant crowd celebrating that a roof had been completed a few hours ago. Mikayla wove her way through as she looked for her friends. Or was she trying to get away from his parents who'd critiqued everything she'd said and done since their arrival? Though he'd asked them to stop, they continued to harangue the girl.

Odd, but he never would have guessed he'd see his parents and Abby's brother as similar, but both seemed intent on having the world match their image of what it should be. They'd been as exacting with him as they were trying to be with Mikayla. Maybe, he realized with astonishment, that was why he'd tried to give his daughter her space. Had he gone too far in the other direction in his attempt not to be the type of parent his own had been?

"If we want to eat," David said, motioning to the queue of people snaking among the tables, "we should get in line."

"No hurry," his mother said. "We can wait, can't we, Ed?"

"Yes," his father replied, "let the others who've worked hard go first."

Puzzled because his father had mentioned how hungry he was several times, David offered to introduce his parents to Glen and some of the other volunteers. Again, they demurred, seeming happy to cling to their corner where they could talk to each other.

He excused himself when Michael Miller motioned

to him. Michael was sitting with his soon-to-be family at a table not far from the pass-through window. Smiling a greeting to Michael's fiancée and children, David congratulated his friend on getting the roof up on the house his team was building.

"It's a *gut* feeling to have that important step done with April showers coming and going." Michael put down his fork. "I was wondering if you could stop by tomorrow or the next day and check on the furnace before we fire it up the first time. Just to make sure we've gotten the connections right."

"Be glad to." He done the same for each of the previous houses. He hadn't found any problems, but he appreciated Michael's sense of caution. "Any time better for you?"

"Whenever you want to stop by."

"Sounds good." His smile wavered when he saw Abby walking toward him. He was glad she hadn't expected him to apologize for kissing her, because he wasn't sorry he had. But since then, nothing had been the same between them.

She refilled Michael's cup with what she assured him was decaf. "David, let your folks know that they can get in line at any time."

"They told me that the people who've worked hard today should have first dibs on the food."

"How kind of them, but let them know we made enough to feed everyone at a mud sale."

He recognized the term from some memory that had been lying quiescent. A mud sale was an auction held in the spring, usually a fund-raiser for a school or a local volunteer fire department. The term *mud sale* had come about because when the sales were held, the earth was no longer frozen and spring rains often turned the grounds around a barn into a quagmire.

More and more as he spent time with Abby, the bits of his past that he'd stashed into a deep corner of his mind were springing to life again. So many were happy memories, and he wondered why he'd pushed them away.

That, he knew with abrupt insight, was easy. He hadn't wanted to upset his parents who had been distraught at whatever had driven them from their Amish lives. Even a young child knew when something caused a parent anguish and would do whatever was necessary to avoid it.

Abby picked up another empty cup and filled it.

When she handed it to him, he said, "I don't like decaf."

"Sorry." She leaned toward him and lowered her voice. "We need to talk. It's important, David." She glanced at his daughter. "Really important."

"Can it wait until tomorrow? With my parents here…" He didn't finish and he guessed he didn't have to because understanding bloomed in her eyes.

"I guess it'll have to. I'll see you then."

Though he wanted to ask her what was wrong, he didn't. Mikayla was unhappy with his parents in the house, and he hoped that was what Abby wanted to discuss. He didn't want to think what other difficulties might lurk in his troubled relationships.

The community center was wrapped in dusk when Abby heard the door open. In astonishment, she saw David skulk into the kitchen. Why was he back now? He'd said they'd talk tomorrow. What had changed his mind?

Earlier, she'd watched him with his standoffish *daed* and *mamm*. They'd sat by themselves and had spoken only when someone stopped by their table to talk to David. When they'd dawdled over their meal, making the kitchen volunteers wait to clean their dishes after the others had been done, she'd been surprised. She'd assumed they'd duck out quickly. Were their unfriendly ways the reason David hadn't spoken much about them? That didn't make sense, because she'd seen that he had affection for them in an almost protective way, as if they were the *kinder* and he the parent.

"Kaffi?" she asked instead of the questions pounding against her lips.

"No, thanks. You said we needed to talk about something important. Something about Mikayla?"

She gestured for him to follow her to one of the tables in the dimly lit main room. Sitting, she waited until he chose a seat facing her. The distance between them seemed too intimate and too vast at the same time.

He listened without comment as she outlined the conversation she'd had with Mikayla earlier. Leaning back in his chair, he sat so his face was too shadowed for her to read his reaction.

"She's hurting, David, and she doesn't know where else to turn. She wants to have a family, but she seems scared of making one with you."

"Scared?"

"Ja. For some reason she believes it'd be different if she lived a plain life. I didn't want to discourage her, but she sees living as we do a panacea for her grief."

"I can think of a sure way to change her mind." His voice coming out of the shadows was grim.

"What is it?"

"I can tell her the truth."

"The truth? The truth about what?"

"Me. Me and my parents."

Now he had baffled her because she opened her mouth to ask another question, but no sound emerged. She took a deep breath and released it before she asked, "Why would the truth about your family have anything to do with her thinking she wants to live a plain life?"

"Because we used to be Amish."

Chapter Fifteen

Understanding how a fish felt out of water, Abby gasped for air. A whooshing grew loud, then receded in her ears. Her voice sounded weird as she asked, "You— you were Amish?"

"Until I was around five or six years old." He slanted toward her and she could see his face was as dreary as his voice. "I don't remember exactly how old because my parents took me away a couple of times before we left for good."

"So you remember that life?" She couldn't believe she was as poised as if he were talking about something no more surprising than how Tuesday followed Monday each week.

"Very little. When I was that age, I did pretty much the same things that any child does. I played with my friends and cousins, enjoyed time and meals with my parents as well as having someone tuck me in at night and read me a story."

"*Ja*, in those ways plain and *Englisch kinder* are much the same." She paused. "Is that why you understand some *Deitsch*?"

"Maybe. I don't know." He rubbed his eyes, then raised them to meet her gaze. "I've understood a few words when you spoke them, but it may have been because they sound like English or I could figure out the meaning through context. My parents stopped speaking *Deitsch*, so I'd thought I'd forgotten it. I know what you're going to ask next. Why did my parents leave?"

She nodded.

"I'm not sure."

Abby was shocked to the depths of her soul. As curious as David was about everything around him, a trait that had led him to learn about how machines worked so he could repair them, she'd expected him to have a quick answer to soothe *her* curiosity about why he and his parents had walked away from their plain community.

She wanted to put her hands up to the sides of her head to make sure it was still in place. With every thought, her mind spun like a mixer set at highest speed. It was difficult to believe she was sitting instead of floating around like a runaway kite.

David had been born plain? He did live a simple life, but so did many of the people in Evergreen Corners.

Then she thought of his parents. Nothing about them had suggested they'd ever been Amish. They wore *Englisch* clothing. Their hair was cut in *Englisch* styles. His *mamm* had been draped in elegant jewelry each time Abby had seen her, and she wore those stilettos Abby couldn't imagine trying to walk in. His *daed* wore a thick gold watch and a mustache. If someone had asked, she would have said the closest they might have ever been to plain folk was visiting the tourist shops in Pennsylvania.

And David… Nothing about how he dressed suggested he'd ever worn broadfall trousers and suspenders and a straw hat with a narrow black band.

"Are you from Pennsylvania, too?" she asked, struggling to enunciate each word because her lips were trembling so hard.

"I'm not sure where we lived before my folks left."

"Your birth certificate—"

"It lists my birth place as Sugarcreek, Ohio, but I do recall that we moved several times before we came here. Once we settled in Evergreen Corners, we never went to visit family again. I don't remember my grandparents' faces, though I sometimes recall hints of their voices."

"Oh, my," she whispered. "Now I understand why your parents jumped the fence."

"Jumped the fence?"

"That means leaving the Amish, and I'd guess your parents did because they were under the *bann*," she whispered. "That's why they ate last and made sure their dishes were the final ones washed tonight."

"I don't have any idea what you're talking about."

"Do you know what 'under the *bann*' means?"

"No." His eyes narrowed. "Are you talking about being shunned?"

"*Ja.* When an Amish person does something that violates the rules of the *Ordnung*, they are shunned."

"Kicked out, you mean? Told to hit the road because they refused to kowtow to rules set by a bunch of old men? I don't understand how a people who preach kindness and nonviolence can treat their own that way. How can kicking someone out of their home be part of Jesus's teachings?"

She wanted to recoil from the venom in his voice but forced hers to remain calm. "That's a misconception many *Englischers* have. Being put under the *bann* isn't an act of retribution. It's an act of love."

"Do you believe that?" he asked with a snort.

"Ja." She leaned across the table and put her hands on his, not caring what she was risking by touching him. He needed to know the truth to deal with the pain that had been a part of him for more than two decades. "David, listen to me. Being under the *bann* means you aren't part of the faith community until you confess your sin. It's a loving act that gives the sinner a chance to see what would be lost and what can be regained if he or she will set aside their *hochmut*—their pride—and admit their wrongdoing. No one is forced to leave their home and their community, but they must eat separately and nothing must pass from their hands to ours. Your parents took their food last and had their dishes washed last, so what have been labeled as their sins wouldn't contaminate the rest of the community."

She was shocked anew the Riehls still clung to some of the beliefs they'd otherwise set aside. Or had they believed someone tonight would have pointed a finger at them, telling them they shouldn't eat with others because of the *bann*? Old habits were hard to break and old fears hard to set aside.

"Is ostracism any better than being kicked out?" David asked in the same razor-sharp tone.

"No, it's not. I had an *onkel* who was put under the *bann* for two weeks because he bet on football games. It was sad when he couldn't sit at the table with us and share in God's grace and bounty. His business didn't suffer because he was under the *bann*. During that time, his customers left money on the counter in his small engine shop so it didn't pass from their hands to his."

"So he knuckled under to the rules in two weeks?"

"He was put under the *bann* for two weeks, and at the end of that time, he was invited to rejoin us during our worship service to confess to his sins. Sometimes there is a specific time limit. In other situations, it's up to the person who's sinned to decide when or if to return." She gave his hand a light squeeze. "David, stop thinking of the *bann* as a punishment. The *bann* is a way for people to come to terms with their mistakes and for the *Leit* to understand the value of forgiveness. We must forgive those who trespass against us so we can be forgiven. Just as the Lord's Prayer teaches us."

"Apparently my parents got the permanent kind of shunning."

"They *chose* to let the shunning become permanent." She sighed. "No, that's not right, either. They've allowed it to continue thus far. If they ever wished to return, they could confess and ask for forgiveness."

"And you're telling me that they'd get it." He withdrew his hand from beneath hers and snapped his fingers. "Just like that?"

"If the *Leit* believed their confession was sincere, *ja*, forgiveness would be offered just like that." She snapped her own fingers. "And the matter would never be spoken of again."

"People aren't like that. They don't forget."

"I didn't say anyone would forget. I said that the transgression would be forgiven. How can we expect God to forgive us and welcome us into His grace if we don't offer the same forgiveness to others?"

"They don't want what you Amish are offering."

She jerked as if he'd struck her. "Each of us must find our own path."

He stood and slid his chair beneath the table. "Now that you know the truth, maybe you can understand why you can't fix me."

"Fix you?"

"Isn't that what you've been trying to do since you realized I'm Mikayla's guardian?"

"No!" She jumped to her feet.

He shook his head. "I never thought I'd see the day you wouldn't be honest with me, Abby. You know as well as I do that you've been trying to fix everything you think is wrong with me. You've tried to prove I can be fun. You've done everything in your power to smooth the differences between Mikayla and me." Bitterness filled his voice as he added, "Now you can see I've got more problems than even you can fix."

"I'm not trying to fix you." She wanted to stamp her foot, but refused to behave like a *kind*. One of them needed to be the adult in the conversation and David was showing it wouldn't be him. "I'm trying to help you."

"What's the difference?"

"There's a huge difference. If I were trying to fix you, it would be because I think there's something wrong with you. Helping you means I see you have a need for someone to offer assistance. That's a big difference."

"I don't see it."

She bit back the words burning in her throat. Instead, she took a steadying breath. "That's apparent, but you're avoiding one vital fact."

"And you're going to tell me what it is."

Again she was tempted to tell him if he was going to act like a toddler, she couldn't see any point in continuing their heated conversation. She couldn't—she shouldn't—lambast him for his obstinacy when he was hurting.

"You know what it is, David. Not knowing why your parents left has been tearing you apart since the first plain volunteers arrived in Evergreen Corners. Before that, you could believe the Amish were the cruel, intractable people your parents taught us we are. You need to know the truth."

He opened his mouth to answer but halted when a shout exploded into the community center.

"Abby! Abby, where are you? Mikayla is gone!"

At Reece's shout, Abby exchanged a horrified glance with David. He flipped on the lights, and Reece and the other teens—the *Englisch* ones and the Amish ones—came to a stop in a squeal of sneaker soles.

"Here I am. What…?" Her voice trailed away.

The kids' expressions ranged from despair to fear to overt terror. Lily had tearstains running through the makeup on her cheeks as she clung to Jack. The other teens were wringing their hands as they looked to Reece, who had become the spokesman for the group.

"Mikayla's gone!" Reece shouted again.

"What do you mean?" Abby asked. "Gone where?"

"That's it. I—we don't know where she's gone."

Abby shook the niggling tendrils of panic out of her mind. She couldn't let the kids' dismay infect her. She needed facts.

"Where was she when you last saw her?" David asked from behind Abby.

She glanced at him. Their gazes caught and locked for a brief second, but it was enough for her to know he agreed their problems must be set aside until they knew Mikayla was okay.

"I saw…" Reece hesitated, glanced at the other kids, then hurried to add, "I saw Mikayla a half hour ago with Hunter."

"With *Hunter*? Hunter Keyes?" Abby could barely believe her own words. "Why would she go with the boy who's been harassing you for weeks?"

Reece shrugged with a nonchalance that didn't match the strain in his voice. "I don't know. I saw the two of them walking together. I was going to follow to make sure he didn't do anything more to hurt her, but Glen wanted to talk to me. By the time I'd explained to him why I had to go, both of them were gone."

"Hunter is sixteen, ain't so?"

"Yes, but his car is in the parking lot. They must have walked somewhere."

"Where?" asked David, the strain to keep his voice calm was obvious in the single word.

"We don't know," cried Cindi as tears washed down her face. "I wanted to call the cops, but Jack—" She glared at him as if everything that had happened was his fault. "Jack said we should talk to you first. That you'd know the best thing to do."

Reece looked distraught. "Sending the cops after them might make things worse." His voice broke on the last word and color sprang up his face.

"How?"

Before anyone could answer Abby's question, Dwight elbowed his way to the front of the group of teens. "I think I know why she went with him."

"Why?" she asked, again fighting the panic roiling through her.

"She was talking at supper about how we need to forgive those who treat us bad. While we can. That's what she said. We have to forgive them while we can."

Abby turned to David. "Do you know why she was talking about that today?"

He nodded. "We had a big discussion about the importance of asking and giving forgiveness at our house last night." His gaze locked with Abby's. "A big discussion."

"Or," Reece said, "she wants to hang out with him rather than with us, and this gave her the excuse."

"No!" Abby didn't care that all eyes turned on her. "I understand how going with a bad boy because he's a bit dangerous can seem enticing, but it's a road to trouble."

"What are you talking about?" David asked.

She waved aside his question, realizing how much she'd almost revealed. "We don't have time to talk about what happened years ago." What would he think of her when he learned how foolish and selfish she'd been? Now, more than ever, she needed to follow her common sense and let her breaking heart fend for itself. "We need to find Mikayla."

David gathered the teens around him and peppered them with questions. Reece, Jack and Cindi were his daughter's closest friends. It was possible they knew something they weren't aware of, the very thing that could lead them to Mikayla.

Two minutes later his hopes were dashed. Reece was the only one who'd seen Mikayla with Hunter, and he hadn't seen where they were headed. Dividing up the kids, David sent them to several of the spots where Mikayla might have gone while he headed to their house to check if she'd shown up there. He directed Jack to find Michael and ask him to round up more help. He told them to have everyone report in at the community center in an hour. What he didn't say was if there wasn't any sign of her by then, he'd alert the authorities.

"I'll stay here," Abby said. "If someone finds Mikayla and Hunter, I'll have one of the *Englischers* send out a text message to Jack's phone. He can alert everyone else."

It was a good plan, but as minutes passed and ten became twenty, then forty, the kids found nothing in the usual places where teens hung out. David's house was empty. His parents must have gone somewhere after supper. He pushed aside his irritation at how they kept him out of the loop of their lives. He needed to concentrate on finding his daughter. Leaving a note on the kitchen table for Mikayla to call him, he wondered where the two kids had gone. Was his daughter okay?

As he returned to the community center, it started to rain. A cold, wintry rain that warned they'd been foolish to think spring had arrived. He ducked his head into it, hoping it wouldn't turn to sleet as the night grew colder.

The community center was a hubbub of activity. He slipped in and saw Michael talking with Isaac. Abby's brother had pulled out a map of the area and was asking questions. David looked for Abby and saw her pouring coffee. Her face was set in determined lines, but he saw the ravages of worry gouged into her cheeks.

"Glen has talked to the police," she said after she wound her way through the crowd to get to him. "They can't do much until a full day has passed, but will keep an eye out for Mikayla and Hunter."

A full day? He couldn't live through twenty-three more hours of not knowing where his daughter was.

Working with Michael and Isaac and other volunteers, David helped make up assignments. The volunteers were about to dash out the door to widen the search, when it opened. He heard a few gasps, including one of his own, but nobody spoke as Mikayla, wearing her light blue spring coat, walked in alongside Hunter Keyes.

The boy aimed a hostile stare at everyone. He raised his clenched hands when David jumped forward.

David paid the boy no attention. He grabbed his daughter by the shoulders and pulled her into a quick embrace. "Mikayla, you're okay!"

"Why wouldn't I be?" she asked, wiggling away.

He released her and frowned at Hunter. "You know why, Mikayla."

With his chin raised in a defiant pose, the boy growled, "Yeah, he thinks I'm going to do something bad to you, Mick."

When Reece bristled at the other boy's familiarity, David put a hand on each boy's shoulder. "Okay, enough of this posturing." He turned to the rest of the room. "Thank you."

The crowd quickly dispersed, happy the kids were safe. Soon, only the teens and Abby stood with David in the main room. He was surprised when Hunter didn't leave with everyone else.

Reece must have been, too, because he snarled, "Some people don't know when they're not welcome."

When Hunter clenched his hands again, David said, "There's no need for anybody to antagonize anyone else."

Hunter stepped away and folded his arms over his chest. "I don't need you telling me what I can or can't do. You're not my—"

"Hunter," Mikayla said, "you promised you'd be nice."

"I know." The boy hung his head, looking like a chastised puppy.

Disbelief appeared on the faces of the other teens, but before anyone else could speak, Abby urged them to sit. She carried a tray of brownies from the kitchen to the largest round table and pulled out a chair.

David waited until each of the kids had chosen a chair, Hunter last of all, before he pulled out one for himself. "Okay, Mikayla, what's going on? You had everyone worried when you went off without telling anyone where you were going."

"I'm sorry to worry you, but I'm doing what Abby taught me to do."

"What's that?" He glanced at Abby, who obviously had no more idea than he did what Mikayla was talking about.

His daughter gave him a lopsided smile. "She didn't come out and tell me, but I've seen how when she makes a mistake, she apologizes and then lets it go. She doesn't dwell on it. Her mistake doesn't take over her life. That's how the Amish are. They forgive."

He was surprised when he saw Abby flinch. Something about Mikayla's words had pricked her. But what? Did it have something to do with what she'd said about her past before she'd clammed up?

Even if he'd known how to ask, he didn't have a chance because his parents walked into the community center. David looked from Abby's distraught eyes to his parents' furious ones. Why had they come now? He had his answer when his father tossed a piece of paper on the table. It was, David saw, the note he'd written to let Mikayla know he was looking for her.

"The Amish forgive?" His mother sneered at Abby. "What lies have you been feeding these children along with your brownies?"

Chapter Sixteen

David ignored the shocked teens as he stood. Lifting the paper off the table, he said, "I would have thought your first concern, after seeing this, would be for Mikayla."

"She's right there." Without another word, his father picked up a pair of gloves from beneath the pegs where they'd hung their coats earlier.

David wondered how much of the conversation his parents had heard. It hadn't been that long ago when he warned Abby how his mother liked to eavesdrop.

"Don't listen to that woman," Mother said with the same icy disdain. "She's filling your heads with nonsense."

He heard the teens shift in their chairs. They were too polite to call out his mother, but they didn't like hearing Abby insulted.

"It's not nonsense, Mother. Abby is helping these young people learn to live a better life."

"A life that doesn't have anything to do with us."

For a moment, he was speechless. Why did his parents think the conversation was about them? Then he understood. Guilt. They carried the same burden he did, but did so knowingly.

Facing his parents, he said, "How would I know that? You've never answered my questions about why you left the Amish."

That brought big gasps from the kids. From the corner of his eye, he saw Abby trying to hush them, but he kept his gaze locked with his parents'.

"We have answered your questions," his mother asserted. "Every single one, haven't we, Ed?"

"Every single one."

David drew in a steadying breath before he said something he'd regret. After years of trying to discover the truth, he'd come to recognize the tricks his parents used to divert him. They agreed with each other, always parroting the other's words, to take over the conversation and steer it where they wanted it to go.

"Then tell me again now that I'm an adult and can understand it."

His parents exchanged an uneasy look then his mother glared at Abby.

"This is a private family matter."

"No," he argued.

Abby interjected to say, "We can leave, David."

David faced her. He couldn't mistake the gentle warmth in her gaze. He didn't want her to go. She was the only one on his side. He froze at the thought, wondering when sides had been chosen and why he was on a different one than his parents.

"Stay, Abby. I can't go on being torn apart between what I used to believe and what you and the others have shown me with your hard work and concern for Evergreen Corners."

When fingers grasped his hand, he looked down to see Mikayla's worried face. With a renewed shock, as if he'd grabbed hold of a live wire, he remembered that the whole discussion about his past had begun because his daughter had approached Abby about becoming Amish. Because she wanted to be part of a family as much as he did?

Standing, Mikayla motioned to her friends. They got up and walked away. The kitchen door closed behind them and then the pass-through window was shut.

"I can go with them," Abby whispered.

"Stay. Please." His voice broke as Reece's had earlier.

"*Ja.* For as long as you want me to."

Her words resonated in his mind. She'd stay for as long as he wanted her to? Was she saying what he hoped she was saying?

He couldn't think of that now. "Tell me the truth," he said as he looked at his parents again.

His father spoke first. "You shouldn't ask your mother to recount what happened again."

"It isn't again. You two have never explained to me why you left the Amish and cut off connections with them. Look. I want to know the truth. I don't want to judge you or what happened to you. What happened to *us*. I want to know what happened."

"We'd hoped you wouldn't remember those days," his mother said with a sigh as she shrank into her coat.

"I don't remember much. Or I didn't until the plain volunteers came to help rebuild Evergreen Corners."

"That woman has twisted your mind." Her nose wrinkled as she glared at Abby.

He wanted to step between Abby and his mother's

scowl, but he knew Abby understood his mother's pain. "She isn't the only Amish person I know."

"But the most important," his mother argued. With her face so pale that every bit of her makeup looked garish, she blinked. Was she trying not to cry? He wanted to apologize that his quest for the truth was bringing her pain.

God, there must be a way for me to know what happened without adding to what they've already suffered. Help me find it.

"Please tell me why you left," he pleaded.

"I suppose he has a right to know, Ed." His mother folded and unfolded her hands as if weaving an invisible garment. "It's part of his history, too."

"Some history should be forgotten." His father wasn't willing to budge an inch.

"Please, Ed."

His father's face crumpled, and David couldn't help wondering if his father was sending up a similar prayer of his own. Wishing he knew which Bible verse stated "the truth shall make you free," David kept his lips closed. He suspected anything he said now would add to his parents' wretchedness.

"All right, Nora. If you want to leave, I can…"

She shook her head and squared her shoulders. "It's my story, too."

David bit his lower lip as he looked from his father to his mother. The love that had knit them together had grown stronger through the years, and he wondered if that was, in part, because they'd felt they were alone in the world except for their only child.

His father sat at the table and clasped his hands on it, his knuckles bleached with tension. "We lived as

Amish youth should. We met at a singing on a Sunday evening, and I asked your mother to let me take her home in my buggy that night. After that, she rode in my buggy every other Sunday after singings, and I often drove over to her parents' house on Saturday nights to take her to other youth events in the area. I asked her to be my wife, and she agreed. We were baptized. And then we were married, and a couple of years later, you were born."

"I thought—" He took care this time not to mention Abby's name. "I thought when you chose baptism, you agreed to follow the rules of your district's *Ordnung*."

"You've learned a lot about plain ways. Has *that* woman—"

He refused to let either of them disparage Abby again. "For the past five months, a lot of Amish volunteers have come to Evergreen Corners to help those who need them most. They've welcomed us with food and with their skills and with their kindness, lifting us up when we were at our lowest."

"Your property wasn't flooded," his mother interjected.

"No, it wasn't, but Mikayla's was." When his parents looked confused, he explained how the St. Pierre house had been destroyed. "It was empty because she was at my house, but it was her home. Her last connection with her father. Now it's gone. That has nothing to do with any of this. Why did you jump the fence?"

His parents looked at each other again then his father said, "Because your mother was accused of something she didn't do."

"What?" He glanced at his mother, who was looking everywhere but at him. "I'm sorry, but I need to know."

"Our bishop's wife had it in for your mother, and she accused your mother of wearing clothing that didn't fit with the rules set forth by the *Ordnung*."

Some strong emotion raced through his mother's eyes, but it wasn't regret. In that instant he knew the accusation had been honest. Why would they give up their families and friends for such a small misdemeanor?

He got his answer when his father said, "*Daed*—who was our bishop—refused to step in to say your mother wasn't wrong."

"That's because," his mother said bitterly, "he was afraid of his wife. She wanted us to be afraid of her, but I refused to be."

David felt as if he'd run headlong into a wall. A disagreement between his mother and his grandmother had created a fissure that had torn the family apart. Two proud women—both of whom would deny their *hochmut*, as Abby called it—had put being right above everything else.

Something released from around his heart. For so long, he'd cradled his guilt as if it were a precious gift. It wasn't. It had fooled him into believing *he* had been the reason his parents had left their Amish family. Instead of bringing his guilt out into the light of reality, he'd empowered it, giving it more strength to torture him.

"Why didn't you ask for forgiveness?" he asked.

"Why didn't *she*?" his mother fired back.

"If you'd asked, wouldn't it have been granted to you? And couldn't you have forgiven her?"

His mother yanked the door open. "Come, Ed. It's time we left where we're not wanted any longer."

David tried to halt her by reassuring them that they'd misunderstood his need to know the truth. Nothing changed their minds or their dramatic exit into the rainy night. The hurt was too old, too deeply ingrained, he realized, to be soothed with common sense.

Arms curved around his shoulders and he bent to put his cheek on Abby's *kapp*. Neither of them spoke, but he knew all her thoughts were for him and his family.

"I'm so—" Her words were lost beneath an abrupt crash.

Running to the door, he threw it open. He took a single look and sped toward the car that had hit a tree at the lower end of the village green. Already fire licked the car's undercarriage.

His parents' car.

Abby called after him, but he didn't slow on the icy road. More shouts came from every direction. People appeared out of the dark. By the time he'd reached the car, others were there, too.

He grabbed the driver's-side door. His fingers were seared. Jerking them back, he pulled down his coat sleeve to cover his hand and tried again. He could see his father, slumped into the air bag.

The door wouldn't open.

Someone shoved a crowbar into his hand. Grabbing it, he shifted his grip to let others seize it, too. He slid it around the door and shouted, "Now!"

Sirens rang as he put his whole weight along with the other two men holding on to the bar. The metal peeled back, but not far enough.

Yanking the crowbar out of their hands, he raised it and slammed it against the window. Glass shattered as the flames near his feet threatened to melt his boots. He used the bar to sweep the shards aside and reached inside. He couldn't reach the seat belt release.

"Move!" shouted Isaac from behind him. "I'll cut him loose."

He obeyed, and Abby's brother sliced through the seat belt with a sharp knife. As the pieces fell away, David and Isaac tugged his father through the window. Other arms appeared out of the sleet to cradle his father so he didn't fall into the strengthening fire.

"Got him!" someone called. "What about Mrs. Riehl?"

David whirled to go around to the far side of the car, but saw another group of people, this one including Abby, carrying his mother away from the car. He breathed a grateful prayer.

The rescue squad and the fire trucks arrived at the same moment. While the firemen pumped water from the brook onto the car, his parents were lifted with care into the ambulance. An EMT told David, while putting salve on his burnt hand and wrapping it, that each of his parents had a broken arm and possibly a concussion from the air bags.

"Go home and put some dry clothes on before you come over to the hospital," the man said. "The ER staff won't let you in for at least a half an hour, so take your time on the slippery roads."

He nodded and stepped aside as the ambulance pulled out with care, not wanting to risk another accident.

"This is my fault," he said into the darkness.

From behind them, Mikayla cried, "No! Don't say that."

Abby moved to put her arms around the distraught girl. As she led the girl and David up onto a nearby porch so they were out of the rain, Mikayla repeated, "No, David! Don't say that!" The teen didn't wipe away her tears as her friends followed them onto the porch. "Abby, tell him what you told me about not letting guilt rule your life as it has mine."

David stared at her. "Guilt? What do you have to feel guilty about?"

"About Dad's death."

Reece grasped her hand. "You weren't driving."

"I've never told anyone but Hunter, because he understands." She shuddered as a police car slowed to a cautious stop by the fire trucks.

Had it looked like this the night Boyd St. Pierre had died? Abby saw the same question in David's eyes, but neither of them spoke.

"The day of the accident," Mikayla went on, "I wanted to go to a big sale in Brattleboro. Dad said the roads were too icy, and we'd go next week. The sale would have been over by then." She faltered but continued when Hunter climbed the stairs to stand a short distance away. "I whined and I pouted and threw a fit until Dad got tired of listening to me. He told me he'd take me. I walked away with bruises. Dad didn't."

She put her head into her hands and wept.

When her girlfriends moved to console her, Abby held them back. The boys looked overwhelmed and unsure.

David enfolded Mikayla in his arms. She clung to him as if she were a little girl. He pulled a handkerchief from his pocket and handed it to her.

After she wiped her face and blew her nose, she said between the hiccupping remnants of her sobs, "I'm sorry, David."

"You've got nothing to be sorry for."

"I've been horrible to you. I know you've been mourning Dad's death, too, but I couldn't add another person's pain to mine, so I shut you out."

"I understand," he said. "Sometimes it's easier to create a shell around yourself and your pain than to have to face the rest of the world. I was doing that, too…at least for a while." He looked at Abby. "Lately my faith has grown stronger, and I've been reaching out to our Heavenly Father to guide me through the shadows."

"If it hadn't been for me, Dad—"

"It was an accident. Nothing you did caused it. Nothing you do now can change it." He bent so his eyes were level with hers. "Here are a couple of things I want you to remember, Mikayla St. Pierre. Your father loved you more than anything or anyone in the whole world. Because he loved you so much, he wouldn't want you to spend your whole life filled with guilt for something that wasn't your fault."

"If I hadn't begged and pouted—"

"Listen to me." He held her gaze, not letting her look away. "It was an accident, and Boyd wasn't at fault. You weren't, either. Nobody was. That's why we call it an accident."

"But people were hurt!" Hunter protested, shocking Abby, who'd forgotten the erstwhile bully was there. "My uncle is in a wheelchair now because someone did something stupid."

"Your uncle was in the accident, too?" Abby asked.

"Yeah, and me, though I wasn't hurt. That's why Mick and I started talking when nobody else was around. If someone hadn't been stupid—"

"The police said more than one car lost control on the ice to cause the pileup," David said.

"And would you feel better," asked Abby as she moved next to Hunter, who towered over her, "if you had the name of someone to blame? Would it change what happened to your uncle? Would it erase your own memories of that night?" She put her fingers on his fist.

She didn't try to pry his fingers open. She prayed he'd find comfort in her touch.

"If you want to blame someone," she went on, "blame God. He loves us enough to let us do that. Go to Him and lay down the burden of your pain and grief at His feet. He shares our pain, and you know, Hunter, a pain shared is a pain lessened. That's what you and Mikayla have been talking about, ain't so? She's come home crying, but not because you were bullying her, but because, together, you were sharing your pain. Now you must do the same with the guilt that seeks to consume both of you."

The teen stared at his boots, his jaw working as he tried to hold in his grief. She looked at David. Did he understand that her words for Hunter were for him, as well?

"Hunter," Abby continued gently, "we plain people learn one thing from the time we're *kinder*. We learn we must forgive in order to be forgiven, whether it's forgiving and asking forgiveness from others or whether it's doing the same for ourselves." She turned to face Mikayla. "And learning to forgive ourselves is one of the hardest tasks we'll ever face."

The sound of weeping came from where Cindi and Lily stood, their arms around each other. The boys shuffled their feet, trying to keep their own emotions in check. Suddenly, Reece threw his arms around Mikayla, squeezing her as he said over and over how sorry he was he hadn't been able to help her.

When David cleared his throat, the boy released Mikayla. Reece wore a sheepish expression, but his face lit with a smile when David offered his hand. Shaking it, Reece nodded, too overcome to speak.

"Is finding forgiveness why you talked to Abby about becoming Amish, Mikayla?" David asked.

Hunter gasped. "You want to be Ay-mi...?" He glanced at Abby and then, lowering his eyes again, repeated the question as he pronounced the word correctly.

Instead of answering him, Mikayla said, "I wanted to become Amish because..." She dragged her hand across her face, smearing her makeup more. "I wanted to be Amish because they don't drive cars, so they don't get into accidents."

"That's not true," Abby whispered.

"What do you mean?" asked Mikayla.

"There are buggy crashes, too. Some are accidental. Some are...not. You asked me, David, about how I mentioned a *gut* girl could sometimes want to step out of line and do something a bit more adventurous."

"You said it was about the past," he said.

"It is. My past. Two buggies crashed while racing. Two young men's lives were changed forever, but it wasn't an accident. Nobody could blame the tragedy on an icy road. They'd both been drinking, and they both were angry." She met his eyes and saw compassion there. He would understand, because he knew how guilt could take over someone's life. Why hadn't she perceived that before? "They were angry because of me.

I was expected to let one of them take me home but I went with the other. If I'd done as I should have to help one of them instead of doing what I wanted to do, the accident might never have happened."

"So?" Mikayla asked. "So what if one guy thought you were going with him and you decided to go with the other? Neither of them owned you, so you could do as you wished. And did it have anything to do with you? No! They might have raced some other time if they hadn't that night, right?"

"I don't know." Abby delved into the deep well of her memories that she'd been avoiding since that awful night. "*Ja*, they might have. They'd been teasing and taunting each other for weeks about which one had the faster buggy. I'd forgotten that."

"Don't forget it again." Mikayla grasped Abby's hands and squeezed them. "That night, you were free to do what you chose to do. Just like I can spend time with Hunter, if I want to, though I know Reece gets upset because he thinks I'm putting myself in danger."

"If Reece gives you trouble..." Hunter began but then halted when the girl gave him a pointed gaze. "I'm sure you can handle it yourself."

"You're learning, Hunter." She patted his arm. "One of these days, you may turn into a human being."

When Reece held out his hand to Hunter, the erstwhile bully hesitated, then took it and pumped it.

Abby smiled as she hugged Mikayla. "*Danki*. Now you're teaching me. It's a lesson I won't forget." Putting her hand on David's arm, she said, "Let's go and see how your parents are. They're going to want to see you."

"Are you sure they will?"

"*Ja*," she said, though she wasn't.

* * *

Hours later, as the clocks showed a new day had begun, Abby pulled on her coat in the ER waiting room. Both of David's parents had been admitted to the hospital for observation because their concussions had left them dazed. One thing they did recall was the argument that had led to Ed Riehl driving too fast and striking the tree, though neither remembered the accident. They were so happy to be alive and see their son they wanted to put the argument behind them.

Abby guessed there would need to be further discussion among the family, but that could wait until the Riehls were healed. As she watched David reach for his gloves, she was flushed with gratitude that God had led them to the truth. What had happened in the past mattered far less than what the future held. Mikayla and Abby had been wrong to take the blame for tragedies on their own shoulders. Now she felt lighter than she had in years as she handed her sense of guilt over to God.

"Hunter isn't the only one who needs God's help," she said as David began to zip up his coat.

"His bullying friends—"

She put a finger to his lips. When he regarded her with astonishment, she said, "I'm talking about us. We need God's help every day to discover the truth that our human foibles prevent us from seeing. I need to learn what Mikayla says I taught her." She laughed as she shook her head in disbelief. "Somehow she figured out what *I* need to learn myself. I hope by watching her, she can be my teacher."

"Doesn't the Bible tell us to become as children?"

"*Ja*, but don't call Mikayla a *kind*. She wouldn't appreciate that."

"True."

Mikayla walked into the waiting room. Holding out her hand to David, she opened her fingers.

"Happy belated Easter." She held out a bright yellow plastic egg.

Or it once had been bright yellow. Now it was covered with glitter and gold stars and tiny pictures of what looked like the sap house they'd visited. They'd been pasted on in every possible direction until most of the egg was covered.

He balanced it on his palm. "Did you make this, Mikayla?"

The girl nodded. "Open it."

"Nothing's going to jump out, is it?"

Abby was amazed when Mikayla gave a quick laugh. What a beautiful sound it was!

When David twisted the plastic egg open, a smaller egg wrapped in foil dropped onto the chair beside him. He snatched it up before it could fall onto the floor.

"Dad and I always exchanged one egg on Easter morning," Mikayla said, her voice rough with emotion. "We made them to remind us of fun times we had together. I had fun the day we went up to the top of Quarry Mountain and to the sap house. It was fun because of you, David." She gave him a quick hug.

"Oh, my stars!" he breathed as Mikayla rushed out of the room saying she'd meet them at the truck. "She made me an egg like she used to do for Boyd?"

Abby smiled. "*Ja.* A special tradition she shares with her *daed*."

"I'm not really her father."

"Maybe not by birth. She didn't give you the egg because you're a substitute for her *daed*. She wants you to know how much she appreciates what you've done for her."

"I haven't—"

"You've done more than you can guess, David. You've given her a home. You've listened to her when she wants to talk, and you've convinced her to open up when she's been afraid to."

"I think that's what *you* have done." He placed the egg on her palm and closed her fingers over it. "Not only for Mikayla, but for me, too. That's why I need to tell you that I love you, Abby Kauffman, and I want you to be my wife."

"Your wife?" Shock pierced her. "You know I can't marry—".

"An *Englischer*. I know, but I wasn't born *Englisch*, and I don't have to stay *Englisch*. If you'll have me, Abby, I'll relearn what I need to in order to live a plain life with you."

"Do you realize what you're saying?"

He nodded. "I know what I'm saying. I've been talking with Michael Miller. He's told me it wasn't easy, but he knows of a few other *Englischers* who have been baptized Amish. I'll have to give up my truck and my electricity, but my job is one other plain men do. It'll take time while I relearn the language and the customs. Will you help me, Abby, so we can spend our lives together?"

"Mikayla—"

"I doubt she was serious about living a plain life, but if she is, I'll support her in that decision. Boyd wanted her to be happy and have the life she wants. I do, too. She'll always have a home with me." He lifted her hand to his lips and gave it a gentle kiss. "With us?"

She faltered. Should she listen to *gut* sense or should

she follow her heart into David's arms? As she saw the joy in his eyes dim when she didn't answer, she knew there could be only one response, though the way ahead of them could be fraught with many twists and turns. Just as her life had always been.

"Ja," she murmured. "With us. I love you, David, and I want to be your wife."

"That's all the incentive I need to do what I must to be the man I was born to be." He put his arms around her and held her close.

This time when his mouth found hers, she soared on the love that had grown between them, even before they'd been aware of it. As she melted into his kiss, Abby savored this one and couldn't wait for the next. She knew it would be that way for the rest of their lives together.

Epilogue

"Here she comes. Be quiet."

"Shh!"

Abby tried not to laugh as the teenagers were so loud in their attempts to warn the others to be silent. The front room was dark because the curtains on the windows had been drawn tight. They waited there, listening for the hesitant steps coming toward them.

"Why are the drapes closed?" asked an elderly voice.

Stepping forward, Abby smiled at Doris Blomgren. The old woman was almost recovered from the effects of her fall. Now that summer was in full bloom, she was able to get around her house with the help of a walker. She no longer lived alone, because her great-niece, Barbara, had moved in to help her remain in her home.

"We're done," Abby said with a broadening smile.

"Done?" Doris's eyes filled with happy tears. "With my... With the project?"

"Ja." Without turning, she said, "Open those drapes."

The teen group, which now included Hunter and one of his former bully friends among their number, sent sunshine falling into the room. It glistened on the black sewing machine that perched atop its refinished stand. The treadle was polished to a sheen, and the useless belts had been replaced with ones that were smooth and taut.

"Oh, my!" Doris put her hands up to her face. "You did it! You brought that old sewing machine back to life."

David, who looked so handsome in the plain clothes he now wore each day, said, "It works now. We fixed each piece of it and oiled it." He grinned. "Abby wound bobbins in every possible color of thread she could find. It's ready to go whenever you're ready to take it for a test-drive, Doris."

"Not me." The old woman linked her arm through her great-niece's. "I've had the sewing machine for a long time. Now it's time for a new owner. It's yours, Barbara."

Her niece's cheeks flushed with happiness as the teens cheered. "They repaired it for you, Aunt Doris."

"No, I asked them to fix it up for you. Enjoy it. Use it." She winked as she added, "And if it breaks down, I know a good repairman."

Abby gave the women a chance to thank the teens, then herded them out. She didn't want to tire out Doris with the excitement.

The kids headed toward the school to watch the younger ones play baseball, leaving her and David alone as they were so seldom. He often traveled by hired van to take classes in what he'd need to know before he could begin baptism classes. She'd been overjoyed when Isaac offered to help. She hadn't been sure if her inflexible brother would be willing to accept David as her future husband, but Isaac had been his usual terse self.

"If he's going to learn to live a plain life, he needs to learn from someone who will teach him properly," Isaac had said without a hint of humor.

Her brother had been as *gut* as his word and taught David almost every day while Isaac helped lay new floors in the big barn for the apartments David hoped to make available to two low-income families. Any animosity between them had faded as they'd come to respect each other's skills and dedication to their tasks.

Walking side by side through the middle of the village, Abby laughed along with David as he told her stories about his mistakes as he relearned *Deitsch*.

"For some reason," he said, making her giggle more, "Isaac and Michael seem to believe I should learn the adult words for things instead of the toddler ones I remember."

They paused when they reached the empty lot where the old St. Pierre farmhouse had stood for almost two hundred years. The ruined covered bridge was a looming shadow over the road, but rumor suggested it soon would be repaired.

"Mikayla has decided what she wants to do with the land." David picked up a stone and tossed it into the shallow water. He spoke *Deitsch* slower than he did *Englisch*, but was getting better with practice. "She wants to donate it to the town for a picnic park. A park named Boyd St. Pierre Memorial Park."

"What a lovely tribute to her *daed*!" Abby laced her fingers among his as she leaned her head on his shoulder. "She has a home with you, so she doesn't need another."

"She told me that in the same breath when she announced she intended to dye her hair purple."

Abby laughed. "At least it's a color we plain women wear, so she and I will match." She grew serious. "David, have you heard from your parents yet?"

His parents were slowly recovering at their home in California, and their prognosis was excellent. Though they'd reported gaps in their short-term memories, they were getting better with assistance from *doktors* and therapists.

"Ja." He took an envelope out of his pocket and handed it to her.

"You want me to read it?"

"I think you should."

She lifted out the single sheet and unfolded it. The letter was brief, but she hadn't gotten past the second sentence before the page blurred in front of her teary eyes.

Taking it back, he read aloud, "'While our first choice for you wouldn't be the life you're choosing, son, we want you to be happy. A plain life wasn't for us, but we will pray that it brings you the happiness a good son like you deserves.'"

She wanted to dance with sparkling steps as the light did on the water. "Thank God He has opened your parents' hearts. What a *wunderbaar* blessing He has given you!"

"Given us, *liebling*." He enfolded her to him for a sweet kiss, and she knew that she'd been wise to follow both her heart's desire and her head's joy to love.

* * * * *

Carrie Lighte lives in Massachusetts next door to a Mennonite farming family, and she frequently spots deer, foxes, fisher cats, coyotes and turkeys in her backyard. Having enjoyed traveling to several Amish communities in the eastern United States, she looks forward to visiting settlements in the western states and in Canada. When she's not reading, writing or researching, Carrie likes to hike, kayak, bake and play word games.

Books by Carrie Lighte

Love Inspired

The Amish of New Hope

Hiding Her Amish Secret
An Unexpected Amish Harvest
Caring for Her Amish Family
Their Pretend Courtship

Amish of Serenity Ridge

Courting the Amish Nanny
The Amish Nurse's Suitor
Her Amish Suitor's Secret
The Amish Widow's Christmas Hope

Visit the Author Profile page at LoveInspired.com.

ANNA'S FORGOTTEN FIANCÉ

Carrie Lighte

Trust in the Lord with all thine heart; and
lean not unto thine own understanding. In all thy
ways acknowledge him, and he shall direct thy paths.
—*Proverbs* 3:5–6

For anyone who has ever suffered a bumped head
or a bruised heart, as well as for those who
have experienced the healing power of love.
With special thanks to my agent, Pam Hopkins,
and my editor, Shana Asaro.

Chapter One

Anna Weaver slowly opened her eyes. Sunlight played off the white sheets and she quickly lowered her lids again, groaning. Her mind was swirling with questions but her mouth was too dry to form any words.

"Have a drink of water," a female voice beside her offered. "Little sips. Don't gulp it."

The young woman supported Anna's head until she'd swallowed her fill and then eased her back against the pillow. Anna squinted toward the figure.

"You've had an accident," she explained, as if sensing Anna's confusion. "You're at home recovering. It's your second day out of the hospital. How do you feel?"

"Like a horse kicked me in the head," Anna answered in a raspy voice. She blinked several times, trying to focus.

"You recognize me, don't you?" the woman asked. "I'm Melinda Roth, your cousin."

Technically, the woman wasn't Anna's cousin; she was her stepmother's niece. *I doubt I could ever forget the person who captured my boyfriend's heart,* Anna thought. Aloud she replied, "Of course I recognize you. Why wouldn't I?"

"The *Englisch* doctors said you still might have trouble with your memory, but apparently you don't," Melinda answered, appearing more disappointed than relieved.

Anna felt a pang of compassion. It was obvious Melinda felt guilty for what had transpired between her and Aaron. Anna had forgiven them both, but forgetting what happened was a little more difficult, especially since she had to live under the same roof—and share the same bedroom—with Melinda. Each time Melinda tiptoed into the room after her curfew, Anna was made acutely aware of how much her cousin was enjoying being courted by Aaron.

"The only trouble I have is that I'm a bit chilled," Anna said.

Melinda placed a hand on Anna's forehead. "You don't have a fever, thank the Lord. The doctor warned us to watch for that. I'll ask Eli to bring more wood inside for the stove."

"The woodstove in August?" Anna marveled. "That would be a first. Please don't trouble Eli on my account. I'm certain once I get up and move around, I'll be toasty warm."

"Lappich maedel!" Melinda tittered as she referred to Anna as a silly girl. "It isn't August. It's the first week in March."

Anna propped herself up on her elbows. Although she figured Melinda probably meant to be funny, her head was throbbing and she was in no mood for such foolishness. She knit her brows together and questioned, "You're teasing, right?"

Melinda shook her head and gestured toward the maple tree outside the window. "See? It doesn't have its leaves yet."

"How could that be?" A tear slid down Anna's cheek.

"Uh-oh, I've said too much." Melinda jumped to her feet and unfolded a second quilt over Anna's legs. "That should keep you warm."

Anna stared at her cousin, trying to make sense of the scenario. Then she began to giggle. "Oh, I understand! I'm dreaming!"

"Neh, neh," Melinda contradicted, giving Anna's skin a small pinch. "Feel that?"

Completely befuddled, Anna bent her arm across her face. First, she'd lost her boyfriend, then she'd lost her father, and now she feared she was losing her mind. It was simply too much to take in and she began to weep fully.

"You mustn't cry," Melinda cautioned. "The doctor said it wasn't *gut* for you to become upset. We don't want to have to take you back to the hospital."

Melinda's warning was enough to silence Anna's weeping. "I don't understand how two seasons could have passed without my knowing." She sniffed.

"The doctors said it's the nature of a head injury like yours. You may remember things from long ago, but not more recently. You've also been on strong medications for your headache and for hurting your backside when you fell, so even your hospital stay might be fuzzy."

"It is," Anna acknowledged. "And I don't recall injuring myself. How did it happen?"

"You appear to have slipped on the bank by the creek, hitting your head on a rock," Melinda replied. "Do you know what you may have been doing there? Or where you were going? It was early Tuesday morning."

Anna tried to remember but her mind was as blank as the ceiling above. She shook her head and then grimaced from the motion.

"That's okay," Melinda said cheerfully. "How about telling me some of the more important events that you *do* remember?"

"My *daed*'s funeral," Anna responded. "It was raining—a deluge of water—and then the rain turned to sleet and then to ice."

She remembered because at the time she felt as if the unseasonably cold weather mirrored her emotions; a torrent of tears followed by a stark, frozen numbness that even the brightest sunshine couldn't thaw.

"*Jah*, your *daed* died a year ago. Last March. What do you remember after that?"

Anna thought hard. The days, weeks and months after her dad's sudden death from a heart attack were a blur to her even before her head injury. "I remember... your birthday party," she said brightly.

"My eighteenth. *Gut.* That was in late August. Do you remember when I got baptized last fall?"

It felt wrong to admit she couldn't recall Melinda making such an important commitment, but Anna said, "*Neh.* I'm sorry."

"That's alright. The doctor said your memory loss probably wouldn't last long, especially if you're at home, surrounded by familiar faces."

"Well then, if that's what it takes to cure me, I should get dressed and join the boys for breakfast," Anna stated, although she would have preferred a few more moments of rest before joining her four stepbrothers downstairs. She slowly swung her legs over the edge of the bed.

"They'll be glad to know you're well enough to rise," Melinda remarked. "But it's nearly time for supper, not breakfast. And the one who is most anxious to see you is your fiancé. He'll stop in after work again, no doubt."

"My fiancé?" Anna snorted. "But I broke up with Aaron after I caught you and him—I mean, Aaron is walking out with you now, isn't he?"

"Jah, jah," Melinda confirmed. Her cheeks were so red it appeared she was the one who had a fever. "You and Aaron broke up over a year ago. Last February, in fact." She hung her head as if ashamed, before looking Anna in the eye again and clarifying, "I was referring to your new suitor. That is, to your fiancé, Fletcher. Fletcher Chupp, Aaron's cousin from Ohio."

"Fletcher?" Anna sputtered incredulously. "I'm quite certain I'm not acquainted with—much less *engaged to*—anyone by that name."

Fletcher stooped to pick up a cordless drywall screw gun and a handful of screws that had fallen to the floor.

"Don't forget to gather all of your tools before leaving the work site for the evening," he reminded Roy and Raymond Keim, Anna's stepbrothers.

"We won't," Roy responded. "But those aren't ours—they're Aaron's. We didn't know if he was coming back or not, so we didn't dare to put them away."

"Where has he gone?" Fletcher inquired.

"Probably buying a soft drink at the fast-food place down the street," answered Raymond as he folded a ladder and leaned it carefully on its side along the wall.

Fletcher wished Aaron would set a better example of work habits for Raymond and Roy. He worried what their *Englisch* clients would think if they saw him taking numerous breaks or leaving early. Aaron's habits reflected on all of them. Although their projects had been plentiful over the winter due to an October tornado damaging many of the office buildings in their little town of Willow Creek, there was no guarantee that future contracts would be awarded to them, especially if their reputation suffered. Fletcher would need all the work he could get when he became a married man with a family to support. *That's* if *I become a married man,* he mentally corrected himself.

Nothing about his future with Anna was as certain as it had seemed when their wedding intentions were "published," or announced, in church on Sunday. Only two days later, on Tuesday morning, Raymond delivered a sealed note to him from Anna. *Fletcher,* it read, *I have a serious concern regarding A. that I must discuss privately with you before the wedding preparations go any further. Please visit me tonight after work. —Anna.*

The message was so unexpected and disturbing that if he hadn't been responsible for supervising Raymond and Roy, Fletcher would have left work immediately to speak with Anna. By the time he finally reached her home that evening, he was shocked to be greeted by a neighbor bearing additional alarming news: that morning Anna suffered a fall and was in the hospital. Although he loathed knowing she'd been hurt, he was simultaneously informed the doctors said she was going to be just fine. But it tormented him that he had no such assurance about the future of his relationship with her.

Each time he visited Anna, she was resting or couldn't be disturbed. Now, it was Friday and he still hadn't spoken to her. Ever since receiving her note, he'd felt as if he'd swallowed a handful of nails, and he'd barely eaten or slept all week. *Please, Lord, give me patience and peace, even as You provide Anna rest and recovery,* he prayed for the umpteenth time that day.

"I suppose Aaron's allowed to take breaks whenever he wants since he's the business owner's son," Roy commented, interrupting Fletcher's thoughts.

Although Fletcher agreed with the boy's observation, he chided, "Enough of that talk. My *onkel* Isaiah showed you special favor yourself in allowing me to apprentice you here, because your *mamm* was married to Anna's *daed* and he was such a skilled carpenter. Isaiah has been a *gut* employer to me, too. Regardless of how anyone else performs their work, *Gott* requires each of us to work heartily in whatever we do."

The boys finished tidying the site before stepping out into the nippy early-evening air. They wove through the rows of *Englisch* vehicles to the makeshift hitching post at the far end of the parking lot. Aaron's sleek courting buggy was nowhere to be seen as Fletcher, Raymond and Roy climbed into Fletcher's boxy carriage, given to him by his *groossdaadi*, or grandfather.

"Go ahead and take the reins," Fletcher said to Roy, the younger of the two teens. "It's important for you to learn to handle the horse during what the *Englisch* call 'rush hour' traffic."

As Roy cautiously navigated his way through the western, commercialized section of Willow Creek, Fletcher gave him instructive hints. He knew what it was like to lose your dad at a young age—and these boys had essentially lost *two* fathers; first, their own dad and then Anna's. He figured they needed all the guidance and support they could get.

"*Gut* job," he remarked when Roy finally made it

through the maze of busy streets and down the main stretch of highway. From there, they exited onto the meandering country back roads that eventually led to the house Anna shared with her stepmother, Naomi, and Naomi's four sons, Raymond, Roy, Eli and Evan.

"Fletcher!" seven-year-old Evan whooped, sprinting across the yard when he spotted them coming down the lane. He tore alongside the buggy shouting, "Anna's awake!"

"Bobblemoul," eight-year-old Eli taunted, referring to his brother as a blabbermouth. He leaped down the porch steps after him. "You weren't supposed to tell. She said she isn't ready to see him yet."

"She said what?" Fletcher asked, hopping from the buggy after Roy brought it to a halt.

"Now who's repeating something they shouldn't?" Evan retorted to Eli.

"Roy, please hitch the horse for me," Fletcher requested and strode toward the porch, his heart hammering his ribs.

Naomi greeted him at the door with a wooden spoon in one hand and a bowl in the other. *"Kumme* in," she invited.

"Hello, Naomi. How are you?" he inquired politely before asking the question that was burning on his tongue.

"I'm *gut*," she said. "I see you're teaching Roy how to handle the horse in *Englisch* traffic? *Denki*—I worry about him around all those cars. He needs the practice."

"He's improving already," Fletcher remarked and then cut to the chase. "Is it true? Is Anna awake?"

"She is," Naomi replied. "But there's something you need to know."

"I've heard," Fletcher acknowledged. "Eli said she isn't ready to see me yet. I realize she probably needs a few minutes to get dressed and find her bearings. I can wait."

"Oh, dear," sighed Naomi. She sat down at the kitchen table and tapped a chair to indicate Fletcher should sit, as well. "I'm afraid that's not what she means by not being ready to see you. Do you recall the doctor said her memory might be impaired after the fall?"

Fletcher moved toward the table but he didn't sit, despite the heaviness in the core of his gut. He braced himself for another distressing disclosure. "*Jah*, I remember."

"Then you recall he instructed us it most likely would only be temporary, so there's no cause for alarm," Naomi continued cautiously. "However, before you see her, you should be aware she's having difficulty remembering anything at all that happened after late August or early September."

Fletcher gulped when he realized what Naomi was getting at. "I moved to Willow Creek in early September."

"*Jah*," confirmed Naomi, answering Fletcher's unasked question. "But the doctor said putting a face with a name may help her recollection. It's possible as soon as she sees you she will remember who you are. However, she might not. At least, not right away."

"Please, will you tell her I'd just like to see her?" he pleaded. "I haven't spoken to her since before her fall."

Naomi nodded. "I'll let her know and I'll ask Melinda to assist her down the stairs. Go through to the parlor. We'll give you two your privacy there. But, Fletcher, keep in mind she's been through a lot. She's very sensitive right now."

"I won't say anything to upset her," he promised.

As troubled as he was by Anna's last communication to him, Fletcher's primary concern at the moment was her well-being. Naomi had a tendency for excessive fretfulness; perhaps she was exaggerating the extent of Anna's memory loss? Pacing back and forth across the braided rug in front of the sofa, Fletcher wiped his palms on his trousers and bit his lower lip. The past few days without seeing Anna awake had seemed unbearably long, but this delay felt even more difficult to endure.

Someone cleared her throat behind him. He turned as Anna made her way down the hall. Her honey-blond tresses, customarily combed into a neat bun, were loosely arranged at the nape of her neck, her fair skin was a shade paler than it normally was and she clutched a drab shawl to her shoulders, but she took his breath away all the same. Rendered both speechless and immobile with conflicting emotions, he choked back a gasp.

Her eyes were downcast, carefully watching her footing as she tentatively stepped into the room. He studied her heart-shaped lips and oval face, her slender nose and the tiny beauty mark on her left cheekbone. But it was the vast depth of her eyes, accentuated with a curl of lashes and gently arched brows, he yearned to behold. Fletcher and Anna had often conveyed a world of feeling with a single glance, and, in spite of everything, he hoped one glimpse into her eyes would convince him of her abiding love.

"Anna," he stated, moving to offer her his arm to help steady her gait.

She looked up and locked her eyes with his. Even in the dim glow cast by the oil lamp, he could appreciate their magnificent emerald green hue. She seemed to be searching his features, reading his expression, taking in his presence. He waited for what felt like an eternity, but his gaze was met by an impassive blankness.

"I've been told you're my fiancé, Fletcher," she finally said, although it sounded more like a question than a statement. His last wisp of hopefulness dissipated when she shook his outstretched hand, as if they were strangers meeting for the first time.

As Fletcher's expectant countenance crumbled into one of stark disappointment, Anna immediately regretted her gesture. What was she thinking, to shake his hand like the *Englisch* would? She wasn't working in the shop, introducing herself to a customer. She didn't understand why everything seemed so jumbled in her mind.

"I'm sorry, but I need to sit," she said and settled into a straight-backed chair, which made Fletcher frown all the more.

He perched on the edge of the sofa nearest her, leaning forward on his knees. His large, sky blue eyes, coupled with an unruly shock of dark hair, gave him a boyish appearance, but his straight nose and prominent brow and jawline were the marks of a more mature masculinity. She wondered how she could have forgotten knowing such a physically distinctive young man.

"I've been very concerned about you," he stated. "How are you feeling?"

"*Denki*, I'm doing better," she said, although she had a dull headache. "Oh! But where are my manners? I should offer you something to drink. Would you like a cup of—"

She rose too quickly from her chair and the room wobbled. Fletcher again offered her his help, which she accepted this time, grasping his muscular forearm until the dizziness passed. Then he assisted her back into her seat.

"I didn't *kumme* here to drink *kaffi*, Anna," he said, crouching before her, still holding her hand. "I came here to see *you*."

Flustered by his scrutiny and the tenderness of his touch, she pulled her arm away and apologized. "I'm sorry I look so unkempt, but combing my hair makes my head ache."

He shook his head, insisting, "I wouldn't care if your hair were standing on end like a porcupine's quills, as long as I know you're alright."

Although she sensed his sentiment was earnest, her eyes smarted. Couldn't he see that she wasn't alright? And didn't he understand his nearness felt intrusive, given that she had absolutely no memory of him? He seemed so intense that she didn't want to offend him, but she wished he'd back away.

As if reading her thoughts, Fletcher retreated to his cushion on the sofa and said, "It's okay if you don't remember me yet, Anna. The doctor said this could happen. They told us your memories might return in bits and pieces."

Anna nodded and relaxed her shoulders. She hadn't realized how uptight she'd felt. She noticed his voice had a soothing quality. It was deep and warm, like her dad's was.

"Melinda told me a bit about you, but I have so many questions, I don't know where to start," she confessed.

"Why don't I give you the basics and if there's anything else you want to know, you can ask?" Fletcher questioned. When Anna nodded in agreement, he said, "Let's see—my name is Fletcher Josiah Chupp and I'm twenty-four. My *daed* was a carpenter. He and my *mamm* passed away by the time I was fifteen. I have three older sisters, all married, and sixteen nieces and nephews. I moved to Willow Creek, Pennsylvania, from Green Lake, Ohio, in September. My *onkel* Isaiah had been in dire need of another carpenter on his crew for some time."

"Because my *daed* died?"

Fletcher glanced down at his fingers, which he pressed into a steeple. "*Jah.* Your *daed* worked for Isaiah and he had a reputation among the *Englisch* of being an excellent carpenter. He left a big gap in my *onkel*'s business. No one could ever fill his shoes."

"No one could ever replace him as a *daed*, either," Anna murmured. After a pause, she asked, "So then, you live with your *ant* and *onkel*, and with Aaron and his sisters?"

"*Neh.* There wasn't room enough for me there. I live in my *groosdaaddi*'s home."

"Elmer! Your *groossdaadi* is Elmer Chupp! I remember him," Anna exclaimed. Then she realized aloud, "But of course I would, wouldn't I? I've known him for years. He was my *daed*'s first employer, before Isaiah took over their family business. You must greet him for me."

Fletcher rubbed his forehead. "I don't want to distress you, Anna, but my *groossdaadi* died in late December from pneumonia."

"*Neh!* Oh, *neh*!" Anna's bottom lip began to quiver.

"His passing was peaceful and it's a blessing to know he's not suffering the pain he endured toward the end," Fletcher said. "He always appreciated the soups and meals you made for him. And you were very consoling to me while I mourned."

"Dear Elmer Chupp." Anna clucked sorrowfully. "Didn't you say you lived with him?"

"*Jah*, I moved in with him when I first arrived in Pennsylvania," Fletcher clarified. "Now I live there alone. After you and I became betrothed, I discovered *Groossdaadi* willed his house to me, as his first grandson to tell the family of my intention to marry. For some reason, *Groossdaadi* chose not to follow the traditional Amish practice of bequeathing it to his youngest son, my *onkel* Isaiah. In any case, there were property taxes due, which you and I paid from my construction salary and your savings from working at Schrock's Shop, so the house is as *gut* as ours."

Anna's mind was reeling. She and Fletcher owned a house? On one hand, getting married and setting up her own household was a desire she'd harbored for years. On the other hand, with every new piece of information revealed to her, she was becoming increasingly uneasy at how seriously her life was intertwined with the life of a man who seemed like a virtual stranger, albeit, an appealingly thoughtful and stalwart one.

Pinching the bridge of her nose, she admitted, "I'm confused about the timing. In Willow Creek, it's customary for most Amish couples to keep their courtships as private as they can. They wait until July or August to tell their immediate families that they intend to marry. Their wedding intentions aren't published in church until October, and wedding season follows in November and December, after harvest. Yet Melinda says it's now March. Why did we already tell our families we intend to marry next fall?"

"We actually intend to marry next month," Fletcher responded. "You don't recall, but last October, Willow Creek was struck by a tornado. So many houses were damaged that Bishop Amos allowed those betrothed couples who needed to help their families rebuild to postpone their weddings until April. Of course, you and I were just getting to know each other last October, so we weren't yet engaged, but by January, we were certain we wanted to get married. We decided to take advantage of the bishop's special provision allowing for spring weddings this year."

"We only met in September and we're getting married in April?" Anna asked, unable to keep her voice from sounding incredulous. Six months was a brief courting period for any couple, and it seemed especially out of character for her. She had walked out with Aaron for over two years. As fondly as she dreamed of becoming a wife and a mother, lingering qualms had kept her from saying yes to Aaron's proposals, no matter how many times he asked. How was it she'd decided so quickly to marry Fletcher?

"Jah," he stated definitively. "As we confirmed to the deacon, we fully and unequivocally believe the Lord has provided us for each other."

Anna understood the implications. Prior to making their engagements public, Amish couples underwent a series of meetings with the deacon during which time the couple received counseling on the seriousness of entering into a marriage relationship. Although Anna had no recollection of those meetings, she knew if she and Fletcher completed the series and announced their intentions, it meant they were resolute about getting married.

"Have the wedding intentions been published in church?"

"They were announced on Sunday," Fletcher replied. "We'll be wed on Tuesday, April 7, five days before Easter and a week before Melinda and Aaron get married."

Anna inhaled sharply. "Melinda and Aaron are getting married?"

"Uh-oh," Fletcher said, smacking his forehead with his palm. "I assumed Melinda already told you."

"She probably didn't want to upset me."

Fletcher cocked his head. "Why would Melinda marrying Aaron upset you?"

"I d-don't know," Anna stammered. "I have no idea why I said that."

She was far more concerned about her own wedding than Melinda's. *I might as well be marrying the prince of England as this man, for as foreign as he is to me*, Anna thought, deeply disturbed. *Perhaps I should consider canceling our upcoming nuptials?*

"You were so excited after the intentions were published that you mailed the invitational letters to all of our out-of-town friends and family members first thing on Monday morning," Fletcher said. "Of course, the *leit* at church were invited and I extended several personal invitations on Monday evening, as well."

Upon hearing just how far their plans had progressed, Anna felt as overwhelmed by the prospect of calling off the wedding as she was by the prospect of carrying through with it. She silently prayed, *Please, Lord, if I really do know and love Fletcher Chupp and believe he's Your intended for me, help me to remember soon. If he isn't, please make me certain of that, too.*

* * *

Fletcher noticed Anna's face blanched at his words and he worried she might cry—or faint. "This must be a lot to take in," he said, trying to reassure himself as well as to console her. "The doctor said your physical well-being is the priority, and if you get enough rest your memories should take care of themselves."

Fletcher could always tell when Anna's smile was genuine because she had a small dimple in her right cheek. He saw no sign of it as she responded, "I can't imagine there will be much time for me to rest, with two weddings planned. I wonder how Naomi has been faring."

From his discussions with her, Fletcher knew how concerned Anna had been about her stepmother ever since Anna's father died. Naomi, who periodically suffered from immobilizing depression, was so grief stricken in the months following Conrad's death that Anna had almost single-handedly managed their household, with sporadic help from Melinda. In addition to caring for Eli and Evan, comforting Naomi and tending to the cooking, cleaning, laundering and gardening, Anna also worked at a shop in town so she could contribute to the household expenses. Her cheerful diligence was one of the qualities Fletcher most admired about her.

"I know you can't remember this," Fletcher said, "but Naomi began to regain some of her…her energy in January when you confided our decision to marry to her. You told me she embraced the distraction of planning for a wedding. She said it gave her something hopeful instead of dreadful to think about, and rather than wringing her hands, she could put them to *gut* use preparing for our guests."

"That sounds like the old Naomi, alright," Anna remarked and for the first time, her dimple puckered her cheek. But her smile faded almost as quickly as it appeared. "So then, if she is doing better, did I return to working at the shop full-time?"

During Naomi's period of bereavement, Anna reduced her working schedule from full time to part-time, much to the dismay of the shopkeeper, who valued Anna's skills. But as efficient as she was at assisting customers, Anna told Fletcher she drew more satisfaction from meeting her family's needs at home. She worked in the store only as much as was necessary to contribute to their living expenses.

"*Neh*, you're still only working there part-time."

A frown etched its way across Anna's forehead. "If I helped pay the property taxes for the house with my savings, and I've still only been working part-time, how has my family been managing financially? Furthermore, what will Naomi do when I move? Raymond's salary as an apprentice won't be enough to cover their expenses."

"*Jah*, you're right. That's why I asked my *onkel* to promote Raymond to a full-fledged crew member and to allow me to apprentice Roy. Raymond had already been satisfactorily apprenticed by your *daed* and there have been plenty of projects in the aftermath of the tornado, so Isaiah readily agreed. The arrangement has worked well for them and you've been happy that instead of needing to work full-time, you've been able to continue helping Naomi, er, recover, especially as you prepare the house for the weddings."

Averting her eyes toward the window, Anna responded in a faraway voice, "It sounds as if we've thoroughly addressed all of the essential details, then."

That's what I thought, too—until I received your message. Fletcher agonized, chewing the inside of his cheek to keep his emotions in check. He knew this wasn't the time to broach the subject, no matter how desperately he wanted Anna to allay his suspicions about her note.

"Supper's ready," Melinda announced from the doorway. "*Ant* Naomi says you're *wilkom* to join us, Fletcher."

"*Denki*, it smells *wunderbaar*, but I need to be on my way," he replied. As little as he'd eaten lately, Fletcher felt as if there were a cement block in his stomach and he doubted he could swallow even a morsel of bread.

As it was, Anna said she felt queasy and she wanted to go lie down.

"May I visit you tomorrow?" Fletcher asked before they parted.

"*Jah*," she replied simply. Her voice sounded strained when she added, "*Denki* for coming by tonight," thus ending their visit on as formal of a note as it began.

Shaken by how drastically his relationship with Anna had changed within the span of a few days, Fletcher numbly ushered the horse along the winding roads leading to his home. Once there, he collected the mail from the box and entered the chilly house. He turned on the gas lamp hanging above the kitchen table to read his sister's familiar penmanship.

Dear Fletcher,
We were so joyful to receive word of the official date for your upcoming wedding that we got together to write you the very moment the letter arrived from Anna!

As your older sisters, permit us to say we knew how disappointed you were when Joyce Beiler abruptly called off your engagement, even though you tried to disguise the tremendous toll the breakup took on you. Ever since then, we have been faithfully praying that the Lord would heal your hurt and help your heart to love and trust another young woman again. We are grateful He answered our prayers for you so quickly in Willow Creek. It still puzzles us that Joyce chose to marry Frederick Wittmer, but we are grateful you have found a woman who truly recognizes what an honorable, responsible, Godly man you are.

Although our interaction with Anna was brief and we weren't yet aware you were courting, we were fond of her the moment we met her in Willow Creek in December. Even during such a somber time as Grandfather's funeral, she demonstrated a warmth and graciousness that lightened our burden. It is no wonder you are as committed to her as she is to you. Surely, your marriage will be blessed.

With love from your sisters,

Esther, Leah and Rebekah (& families)

Sighing heavily, Fletcher folded the letter and slid it back into its envelope. He understood the sentiments were well-intentioned. But under the circumstances, they opened old wounds of the nearly unbearable heartache and humiliation he suffered when Joyce canceled their wedding.

A single tear rolled down his cheek when he lamented how wrong his sisters were. Anna didn't even recognize his face, much less his character. While he didn't doubt her memory would return eventually, he was far less certain about her commitment to him. His sisters were right: the breakup with Joyce had nearly cost him his physical health and emotional well-being. He didn't think he could endure it if another fiancée called off their wedding.

He knew the message Anna had sent him by heart, but he picked up her note from the table where he'd left it that morning and held it to the light. *I have a serious concern regarding A. that I must discuss privately with you before the wedding preparations go any further.*

There was only one person she could have been referring to when she wrote "A."—Aaron, her former suitor. Fletcher shook his head at the thought. Even though his cousin had become romantically involved with Melinda, Fletcher long sensed Aaron was still in love with Anna. But once when Fletcher expressed his concern to Anna, she dismissed it out of hand.

"That's ridiculous. He broke up with me to court Melinda. She's the one he loves now," she argued. "Besides, you should know from all of our conversations that *I* haven't any feelings for *him* anymore. And whatever feelings I once had pale in comparison with how I feel about you. I may have liked Aaron, but I love—I'm *in* love with you, Fletcher Josiah Chupp."

On the surface, her response reminded him of the many conversations he'd had with Joyce, whom he suspected had developed a romantic affection for her brother-in-law's visiting cousin, Frederick. Joyce vehemently and consistently denied it, until four days before she and Fletcher were scheduled to wed, when she finally admitted the truth. But there was something fundamentally different about Anna, and as she declared her love for Fletcher, she stared into his eyes with such devotion that all of his worries melted away.

Fletcher remembered how, a few weeks after he and Anna confided their marriage intentions to their families, Melinda and Aaron announced they'd begun meeting with the deacon and they also planned to wed in the spring. Because Melinda seemed especially immature, their decision surprised Fletcher, but he was relieved to confirm Anna was right: Aaron was wholly committed to Melinda. Or so he'd thought at the time. But Anna's recent note shook his confidence to the core.

What in the world could have transpired concerning Aaron to make Anna hesitant to carry on with preparations to marry me? Burying his head in his hands, Fletcher shuddered to imagine. He knew from experience that people changed their minds. Engagements could be broken, even days before a wedding. There was still time. Was he was about to be forsaken by his fiancée for another man again? The possibility of having to withstand that kind of rejection a second time made Fletcher's skin bead with sweat. The only way he'd know for certain was to talk to Anna about her note. But first, she'd have to remember what she meant when she'd penned it.

Chapter Two

As the sun began to light the room, Anna peered at her cousin asleep in the twin bed across from her. She rose to make the boys' breakfast, but when her feet touched the chilly floor, she pulled them back into bed, deciding to snuggle beneath the blankets just a little longer.

The tiny room on the third floor of the house was actually a part of the attic her father had sectioned off especially for her. More than once she'd knocked her head against the sloping ceiling and the room tended to be hotter in the summer and colder in the winter than the rest of the house, but she had always relished the privacy it afforded her from the four boys.

She'd had the room all to herself until Melinda's father sent Melinda to live with Anna's family a year ago in January because he wanted her to have better influences than he could provide. Naomi's sister had died twelve years earlier and her brother-in-law never remarried, so Melinda had grown up without any females in her home. It was said by many that she was capricious, or perhaps undisciplined. Some went so far as to call her lazy, a quality condemned by the Amish. Anna ob-

served that the girl was generally willing to perform almost any chore, but she often became distracted in the
middle of it and moved on to another endeavor.

"Half-done is far from done," was the Amish proverb
Anna most often quoted to Melinda the first year of her
residence with Anna's family. Serving as Melinda's role
model had been a frustrating effort, yet Anna mused
that if Melinda had committed herself to following God
and had been baptized into the church, then her living
with them had been worthwhile. It meant Melinda had
put her wild *Rumspringa* years behind her; surely if
she'd made that change, there was hope for other areas
of her behavior, as well.

Melinda's eyes opened. *"Guder mariye."* She
yawned. "I'm Melinda, your cousin."

Anna giggled. *"Jah*, I know. Are you going to introduce yourself to me every time I wake?"

Melinda laughed, too. "You were staring at me. I
thought you didn't know who I was."

"I was marveling that such a young woman has decided upon marriage already."

Melinda sat straight up. "You remembered Aaron
and I are getting married!"

"Neh, Fletcher mentioned it. He thought I already
knew."

"Oh. Well, I'm not that young—I'm eighteen now.
You're only four years older than I am," Melinda reasoned. "Besides, I've known Aaron over twice as long
as you've known Fletcher. I think that makes us far better prepared to spend our lives together."

"Hmm," Anna hummed noncommittally. Melinda
may have been eighteen, but at times she acted fourteen.
Yet Anna couldn't deny she made a valid point about

the brevity of Anna's relationship with Fletcher. Then she raised her hands to her cheeks as her cousin's words sank in—she herself was older than she remembered.

"That's right, I must be twenty-two now since my birthday was in September! Time flies when you have amnesia."

Melinda giggled and the two of them made their beds, got dressed and followed the smell of frying bacon down the stairs. When everyone was seated around the table, Raymond said grace, thanking the Lord especially for Anna's recovery. She was so hungry that she devoured as large a serving of food as her brothers did.

"If it's Saturday, that must mean you're working a half day today, right?" she asked Raymond and Roy, who both nodded since their mouths were full. "I can drop you off on my way to the shop. Joseph Schrock will be relieved to have me back."

"Neh," Naomi answered. "The doctor said you couldn't return to work until after your follow-up appointment. In fact, he said you should limit activities of exertion and anything that requires close concentration, such as sewing or reading, until he sees you again."

"Nonsense," Anna argued. "I'm as healthy as a horse—physically, anyway. There's no reason I can't ring up purchases and help *Englisch* customers decide which quilt to purchase or whether their grandchildren might prefer rocking horses or wooden trains. Besides, we need the income and Joseph needs the help."

Naomi began twisting her hands. "You have a doctor's appointment on Wednesday. Please, won't you wait until you receive his approval before returning to the shop?"

Not wishing to cause Naomi any undue anxiety,

Anna conceded. "Alright, I'll wait. But you must at least allow me to help with the housework. How about if I prepare an easy dinner?"

"That sounds *gut*," Melinda interjected. "If I drop the boys off at the work site before I go to the market, I'm certain Fletcher or Aaron will give them a ride home. Perhaps we can invite them for dinner, since Fletcher wanted to check in on Anna again today anyway?"

Anna caught Naomi's eye and gave a slight shrug. Melinda's habit of finagling a way out of chores in order to spend time with Aaron predated Anna's accident and she remembered her cousin's tactics well.

"Jah," Naomi permitted. "They're both *wilkom* to eat dinner with us. But I'll drop the boys off and go to the market myself. You may begin the housework and assist Anna in the kitchen if she requires it. Evan and Eli have yard and stable chores to complete."

Although Anna made a simple green bean and ham casserole for lunch, with apple dumplings for dessert, it took her twice as long as usual and she was grateful when Naomi suggested that she rest before everyone arrived. She felt as if her head had barely touched the pillow when Melinda wiggled her arm to wake her again. She disappeared before Anna could ask for help fixing her hair, because it still pained her head when she attempted to fasten her tresses into a bun. She winced as she pulled her hair back the best she could and pinned on her *kapp*.

"Guder nammidaag, Anna," Fletcher said when he crossed the threshold to the parlor. Warmth flickered along her spine as she took in his athletic, lanky build and shiny dark mane, but she wasn't flooded with the rush of additional memories she'd been praying to expe-

rience at the sight of him. "How are you feeling today?"
he asked.

"I'm fine, *denki*," she answered. Standing rigidly before him, trying to think of something to say that didn't
sound so punctilious, she impulsively jested, "You're
Aaron, right?"

Fletcher looked as if a horse had stepped on his foot.
"Neh!" he exclaimed. "I'm Fletcher. Fletcher Chupp,
your fiancé. Aaron is my cousin."

"I'm teasing!" she assured him, instantly regretting
her joke. "I know who you are."

"You do?" he asked, raising his brows. "Your memory has returned?"

"Oh dear, *neh*," she replied. "I mean, I remember you
from last night. I know that you're my fiancé. But *neh*,
I don't remember anything other than that."

For a second time, he grimaced as if in pain, and Anna
ruefully fidgeted with her *kapp* strings, wary of saying
anything more for fear of disheartening him further.

"Naomi and Melinda are putting dinner on the table,"
someone said from the doorway.

When Fletcher moved aside, Anna spotted the familiar brunette hair, ruddy complexion and puckish grin.
Although the young man bore a slight family resem-
blance to Fletcher, he was shorter, with a burly phy-
sique.

"Aaron!" she squealed, delighted to have recognized
another person from the past, even if it was someone
who'd brought her considerable heartache.

"I'm happy to see you, too, Anna," he replied before
leading them into the kitchen.

Because there were two extra people, everyone had
to squeeze together to fit around the table and Anna

kept her elbows tightly to her side to avoid knocking into Fletcher, whose stature was greater than the other young men's.

"You made my favorite dish," Aaron declared appreciatively after grace had been said and everyone was served.

"Did I?" She didn't remember Aaron liking this casserole in particular.

"Don't pay any attention to him," Melinda piped up. "He says every dish is his favorite so the hostess will serve him the biggest helping."

Anna thought that sounded more like the jokester Aaron she remembered.

"Don't scare me like that," she scolded. "I panicked my memory loss was getting worse."

"Sorry, I didn't mean to," Aaron apologized. "But honestly, this casserole is Fletcher's favorite dish. Right, cousin?"

Without warning, Fletcher spat the mouthful of noodles he'd been chewing onto his plate and guzzled down his water. Scarlet splotches dotted his face and neck.

"Does this have mushrooms in it?" he sputtered.

"Cream of mushroom soup, *jah*," Anna answered, appalled by his lack of manners. "I didn't realize you don't like them."

"I'm *allergic* to them!" Fletcher wheezed.

"Quick, bring me the antihistamine we use for Evan's bee sting allergy," Anna directed Melinda, who darted to the cupboard and produced the bottle.

Anna poured a spoonful of syrupy pink liquid, which she thrust toward Fletcher's lips. After he swallowed it, she gave him a second dose.

"Perhaps Raymond should run to the phone shanty and dial 9-1-1," Naomi suggested.

"*Neh*, the redness is starting to fade," Anna observed.

Indeed, Fletcher's breathing was beginning to normalize and within a few more minutes, his heart rate slowed to a more regular pace. Anna, Melinda and Naomi encircled his chair while the boys remained motionless in their seats, too stunned to move. Aaron nervously jabbed at his noodles with a fork, but didn't lift them to his mouth.

Fletcher coughed. "I feel quite a bit better now. Please, sit back down and eat your meal, if you still can after my unappetizing display. I'm sorry about that."

"I'm the one who is sorry, Fletcher." Anna's voice warbled and her eyes teared up. "I didn't know you were allergic. I could have killed you!"

"That's one way to get out of marrying him," Aaron gibed, reaching for the pepper.

"Aaron Chupp, what a horrible thing to say! Anna didn't do it on purpose," Melinda admonished, swatting at him with a pot holder in mock consternation as Anna fled the room.

"It was only a joke," he objected contritely. "No need to be so sensitive."

Fletcher pushed back his chair. "If you'll excuse me, a little fresh air always helps me feel as if I can breathe better after one of these episodes."

He stalked across the backyard, stopping beneath the maple tree. Inhaling deeply, he took a mental inventory of his grievances. First, Anna pretended she thought he was Aaron and then when Aaron actually entered the room, she seemed more delighted to see him than she'd been to see Fletcher. Second, he felt slighted by how carefully Anna avoided his touch. Of course, spitting his food out at the table—even if it was necessary—wasn't likely going to cause her to draw nearer to him anytime soon. But most irksome of all was Aaron's jape, *That's one way to get out of marrying him.* Was that just another one of his cousin's goofy attempts at humor, or did the joke have a more weighty meaning?

Fletcher picked up a stone and threw it as hard as he could in the direction of a wheelbarrow across the yard. With all of his might, he pitched another and another.

"*Gut* aim," Naomi said after each rock had clattered against the metal and he was empty-handed again.

"I didn't know you were behind me," he answered, embarrassed she'd seen his temperamental behavior.

"I wanted to be certain you were okay. Whenever Evan gets stung, the effects of the adrenaline linger for him, too. He says he has the most irritable thoughts, claiming it's as if the bees are buzzing around in his brain as well as under his skin."

"I don't know if I can blame my thoughts on adrenaline," Fletcher replied.

"Sometimes, we're not quite ourselves when we're ill or upset. Not Evan. Not you. Not me. Not Anna," Naomi said pointedly. "You have to give it time. Things will work out."

Naomi Weaver's gentle way of imparting wisdom reminded him of his own mother. "*Jah,*" he answered. "I understand."

"*Gut.* Now *kumme* inside for dessert."

Melinda was placing fresh bowls on the table, where the boys sat in silence. Anna had returned to the kitchen and was preparing dessert at the counter with her back to the others.

"Since I didn't eat any dinner, I should be allowed two helpings of dessert, don't you think?" Fletcher questioned Evan, tousling the boy's hair to break the tension in the room.

"How do you know if you'll like it, when you don't know what it is?" Evan asked.

"Well," Fletcher said, winking at him as Anna turned with a tray, "I've got high hopes it's molasses and mushroom pie."

Anna paused before pushing her features into an expression of exaggerated dismay. "Oh, dear! I've made the wrong thing—I thought mushroom *dumplings* were your favorite."

Fletcher clutched his sides, laughing. Now *this* was more like the kind of interactions he and Anna usually shared. Hilarity filled the room and when it quieted, Anna announced, "I am truly sorry for my mistake, Fletcher. I meant you no harm."

"There's no need to apologize—I'm the one who should have reminded you."

"Do you have any other allergies I should know about?"

"Just mushrooms," he stated.

"Gut." Then she addressed everyone. "What else has happened around here since early September? *Gut* or bad, I want to know. I *need* to know. It may help my memory *kumme* back. Also, I'd prefer that no one outside of this room, with the exception of the Chupp family, finds out I have my amnesia. In order to ensure that, I'll need to be made aware of what's been going on in Willow Creek."

"Grace Zook had a *bobbel*—a girl named Serenity—in January," Naomi told her.

"How *wunderbaar*!" Anna's fondness of babies was reflected in her tone.

Melinda added, "Doris Hooley married John Plank last fall, shortly after the tornado."

"Was anyone from Willow Creek hurt in the storm?" Anna asked.

"*Neh*, not seriously, although many houses and offices needed repair," Naomi said.

"*Jah*, the tornado was *gut* for business. For a while, we couldn't keep up with the demand. So I took over as foreman for my *daed*'s Willow Creek clients in May," Aaron stated. "He's handling the Highland Springs clients. They were hard hit, too."

Anna raised her brows and Fletcher wondered whether her expression indicated she was dubious or impressed to hear about Aaron's promotion to foreman. She extended her congratulations.

"We lost a beloved family member," Evan reported, his lower lip protruding. "Timothy."

Anna gasped. "Who is Timothy?"

"He was my turtle. I found him at the creek in October. His foot was injured from a fishing hook and I was caring for him until he was well again."

"That's very sad he died," Anna said, her mouth pulling at the corners.

"He didn't die," Evan clarified. "We lost him. *You* lost him. You were supposed to be watching him in the yard after church when it was our Sunday to host, but he crawled off. How could that happen? Turtles are naturally slow on land—and he was injured."

It happened because she wasn't watching the turtle, Fletcher reminisced as wistfulness twisted in his chest.

She was with me behind the maple tree and we were sharing our first kiss.

"I'm sorry but I don't remember anything about that," Anna said and it took Fletcher a moment to realize she was speaking to Evan, not him. "How about if you, Fletcher, Eli and I take a walk to the creek to see if he has returned for the spring? Just let me do the dishes first."

"I'll do the dishes," Naomi insisted. "You ought not to touch any mushroom leftovers, lest your hands *kumme* into contact with Fletcher and he suffers another allergic reaction."

But there was little danger of that. Despite the temporary connection he'd just shared with Anna, Fletcher noticed she stayed closer to Eli and Evan than she did to him as they strolled down the hill, through the field and along the creek. Fletcher knew Anna's amnesia prevented her from recalling they rarely walked anywhere together without interlocking their fingers, but he felt too tentative about their relationship now to take her hand.

This early in March, they failed to spot any turtles, with or without injured feet. Once they returned home, Anna thanked Fletcher for his visit. Before leaving, he arranged to call on her the next day after dinner.

"Perhaps by then I'll be able to remember what your favorite dessert really is," she jested. "Although I suppose once my memory returns, we'll have more serious concerns to discuss."

"No doubt," Fletcher agreed as anxiety surged within him at the mention of "serious concerns," the same phrase she'd used in her note. Speaking to himself as much as to her, he added, "I guess we'll just have to wait and see what tomorrow brings."

* * *

"You look a little peaked," Naomi said when Anna entered the parlor where she was sewing. She folded the material into a square and stowed it in her basket.

"The glare of the sun bothered my eyes," Anna admitted. "And I feel a bit nauseated."

"Uh-oh, the doctor told us to let him know if you became sick to your stomach."

"I wasn't sick, just nauseated. But I don't think it's from my head injury," Anna rationalized. "It's probably because I ate too much too soon after going without."

"Kumme." Naomi extended her hand. "Take a little nap in my room. That way, you needn't climb the stairs."

"But I've been so lazy. I've hardly helped with a thing today."

"And well you shouldn't—I keep telling you that. Now go lie down on my bed and I'll fix us a cup of ginger tea. That should settle your stomach."

Anna removed her shoes and reclined on the side of the bed her *daed* had always slept on. His dog-eared Bible still lay on the nightstand. She picked it up and tried to read the print in German, but she felt too woozy to focus. Squeezing her eyes, she imagined her father poring over Scripture whenever he had a free moment toward the end of the day. She lifted the Bible to her nose, hoping to smell the honey and oatmeal scent of the salve he used on his cracked, calloused hands in winter, but she couldn't.

"I used to keep your *daed*'s sweatiest shirt hidden in my drawer so I could smell it whenever I missed him," Naomi said when she came in and saw Anna sniffing the Bible.

"Used to?"

"After a while, it stopped smelling like him and just smelled musty," Naomi reflected. "And I was ready to let the shirt go, because my memories of him are more tangible and comforting to me now. As the saying goes, 'A happy memory never wears out.'"

Bursting into tears, Anna placed her cup on the nightstand so she wouldn't spill her tea.

"Oh, Anna." Naomi sighed. "I'm so thoughtless. I shouldn't have mentioned my memories when you're struggling so hard to recall your own."

"*Neh*, it's fine, truly. I'm relieved to know you've been doing a bit better, Naomi. I wanted to ask, I just didn't know how to talk about…about your grief."

"Your faithful prayers and your quiet strength, along with all of your hard work, have kept our household going, Anna. I'm grateful for all you've done, even if it seemed I was too sorrowful to notice." Naomi squeezed her hand. "You remind me so much of your *daed*. I'll miss having you here every day, but I'm grateful *Gott* provided you such a *gut* man as Fletcher."

"Is he such a *gut* man?" Anna wondered aloud. "How do you know?"

Naomi blew on her tea before responding. "I suppose I don't know for certain. You and Fletcher were very secretive about your courtship—even more than most Amish couples customarily are. But I have observed how sincerely considerate he is of me and how helpful he has been to Raymond and Roy at work. Beyond that, I trust your judgment. I know there must have been very sound reasons you decided to marry him."

"I want to believe that," Anna said. "But I honestly don't remember what they are."

"Give it time, it will *kumme*."

"But there's hardly any time left! Aaron courted me for two and a half years and I still wasn't sure whether to marry him. How was it I was certain I should marry Fletcher after knowing him for less than half a year? What if the reasons don't return to me within this next month?"

"We'll build that bridge when we *kumme* to the creek," Naomi responded with Anna's father's carpenter variation on the old saying, "We'll cross that bridge when we come to it."

The two of them shared a chuckle before Naomi continued, "Even if it takes a while longer for your memory to fully return, I'd suggest you wait to make any changes to your wedding plans until the last possible moment. After all, if you postpone the wedding now and your memory suddenly *kummes* back, you'll have to wait until autumn's wedding season to get married. That delay can seem like forever to a young couple in love! Plus, you've already invited all of your guests. And, if you and Fletcher don't marry in the spring, it's my understanding the house could possibly go to Aaron and Melinda, which hardly seems fair since the two of you have already paid the back taxes. But you needn't think about any of that today. Right now, rest is the best thing for you."

Feeling reassured, Anna dropped into a deep slumber until she woke to someone rapping at her door. It was Melinda, declaring, "*Guder mariye*. Time to get up, *schlofkopp*."

Noting her surroundings, Anna suddenly understood why her cousin referred to her as a sleepyhead. "I slept here all night? Where did Naomi sleep?"

"Upstairs, in your bed," grumbled Melinda. "When I

came in after curfew, she lectured me about how I must guard my reputation, even though I'm soon to be wed. By the time she finished her spiel, I hardly got a wink of sleep, but she let you sleep in, since it's an off-Sunday."

Although she felt completely refreshed, Anna was just as happy that church wouldn't meet again until the following Sunday—she didn't feel prepared to field questions about her injury from the well-meaning *leit* of her district. After breakfast, the family read Scripture and prayed together. They followed their worship with a time of writing letters, individual Bible reading and doing jigsaw puzzles, but since Anna was prohibited from activities that required using close vision, Evan and Eli took turns reading aloud to her. Then, after a light dinner, the boys were permitted to engage in quiet outdoor leisure and games.

"What will you and Fletcher do when he visits today?" Melinda asked her.

Anna shrugged. "I have no idea what kinds of things we enjoy doing together. I suppose we'll take a walk and talk." She secretly just hoped to get to know him better.

"That sounds rather boring. Why don't you *kumme* out with Aaron and me?" Melinda suggested. "We're going for a ride to the location where Aaron plans to build our house later in the spring. It will be a tight squeeze in his buggy, but we can fit."

"Are you sure you won't mind if we accompany you?"

"Of course not. After all, think of how many times you and Aaron let me tag along on your outings," Melinda said.

Anna remembered. She'd intended to demonstrate how a young Amish woman ought to behave in social

settings and she naively believed Aaron was being for-
bearing in allowing Melinda to join them: she didn't
realize he was interested in Melinda romantically.

"Besides," Melinda chattered blithely, "Naomi won't
fret about my reputation if I'm out with you."

Anna sighed. So that was the reason she was being
invited. Still, it seemed she and Fletcher had an easier
time conversing when there were more people around.
"I'd like that," she said. "As long as Fletcher doesn't
mind."

Because they'd been so discreet about their relationship, Anna and Fletcher usually favored spending any
free time they had with each other instead of attending social events within their district, such as Sunday
evening singings. They'd certainly never accompanied
another couple on an outing before, so Fletcher was
startled when Anna asked if he'd like to join Aaron and
Melinda on a ride to see the property Aaron intended
to buy. But, realizing Anna wouldn't have remembered
their dislike of double dating, Fletcher deferred to her
request. Besides, he was heartened by the fact Aaron
was considering buying property—perhaps it meant
he was as dedicated as ever to marrying Melinda,
and Fletcher's concerns about him and Anna were for
naught.

The afternoon was unseasonably sunny and warm,
and the tips of the trees were beginning to show dots of
green and red buds. As the two couples sped up and down
the hills in Aaron's buggy, Anna kept marveling at the
changes in the landscape. She noticed nearly every tree
that was missing and each fence post that had been replaced after the October tornado. She seemed especially

aghast to discover the schoolhouse was one of the buildings that had suffered the worst damage, but she was relieved to learn none of the children had been harmed.

"Now that you've had more rest and you've seen the destruction, surely you must remember the storm," Aaron suggested. "It was so violent that I couldn't forget it if I tried."

Anna shrugged. "I still have absolutely no recollection of anything that happened in the past six months, whether big or small, positive or negative."

"I guess that's *gut* news for you, huh, Fletcher? Anna can't remember any of your faults," Aaron needled his cousin. "On the other hand, she probably can't remember why she agreed to marry you, either."

Fletcher's mouth burned with a sour taste but before he could respond, Anna abruptly shifted the subject, asking Melinda, "Where will the two of you live until Aaron has time to build a house?"

"With Naomi and the boys," she replied, clutching Aaron's arm as he rounded a corner. "It will be crowded but I'm trying to convince Naomi to temporarily move into the room in the attic so we can have her room downstairs."

From the corner of his eye, Fletcher caught Anna frowning. He usually felt as if he could read her expression as easily as the pages in a book, but today he couldn't tell if she was scowling because of Aaron's rambunctious driving, Melinda's gall in asking Naomi to take the attic room, or some other reason altogether. The uncertainty caused his mouth to sag, too.

"Here we are," Aaron announced as he swiftly brought the horse to a standstill. He made a sweeping motion with his hand to indicate the field to their right.

"The old Lantz homestead?" Fletcher asked.

The modest square of land on the corner of the Zooks' farm used to belong to Albert Lantz, who resided with his granddaughter, Hannah. After their home was flattened by the tornado, they chose not to rebuild because Hannah married a visiting cabinetmaker from Blue Hill, Ohio, and thus moved out of state. Her grandfather accompanied her, but first he sold his property back to the youngest generation of the Zook family, who now lived on the farm.

"Their old homestead and then some," Aaron boasted. "The Lantz plot was barely as big as a postage stamp. I'm in negotiations with Oliver Zook to purchase the acreage running all the way down the hill to the stream."

"Isn't it *wunderbaar*?" sang Melinda, spreading her arms and twirling across the grass.

"*Jah*, it's lovely," Anna answered, but Fletcher noticed how taut her neck and jaw muscles appeared. Was she jealous? Was she imagining herself, instead of Melinda, owning a house with Aaron in such a picturesque location? Fletcher stubbed his shoe on a root as the tumultuous thoughts rattled his concentration.

"*Kumme*, have a look at my stream," Aaron beckoned.

"I believe the stream belongs to *Gott*, although He's generous enough to allow it to run through your property—or actually, through Oliver Zook's property," Fletcher stated wryly.

"Lighten up. Worship services are over for the day," Aaron countered. "Or if you're going to preach at me, how about remembering the commandment, *Thou shalt not covet*?"

"Stop bickering," Melinda called. "This is a happy occasion, remember? Hooray!"

She picked up a handful of old, dried leaves and tossed them into the air and then tried to catch them as they fluttered around her. Then she and Aaron cavorted down the hill like schoolchildren, racing to tag each other's shadows until they disappeared into the woods, while Fletcher and Anna followed at a slower pace, neither one speaking.

When they reached the stream, Anna closed her eyes and inhaled deeply. "Mmm, it smells like spring," she said, and then raised her lids to view the bubbling current, the gently sloping embankment and the thick stand of trees. "What a beautiful place."

"I have to agree, it's a fine fishing spot," Fletcher responded. Thinking aloud, he added, "But Aaron's too impatient to fish and even if he weren't, Melinda's such a chatterbox, she'd frighten the fish away."

Anna narrowed her brows. "That may be true of them now," she said, "but people change. They grow. With *Gott*'s help, we all do."

Fletcher hadn't intended to be insulting. He simply meant the location seemed better suited to his and Anna's preferences than to Aaron and Melinda's, since he enjoyed fishing and Anna appreciated solitude, so he was surprised by how quickly Anna seemed to defend them. And what did her comment about people changing and growing mean, anyway? Was she indicating that she had changed? Was she implying she thought Aaron had grown? Fletcher's brooding was interrupted when Melinda capered up the embankment.

"Help!" she squealed. "Aaron's trying to splash me and that water's freezing!"

Aaron reappeared and the four of them ascended the hill. At the top, they were greeted by Oliver Zook. "*Guder nammidaag.* Grace sent me to invite our prospective new neighbors and their future in-laws for cookies and cider."

"That sounds *wunderbaar*," Melinda said, accepting the invitation for all of them.

The fragrance of hot cider and freshly baked cookies wafted from the kitchen when Grace ushered everyone inside. As they situated themselves in the parlor, where Doris and John Plank were also visiting, the Zooks' baby began wailing in the next room.

"I'll get her while you prepare the refreshments," Oliver said, squeezing his wife's shoulder.

"Wait till you see how much she's grown since the last time you saw her, Anna," Grace remarked before leaving the room, understandably ignorant of Anna's amnesia.

When Oliver returned, jostling the fussy baby, Aaron suggested, "You should let Anna take her. She has such a soothing, maternal touch. She was always able to comfort my eldest sister's son when he was a newborn."

"*Jah*, I remember," Anna said, smiling as she lifted Serenity from Oliver's arms. "Your nephew had colic and your poor sister was exhausted because he gave her no rest."

Although he knew it wasn't Anna's fault, Fletcher felt a slight twinge of sadness that she could remember everything that happened during her courtship with Aaron, but not a thing that happened during her courtship with him. And who was Aaron to openly flatter Anna, as if he were still her suitor? Of course, Aaron's compliment was well deserved: within a few moments of cooing and swaying, the *bobbel* had fallen asleep in

Anna's arms. She sat back down and accepted a cup of cider from Grace with her free hand.

"See that, Fletcher? The *bobbel* in one hand, a cup in the other." Oliver laughed. "Anna will have no problem keeping your household in order."

Anna demurely glanced at Fletcher from beneath her lashes and a tickle of exhilaration caused his nerves to tingle. He momentarily forgot all about her note as a glimpse of their future *bobblin* flashed across his mind's eye.

"You're a fortunate man, indeed," Doris Plank interjected. "But I have to say, you could have knocked me over with a feather when the intentions were announced. For the longest time, I suspected Aaron was betrothed to Anna. Even after it was rumored he'd begun walking out with you, Melinda, I always assumed he'd eventually wind up with Anna again, don't ask me why. But then, I never expected I'd marry John, either, so I guess it's a *gut* thing I'm not a matchmaker!"

As Doris gleefully tittered at her own humor, Fletcher's ears burned and his jaw dropped. Doris had a reputation for making bold remarks, but he'd personally never been on the receiving end of one and he didn't know how to respond without sounding rude himself.

"*Jah*, life is full of *wunderbaar* surprises for everyone, isn't it?" Grace diplomatically cut in. She passed the tray to Anna. "Here, Anna, you haven't had a cookie."

"*Denki*, but *neh*," Anna declined. "I… I…"

"She has to watch her figure," Melinda finished for her. "But I don't, so I'll take some."

"Ah, you must have finished sewing your wedding dress then, Anna?" Grace's eyes lit up. "You don't want to have to make any last-minute alterations, is that it? If you're anything like I was, you're counting down the days!"

Blushing, Anna gave a pinched smile and a slight shrug but didn't answer.

"You're fortunate your intended is so calm, Fletcher," Oliver remarked, as he patted his wife's hand. "As soon as our intentions were published, the wedding preparations were all Grace talked about to anyone who would listen. And even to some people who wouldn't!"

As everyone else laughed, Fletcher did his best not to frown, acutely aware that Anna's last communication about their wedding preparations had been anything but enthusiastic.

Suddenly, Melinda sniffed exaggeratedly and declared, "Oopsie! I think Serenity needs a diaper change."

All three couples soon made their way out the door. As they departed the farm and headed back toward Anna's house, Fletcher thought, *The* schtinke *of a dirty diaper makes a fitting end to this afternoon.* Disappointed that he and Anna hadn't exchanged a private word between them, and feeling even less certain about their future today than he'd felt all week, Fletcher decided the next time he went out with Anna, they were going out alone.

Chapter Three

The Sabbath was supposed to be a day of rest, but Anna felt utterly exhausted by the time she said her prayers and slipped into bed. Yet as achy and tired as her body was, her brain was wide-awake, reliving the afternoon's unpleasant events.

First, the buggy lurched about so much, she'd become increasingly nauseated as they journeyed toward their destination. Second, she was nettled by Aaron's wisecrack about her continued inability to remember Fletcher—and judging from Fletcher's expression, he was equally peeved. Third, Melinda's prancing and twirling caused Anna's head to spin. Then, Fletcher and Aaron squabbled like two boys on a playground. Finally, when she tried to focus her attention on something positive by commenting on the beauty of the scenery, Fletcher pulled a face. His remarks about Aaron's and Melinda's personalities may have been true, but they weren't especially generous, which made her wonder if he was characteristically judgmental.

Not that Aaron or Melinda took much care to measure their own words about others: Melinda's pronounced insinuation that Anna needed to watch her weight would have been humiliating, had it been true. In reality, she'd been far too nauseated to eat any cookies, but she didn't want to draw attention to herself by saying so.

Of course, all eyes had been on her when Grace questioned Anna about whether she'd sewn her wedding dress or not. Making her dress was one of the wedding preparations an Amish bride reveled in most, but Anna couldn't even recall if she'd bought her fabric yet. Nor did she know if she'd selected her *newehockers*, also known as sidesitters or wedding attendants, and given them the fabric for their dresses, which would match hers. Had she made Fletcher's wedding suit for him, as was the tradition?

If she hadn't begun sewing yet, should she bother starting now, given that her memory might not return in time to carry through with the wedding? On the other hand, if she delayed making the garments until her memory returned, it was likely she'd have to rush to finish them, since there were only a few weeks until the wedding as it was.

Of course, her dilemma about their wedding clothes wasn't nearly as disconcerting as her growing concern about whether or not they should get married at all. Anna hesitated to bring up the subject with Fletcher, who demonstrated no signs of hesitation about carrying through with their plans. Considering all they'd apparently invested in their relationship, their house and their wedding, how could she tell him she had doubts about their future together? Once her misgivings were voiced, there'd be no taking them back. Even if her concerns were legitimate under the circumstances, Anna was aware of how deeply they might hurt Fletcher. Completely exasperated, she cried herself to sleep, stirring only once when Melinda's footsteps creaked on the stairs.

By morning, she resolved to exercise more patience as she waited upon the Lord to guide her about what to do next in regard to the wedding. After praying once again for her memory to return—and for a sense of peace in the meantime—she managed to comb her hair into a loose likeness of a bun. She had breakfast on the stove before Naomi could forbid her to help. She knew her stepmother was only concerned for her health, but Anna was growing increasingly restless from being told she couldn't do her share of work around the house.

Naomi chided her anyway. "The doctor said for you to take it easy. Where is Melinda hiding this morning?"

"Here I am," Melinda answered, skittering into the room.

"*Gut.* Since you and Anna need the buggy to go into town today, I'll drop Raymond and Roy off at work," Naomi suggested. "While I'm gone, I'd like you to clean the breakfast dishes and wring and hang the laundry, please. And remember, Anna isn't to help with any housework until she's seen the doctor again."

The ride to the mercantile was much smoother than it had been in Aaron's buggy, and on the way, Anna asked Melinda about their shopping list. She assumed they were picking up grocery staples for the week and she thought dividing the list would make the task easier.

"Oopsie, you must have forgotten our plan, since we arranged today's outing prior to your accident," Melinda replied. "We're not buying groceries. I'm buying organdy for my wedding apron. I also need to check to see whether the fabric has arrived for my dress and my *newehockers'* dresses. Aaron's mother is sewing his wedding suit, so I needn't concern myself with that. What do you intend to purchase today?"

Anna swiveled toward her and cocked her head, racking her brain. If only Melinda had reminded her they were going fabric shopping, she might have had an opportunity to discuss the matter with Naomi, whose practical and Godly advice she valued.

"I don't know that I'll purchase anything," she finally responded. "After Grace's question yesterday, I checked my sewing basket and the closet this morning and I didn't find evidence I've been working on my wedding dress, but I didn't have a chance to ask Naomi if I might have hung it somewhere else. Nor do I know if I've finished Fletcher's suit. I don't even know whether I've chosen my *newehockers* or who they might be."

Melinda clicked her tongue. "That's the trouble with being so secretive. To be honest, it hurt my feelings a bit that you never confided in me about your relationship with Fletcher. Perhaps if you'd told me more, I'd be able to help determine your sewing needs now. But, as Aaron and I agree, it makes sense that you and Fletcher hid your courtship from everyone, especially from us."

Anna silently counted backward from ten before responding. "Plenty of Amish couples still practice discretion about sharing their courtship—the custom isn't intended to insult anyone, so I'm sorry if you felt that way," she said. Taking a deep breath, she asked, "But what do you mean it made sense we'd keep our courtship hidden, especially from you?"

"Oh, you know," Melinda prattled on obliviously, working the reins. "I imagine you might have worried if you brought Fletcher around socially, he would have been drawn to me, the way Aaron was. Not that I'd ever be interested in Fletcher, of course, but you must have some lingering worries. It's only natural. Also, Aaron said the two of you never kept your courtship such a secret. He thinks that you and Fletcher didn't let anyone know you were courting because you were worried Aaron might tell Fletcher that he was your second choice."

"Oh really?" Anna asked drily. What hogwash! She was the one who begged her father and Naomi not to send Melinda back to Ohio after she discovered her shenanigans with Aaron! And she was the one who insisted she was glad Melinda had found an Amish boyfriend instead of an *Englischer* because maybe he'd be a good influence on her! As for Aaron, she'd gotten over their breakup within a couple of weeks. Some of his ideas were so preposterous Anna wondered why she'd ever accepted him as her suitor.

They continued in silence until they reached the designated horse and buggy lot on the far end of Main Street. After they'd secured the animal at the hitching post, Anna said, "I'm going to Schrock's while you're at the mercantile. I expect you back within half an hour, please."

The bells jingled when she pushed open the door of Schrock's Shop, and Anna's agitation was replaced with a sense of nostalgia. She took special pleasure in the resourcefulness and creativity of the Amish *leit* from her district, who consigned their handiwork in the large store. Today the gallery bustled with tourists in search of specialty Amish items such as quilts, toys, furniture, dried flower wreaths and naturally scented candles. She knew Joseph Schrock must have been pleased so many people were making purchases, although he looked overwhelmed by the line stretching from the register to the door. It seemed such a shame Anna couldn't work that afternoon, but she decided not to add to Joseph's burden by interrupting him with small talk.

She browsed the aisles, noting the price and location of the inventory. *I don't recall any of these items being stacked here*, she thought. She took a square of paper and a pencil from her purse and jotted down the contents on the shelves so she could study them before returning to work. When she finished, she turned to leave, nearly bumping into another young Amish woman whose arms were loaded with bars of homemade soap.

"Excuse me," she apologized, bending to retrieve the bars that had spilled from the woman's grasp.

"Anna!" the woman declared. "It's so *gut* to see you—I wasn't sure if you'd be stopping in today. We've been praying for you since we heard about your head injury. How do you feel?"

Anna surveyed the woman's olive complexion, pronounced cheekbones and deep-set eyes. She couldn't register who she was, although she deduced the woman also worked in the store.

"I'm much better," she said slowly. "*Denki* for your prayers."

"Of course," the woman replied. "As you can see, there's a long line now, but if you give me fifteen minutes, I'll be able to take my break and we'll catch up on everything."

"Actually, I was just popping in for a moment. Will you kindly tell Joseph I'll return to work on Thursday if the doctor approves? I'm sorry, but I have someone waiting and I can't stay." Anna backed away before it became apparent she couldn't recall the woman's name.

On the way home, Melinda jabbered nonstop about how irritated she was because the particular shade of purple fabric she'd ordered for her wedding dress hadn't arrived yet. Anna didn't get a word in edgewise until they sat down for tea at home, where she told Melinda and Naomi about her puzzling interaction with the unfamiliar woman.

"She's clearly new to Willow Creek. She's about my height and has dark hair and a ready smile," Anna commented.

"It must have been Tessa, one of the Fisher sisters," Melinda guessed. "Was she a homely woman with a big nose?"

"Melinda!" Naomi snapped.

"What?" Melinda chafed. "I'm only giving an honest description of what she looks like. Doesn't *Gott* require us to be honest?"

"First, beauty is in the eye of the beholder, and second, *Gott* requires us to be kind," replied Naomi. "And in this house, so do I."

Anna seldom heard Naomi raise her voice like that and Melinda looked as surprised as Anna felt. The young woman snatched her coat from the hook and stomped outside.

After the door banged shut behind Melinda, Naomi confessed, "Even though she's my dear departed sister's *kind*, there are times when her churlish behavior tries my last nerve and I fear I don't have any patience left."

"She's young and she doesn't always weigh her words," Anna acknowledged, consoling herself as much as Naomi. "I suppose that's the result of not having a *mamm* or sister in her home for so many years and then running around with the *Englisch* as often as she did."

Naomi sighed. "'Tis true, I suppose. In any case, Tessa Fisher and her older sister, Katie, moved to Willow Creek together in the fall. They rent Turner King's *daadi haus*. Katie took Doris's teaching position when Doris got married. Tessa works at Schrock's. The three of you became fast friends—you've spent many sister days and Sunday visits at their house."

"No wonder she looked so perplexed," Anna said. "She must have thought me terribly rude not to even greet her by name."

"I'm certain she'll understand once you explain the reason. But even without having all the facts, a *gut* friend will always give another the benefit of the doubt."

"*Jah*, that's true," Anna agreed, sipping her tea. As she reflected on Naomi's words, Anna decided that although she didn't have all of the facts about Fletcher, she was going to try to be more open about giving him every benefit of the doubt, too. As her fiancé, he deserved that much.

"I'll take Roy and Raymond home," Aaron offered at the end of their workday.

"*Neh*, I gave Naomi my word I'd do it when I saw her this morning," Fletcher countered. He had also been asked to stay for supper.

Aaron shrugged. "Suit yourself, but I'm going that way anyhow, since I'm picking up Melinda. She and my *mamm* and sisters are working on the wedding clothes together."

Fletcher was relieved Aaron and Melinda wouldn't

be at the house. While he didn't expect to be able to spend much time alone with Anna, he was already on tenterhooks about his relationship with her; he didn't want to be harried by Aaron's snide remarks or Melinda's animated mannerisms. Besides, his appetite was beginning to return and he looked forward to eating another home-cooked meal instead of the soup and sandwich supper he usually prepared for himself.

After supper, he turned to Anna. "It's a clear night. Would you like to take a drive in the buggy or a stroll down to the creek?" he asked. "I'll bring a flashlight."

She hesitated. "How about if we sit on the porch instead? I'm afraid my energy is lagging. Would you like a cup of hot tea?"

"*Jah*, please," Fletcher answered.

They carried their steaming mugs out to the porch and peered over the railing, up at the starry sky, standing so close that Fletcher could hear the soft puff of Anna's breath as she pursed her lips to blow on her tea. A week ago, he would have draped his arm around her shoulders and nestled her to his chest, but tonight he had no assurance the gesture would be welcome, so he stepped away so as not to bump her with his elbow when he lifted his own mug to drink.

"I think spring might be coming early this year. Listen, you can hear the peepers," he said, indicating the chirping call of nearby frogs.

"Speaking of peepers, don't turn around," Anna instructed, glancing sidelong. "Evan is doing something he's expressly been forbidden to do—he's eavesdropping at the window. Ignore him. He can't hear us anyway."

Despite her admonishment not to look at him,

Fletcher wheeled around and made a monstrous face to send Evan scampering, which sent Anna into a fit of giggles.

"Let's sit," she suggested, but no sooner had they settled into the swing next to one another than Anna got up and moved to the bench.

"Do I smell bad or is something else wrong?" he asked, suddenly fearful she'd remembered the misgiving that caused her to write the note the day of her accident.

"*Neh!* Of course not. I'm sorry, I should have explained... I've been so nauseated that even the rocking of the swing causes my stomach to flip. I haven't wanted to say anything because I didn't want to alarm anyone."

"Oh, I see," Fletcher said and his muscles immediately relaxed. So that was all it was. "Are you sure you shouldn't call the doctor?"

"*Neh*, I'm not sick," she assured him. "They told me I might temporarily have motion intolerance and I think I'm still recovering from Aaron's handling of the buggy yesterday. It seems lately I've been sensitive to certain smells and sights, too. And even though Melinda was the one twirling in circles yesterday, I felt as if I was the one becoming dizzy just from watching her."

"Is there anything I can do to help?" Fletcher asked.

"Don't twirl in circles," Anna quipped.

Fletcher chuckled heartily; Anna always could make him laugh. "I hope the bouts of nausea pass soon."

"*Denki,*" Anna replied. "To be on the safe side, I'll mention it to the doctor when I see him on Wednesday, although I'm more interested in knowing when he thinks my memory will fully return. Meanwhile, it would be helpful if I could ask you a few questions."

"Of course," Fletcher agreed.

"Well, right now, my immediate concerns are actually about the wedding preparations."

Fletcher's hand trembled so noticeably he had to set down his mug of tea. Squaring his shoulders as if to brace himself for whatever Anna was about to disclose, he could only utter, *"Jah?"*

"For starters, I don't know if I've made your suit yet. Do you?"

There was a pause while her question sank in and when it did, Fletcher was nearly woozy with relief. *"Jah,"* he answered, half coughing and half choking on the word. *"Jah*, you've already made my suit and I feel pretty dapper in it if I do say so myself."

"Oh, *gut*." Anna's teeth shone in the moonlight. "How about my wedding dress? Have I mentioned anything about that?"

"Only that you might plan a sister day to work on it, along with your *newehockers*."

"Have I told you who they are?"

"Katie and Tessa Fisher."

Anna exhaled. "It's so *gut* to know these things. Now I can get back to working on the preparations before too much time elapses and I fall behind with the things that need to be done. I mean, obviously, there's so much I want to remember about you and about our relationship, too, but I've been praying fervently that my memory will return any moment now and all will *kumme* clear in that regard."

"Jah, any moment now, all will *kumme* clear," Fletcher repeated. But what would happen once it did? A shiver made his shoulders twitch.

"Oh, you're cold," Anna observed. "We should go inside."

"Actually, it's getting late and I ought to head home." Fletcher felt drained from the gamut of emotions he'd just experienced. "Unless you have any other urgent questions for me?"

"Only one. Actually, it's more of a favor. As I mentioned, I have a doctor's appointment on Wednesday. It's all the way in Highland Springs and it's at three o'clock, the middle of your workday. But I'm not supposed to take the buggy out until I've gotten the all-clear from the doctor and you know how nervous Naomi gets. I'd ask Melinda, but she isn't too careful on the major *Englisch* roadways... More important, I'd like you to be able to ask the doctor any questions you might have, too."

"Of course I'll take you," Fletcher agreed, although he very much doubted the doctor was the person who could give him the answers he most needed to know.

When Anna told Naomi about the plan for Fletcher to bring her to the medical center, Naomi seemed relieved not to have to take the buggy through city traffic.

"You promise you'll ask the doctor whether or not you're able to return to work?" she prodded.

"Of course I will," Anna reassured her. "What I'm more concerned about is helping you with preparations for the weddings."

"Don't worry about that," Naomi said, cupping Anna's face in her hands. "Having to prepare for the weddings was the best thing that could have happened to me. Without the deadline of your wedding dates, who knows how long I might have lolled about in misery?"

"I'm glad you're feeling more energetic, but I still

intend to help. There's so much cooking, cleaning and organizing to do. And wherever will our guests stay?"

"I'll *wilkom* your help if the doctor allows, and for what it's worth, I intend to put Melinda to work, too. As for our guests, some of them will stay here and those who are related to the Chupps will stay with Aaron's family. We'll make do. I'm just pleased to hear you're more certain about going through with your wedding now."

Anna hardly felt certain, but Naomi was so upbeat that Anna didn't want to discourage her by rationalizing that even if she canceled her wedding to Fletcher, their household preparations wouldn't be in vain, since Melinda's wedding was only a week later. Instead, she replied, "As you've said, there's still time to decide. And I'm hopeful the doctor will have something promising to say about when I can expect my memories will return."

The medical center was on the opposite end of Highland Springs and although Fletcher worked the horse into a fast clip, he took care to ensure the carriage remained steady. They arrived in plenty of time for Anna to check in and he dropped her off in front of the building so he could take the buggy around the corner to the designated lot. Aaron had rarely been heedful of her comfort, so Anna was pleasantly surprised by Fletcher's chivalry, especially in light of her anxiety about the appointment.

"Would you like me to *kumme* into the examining room with you?" Fletcher asked when he reunited with her in the waiting area.

"*Jah*, I think the doctor is only going to look into my eyes and talk to me about my progress. And this way, you can ask him your questions, too," she suggested.

The truth was Fletcher's presence had a calming effect on her, and she needed that right now.

The doctor was a rotund bald man, who shook hands with both of them. "I'm Dr. Donovan," he said. "I've met you and your family in the hospital, Anna, but you may not remember me. Many patients don't after they've had a head injury. Sometimes it's because of their concussions and sometimes it's because of the medication we give them."

Anna squinted at the doctor and then apologized. "I'm sorry, I don't."

"That's okay, I've been told I have a forgettable face, although my wife likes it," the doctor jested. "How have you been feeling?"

"Fine," Anna answered, clasping her hands on her lap.

"*Fine* as in you don't want to complain in front of your fiancé, or *fine* as in you haven't had any nausea, fatigue, headaches or blurred vision at all? Most patients do, you know," the doctor stated, settling into a chair.

"Well, my head feels a bit heavy but I wouldn't say it aches, and I suppose my energy isn't what it usually is," she admitted. "The other day I had a pretty severe bout of nausea, too."

"Has that happened often?" the doctor asked.

"Only once." Anna dipped her head and scraped at her thumbnail. "But it was because my friend handles his buggy like a madman."

"I see. Well, that's understandable. And how about your moods, how are they?"

Anna bit her lip. "With the grace of *Gott*, I try to be *gut*-natured, but I'm afraid I don't always succeed."

"I'm sure you do your best, Anna," Dr. Donovan

said and his eyes twinkled. "But what I mean is, are there times when you experience extreme mood swings? Times when you've felt exceedingly angry or despondent, or even elated? Anything like that?"

She hesitated, wondering if her ambiguous feelings about the wedding qualified as mood swings, before shaking her head.

"It's not extreme, but I have noticed Anna is weepier than she was before the accident," Fletcher offered. "She seems on the verge of tears more often than not."

"Does she—" Dr. Donovan began to ask Fletcher, but then rephrased the question and directed it toward Anna instead. "Do you suffer any prolonged periods of crying? Times when you just can't stop? Or any other unprovoked outbursts of emotion?"

"*Neh*, nothing like that," she stated.

The doctor smiled. "I suppose with four brothers at home, there's plenty to provoke an outburst now and then, isn't there?"

The three of them chuckled before Dr. Donovan continued, this time asking Fletcher, "Have you noticed any other differences in Anna's temperament?"

Fletcher replied carefully, "She's, er, less relaxed than she used to be. Not as easygoing."

Heat rose in Anna's cheeks. She realized she'd felt tearful and tense lately, but she regretted it was so obvious to others. Was her behavior off-putting to Fletcher?

Dr. Donovan must have caught her expression because he winked at her and joshed, "When your fiancé suffers a traumatic brain injury, we'll see how relaxed he feels, right?"

"I didn't mean to sound critical," Fletcher said, and

it was his turn to blush. "I only meant to point out a difference."

"It was good you did," the doctor replied. "I asked about it because it's important for me to be informed immediately if Anna experiences any extreme mood changes, like those I mentioned. That said, many head and brain injury patients are generally out of sorts following their accidents. Some of that is due to residual pain, some of it's a medication side effect and some of it is because they're quite literally not themselves. At least, not until their brains are fully recovered. It takes patience. Which may be very frustrating and even frightening for them as well as for the people who care about them. But it's all part of the healing process."

Anna leaned back in her chair, reassured by the doctor's assertion that what she was experiencing was both normal and temporary.

"How is your memory, Anna?" he asked. "Do you recall what happened the day before the accident? How about the week before? The month?"

With each question, Anna shook her head. They discussed what she did recall—confirming her latest pre-accident memories were of late August—and then the doctor performed a brief examination, looking into her eyes and checking her neurological reflexes.

"Overall, I'm pleased with your progress," he said when he completed the exam. "Your scans look good—great, in fact. I think the nausea you described will subside in time, especially now that you're not taking any medication."

"I'm glad to hear that," Anna responded politely. "But what about my memory loss?"

"You do have a longer period of amnesia than most,"

Dr. Donovan admitted. "It's called retrograde amnesia—meaning, you can't recall things that happened before the accident. Most people lose a few minutes, a couple of hours or even a day or two. You've lost about five or six months of memory. Now, before you get too worried, I'll tell you I've had patients who have lost up to three years!"

This fact was little consolation to her and judging from the wrinkles across Fletcher's forehead, he wasn't finding it to be reassuring, either.

"Your memories could return like that," Dr. Donovan said and snapped his fingers. "Or, more likely, they could come over time. Sometimes, patients will experience random memories we call *islands of memory*, because they might recall certain details of an event, but not the surrounding circumstances."

Anna bent toward him, her hands folded as if in prayer. "But isn't there anything I can do to hasten my memories to return?" she asked.

Fletcher heard the note of desperation in Anna's voice and it echoed his own feelings.

"I've had patients' families and friends try to recreate lost memories for them. Others surround themselves with familiar scents. Some people insist sage tea helped their memories return. I've even known people to try hypnotism," answered Dr. Donovan. "What I recommend is getting plenty of rest."

"I've been resting all week," Anna asserted. "But I have a job. I'm a clerk at a shop in town and I think I'm ready to return to work now."

Dr. Donovan crossed his arms. "I'd highly recommend you don't. In fact, you shouldn't do any more than what you've done at home this week, both mentally and physically. It will sound funny, but you need to avoid thinking too much. I'd also advise minimal reading and problem solving. Nothing involving lengthy periods of close concentration, such as sewing. And no strenuous activities. No pitching hay, no floor scrubbing, nothing more vigorous than collecting eggs from the henhouse. I'd suggest limiting your exertion to a slow, daily stroll in the fresh air."

"But I have to help prepare the house for the wedding," Anna protested and her eyes welled.

Dr. Donovan raised his brows at Fletcher. "I'm certain your fiancé would rather have his bride healthy than anything else, right?"

Whether Anna actually became his bride or not, Fletcher agreed her health was paramount. "Anna, if rest is what it takes for you to recover and your memory to return, I'm sure Naomi will take over until you're better," he reasoned.

Dr. Donovan held up his hand. "I want to caution you both that while rest *may* be helpful in restoring Anna's memory, there's no guarantee. But the benefits of rest—for both body and mind—greatly outweigh the risks of overexertion at this point. Further, the more pressure Anna is under, the less likely she is to get the memory results you both want. So, take each day as it comes and keep your expectations in check. And remember, it's crucial that Anna doesn't experience a lot of stress or become too upset."

Fletcher and Anna both nodded without replying.

"Why such long faces?" the doctor inquired. "Anna is recovering well, whether or not her memory returns. There's a good chance it will, but if it doesn't, it's a loss but it's not the end of the world. You have your entire lives together to make new memories, right?"

Fletcher cleared his throat and spoke deliberately. "Anna and I only met in September. She has no recollection of me and we're scheduled to be wed in about a month. We have certain…certain concerns."

Dr. Donovan blew the air out of his cheeks and took off his glasses to rub his eyes. "Ah, I understand now," he said, before readjusting his frames behind his ears. Slanting forward, he said, "I see how that could be problematic. But it also might be one of the best blessings a couple could ever receive. There's no thrill like falling in love with each other for the first time. It sounds as if you two have the opportunity to experience that joy twice!"

From the corner of his eye, Fletcher could see Anna's cheeks blossom with pink. Amish couples didn't usually speak of such intimate matters to anyone, much less to *Englisch* acquaintances, but Dr. Donovan didn't seem to notice their embarrassment.

He rolled his chair back, saying, "Alright, then, I'd like to see you back here in two weeks unless any of your symptoms worsen instead of improve. Meanwhile, have a little fun getting to know each other again. Falling in love is a gift. It's something to celebrate."

Fletcher realized the kind man meant his words to be encouraging, but as he shook the doctor's hand goodbye, he thought this felt nothing like a time of celebration. Indeed, while they journeyed back toward Willow Creek, Anna seemed somber, as well. He wasn't ready to discuss what the doctor said about her memory returning or how they might spend the next couple of weeks, so Fletcher was relieved when she didn't broach those topics, either. But she remained quiet for so long he finally asked if the journey was nauseating her.

"*Neh*, not at all. This has been a very smooth ride," she replied. "I was just thinking how disappointed Joseph will be to learn I can't yet return to the shop."

"Are *you* disappointed?" Fletcher asked.

Anna giggled. "To be honest, *neh*, not really. I'd much rather help Naomi manage the household. And I'll admit that it's been necessary for me to rest in between tasks recently, which I couldn't do at the shop. I worry I wouldn't be efficient there, even if I were allowed to return. But I feel bad leaving Joseph shorthanded. The store was packed with customers when I stopped by the other morning."

Fletcher pulled on the rein and the horse turned toward the right, exiting the main roadway. "Would it be possible for Melinda to temporarily take your place?"

"Jah!" Anna practically hopped up from the seat. "What a great idea, Fletcher! I'm sure she'll prefer working in town, and I dare say Naomi will appreciate having her out of her hair for a while."

Fletcher grinned, pleased he could provide Anna with a satisfactory solution to at least one of the problems she was facing. Her praise always made his chest swell and today, it gave him hope that they might be able to work out whatever other concerns she had, too. But first, he'd have to help her remember them, of course. So, before dropping her off for the evening, he said, "I'll have to work late tomorrow and Friday night because I left early today, but I'd like to take you out alone on Saturday, if I may?"

"*Denki*, I'd like that." Her cheek dimpled as she replied.

Fletcher felt so encouraged that when he returned home, he took out his toolbox for the first time since receiving Anna's note and began working on his wedding gift for her: he was resectioning one area of the parlor into an alcove so she could have privacy for reading and writing in her journal. As he was sanding a length of board, he began thinking about ways in which he could help jog Anna's memory without pressuring her. By the time he put away his tools for the night, he was so eager for the date he'd planned that he almost hoped her memory wouldn't come back before he had a chance to see her again.

Chapter Four

Upon waking on Saturday morning, Anna kept her eyes closed, hoping her memory had been restored overnight. Once again, she was disappointed that nothing from the past six months came to mind. She blinked to see Melinda rummaging through a drawer. Usually Anna was awake long before her cousin, who required considerable rousing to get out of bed, especially after she'd been out with Aaron the previous night. Anna figured Melinda must be excited about beginning her first day of work at Schrock's Shop.

"Guder mariye," Melinda sang out. "Do you suppose I might borrow a few hair clips?"

Anna yawned as she pushed herself onto her elbows. "I gave you my hair clips earlier in the week. Did you misplace them?"

"Neh, you never gave them to me," Melinda replied. "Perhaps you gave some to Naomi, but not to me."

"I'm certain I gave them to you," Anna insisted. "In fact, I was running low myself but I let you use them because it hurt my head to gather my hair tightly. Don't you remember?"

Melinda shrugged. "*Neh*, but that's okay. Naomi probably has extras."

Anna didn't mind about the hair clips in particular as much as she minded the fact Melinda denied Anna gave her the accessories in the first place. How could Melinda be that inattentive? Before Anna could think of a kind way to point out her carelessness, the young woman hurried from the room.

Anna dressed quickly and scurried into the kitchen, too. Fletcher had already picked up Roy and Raymond for their half day of work, and he'd bring them home at dinnertime, too, since he was taking Anna on an outing. Meanwhile, she decided to offer to transport Melinda into town. Whether unintentionally or not, the doctor hadn't expressly prohibited Anna from handling the horse and buggy, and she was feeling cooped up. Besides, she wanted to purchase more hairpins so she could tidy her appearance before going out with Fletcher.

When Anna suggested to Naomi that she wanted to take Melinda to Schrock's, her stepmother replied, "*Denki*, but I have to go to town anyway to buy baking supplies."

"Why don't you let me pick them up?" Anna asked, knowing the heavy Saturday traffic would be unsettling to Naomi, who was easily flustered by the *Englisch* trucks and tour buses.

"*Neh*, I need to buy in bulk, in preparation for our wedding guests," she countered. "The items will be too heavy for you to carry. The doctor's list prohibits heavy lifting, remember?"

"I'll take Eli and Evan with me. They're strong— they can carry the packages. If they're especially helpful, we might even stop at Yoder's Bakery for a treat afterward," Anna bargained. "I'll be fine."

"*Jah*, we'll help Anna. Please can we go, *Mamm*?" pleaded Evan.

"It will keep us out from underfoot," Eli reasoned, using one of his *mamm*'s expressions for effect, "instead of muddying your freshly scrubbed floors."

"*Jah*, alright, but you'll still have to complete your chores when you return," Naomi warned the boys as they shot out the door ahead of Anna and Melinda.

On the way, as Eli and Evan were distracted in the back seat with dividing the shopping list between them, Anna again brought up the topic of the hair clips. "I can replace the pins, Melinda," she said. "But it troubled me to hear you say I never gave them to you. You need to be more focused. If a customer at Schrock's gives you a large bill and you aren't paying attention, you may neglect to give them their correct change. That will create problems for everyone."

"I'm quite certain that won't happen," Melinda said breezily. "After all, I'm not the one with amnesia."

Anna's ears were ringing, but she responded calmly. "What do you mean by that?"

"Only that I don't recall you ever giving me your hairpins, so I have to believe you're mistaken. It's not your fault, necessarily. You're probably just remembering it wrong."

Anna squeezed her eyes shut and inhaled through her nose and then blew the air out through her mouth. She opened her eyes and moderated her voice to state, "Melinda, I gave you the hairpins after my accident and after I ceased taking any medication. I remember everything from the past week perfectly."

Melinda wrinkled her nose. "Why are you getting so prickly about such a trivial matter?" But before Anna responded, Melinda shrieked, "Oh, take the reins, will you? I can jump out at this stop sign instead of walking to Schrock's from the horse and buggy lot. See you later!"

As Melinda bounced down from the buggy and tore through traffic, Eli exclaimed, "Everyone knows you're not supposed to do that! Doesn't she have any common sense?"

Shaking her head, Anna wondered the same thing herself. In the pause it took for traffic to start moving again, Melinda scudded across the street and pulled open the door to Schrock's. Watching her, Anna feared her cousin might not even last a week in the shop before Joseph would have to let her go. He'd be short staffed again and Anna would feel obligated to return, since she was the one who recommended Melinda for the temporary position. *In that case, I better make hay while the sun shines*, she thought. *Or at least make my dress while I have a chance.* Although the doctor had prohibited prolonged periods of sewing, Anna figured she could stitch it together a bit at a time, but first she'd need to purchase her wedding dress fabric.

After all of the groceries had been secured in the buggy, Anna shepherded the boys into Yoder's Bakery, where she treated them to a cup of cocoa each and allowed them to split one of Faith Yoder's renowned apple fry pies.

"How are you?" Faith asked with a look of concern. "We heard you took a bad fall."

"*Denki*, I feel fine now." Anna deliberately kept her answer vague; she didn't want to lie, nor did she wish to tell anyone else about her memory problems, lest they question her about her wedding plans, as well. "How about you? Is your business thriving in its new location?"

"*Jah*. It's made such a difference to have a shop on Main Street instead of working out of the kitchen at home," Faith said. "I'm already up to my eyeballs in Easter orders for my *Englisch* customers' celebrations. Oh! That reminds me, are you planning to order a wedding cake?"

Although many of the desserts at Amish weddings were homemade by the bride's family and friends, it was common for the bride to order at least one special-made cake from a professional baker, as well, and Anna didn't know quite how to reply. She figured it was one thing to buy fabric for a wedding dress at this point, but it was entirely another to order a wedding cake.

Despite experiencing the first sweet stirrings of infatuation for Fletcher, Anna realized that if her memory didn't return in full, there was still the possibility they wouldn't marry. If the wedding was called off, she could always wear her dress to church, since it would be in the same pattern as the rest of her clothes. But if she placed an order for a cake, Faith might turn down future business so that she would have time to fill Anna's order. Anna didn't want to inconvenience Faith and affect her business like that.

"Er," she hedged. "I'm not quite certain."

Faith's creamy complexion splotched with pink. "Of course, that's fine. I only asked because your wedding date is so close to Easter, I wanted to be sure to reserve time to make your cake if you wanted one. I wasn't trying to pressure you into ordering anything from me—"

"*Neh*, I didn't think you were." Anna stammered, "It's just that I… I haven't made up my mind yet."

"Better you should wait, then." Faith chuckled. "Your cousin Melinda ordered hers last week and she's already changed her mind three times. I'm not going to stock up on any specialty ingredients for hers until the week before the wedding, when I give her a final deadline."

"*Gut* idea." Anna laughed. "I'll be sure to place my order as soon as I've given it more thought. Meanwhile, would you mind if I leave Eli and Evan here to finish their cocoa? I need to make a last-minute purchase from the mercantile. They'll behave themselves, won't you, boys?"

"With six brothers, I know how to keep these two out of mischief," Faith jested.

Anna was glad for the opportunity to shop for the fabric without the boys around. The two of them had eyes and ears for everything, and she was concerned they might report her purchase back to Naomi, who would fret endlessly about Anna sewing, no matter how many breaks she took. Anna swiftly backtracked down Main Street to the mercantile, but selecting the color took more time than she'd anticipated. Brides in her district tended to choose a traditional blue for their wedding dresses, although some, like Melinda, favored brighter variations, such as shades of purple. Anna liked both colors, but neither particularly appealed to her over the other.

She was fingering a swatch of navy blue cotton when she caught sight of a bolt in a deep green hue. It reminded her of the shade of the grass beneath a willow tree. She'd be pleased to have a new dress in that color, regardless of whether it ended up being her wedding dress or not. And somehow, just the act of selecting the fabric made her feel more confident about the future. She bought enough for herself and her two *newehockers* and hustled back to the bakery, knowing Naomi would begin to worry if she and the boys didn't return home soon. A young Amish woman was exiting Yoder's with a stack of cardboard boxes full of treats in her arms and two bags of doughnuts swinging from her hand as Anna was entering.

"Excuse me," Anna apologized, peering around the large package of fabric she carried.

The woman held the door open for her with her elbow as she balanced her own packages.

"*Denki*, but I don't think there's room for me to squeeze by. I'm just here to summon my brothers anyway." Anna smiled, calling, "Eli, Evan, *kumme* please."

The woman made a discontented huffing noise as the boys passed her.

When they were out of earshot, Anna instructed, "Boys, it's only proper to hold the door for someone who has packages in her hands, even when she's being very polite and holding it for you. I think you offended that lady."

"I'm sorry, Anna. We'll remember that next time," Evan promised.

"*Jah*," agreed Eli. "I didn't want to get my handprints on the door handle. But we'll apologize to Katie Fisher at church on Sunday."

"That was my friend Katie Fisher, Tessa's sister?" Anna asked abashedly.

Suddenly she understood why Katie had acted so crabby: it must have seemed as if Anna was snubbing her, just as she'd apparently snubbed her sister, Tessa.

Anna pressed her lips together, silently praying for her memory to return before she hurt anyone else's feelings or had to tell another person about her amnesia.

Fletcher pried the lid off a paint can. Painting was no one's favorite part of the job, but it was a necessary one. He wanted to be certain Raymond and Roy took as much care performing the mundane aspects of their responsibilities as they did the more challenging tasks.

"We'll have to move up our completion date on this site," Aaron announced. "I accepted another project that begins next week."

Fletcher voiced his surprise. "This office suite is going to require hanging more than the usual amount of trim, which we don't even have on hand yet."

"*Jah*, that's why I'm heading to the lumber store now."

"Now?" Fletcher repeated. If Aaron left, they'd fall behind on the painting.

"It's not as if I can call them on my cell phone, is it?" Aaron cracked. "If I don't talk to them today, I won't know if they have what we need in stock."

Fletcher hesitated. "The boys and I could stop on our way to their house after work today," he suggested.

"*Neh*, I'll go now," Aaron insisted.

To Fletcher, it seemed a waste of time and manpower for Aaron to run errands during the workday when Fletcher offered to do it off the clock, but he knew that was Aaron's decision to make, not his, since Aaron was the foreman. After giving it more thought, Fletcher concluded he'd prefer to arrive at Anna's sooner rather than later anyway, so he could finally spend an afternoon alone with her, helping her to recall the past. As he painted he silently asked God to bless their time together, and before Fletcher knew it, Roy signaled that it was nearly dinnertime.

At Anna's house, Evan and Eli zipped pell-mell across the yard to greet them.

"Fletcher!" Eli shouted. "*Mamm* says you're joining us for dinner. We made certain to taste test your food for mushrooms—just like Nehemiah did for King Artaxerxes in the Bible."

"Really?" asked Fletcher. "I didn't realize King Artaxerxes was allergic to mushrooms, too."

"Not mushrooms but anything poisonous," Eli explained solemnly.

Fletcher nodded seriously and clapped Eli's shoulder in return. "I appreciate that."

When Fletcher entered the kitchen, Naomi was slicing bread. Anna had just slid a pan from the oven and her cheeks were glowing. She gave him a little half wave with the oversize oven mitts she wore on her hands and then giggled at herself. He hadn't realized how much he'd missed her spontaneous sense of humor and he suddenly felt unnerved by her charm.

"Hello, Naomi. Hello, Anna," he said. "You smell *appenditlich*."

He'd meant to say the *food* smelled delicious, but before he could correct his mistake, Evan hooted, "Fletcher said, 'you smell *appenditlich*' instead of 'the food smells *appenditlich*'!"

"*Beheef dich,*" Anna shushed Evan with the command to behave himself before giving him a playful swat with the oven mitt. "Go wash your hands, please."

"I'd better wash my hands, too." Fletcher quickly ducked into the washroom until his ears lost their crimson flush.

After the meal, he informed Anna she might want to wear a heavier shawl, as they'd be spending time near the creek, where the air was especially cool.

"You're going to the creek?" Eli asked. "Can we *kumme*, too? We finished all of our chores."

"*Jah.* We can look for Timothy again," Evan begged. "Please?"

For a split second, Fletcher feared Anna would allow Eli and Evan to accompany them, but then she glanced in Fletcher's direction and gave him a wink.

"I think the turtles are still in brumation," she said. "Besides, you boys already went on an outing with me today. Now it's Fletcher's turn."

Satisfied, Fletcher uncrossed his arms, but there was still a delay before he set out with Anna: she insisted on washing and drying the dishes, despite Naomi's protests. When they were finally seated in the buggy and traveling down the lane, he glanced sideways to see Anna smiling broadly.

"Look!" she exclaimed, pointing to a robin in the field. "I guess that means winter is officially over, although our winter was so mild this year, it was as if it hardly happened."

"You remembered our mild winter?" Fletcher asked, unable to keep the tension from his voice.

"*Neh*, Naomi told me," Anna confessed. "I'm sorry if I got your hopes up. I assure you, as soon I remember anything from the past six months, I'll let you know."

"Of course you will." Fletcher hadn't meant to sound as if he were pressuring her. He loosened his grip on the reins and lightened his tone. "We did have a white *Grischtdaag*, though. The landscape was blanketed in pristine perfection."

"So then, white must be your favorite color?" Anna asked him cheekily. "And winter must be your favorite season?"

"*Neh*, spring is my favorite season—same as yours. And green is my favorite color," he answered, thinking in particular of the green radiance of Anna's eyes.

"Oh, that's interesting to know," Anna replied. "Because today I purchased green fabric for my wedding dress."

Fletcher again felt a surge of apprehension. She was making her dress, which was another significant step in the wedding preparations. Although that was a good sign, he had to remind himself that once Anna's memories returned, it was possible she'd cancel the wedding to him in favor of a renewed courtship with Aaron. Even so, Fletcher allowed himself a small measure of optimism.

They rode in silence until they came to the public park that hosted the stony path running adjacent to the creek. Following the trail, they eventually arrived at the same spot Anna and her brothers frequented by cutting down the hill and through the meadow directly behind their house.

"We could have walked straight to the creek from my house," Anna noted. "I'm not as fragile as everyone seems to think I am."

"*Jah*, but the creek isn't the only stop on our itinerary," Fletcher replied as he pulled a blanket and thermos from the back of his buggy. "We'll need the buggy to travel to the other place we'll visit today."

"As long as our next destination isn't Tessa and Katie Fisher's house," she remarked. "I'm afraid I've managed to slight them both on separate occasions. I had no idea who they were and I feel awful I don't remember them." Anna sighed.

"You'll remember them yet," Fletcher encouraged her.

When they reached the water's edge, Fletcher spread the blanket he'd been carrying beneath a barely budding willow tree and motioned for Anna to have a seat. Then he poured fragrant hot liquid from the thermos into a cup and presented it to her.

"What's this?" she questioned.

"It's sage tea," he replied, filling a cup for himself. "Remember? Dr. Donovan said he had patients who claimed it helped their memories return."

Anna pursed her lips to blow on the steaming drink. "He also said some of his patients practiced hypnotism. You're not going to try to hypnotize me, too, are you?"

Fletcher could tell by the way her cheek dimpled that she was pleased rather than annoyed. "*Neh*. But he did say it was important to get rest—which is why we're going to relax here for a while."

"Oh, I see," Anna said with a lilt in her voice. "We're not merely whiling away a Saturday afternoon. We're actually following doctor's orders?"

"Doctor's orders," Fletcher reiterated, enjoying their flirtation. "Actually, we're following his orders and his patients' suggestions. He mentioned some of their families and friends tried to recreate memories in order to jog the patients' recollection. There's no pressure, but I hope these surroundings might prompt memories of our early days together. You see, I hadn't been in town for more than a week when I first met you fishing down at the bend in the creek."

"I was fishing?" Anna was surprised. "But I've never liked handling grubs."

Fletcher gave a hearty laugh, exposing nearly perfectly aligned teeth, except for one at the top left corner, which was slightly crooked, as if it didn't quite fit among the others.

"*Neh,*" he said. "I meant *I* was fishing. You were leaning against a willow on the embankment."

"Just loitering there?" That didn't sound like something she would have done, either.

"Actually, you were weeping," Fletcher admitted.

Anna's cheeks went hot when she heard Fletcher had first encountered her in such a vulnerable state. "I'm afraid I did a lot of crying in the months following my *daed's* death."

"Perhaps, but when I made a dumb joke about suddenly understanding why the tree was called a *weeping* willow, you were gracious enough to laugh."

"You don't expect me to start weeping under this willow again now, do you?" Anna bantered.

"*Neh,*" Fletcher replied. "If there's one thing I hate, it's seeing you in tears."

Fletcher's response was so earnest it warmed Anna to the tips of her toes. She looked around and noted, "I've always appreciated what a peaceful place this is."

Fletcher guffawed. "That's the very thing we first argued about."

"We did?" Anna's curiosity was piqued. "Why?"

"Well, after I met you here the first time and you were crying—you hadn't yet confided the reasons behind your tears—I made that dumb joke, but then I contrived an excuse to leave, so you'd have your privacy."

"That was kind of you," Anna commented.

"Not really," Fletcher admitted. "I was agitated because I believed our voices had scared away the fish. See, I'd specifically chosen this spot instead of the location upstream where everyone else was fishing because it seemed more peaceful here. So, when you showed up the next evening, we got into a bit of an argument about who had more of a right to be here."

"You were a newcomer to our community," Anna said. "I'm sorry I wasn't friendlier. That was rude of me."

"*Neh*, what's rude is what I did on the third evening."

Listening to Fletcher talk about their first encounter was like reading a very good book: Anna wanted to hear all of it at once yet she didn't want the story to come to an end.

"What did you do on the third evening?" she asked.

"I presented you with a pen and a journal and suggested you might benefit from writing about your heartache instead of reflecting on it here at the stream," Fletcher said, cringing at himself. "What a heel."

"You weren't a heel. I can be a bit territorial—my *daed* always said it came from living as an only child for so long and not having to share my space. I was being selfish."

"*Neh,*" Fletcher countered. "*What a heel* is what you wrote about me on the first page of the diary I'd given you. You scribbled, *This journal was given to me by Fletcher Chupp, what a heel*. And then you thrust the diary under my nose to show me what it said."

"I did?" Anna was mortified. "That was childish."

"It was *true*. I was being a heel. I cared more about fishing than about your feelings. And I tried to disguise my self-centeredness with a gift."

"How did we ever end up courting after introductions like ours?" she asked.

"It's simple—we got to know each other. I kept com-

ing here to fish and you kept coming here to be alone
with your thoughts. Neither of us had the privacy we
needed to accomplish our purpose, but we were both
too stubborn to budge, so we began talking to each
other instead. Soon, there was nothing we didn't tell
each other. Nothing," Fletcher said.

When he looked at her, his eyes were dark as the
midnight sky and his voice was husky with ardor. A
subtle yet familiar emotion stirred inside of Anna and
she shivered.

"What is it?" Fletcher asked, sitting up straight. "Did
you remember something just then?"

"Almost," she said, sorry to disappoint him. "But it
was more of a feeling than a memory."

"A happy feeling?"

"Decidedly so." She smiled, holding his gaze.

"Gut." He stood and took her empty cup. "There's
another important stop along our stroll down memory
lane, so we ought to get going now."

As they were returning to the buggy, Anna suddenly
uttered, "The journal you gave me! Surely I must have
recorded my memories in there."

"I hadn't even thought of that, but you're right,"
Fletcher agreed. "When was the last time you wrote
in it?"

"Wrote in it? I didn't even know it existed! Where
do I keep it?"

"I don't know. You told me you wrote in it all the
time but you had to squirrel it away in a secret place
because you didn't want the boys happening upon it."

"Really?" Anna was deflated. "Well, what did it look
like?"

"It was about this big," Fletcher answered, squaring his hands, "and it had a brown leather jacket with a little gold lock attached at the side."

"I'll search for it as soon as I get home," Anna said enthusiastically as Fletcher supported her into the buggy. "It must hold a storehouse of memories."

Fletcher's palms grew sweaty as he contemplated what Anna might find written in her journal. He'd gotten so caught up in the nostalgia of first meeting her that he'd momentarily lost sight of the fact his ultimate intention for the outing was to help her recall her hesitation about marrying him, so he could address it. He removed his hat and swept his hand through his hair, as if to brush away the troublesome thoughts.

"Someone's been painting today, I see," Anna noticed. "You've got flecks of white in your hair."

"If you think my hair is bad, you ought to see Roy's and Raymond's," he replied. "Their saving grace is that they're blond, rather than dark like me, so it doesn't show up as much."

"*Denki* for mentoring them, Fletcher. I don't know what Naomi would do without a man around to train them in a vocation."

"It's a privilege," Fletcher said soberly. "Now, as you know, to the right is Turner King's *daadi haus*, but we won't drop in there until you resolve your misunderstanding with Katie and Tessa. A little farther along the lane is our house."

Anna hesitated when Fletcher turned in the driveway. "I'm not sure it's appropriate for the two of us to spend time together unchaperoned here. I wouldn't want people to see us and think—"

"Of course not. Neither would I," Fletcher said. He

shared Anna's commitment to modesty and decorum. "I only want to show you something. Wait here and I'll be right out with it."

He scooted into the house and emerged carrying a black suit on a hanger.

"I don't suppose you recall making this?" he asked.

"Hmm, I don't know." Anna scrunched her brows together and teased, "That stitching doesn't look like mine. Are you sure *you* didn't make the suit?"

"These hands can work a hammer, but not a sewing needle," Fletcher argued.

"*Jah*, that would explain why the side seam appears crooked."

"It's not crooked, you're looking at it askance."

Anna giggled. "One thing is certain—you will look very dapper in that, indeed. Now please go put it away. I'm freezing," she said.

Despite his best efforts to guard his emotions, Fletcher felt his knees go weak and his hopes grow strong because of Anna's compliment. He whistled as he brought the suit inside and quickly returned to take Anna home. He idled at the end of the lane as another buggy sailed past. Even if he hadn't recognized the familiar style of the carriage, he knew only one person who worked his horse that hard.

"That was Aaron," Anna said, as if reading his thoughts. "He probably picked Melinda up after her first day at the shop. Look at him go! I'm queasy just watching him."

Anna's remark cast doubt on Fletcher's concern about her affection for Aaron, and he chuckled zealously. As they rode, she peppered him with questions about his work as a carpenter, his sisters and their families, his likes and dislikes, and other important aspects of his life.

Finally, he teased, "There isn't going to be a quiz about this, Anna."

"*Neh*, but I want to learn as much about you as I can as quickly as I can, Fletcher Chupp."

Fletcher drew the horse to an abrupt halt and shifted to study her face in the waning light. "Why did you say that?" he asked, his voice throaty.

She tipped her head. "I said it because I meant it."

"That's exactly what you said—and I do mean word for word—when I first began walking out with you," he explained. "I thought maybe you'd remembered saying it."

"*Neh*, but it's still true," she responded. "Rather, it's true again."

As he clicked to the horse, Fletcher's stomach turned somersaults. Dr. Donovan was right: there was nothing more exhilarating than falling in love, and he was on the brink of falling for Anna a second time.

"Whoa, steady," he commanded the horse, directing it down the lane to Anna's house. He might as well have been talking to his own heart, which seemed in danger of rearing wildly and galloping away with him. He couldn't allow himself to forget Anna's note, even if she had.

"Look, Aaron has hitched his horse," Anna pointed out. "That must mean he's staying for supper. You're *wilkom* to join us, too."

"*Denki*, but I have work to do at home," Fletcher said. He needed to clear his head. Besides, he didn't want to take advantage of Naomi's hospitality, even if his cousin was staying, so he walked Anna to the porch, but before he could say goodbye, the door swung open. The tantalizing aroma of pork chops filled Fletcher's nostrils and when Naomi insisted he stay for supper, he couldn't refuse. This time when everyone joined hands for grace, Anna gave his palm a quick squeeze before letting go, and when he accidentally knocked his knee into hers, she didn't flinch or move her chair.

"How was your first day at the shop?" Anna asked Melinda as they were eating dessert.

"Easy as pie," Melinda replied. "No wonder you prefer working there to helping us at home."

"Anna's reputation for industriousness is what afforded you a temporary position at Schrock's Shop," Naomi diplomatically reminded her niece. "But because you've had such an easy day there, Melinda, you may clear the table and wash and dry the dishes, as well. I'm sure Aaron has chores to get to at home and will be leaving straightaway, too. As it is, I've got mending to do and the boys need to take a bath. *Kumme*, Evan and Eli, say *gut nacht* to everyone. Roy and Raymond, the wood bin is running low."

"I'll walk outside with you," Fletcher suggested to Aaron after Naomi and the boys left the room, fearing his cousin wouldn't take the hint that it was time to leave.

"Okay," he agreed amiably. "But first I have something to give Anna. It's in my buggy."

Anna stopped rinsing the pan in her hands long enough to shrug her shoulders and cast a puzzled look at Melinda. Fletcher stood by the door of the mudroom until Aaron returned with a pot of pale blue flowers.

"For you," he said, extending it to Anna.

She looked confused. *"Denki,"* she said, accepting the pot. "How thoughtful."

Melinda clapped her hands and tittered. "They're forget-me-nots, get it? You know, because you have amnesia. I was telling Aaron about the hair clips as we drove by the nursery in town and he was suddenly inspired. He said the flowers would make the perfect get-well gift for you!"

"I get it. *Denki,*" Anna repeated, red-faced, before abruptly saying good-night to everyone and excusing herself from the room.

Fletcher strode to his buggy without waiting for Aaron to stop laughing with Melinda. Filling his lungs with the night air, he tried not to rush to conclusions about the name of the flower Aaron had chosen for Anna. He was familiar enough with Aaron's sense of humor to know that his cousin's jokes were often misplaced. It was entirely possible there was no hidden message—other than the obvious pun in reference to amnesia—intended by his choice of flowers. As for Anna leaving the room so quickly, perhaps she merely felt nauseated or tired.

Yet as the horse pulled his buggy toward home, Fletcher noticed the optimism he'd felt earlier in the day was replaced by a gnawing insecurity that he couldn't seem to shake. *Dear Lord,* he began to pray, but then he stopped. Unsure of what to ask for, he kept his request simple: *please help.*

Chapter Five

After retreating to the washroom to splash water on her face, Anna patted her cheeks dry with a towel. Over the course of her relationship with Aaron, she'd grown accustomed to overlooking his jokes and pranks, and once again she reminded herself that his intention was to her laugh, not to mock her condition. Recalling that Dr. Donovan said it was normal for head injury patients to be hypersensitive during their recoveries, she decided rather than to waste any more time feeling irritated, she'd turn her attention to searching her bedroom for the journal Fletcher had given her.

When she didn't find it, she searched again a second time, patting beneath her mattress, opening every drawer and examining the shelf in her closet. Like most Amish homes, theirs was furnished simply and contained little clutter, so finding lost items was usually only a matter of retracing one's steps. Unfortunately, Anna's amnesia kept her from being able to do that.

She shone the flashlight into the other half of the attic, which was completely empty except for the package containing the wedding dress fabric she'd stashed there that afternoon because she was afraid Naomi might reproach her for sewing if she happened upon it in Anna's closet. Although Anna knew it would be unlikely for her to keep a personal item like a journal elsewhere in the house, she checked each room and asked each family member if they might have known where she'd put it.

"You're always writing in it, so you'd better find it soon," Melinda answered as she furiously scoured a pan. "It would be a shame if someone discovered your secrets."

To Anna's ears, that almost sounded like a taunt. Did Melinda know something she wasn't saying about the journal? Had she read it? Almost immediately, Anna was filled with shame. Assuming ill of another person was not the Amish way. Besides, Fletcher said the diary had a lock, so when Anna found the key on a string inside her drawer, she immediately looped it around her neck.

"I'm not concerned about someone discovering my secrets," she replied affably, picking up a towel to dry the dishes stacking up next to the sink. "But the diary could go a long way in helping me regain my memory, so please keep your eye out for it. Now, how about if you tell me more about your first day at the shop?"

Melinda was pleased to regale Anna with descriptions of the *Englischers* who came into the shop, recounting their questions and comments, and detailing their purchases. Listening to Melinda's exuberance about the experience, Anna was glad her cousin had the opportunity to work outside their home. Perhaps by representing the Amish community's wares to *Englisch* customers, Melinda might take better care to reflect Amish values, too.

By the time they finished cleaning the dishes, any tension Anna experienced concerning Aaron's gift had been washed away, as well. But her head felt as heavy as an anvil and she retired to her bedroom early. She searched her drawers and under the bed one last time, wishing she could find her journal. Not only did she want to read what she'd already written there, but she wanted to record her current feelings about Fletcher, in order to make sense of them. She found him to be thoughtful, respectful and fun, as well as strong, handsome and Godly. It was no wonder she'd been smitten with him from the start.

Yet, as she leaned against her bed to unlace her shoes, she ruminated that being infatuated wasn't reason enough to marry someone. She didn't doubt she professed to the deacon after their meetings concluded that she believed Fletcher was the husband the Lord provided for her. But despite her growing affection for Fletcher, Anna just didn't know if she could honestly make that same vow again when the bishop asked her to affirm it during the wedding ceremony in church.

Anna slipped into a kneeling position on the floor and folded her hands, beseeching, *Please, Lord, return my memory to me soon. And if it's Your will, help me find my diary, as well.*

"Oh, *gut*, you're still up," Melinda said when she burst through the door. "Do you want to see the material for my wedding dress? It arrived at the mercantile today and I picked it up after work."

"Sure." Anna straightened into a standing position.

Melinda unwrapped a layer of brown paper from a large package.

"It's beautiful," Anna gushed about the violet fabric,

fingering it along the edge. "This will look lovely with your brunette hair and big brown eyes."

"That's what Aaron said, too," Melinda commented as she secured the string around the bundle again.

As they donned their nightclothes, Anna realized perhaps Melinda simply didn't realize how she came across when she repeated Aaron's remarks, whether kind or far-fetched. She extinguished the lamp.

"Melinda?" Anna asked into the darkness. "Remember how you were talking about secrets and wishing I'd confide in you more often? I have a secret I'd like to share with you."

Anna could hear Melinda scramble into an attentive position. "What is it?"

"I bought my wedding dress material today, too. It's forest green. I'm not supposed to concentrate on sewing for long periods of time, but I figure I can work on it now and again, provided Naomi doesn't catch me and start to fret."

"I promise not to tell," Melinda said and flopped back down against her pillow, sighing. "I don't know where I'm going to find time to make mine now that I'm working at the shop."

"I'll tell you what," Anna offered. "The light in our room isn't the best, but perhaps we can spend a few evenings a week sewing up here together. And I'm happy to help sew yours if you find it becomes unmanageable while you're working at the shop."

"*Denki*, Anna." Melinda yawned. "I'd really appreciate that."

After a few minutes of silence, Anna was on the brink of sleep when Melinda mumbled, "I'm so happy you decided to buy your material even though you can't remember your groom. Aaron told me today that he didn't think Fletcher could handle another fiancée calling off the wedding. The first time nearly crushed him."

"What?" Anna whispered. When there was no reply, she asked again, "What did you just say?" but Melinda's breathing rose and fell in the steady pattern of sleep.

Anna listened to it all throughout the night as she tried to drum up a satisfactory reason for why Fletcher neglected to mention his previous fiancée. Instead, she just came up with additional questions, each one more alarming than the last: Why did Fletcher's first fiancée call their wedding off? If Anna had known the reason, would she still have agreed to marry him so quickly? Was there anything else he was keeping from her? If so, how would she know?

She was relieved when daylight filled the windows and she could rise and ready herself for church. The family squeezed into the buggy, three seated in the front and three seated in the back, with Evan balanced against Naomi's knees. This Sunday, they traveled to James and Amelia Hooley's home on the other end of town. Their basement was used as the gathering room for the worship service; afterward, the men flipped the benches, fashioning them into makeshift tables for lunch. Anna was eager to speak to the Fisher sisters and she figured she'd find them in the kitchen, helping serve and clean up.

"Look who's here!" Tessa exclaimed, nudging her sister.

"I'm Ka-tie," her other friend greeted her, pronouncing her name very slowly.

"And *I'm* sorry," Anna apologized. "I'm afraid you both must think me terribly rude—"

"It. Is. Okay," Katie enunciated loudly. "Why. Don't. You. Sit. Down?"

Anna didn't know what to make of Katie's manner of speaking. Did she always talk like that? She squinted at her.

Tessa explained in equally deliberate speech. "Please don't cry. We aren't angry with you. We know about your brain injury."

"Is that why you're talking like that?" Anna inquired, suddenly realizing their strange intonations were supposed to be for her benefit. "*Jah*, I had a traumatic brain injury, which is another name for a concussion, and I'm experiencing something called retrograde amnesia, but there's nothing wrong with my hearing, I'm not about to cry and I don't need to sit down."

Tessa threw her hands in the air. "Ach! Melinda told everyone at the shop your faculties haven't been the same since your fall. Oh dear, Anna, now *we're* the ones who are sorry!"

Katie covered her face with the dishtowel. "I'm so embarrassed I could cry!"

Anna should have known Melinda was at the heart of the misunderstanding—she was such a *bobblemoul*, as Evan would say! Nevertheless, she sympathized with her friends. "That's exactly how I felt when I learned I'd accidentally slighted each of you."

"It wasn't like you at all," admitted Tessa. "I couldn't understand why you were standing me up—we'd made a date to walk over to the mercantile during my break to look at material. I thought perhaps you'd changed your mind about asking me to be a *newehocker*."

"*Jah*, and when you made a remark about not being able to get past me at the door of the bakery, I took it as a judgment on my weight," Katie confessed. "Especially since I was carrying a load of goodies. Which, by the way, I was purchasing to bring here for dessert—it was my turn but I'd had a cold and I didn't want to spread germs by baking for everyone."

"*Neh*, not at all!" Anna assured them. "I simply couldn't—I *can't* remember any part of my life after August. The doctor says those memories may return soon and I hope they do because by all counts, I've heard we've had many *gut* times together."

"We still can," Katie suggested. "And nothing makes for a *gut* time like a treat from Faith Yoder's bakery. Follow me and I'll show you where I'm keeping a secret stash!"

Fletcher scanned the yard for Anna, wondering if she'd stepped outside for a breath of air. They had a long-standing practice of "bumping into each other" under the tallest tree in the church hosts' yards after he helped put the benches into the bench wagon and she participated in dish cleanup. He wondered if there was any chance she'd remember and meet him there that day. But beneath the Hooleys' oak, he happened upon his uncle instead of Anna.

"My knee acts up when I sit that long so I have to get out and move around," Isaiah explained to his nephew. "Especially when the weather is damp and dreary like it is today."

"It must run in the family," Fletcher replied. "My *daed* suffered from arthritis, too."

"*Jah*, I remember. Speaking of suffering, how is Anna?"

"She's not in much physical pain anymore, but her memory still hasn't returned."

"It will, son." His uncle's confidence was comforting. Isaiah continued, "She's young. It's not like when you get to be my age. The memory just goes. The other day I climbed down a ladder to get a tool and couldn't remember what I was looking for. I climbed back up, remembered, climbed back down and forgot again by the time I reached the landing."

"No wonder your knee hurts, with all that ladder climbing." Fletcher chuckled. Then he confided, "I wish it were just a single item Anna couldn't remember. But she doesn't remember events, she doesn't remember people... She doesn't remember me."

"*Mamm* sent me to round you up, *Daed*," Aaron interrupted, suddenly present at Fletcher's side. "One of the girls has a headache and needs to get home."

"*Jah*, alright. But speaking of headaches, if you need to take Anna to her doctor appointments, you go right ahead, Fletcher, you hear?" Isaiah ordered.

"I'm glad you mentioned that, because she has a follow-up appointment on Tuesday afternoon in Highland Springs. It's possible Naomi or Ray—"

"*Neh*, it's better if you're the one who brings Anna to Highland Springs," Isaiah interjected. "I trust you to manage your workload. As for Anna not remembering you, she will. Just wait a little longer, pray a little harder and keep spending every spare moment you can with her. Either way, the more she's with you, the more she'll know you. And as they say, to know you is to love you."

"*Denki, Onkel*, that's *gut* advice," Fletcher said as Isaiah clapped him on his shoulder before meandering away. He was heartened by his uncle's perspective.

"Like *Daed* said, it's okay if you leave early Tuesday afternoon, but you'll need to clear it with me in the future if you change your schedule," Aaron remarked. "You can't just leave the site without notifying anyone where you're going or when you'll be back."

"Of course," Fletcher agreed, even though he was thinking that Aaron was the one who left the work site without telling anyone where he was going. Upon waking that morning, Fletcher had asked the Lord to forgive him for his annoyance about Aaron's get-well gift, so he didn't want to slip back into a resentful attitude. He also prayed that while he waited for Anna's memory to return, he'd be able to maintain a more positive outlook about their future. "Have you seen Anna around?"

"She and the Fisher sisters were eating doughnuts on the side porch a few minutes ago."

Approaching the house, Fletcher heard the trio's laughter before he saw them. "That's the sound of old friends," he said as he hopped up the porch steps.

"Who are you calling old?" Katie teased him.

"I meant to say it's the sound of *gut* friends," Fletcher clarified. "*Gut* friends and *gut* women."

"For that, you may have the last doughnut." Tessa passed him a cream-filled pastry.

As Fletcher chewed, he noticed how reserved Anna seemed. She had dark circles under her eyes and he hoped he hadn't exhausted her with yesterday's activities. Or was there another reason she appeared fatigued? What happened after he left the previous evening? Did she remember something? Was it about Aaron? Determined not to let his dread get the best of him, he wiped his lips with the back of his hand and stood up.

"May I take you home, Anna?" he asked. "I know your family must have had a full buggy this morning."

"*Jah, denki*, Fletcher," she answered formally. "*Mach's. Gut.* Ka-tie. And. Tes-sa," she said slowly, and for some reason, this elicited peals of laughter from the Fisher sisters.

"Why did you use a funny voice when you said good-bye to Katie and Tessa?" Fletcher asked conversationally as they rode away.

"It was a private joke," was Anna's terse reply.

"Oh, I understand," Fletcher said, although usually Anna enjoyed sharing her funny stories with him.

"*Jah*, I figured you might, since you like to keep certain matters private yourself," she replied stiffly.

Now Fletcher knew something was wrong. He jerked the reins, causing the horse to detour down a gravelly side road overlooking a meadow where stubbles of crocuses, tulips and wildflowers were beginning to poke through the rich soil.

When they stopped, he said, "If there's something troubling you, Anna, I wish you'd tell me outright."

"Ha!" she declared. "You're one to talk, considering what you haven't told me!"

"I honestly have no idea what you're referring to."

"I'm referring to the one very important, very personal thing you neglected to tell me!" Anna harrumphed, crossing her arms over her chest.

Fletcher was utterly baffled. Was the issue that was upsetting Anna now the same issue that caused her to write the note? "I'm sorry, but I still don't know what you're talking about."

"I'm talking about your first fiancée," she said, staring straight ahead.

Fletcher noticed he'd curled his fingers into a fist. The mention of Joyce always caused him to tense up. He loosely shook his hands and then rested them on his knees. "What about her?"

"Then you don't deny you were engaged to someone else before me?"

Fletcher snickered. "Of course I don't deny it. I told you all about her shortly after we first met."

Anna wasn't satisfied. "Perhaps, but why didn't you tell me about her after my accident?" she pressed. "You knew I wouldn't have remembered hearing about her."

Fletcher's temper flared, imagining how Anna might have learned about his first engagement. "Who has been telling you about these things from my past anyway? Was it Aaron? Melinda?" he guessed. "Or did you find your diary and read something there?"

"The question isn't who told me about your past, Fletcher. The question is why didn't *you* tell me about it?"

"It didn't seem important," he stated.

"Not important?" she challenged. "How can you say being engaged isn't important?"

She was sobbing into her hands now, and Fletcher recalled Dr. Donovan's concern about unprovoked emotional outbursts. He was worried that this might qualify. Then he realized that if it did, he also probably needed to consult a doctor because he felt disproportionately emotional, too. He had to calm down himself if he was going to be a comfort to Anna.

"Anna," he said, nudging her shoulder with his. "I didn't tell you about my allergy to mushrooms, either. Now *that* was important, but I didn't bring it up because at the time, it didn't seem relevant. That's the phrase I should have used. My first engagement didn't seem relevant."

Anna's giggle reassured Fletcher there was no need to seek medical attention: her tears had nothing to do with her concussion. His mind eased, he offered her a handkerchief, and soon her sniffing had quieted and she'd dabbed her cheeks dry.

"I'm sorry," she apologized and carefully folded the handkerchief into a triangle, ashamed to face him. "I didn't sleep a wink last night, but even so, that wasn't a very mature way for me to approach this topic."

"I should be more understanding," Fletcher acknowledged. "I can't imagine what it feels like to lose your memory."

"It feels like the sky looks," Anna said, pointing to the white, overcast expanse. "It feels vast and empty and colorless. I want to remember, but when I try, there's nothing there."

"Then it's up to me to do a better job of filling in the blanks," Fletcher stated firmly. "Joyce Beiler was the name of my first fiancée. We courted for a year and although in hindsight I wouldn't say we were in love, I did care deeply for her and believed she felt the same way about me. Anyway, the summer before we decided to get married, Joyce's brother-in-law's cousin, Frederick, came to live with him and Joyce's sister, to help with growing and harvest seasons. I thought it was only natural that Joyce spent a lot of time with Frederick, since she was responsible for helping her sister and brother-in-law at the farm, too."

Noticing Fletcher's voice drop, Anna said softly, "It's okay, you needn't explain. I think I understand what happened."

But Fletcher cleared his throat and continued talking. "Eventually, I had a conversation—I had *several* conversations—with Joyce about my concerns, but she assured me she felt nothing but a sisterly type of fondness for Frederick. She and I completed our meetings with the deacon and announced our wedding intentions to our families and to the *leit* in church. Four days before the wedding, she told me she couldn't go through with it—she was in love with Frederick."

Anna gasped and touched Fletcher's forearm. "Oh! That must have been so painful for you."

"It was." He grimaced and hung his head. "At the time it felt personally excruciating and publicly disgraceful. I have to admit, I was relieved to leave Green Lake."

Anna understood only too well; Aaron's betrayal had wounded her deeply, too. But her relationship with Aaron hadn't progressed nearly as far as Fletcher's relationship had with Joyce, nor was the reason behind Anna's breakup public knowledge. She winced to imagine the extent of disbelief, disappointment and dejection—not to mention, embarrassment—Fletcher must have had to overcome, and her admiration for him burgeoned.

The air was silent except for the sound of the horse occasionally swishing his tail or shuffling his hooves, and after a few moments, Anna apologized. "I wish I hadn't made you relive that memory."

"It was necessary in order for me to clear it up with you," he replied. "I have nothing to hide so I don't want you to feel as if I'm keeping anything from you. I don't want you to feel as if there's something you need to keep from me, either. No matter what it is."

"Of course," Anna pledged pensively, noting the edge in Fletcher's tone. Did he think she was keeping something from him? If so, what? There was no other man in her life. The only person she'd ever walked out with was Aaron, and they'd broken up more than six months before Fletcher arrived in town. Since Fletcher was Anna's intended, she assumed she must have confided her intimate secrets to him, just as he'd confided his to her. That meant she must have told him what happened with Aaron and Melinda, didn't it? But, maybe she hadn't. Without asking, she couldn't be certain.

"What have I told you about my past?" Anna questioned.

Fletcher looked taken aback. "What do you mean?"

"I must have told you things about my life, but I can't remember what they are. What do you know about me?"

Fletcher wiped his upper lip. "Well, you told me about your *mamm* dying when you were a *bobbel* and how your *daed* and you lived with your *groossmammi* until she passed, too. I know that your *daed* married Naomi when you were sixteen, and it was a big adjustment for you to suddenly have four brothers around. You felt as if they were forever underfoot or spying on you."

Anna giggled. "Sometimes, I still feel that way about Eli and Evan."

"*Jah*, but you also said that helping Naomi care for them as young *kinner* made you eager to have *bobblin* of your own one day."

"What did I tell you about Melinda?"

Fletcher tilted his head from side to side, as if to work a kink out of his neck, before he said, "You said her *daed* sent her to stay with you because she was getting into trouble during her running-around period. He thought you might be a *gut* influence on her, since her *mamm* died long ago and she hadn't any female relatives living nearby."

"Go on," she prompted him.

"You tried to set a *gut* example and invited her to attend social events with you and Aaron, whom you'd been walking out with for about two and a half years. But then last February, you discovered Melinda and Aaron, um…"

Anna concluded his sentence for him, "Kissing behind the stable."

"Jah," Fletcher acknowledged.

"Did I tell you how I felt about that?"

"How you felt?" he repeated hesitantly. "Anna, are you sure you want to relive this?"

"I have no need to relive it—I already distinctly remember that part of my life. It happened long before my accident. What I want is to know what I told you about it. As your betrothed, I must have confided my innermost secrets in you. What did I tell you?" she challenged.

"You told me you were devastated at first, of course. But you said you soon realized it wasn't that Aaron had broken your heart as much as he'd broken your trust that pained you. Compared with losing your *daed*, you said ending your courtship with Aaron was easy. That's how you knew you hadn't truly been in love with him— because losing Aaron didn't split your heart in half."

"That's right." Anna nodded, contented to confirm Fletcher knew exactly how she felt. "What else did I tell you about the months following the breakup and my *daed*'s death?"

Fletcher's voice was gentle with compassion. "You told me spring was a blur. That everyone said how strong you were in the wake of your *daed*'s passing, caring for Naomi and the boys and putting up with Melinda's antics besides. You told me your secret was that you made yourself numb and kept as busy as you could.

You said the only thing you looked forward to was the half hour you allowed yourself each day to weep in private—in the hayloft during the spring, and then beneath the willow by the creek in the warmer summer months. Which, as I've indicated, is where we first met."

Anna's eyes smarted. *I must have trusted him wholeheartedly to confide those emotions in him,* she realized.

Aloud, she said in a raspy voice, "*Denki* for telling me all that. It helps me to know we've both shared our feelings and experiences so openly."

"Of course," Fletcher replied. Although time would tell if she'd come to remember she hadn't quite been open about sharing *all* of her feelings, he was grateful for the sense of calm that seemed to have settled over Anna. He wouldn't have forgiven himself if she'd gotten so upset they needed to call Dr. Donovan.

"Melinda told me I've seemed prickly since my accident," Anna said, interrupting his thoughts. "I don't mean to be that way, but it's frustrating trying to make sense of things. So I'll probably continue to ask you a lot of questions."

"Please do. As I said, we spent our early courting days down by the creek, just talking. We told each other all about our dreams and disappointments, our triumphs and our failures. We used to spend hours talking about our faith and our families, and we shared other details from our lives, too. For example, I even know that when you were a girl, you believed lightning bugs were actually made out of lightning."

"You mean they're not?" Anna laughed before requesting, "Now tell me some little thing I know about you that I don't know I know about you."

Relieved to engage in a little levity after such an intense discussion, Fletcher pushed up his coat sleeve and lifted his arm. "See this scar? You know that I got it hurtling over a fence."

"Who was chasing you?"

"It wasn't a *who*, it was a *what*. It was Thistle, the neighbor's goat, to be precise."

"Ach! The mischievous animal!"

"Actually, I was the one who was mischievous. I was taking a shortcut, which amounted to trespassing. My first and last time."

"How old were you?"

"Oh, around twenty-two," Fletcher said.

"Neh!" Anna exclaimed. "Really?"

"Neh," he admitted. "Not really. I was about eight or nine. Definitely old enough to know better."

Laughing, Anna asked, "Did I confess any of my wayward escapades to you?"

"Only that you once burned your finger snatching an oatmeal cookie from your *groossmammi*'s oven. And that you used to climb trees to hide on your brothers."

"I still do that sometimes."

"Really?" Fletcher questioned.

"Neh, not really," Anna echoed impishly. "I'd like to think my behavior is a little more mature than that now. Although I haven't forgotten how to climb so I still could if I wanted to."

"Perhaps in warmer weather, you'll teach me, then," Fletcher suggested, caught up in their whimsical banter. "That's one skill I never mastered. I have a slight fear of heights, which isn't one of the best qualities in a carpenter, so please don't tell Melinda. I don't want Aaron finding out about it and giving me a hard time. On the job, I do whatever needs to be done, including roofing—but how I feel about doing it is our little secret."

"I won't tell a soul, especially not Melinda," Anna agreed conspiratorially. "I don't think she intends any harm, but she has a habit of blurting things out before she's really thought them through."

"I've noticed that, too," Fletcher said. "Not only does she seem to share things she shouldn't, but half the time her perspective isn't exactly reliable."

"Is that why we were so discreet about our relationship, because we didn't want her to tell everyone and share her thoughts on the matter?" Anna wondered aloud.

"That was one of the reasons, I suppose," Fletcher confirmed. "I had similar misgivings about Aaron finding out. It was also that you wanted to be respectful of Naomi's mourning period. I think you felt a little guilty for being so happy when…"

"When my *daed* had recently died?"

"*Jah.* But there were a few people who knew we were courting early on, before we officially told our families."

"Who?"

"Well, Tessa and Katie. And my *groossdaadi*. Mind you, I never told him myself. He just knew. After you'd visit, he'd say, 'Fletcher, your Anna makes the best beef barley soup I've tasted since your *groossmammi* was alive.' Or, 'Your Anna's eyes were sure sparkling today, weren't they, Fletcher?' It was always 'your Anna,' not just 'Anna.' We never discussed it, but I think that was his way of letting me know he knew we were courting and he approved."

"I'm glad—on both counts," Anna said, rubbing her hands together.

The tip of her nose was pink and Fletcher's heartbeat quickened as he regarded the brightness of her lips, recalling how silky they used to feel against his own.

Her voice cut through his thoughts. "I'm afraid I'm getting a little chilly."

"Me, too," he said reluctantly. He picked up the reins and directed the horse back onto the roadway so he could drop Anna off and head toward his own house. The rhythmic cadence of the horse's clopping along the road made his eyelids droop and he decided that when he got home, he'd lie down for a much needed nap. After stabling the horse, he realized he'd had such a full day with Anna on Saturday that he'd neglected to collect the mail that evening. Checking the box, he found an envelope addressed in penmanship he didn't immediately recognize. He quickly read its contents.

Fletcher,
We've received the invitation to your wedding from Anna, along with the note from you asking us to be your *newehockers*. We already have our suits from the last time you almost got married, so how could we say no?

In all sincerity, we're both glad you found a good woman and we look forward to meeting her and celebrating your marriage.

We expect to arrive on Monday, the sixth of April.
Your friends,
Chandler Schlabach & Gabriel Ropp.

In the turmoil following Anna's accident, Fletcher had forgotten he'd asked Chandler and Gabriel to be his *newehockers*. Recalling how supportive they'd been after his wedding debacle with Joyce, he knew their reference to it was intended lightly, and he was grateful he had friends who'd gladly make such a long journey on his behalf. Still, the remark touched upon his concerns that this wedding might not happen, either.

Yet as his head sunk into the pillow, he was cautiously upbeat as he reflected on the discussion he'd just had with Anna. Simply repeating what she'd told him about her breakup with Aaron made Fletcher feel more confident. Nothing about Anna's comments or behavior, past or present, indicated she held any enduring affection for his cousin. Fletcher still didn't know what to make of Anna's note, but maybe it was time for him to stop worrying about it. Perhaps the note only represented a single moment of hesitation, compared to an entire courtship of certainty. Could it be that today's conversation with Anna was further proof that there was nothing the two of them couldn't work out together if they talked it through? As Isaiah suggested, the best course of action might be to spend as much time with Anna as he could. *To know me is to love me*, he thought drowsily.

His mind made up, Fletcher felt more relaxed than he had since Anna's accident and he drifted into a languorous snooze.

Chapter Six

The house appeared to be deserted when Anna entered it, but she knew from experience that even if Melinda and the boys were out, it was likely Naomi was resting in her room. Tiptoeing down the hall, Anna hoped her stepmother wasn't relapsing into a period of depression and fatigue. If Naomi was sleeping, she didn't wish to rouse her, but if she was awake, Anna hoped she could be of some comfort.

"Are you asleep?" she asked quietly as she paused outside the closed bedroom door.

"I'll be right there," her stepmother called and Anna heard the patter of footsteps followed by what sounded like a drawer closing. When Naomi opened the door, her face was flushed. "Oh, *gut*, it's you, Anna."

"I'm sorry to disturb you. I wanted to see if you were alright and if there's anything I can do for you."

"Anna, dear, you're always so considerate of me, but I'm fine," Naomi said. She stepped aside and motioned Anna into the bedroom. "Actually, I was in here looking for some fabric. Mind you, I wasn't sewing on the Sabbath—I was only looking to assess what I might have left over. I wanted to make new trousers for Raymond, as I've let down the hems in his church pants as far as they'll go and today I noticed they're still too short. I remembered starting a pair for your *daed* that I never finished. I'd tucked the material away until I could face seeing it again. While I was searching for it today, I found this. I'd forgotten all about it…"

She opened the bottom drawer of her bureau and removed a thick, neatly folded bundle of eggplant-colored fabric.

"Oh! That would be such a becoming color on you, Naomi," Anna replied, fingering the material. "Are you going to make yourself a new dress?"

Naomi's eyes shimmered. "I haven't sewn a dress for myself in so long, I've forgotten my measurements!"

"Then it's past time for you to have one."

Naomi laughed. "That's exactly the kind of remark your *daed* would have made, Anna."

"Well, he would have been right. Anyway, now that you've found the material, it would be wasteful to allow it to continue to sit in the drawer."

"You know what?" Naomi asked, patting the fabric. "I think I *will* make a new dress for myself. A wedding is such a special occasion and I'll wear the dress again to church for years."

Naomi's exuberance delighted Anna. In the past when her stepmother mentioned Anna's *daed*, she sounded so forlorn but today she conveyed only a sense of mirth and anticipation for the future, and her hopefulness felt contagious. Naomi set the material atop her sewing basket and the two women ambled into the kitchen for a cup of tea.

"Where are the boys this afternoon?" Anna asked.

"The four of them loped off to the creek. Roy and Raymond wanted to practice their casting and Eli and Evan tagged along for the fun of it. They were all hoping Fletcher might *kumme* down and join them for a while, too."

"He would have enjoyed that, but he left after he dropped me off."

Naomi narrowed her eyes. "Is something the matter? I assumed he'd stay for supper. We're only having leftovers because it's the Sabbath, but I figure our leftovers are tastier than whatever he might make on his own."

"*Neh*, nothing's wrong," Anna assured her. "I think he didn't want to wear out his *wilkom*, that's all."

"Ach! That's because I was so cranky the other night, isn't it? I didn't mean to be inhospitable, but I was short-tempered because of Melinda's comments. The truth is, both she and Aaron seem to be lacking in diligence. I think if they spent less time frolicking and more time tending to their responsibilities at home, instead of just those at their paid jobs, they'd have a better idea of what it means to manage a household. But it wasn't charitable of me to chase Aaron away as I did and I certainly wasn't hinting that Fletcher should go, too."

"I doubt Fletcher thought twice about leaving when he did," Anna replied. "As it was, I think he was surprised to be invited for supper since he'd already had dinner with us. He wouldn't take advantage of your generosity—he's very considerate in general."

"*Jah*, but I want you both to know he has an open invitation to join us for dinner or supper whenever he pleases. I know how important it is for the two of you to…to get to know each other again."

"*Denki*, Naomi, I'll tell him that," Anna said as she

lifted the whistling kettle from the front burner of the gas stove. "I have my follow-up doctor's appointment Tuesday afternoon, which he intends to take me to. It would be convenient if he could eat with us that evening, since we'll be returning home around five thirty or six o'clock."

"Of course," Naomi agreed, arranging several thimble cookies on a plate. "So, have you learned anything else about him other than that he's 'very considerate in general'?"

Anna carried the teacups to the table. Although she and Naomi shared an unusual closeness, most Amish couples in their district seldom discussed their romantic relationships.

"Well," she said, hesitating. Then her face broke into a huge grin. "I think the most important thing I've discovered is the more I know him, the more I like him."

"Look at you blush," Naomi gushed. "That's *wunderbaar*. Then do you still plan to marry him even if your memories don't fully return by your wedding date?"

"Oh, I haven't given up hope that my memories will *kumme* back!"

"That's what I'm praying will happen, too, and I have faith *Gott* will answer our prayers in His time and in His way."

Anna pensively bit into a cookie. After she swallowed, she said, "I guess at this point—without having my memories restored—I'd say I might not be ready to marry Fletcher yet, but I can clearly see he has the qualities I'd want in a husband." She was referring to his fortitude and candor, and to how respectful, protective and understanding he'd shown himself to be.

"And are you drawn to him?"

"Drawn to him?" Anna repeated, drizzling honey into her tea.

"A number of men might have the qualities you'd desire in a husband, but they don't set your heart aflutter," Naomi stated candidly.

Anna thought of how her heart melted within—like honey in tea—whenever Fletcher's eyes met hers. *"Jah,"* she said, "I'm drawn to him."

"Then it sounds as if you just need a little more time," Naomi suggested.

"Or for my memories to return," Anna replied, frowning. "Although I'd settle for finding my journal. As fond as I'm growing of Fletcher, I'm still surprised I made the decision to marry him so quickly."

"It's wise to know someone well before committing to marriage, but knowing someone well doesn't necessarily mean having a long courtship," Naomi reasoned. "I only knew your *daed* for four months before I married him. I had a solid sense of his character from the first day I met him and that never changed. I loved your *daed* early on and I knew he loved me. We were meant for each other. There was no other way to explain it and no other explanation needed."

Anna kissed Naomi's forehead as she stood to bring the empty teacups to the sink. "I'm so blessed you and my *daed* got married, Naomi. I'm sorry for how cross I acted that first year because I had to give up my bedroom to Raymond and Roy."

Naomi laughed. "You've more than made up for it by sharing your room with Melinda so graciously." Then, in a serious tone, she said, "I must admit I hoped—even prayed—Melinda and Aaron might have second thoughts about getting married. I think they both could benefit from maturing a little individually before they begin a life together as husband and wife."

"Well, as you've been reminding me, there's still time..."

Anna's comments were disrupted by the sound of footsteps on the porch as the four boys burst through the mudroom into the kitchen.

"Don't worry, *Mamm*, Evan's fine, he's just wet," Raymond immediately announced as he placed his soggy brother down on the floor.

"And cold," Evan said, shivering.

"Haven't we had enough accidents in this family? Didn't I warn you to keep a close eye on him?" Naomi upbraided Raymond and Roy as she rushed Evan to the washroom for a hot bath.

As Anna pulled plates from the cupboard to set the table for supper, she couldn't help but think that if Fletcher had gone fishing with the boys, he would have snatched Evan out of the creek before the boy had a chance to get wet. Because not only did Fletcher have the most striking eyes she'd ever gazed into, but Anna noticed he had particularly strong arms, too.

On Monday morning, Raymond delivered a note to Fletcher from Anna. *Fletcher,* it said, *would you like to join us for supper? I'm making meat loaf and brown-butter mashed potatoes, with butterscotch cream pie for dessert. Naomi wanted to be sure you know you are wilkom to join us. —Anna.*

Fletcher's mouth watered at the thought of Anna's cooking, but he had to decline. He had to work late in order to make up for the time he'd miss the next day when he left early to take Anna to Highland Springs.

As it was, he, Aaron, Raymond and Roy would have to struggle to keep up with their contracts. The trim Aaron ordered for the first site wasn't delivered that morning, so Aaron suggested they temporarily abandon the location to begin working on the new project at a second site. Fletcher was concerned the first customer would be upset by the delay in the completion of the assignment, but Aaron shrugged it off.

"It's unfortunate, *jah*, but when I explain to the customer that our supplier hasn't delivered the trim yet, he'll understand," Aaron said. "The *Englisch* crews are usually much farther behind their deadlines than we are, so the customer won't think twice about it."

Fletcher had gritted his teeth. Aaron was a good carpenter, but he lacked the kind of drive and the organizational skills his father possessed. If Isaiah had been managing this project, he would have seen to it the supplies were ordered ahead of time.

"Perhaps, but our purpose is to honor our word and bring glory to *Gott*, not merely to do better than our *Englisch* competitors," he reminded his cousin.

"If you're so worried about it, tonight you can stop at the lumber store after you're done making up your time and ask the clerk to expedite the order. I've also made a list of supplies we need for our next job. Most of it is small enough to load into your buggy. The rest they can deliver with the trim."

"How will I pay for it?" Fletcher asked.

"Here, take the card. Just sign the receipt 'Chupp,' like you usually do."

Fletcher knew he was the only crew member Aaron entrusted with this task, but it wasn't a job Fletcher appreciated being assigned. The purchasing of supplies was usually the foreman's responsibility. Fletcher was only willing to do it because it would expedite progress on their customers' projects. It wasn't until later in the evening, when he was alone, wolfing down a cheese and bologna sandwich, that it dawned on Fletcher what the real reason was Aaron tasked him with visiting the lumber store that evening: Aaron didn't want go himself because he feared he'd miss the opportunity to be invited to Melinda's house for supper. In fact, he was probably devouring a thick slice of Anna's meat loaf at that very moment.

Fletcher relished Anna's cooking, knowing the satisfaction she took in providing healthful, tasty meals for her family, her friends or *leit* in the church who happened to be visiting or ailing. Yet he realized even she needed a break from her responsibilities from time to time, and he decided he'd like to treat her to supper out after her doctor's appointment. It would be a surprise— a good one, for once.

The very thought carried him through his work that evening and the following day, and before he knew it, he was knocking at her door. Knowing Naomi would fret if he and Anna were late returning from the medical center, but anticipating he might not be able to speak to Naomi in private, Fletcher carried a folded note. *Naomi,* it read, *I'd like to surprise Anna by taking her out for dinner after her appointment. We may not be returning until later in the evening. Is that okay with you? —Fletcher.*

When Anna went to retrieve her shawl, Fletcher slipped Naomi the note and gestured for her to read it. She quickly scanned the slip of paper and crumpled it in her fist just as Anna came back into the room. With a wink at Fletcher, Naomi bid them goodbye. They were about to board the buggy when she called from the porch, "Be careful and have an *appenditlich* time, you two!"

Waving back at her, Anna asked Fletcher, "What do you think she meant by that?"

Fletcher recalled the time he told Anna she smelled *appenditlich* and his cheeks burned. Avoiding her question as he assisted her into the buggy, he advised, "Watch your step."

The sunlight played off the trees, which waved their branches in a light breeze, and the landscape was beginning to blossom with azaleas, crocuses and daffodils. As Fletcher and Anna passed them, he recognized how much more buoyant he was during this trip than he'd been the last time he'd taken Anna to Highland Springs, and he hummed a few measures of the hymn they'd sung in church on Sunday.

"How are you feeling, Anna?" Dr. Donovan asked when he entered the exam room.

"Wunderbaar," Anna answered in Pennsylvania Dutch. She quickly clarified, for the doctor's benefit, "I mean, wonderful."

Dr. Donovan's round cheeks grew even rounder when he chuckled. "Even if I hadn't known what you meant by the word *wunderbaar*, I could have guessed by the color in your cheeks and the glint in your eye. *Wunderbaar* is a big improvement from *fine*, isn't it?"

"It is," Anna agreed.

After questioning her about any ongoing nausea or headaches, he told her to hop onto the examining table, where he looked into her eyes and quickly tested her reflexes before telling her to take a seat in the chair next to Fletcher again.

"Physically, you're in great shape," the doctor reported. "I'm glad to hear the nausea has subsided. The dull headaches you mentioned are probably a sign you're doing a bit more focused concentrating than you ought to be doing. Have you been heeding my advice not to do too much sewing or reading?"

"Oh, I haven't been reading at all," Anna stated with a wide-eyed innocent look.

"Aha!" Dr. Donovan pointed his finger in mock accusation, grinning. "You'll need to cut back on sewing, then. I'd advise that you don't return to your job at the shop yet, either. Now, how about your memories, have they returned yet?"

Anna shook her head. "Not yet."

"Hmm," the doctor murmured thoughtfully. "Well, they still might. Although, as I said before, there's no guarantee. But something tells me the two of you may have gotten reacquainted, perhaps rediscovered some of the qualities in each other that made you fall in love in the first place. Am I right?"

Anna modestly dipped her head so Fletcher answered for them both, saying, "We've enjoyed spending time together recently, *jah*."

"*Wunderbaar!*" Dr. Donovan exclaimed, smacking his desktop, and Anna and Fletcher both laughed. "Have faith and keep heading forward and things will turn out alright, one way or the other."

While Anna was scheduling an appointment to return in four weeks, Fletcher went to retrieve the buggy from the lot. After picking her up, he skillfully maneuvered the horse through the heavy traffic along the main road. Oddly feeling as skittish as he did the first time he formally asked to court her, he didn't speak until they turned down a side street.

"If you're hungry, I'd like to take you to supper," he said.

"*Denki*, that's a very nice invitation," Anna replied slowly, as if considering the offer, "but Naomi will grow concerned if we're not back by six or six thirty."

"It's okay, I cleared it with her first," Fletcher confessed.

"Really? You're so thoughtful!" Anna said, clasping her hands and shuffling her feet. "Is there a special place we've frequented?"

"*Neh.* We've never actually eaten out together, but I think it's time to do something new to both of us, not just new to you. Don't you agree?"

"I'd like that," Anna said and Fletcher stared into her eyes so long a driver from behind tapped on his horn to indicate the signal light had turned green.

They chose to dine at a pizza place Anna had heard some *Englisch* customers rave about in Schrock's Shop, and the food lived up to the recommendation. Together Anna and Fletcher polished off a medium Hawaiian pizza as well as a pitcher of root beer, which gave Anna hiccups that lasted all the way home.

"*Gut nacht*, Fletcher," she said when he walked her to her door. "I *hic*—had an absolutely *scrumptious* time. *Hic.*"

By the time he turned in for the night, Fletcher's jaw ached from grinning but he still couldn't stop smiling. Their evening out seemed to underscore what Dr. Donovan suggested: Anna and Fletcher needed to move forward, not backward. They needed to have faith and to focus on the future, not on the past. As the doctor said, there was no guarantee Anna's memory would ever return. If not, she wouldn't ever be able to tell him what she'd meant when she sent her note the day of her accident. But since nothing about her actions or attitude indicated any special affinity for Aaron, Fletcher decided it was time to put the note behind him for good. He turned off the lamp and floated into sleep.

On Wednesday, Anna woke to the thrumming of rain on the rooftop and the low rumble of distant thunder, which struck her as odd. It seemed early in the season for thunder. The last storm they had was in October, on Fletcher's birthday. She lay there thinking about how upset she'd been when the cloudburst ruined her carefully planned picnic beneath the willow at the creek. Making a dash for Fletcher's buggy, she'd tripped on a tree root, stumbling face-first toward the ground. When Fletcher lunged to catch her, he'd dropped the basket he'd been carrying, upending its contents beside her. They both ended up splattered with cake and mud. She wondered how she ever explained her appearance to her family that day.

Then she sat bolt upright in bed: she had remembered something from the last six months!

She tucked her hair into her prayer *kapp* and knelt by her bed. "Dear Lord, *denki* for restoring my memory. *Denki, denki, denki!*"

"Shh," Melinda groaned. "I can't take a nap in the middle of the day like you can and I still need to sleep."

"But I remembered! I remembered!" Anna said, shaking her cousin's shoulders. When she elicited no further response, she dressed and hopped down the stairs and into the kitchen.

"I remembered something!" she announced, hugging Naomi, who was standing at the stove scrambling eggs.

"*Gott* is *gut*," Naomi proclaimed, dropping her wooden spoon to take Anna's face in her hands. "See? It just took time."

"Why are you two crying?" Raymond asked when he entered the room.

Anna leaped to hug him. "Because *Gott* is *gut*!"

"What's all the noise? Is there a party going on in here?" Roy asked a few seconds later.

"Not yet, but there will be tonight, if your *mamm* allows it," Anna said. "We'll invite Fletcher, Aaron, Katie and Tessa for supper and a cake. I'll buy the ingredients and do all of the work myself, I promise."

"Anna, you know what the doctor said about overexertion—"

"He only warned me about up close activities. Besides, it won't be any different than preparing a meal for our family—it will just be a bigger meal. If I truly need help, Katie and Tessa will pitch in," Anna countered. "I had a great sleep last night and I'm obviously getting better or else I wouldn't have experienced one of my memories returning."

Eli rubbed his eyes as he took his seat. "Your memory came back?"

"Now maybe you'll remember what happened to Timothy!" Evan added, picking up a fork.

"It was only a single memory and it wasn't about your turtle, Evan, but it's still a cause for celebration."

"*Jah*, okay," Naomi agreed. "As long as you don't overdo it."

"*Denki*," Anna said. "I'll drop Melinda off, so I can go to the market. She can invite Tessa and Katie when she sees Tessa at work. They'll probably give her a ride home, too. Raymond, I'll give you a note to give to Fletcher. But whatever anyone does, you mustn't let him know I started to remember again—even after he arrives here. I have an idea for how I want to surprise him with the news. So, mum's the word, right, Eli and Evan?"

"Right," said Evan, pretending to seal his lips shut. Then out of one corner of his mouth, he squeaked, "I won't say a word."

"You'd better not," Eli warned. "Terrible things happen when you spy or share other people's secrets."

"I don't know if that's true," Anna commented as she searched a drawer for a piece of paper. She and Naomi were concerned about Melinda's influence on the younger boys, so they'd been trying to teach Eli and Evan the value of discretion, but Anna wondered if they'd been too strict on the subject. "I would just appreciate it if we kept this a secret. This way, we'll all have the pleasure of seeing the surprised look on Fletcher's face!"

Dearest Fletcher, she wrote on a piece of paper. *Please come to supper tonight at six. You will like what I am making. —Your Anna.* Sealing the note with a piece of tape, she instructed Raymond to give it to Fletcher as soon as he got to the work site.

"And please tell Aaron he's invited, too," she added, knowing that when Melinda finally dragged herself from bed, she'd be as pleased about her fiancé joining them for supper as Anna was about hers.

Fletcher began whistling the moment after reading Anna's message. It wasn't just that he was happy he'd get to see her again this evening; it was that she used not one but *two* terms of endearment in her note. Even before her accident, she was careful about what she expressed to him in writing. She said she trusted Raymond not to read her messages, but she wasn't as certain she always trusted him to remember to deliver the notes and she didn't want her "sweet nothings" ending up in someone else's hands by accident.

He was still whistling when he, Raymond and Roy packed up their tools for the day. Despite the fact that Aaron had left early to go to the lumber store again, they were managing to keep on schedule with their new project. Anna's *daed* had trained the boys well. They were hard workers and applied whatever techniques he taught them. Raymond was already nearly as handy of a carpenter as Aaron was, and what he lacked in skill, he made up for in perseverance.

"It's rainy, getting dark and there's a lot of traffic. Roy, you need more practice," Fletcher instructed, handing the boy the reins.

Roy gladly accepted the responsibility and soon they were situating Fletcher's buggy next to Tessa and Katie's at the Weavers' house. As Fletcher was hitching the horse to the post, Aaron arrived.

"Looks like quite a gathering," Fletcher remarked, pulling a carrot from a sack he kept for the animal. "It should be a pleasant evening."

"*Jah*, provided Anna doesn't sicken anyone with her cooking tonight." Aaron laughed. "Although Katie Fisher probably eats the most, so she's in the greatest danger."

Fletcher didn't know whether Aaron's remarks were intended to be as derisive as they sounded or if they were only another misguided attempt at humor. "I wish you wouldn't talk about Anna or her friends like that. Or anyone else, for that matter," he said. "Some of your remarks aren't funny. They're unkind."

"If I'm so unkind and unfunny, why did Anna date me for almost three years?" Aaron asked as water dripped off the brim of his hat. Then he answered his own question. "She dated me because she liked me."

Surprised but undaunted by his cousin's bluster, Fletcher lifted his chin and straightened his posture. "And yet, she's marrying *me*," he said defiantly.

"Only because I chose to walk out with Melinda instead," Aaron challenged. He patted his horse on the flank before adding, "And whether or not Anna marries you is yet to be seen." Then he strode toward the house.

Fletcher removed his hat and looked toward the sky, allowing the rain to cool both his skin and his temper before he joined the others inside. *Please, Lord, forgive me my anger. Give me patience and bless our fellowship tonight.*

"*Denki*, Naomi, for having me over again," he said after he'd removed his muddy boots and was standing in the kitchen.

"This is all Anna's doing," Naomi explained, "but you're always *wilkom*, Fletcher."

As Anna glided into the room, he noticed her eyes were luminous and her creamy complexion was tinged with pink. He sensed something about her had changed. Rather, something was very much the same as it used to be. He didn't know exactly what it was, but the width of her smile was accentuated by the sincerity of her tone when she said, "Hello, Fletcher. I'm very glad to see you again."

After they were seated, said grace and filled their

plates with creamed chicken, noodles and chow chow, Katie complimented Anna. "This chicken is so yummy. You've done something different with the recipe, haven't you?"

To Fletcher's consternation, Aaron butted in, spouting, "*Jah*, she left all of the poisonous ingredients out this time."

Before Fletcher could defend Anna, she was gripped with paroxysms of laughter and then Eli and Evan were, too. Their laughter was so infectious it wasn't long before Katie and Tessa were clutching their sides, although they had no idea why, so Anna recounted the incident, with the younger boys performing an exaggerated re-enactment that included Fletcher's eyes bulging before he fainted to the floor, gasping for air.

Whether Anna realized it or not, her ability to turn something that was intended as a barb into a source of amusement was one of her former qualities he deeply appreciated, and Fletcher chuckled in spite of himself. The rest of the meal was also accentuated by spirited conversation and peals of laughter. Afterward, Katie and Tessa cleared the dishes from the table while Anna prepared the dessert.

"Okay, now, Evan," she said to her youngest brother, who dimmed the lamp.

Fletcher didn't understand why until Anna turned from the counter balancing a large cake aglow with candles. *She looks so pretty*, he thought. *But I wonder whose birthday it is.*

"Happy birthday to you," Katie started to sing.

Although he didn't know who they were singing to, Fletcher joined the others. He was surprised when Anna hovered near his shoulder and everyone sang, "Happy birthday, dear Fletcher, happy birthday to you."

"Denki," he said hesitantly when she placed the cake in front of him. He didn't want to embarrass her in front of everyone by telling her it wasn't his birthday.

"Make a wish and then blow them out," she instructed merrily.

As soon as he extinguished the candles, everyone burst into applause. When Naomi turned up the lamp again, he noticed the cake Anna had prepared was his favorite: turtle cake, a gooey, melt-in-your-mouth chocolate cake that included pecans, chocolate chips and caramel.

"This is a *wunderbaar* celebration!" he said, "I haven't had turtle cake since—"

"Since I made one for your actual birthday in October and you were carrying it and you tripped. We both ended up wearing it instead of eating it," Anna said, her eyes gleaming.

"That's right. You were so—" Fletcher began to speak but his mouth dropped open midsentence. "Anna! You remembered?"

She nodded and his heart palpitated. He was torn between feelings of absolute jubilance that Anna might begin to remember their courtship and utter despondency that she might also recall her hesitance to marry him.

"Stop catching flies," Aaron ribbed him. "Don't you have anything to say?"

"You remembered?" he asked again, quieter this time, staring into Anna's eyes.

"I remembered," she confirmed. "I still can't recall anything else from the past six months, but I definitely remember your last birthday."

"Are we going to get a piece of cake before his *next* birthday?" Roy interrupted and the others all laughed.

While they were devouring their cake, Fletcher's mind reeled. He could hardly concentrate on the anecdote Anna was sharing about his birthday picnic mishap, which kept everyone in stitches, especially when she got to the part about trying to salvage the cake from the puddle it landed in.

"I guess that's why they call it *turtle* cake," Evan punned.

"They're going to call *you* a turtle at school tomorrow if you stay up much later," Naomi said. "*Kumme*, it's time for you and Eli to get ready for bed."

Since Anna refused Tessa's and Katie's help with the remaining dishes, they bid their goodbyes. To Fletcher's surprise, Aaron gamely offered to walk them to their buggy.

"I'll *kumme*, too, since I have a flashlight," Melinda chimed in and followed them out the door.

As Fletcher was lacing his boots in the mudroom, Anna brought him the remainder of the turtle cake, which she had secured in waxed paper for him to take home.

"*Denki*, I will savor this," he said, although eating was the last thing on his mind.

"There's something else." She handed him a small package wrapped in bright green cellophane. "What's a birthday party without a present?"

He untied the silver bow and pulled out a round jar with a black top. "Honey and oatmeal salve," he read. "This is something I definitely need."

"It's the kind my *daed* always used. I noticed your hands are a bit dry, too. *Daed* often said if the floors he installed cracked as badly as his skin, he'd be out of work," she quoted. "Here, try it."

She unscrewed the lid and dipped her finger into the salve. After applying it to the back of his hand, she began caressing it into his skin in gentle circles. "Doesn't that feel better?" she asked, reaching for the jar again.

Agitated by her news and fearful she'd notice his hand shaking, Fletcher pulled away, saying, "*Denki*, but it's getting late. I should go."

"Oh, okay," she said, quickly wiping her fingers on her apron.

The pained, perplexed look that crossed Anna's face rivaled Fletcher's aching inner turmoil. In bed that night, he shifted his body from side to side as his mind leaped from one thought to another. How long before Anna recalled what she meant by her note? Should he tell her about it before she remembered, or would that only upset her? And what about him? Could he really bear to know the truth, now that the past was no longer past?

Chapter Seven

On Thursday morning, Anna lay in bed, thinking about the previous evening. As euphoric as she was that her memories were starting to return, she simultaneously felt let down by Fletcher's subdued reaction. In response to her news, she had imagined a scenario in which he would have picked her up, twirled her around and declared there was no better "birthday" gift he could have received than having her memory come back. Instead, he hardly uttered a word about it and he noticeably flinched when she later took his hand in hers to soften it with salve.

Wasn't he a physically demonstrative person? Try as she did to recall, she couldn't summon any recollection of the two of them holding hands or embracing before her accident. After her accident, he'd occasionally offered his hand or arm to steady her, but not as a spontaneous gesture of affection. Perhaps his reticence was simply part of his personality. Or was he upset by something else? Had she done something to perturb him? Was he taken aback that she shared the story of his original birthday party with everyone else?

There was only one way to find out: talk to him. He'd indicated he wanted them to be open with each other, didn't he? That was her desire, too. Anna quickly rose, donned her *kapp* and thanked the Lord for the memory He'd restored and for those yet to come. Then she finished dressing, made her bed and tiptoed out of the room in order not to wake Melinda.

After making oatmeal with raisins for her brothers, she scribbled a quick note for Raymond to deliver to Fletcher. *My dear Fletcher*, she began, but then she feared he might think it sounded too coquettish. She ripped up the paper and started again. *Fletcher, will you join us for supper at six o'clock? There's something I'd like to discuss with you. —Anna.*

Aaron had arranged to pick Roy and Raymond up that morning, and as soon as his buggy departed the lane, Eli and Evan entered the kitchen.

"Eggs, oatmeal, or cinnamon raisin French toast, boys?" she asked them.

"French toast, please!" they chorused.

"How did I know?" Anna chuckled as she sliced the loaf of bread Naomi made the day before.

The boys sat quietly at the table, rubbing their eyes and chatting with Anna as she made their breakfast. She was glad her stepmother was catching a few extra minutes of sleep; she always relished spending time alone with Eli and Evan. When they were younger, she used to pretend they were her children, not Naomi's, and she suddenly realized how quickly they were growing and how much she'd miss their familiar childish expressions and antics.

"Have you remembered anything else, Anna?" Evan asked, stifling a yawn.

"*Neh*, not yet. But I trust it won't be long until everything returns to me, so if you've done anything naughty in the past six months that I never found out about, don't think you've gotten away with it!" she joked, kissing the tops of their blond heads as she reached over them to set the platter of French toast on the table.

"Don't worry," Evan said, shaking his head vigorously. "*Mamm* already reprimanded me for anything I did that I shouldn't have done!"

Anna had to pinch the skin on her wrist to keep from laughing so she could say grace. After she lifted her head, she picked up the serving fork and asked, "How many slices would you like, Eli?"

"I'm… I'm not hungry," Eli whimpered. "My stomach hurts."

"Your stomach hurts?" Naomi sounded alarmed as she entered the kitchen. Placing a hand on Eli's head, she said, "He doesn't seem hot to me. What do you think, Anna?"

Anna felt his forehead and then slid her hand down to his cheek. "*Neh*, he's not warm. But if you think he should stay home from school, I could—"

"I don't want to stay home from school," Eli insisted. "I'm just not hungry. May I be excused from the table?"

"Of course," Anna said. "Why don't you go lie down on the sofa and I'll fill a hot water bottle for your tummy? Evan and I will do your morning chores for you before school starts—how's that?"

"*Gut*," the boy replied, shuffling out of the room.

"If he's too sick to eat, may I have his pieces of French toast?" Evan asked.

"*Neh*, we don't want you getting a tummy ache, too," Anna replied. "But you may have *one* additional piece, since you'll need extra energy to help me with his chores."

"*Denki*, Anna!" Evan said, leaning over his plate.

"Why are you smiling like that?" Anna whispered to Naomi above Evan's head. "Is it because of his appetite?"

"*Neh*, it's because of your aptitude. You're going to make a *wunderbaar mamm*."

Anna couldn't keep the bliss from her voice when she replied, "That's because I had you as my example."

"Some example I am—I almost slept as late as Melinda did today!" Naomi pointed to the window. "It's cloudy, but it's supposed to be warm again. I think I'll take advantage of the weather and begin some gardening today."

"While you're doing that, I'll wash the windows," Anna suggested.

"I don't know if that's wise. Did Dr. Donovan say it's okay to resume strenuous activities?"

"It's hardly strenuous. In fact, it gives my brain time to wander and that's when the memories seem likely to return."

Naomi reluctantly approved. "Well, the windows do need cleaning. I suppose if you take breaks, it might be alright. It will also give me time to work on preparing bedding arrangements for our guests' *kinner*. I'm thinking of putting all the boys on the second floor. Do you think it's warm enough for the girls to sleep in the attic room next to yours?"

"It will be if they're all tucked in side by side," Anna said.

Naomi's question reminded Anna that she needed to retrieve her new material from the other side of the attic and store it in her closet. She'd been helping Melinda with her dress so frequently that she hadn't taken her own fabric out of its wrapping, except to discreetly give Katie and Tessa their share of the material the evening before. Because she didn't want Naomi to hear her talk about sewing, Anna hadn't had the chance to ask her friends if they wanted to schedule a sister day to work on their dresses. Worried about whether they'd finish them on time, Anna thought, *Katie's a terrible procrastinator. A day before* Grischtdaag, *she still didn't even know what gifts she was going to give to her* mamm *and* daed.

It took a moment for Anna to realize she'd recalled another memory, and when she did, she was nearly as ecstatic as when it happened the first time. Throughout the day, additional remnants of the previous six months flitted through her mind. Her recollections were random and relatively minor—she recalled quilting with other women from the church, wading with the boys at the creek and the day an *Englisch* customer inquired about purchasing a dozen *kapps* in the shop. Many of the memories were fragmented and some were hazier than others, but there was no doubt her recollections were authentic, since no one had given her any hint about the events she recalled. She was so invigorated that she breezed through washing all of the windows in the house.

She was wringing out her rag after wiping the final pane when Evan and Eli returned from school and Melinda from the shop. Shortly afterward, as Anna was peeling potatoes for supper, she heard a buggy in the lane and had to restrain herself from throwing open the door to greet Fletcher. But it was Aaron who walked in with Roy. A minute later, Raymond followed, bearing a return message for her.

Anna, Fletcher wrote at the bottom of her own note to him, *I have to work late tonight and again tomorrow installing trim. Perhaps I can see you on Saturday? —Fletcher.*

Her eyes stung as she reread the note. Fletcher had told her how eager he was to complete the remaining trim for their first customer, so she understood why he needed to work late, but she was disappointed his message didn't contain so much as a jot of endearment or tittle of appreciation for the invitation. She supposed he could have simply been in a rush when he replied, but again she wondered if he was displeased with her. Or could it be he was tiring of eating at Naomi's with Anna's entire family?

Not knowing what to think, Anna penned a simple response under Fletcher's signature: *I'll be doing housework and gardening, so I should be home if you stop by on Saturday.* There wasn't room left on the page for her full name, so she merely scrawled her first initial.

There, she thought. *That doesn't sound the least bit cloying, so he shouldn't feel obligated to visit.* But deep down, she hoped by Saturday afternoon Fletcher would be as eager to see her as she was to see him.

Fletcher couldn't shake his apprehension that any second now, Anna would recall whatever it was that had caused her to write the note on the day of her accident. He felt as if his temples were being compressed by a vise, and his persistent nausea was exacerbated by the messages Raymond delivered. The first one, which read, *there's something I'd like to discuss with you,* was reminiscent of her preaccident note, *I have a serious concern regarding A. that I must discuss privately with you.* The chilly tone of her second inscription further heightened his jitters.

He was actually relieved to have a valid excuse for turning down her supper invitation: the trim had finally been delivered for the first project and he wanted to hang it as soon as possible. Aaron wouldn't release him from the second customer's site during the day, claiming the trim could wait another week. As a matter of providing good service, however, Fletcher assured the first customer he'd hang the trim after hours, completing it by Friday evening.

By Saturday morning, however, Fletcher was so sleep-deprived, miserable and beside himself with agitation, he could hardly wait to talk to Anna about the topic he'd been dreading for so long. As devastating as he anticipated their discussion would be, he knew it was better to face the truth than to suffer the agony of waiting for the issue to come to light.

Bleary-eyed, he whacked his thumb with his hammer, a carelessness even Roy hadn't demonstrated after his first month on the job.

"Ouch!" he yelled and flung the hammer to the floor.

"You need ice?" Raymond asked.

"I need air," Fletcher responded, heading out the door.

In the parking lot, he paced in circles, trying to shake off the pain. When it didn't subside, he took a short jaunt to the corner store to purchase three cups of coffee and what passed for glazed doughnuts in the *Englisch* community. Upon returning, he crossed paths with

Aaron, who had just arrived to work and was hitching his horse.

"Where have you been?" Aaron asked.

Fletcher held up the tray of coffee to indicate his response. "Where have you been?" he asked in return.

"Not that I have to answer to you, but I was assessing another project," Aaron said. "I told you once before, if you're going to change your schedule, you need to let me know. You shouldn't leave Roy and Raymond unsupervised at the work site."

"I didn't change my schedule," Fletcher explained, thrown off by Aaron's tone. "I was gone all of five minutes."

"Don't let it happen again," Aaron warned before helping himself to a cup of coffee from the tray and strutting away.

Fletcher kicked at the dirt. The throbbing in his thumb was nothing compared to the pounding in his head. *Please* Gott, *give me grace,* he prayed. *The grace to deal with Aaron's attitude and the grace to accept whatever Anna has to say this afternoon.*

His morning progressed without further injury and Fletcher was pleasantly surprised when Isaiah arrived midmorning and took him aside to thank him for finishing the trim at the other customer's site. After his shift ended, Fletcher stopped at home to change his shirt before traveling to Anna's house. The closer he drew, the drier his mouth grew and by the time he pulled into the yard, he felt as if his tongue were made of wool.

"Fletcher!" Evan beckoned from behind a tree near where Fletcher hitched his horse. "Don't tell Anna you saw me—we're playing hide-and-seek."

"Too late, Evan," Anna said, creeping up from behind and tagging him on the shoulder. "You're it!"

"Aww, alright," Evan moaned. "Fletcher can play, too."

"*Neh*, Fletcher and I are going to take a walk to the creek, aren't we, Fletcher?"

"*Jah*," was all he could say.

Before ambling away, Anna instructed Evan, "After you find Eli, I'd like both of you to take that basket of laundry inside the house and wash your hands for dinner. Then ask your *mamm* if there's anything you can do to help her."

As she and Fletcher traipsed down the hilly field, they chatted about the spring birds they spotted, Fletcher's new project at work and Isaiah's visit to the site. Fletcher assumed Anna was stalling until they arrived at the creek before discussing her note, and with each step he felt as if he wore cinder blocks strapped to his feet.

When they reached the embankment, he viewed the rushing water and remembered a saying his sister Leah often quoted, "If the river had no rocks, it would not have a song."

"What?" Anna questioned.

Fletcher didn't realize he'd spoken aloud. "Oh, that's a proverb my sister often says. I think it means you can't have something beautiful without also having some rocky, difficult patches."

"That's true," Anna said, thoughtfully furrowing her brow.

Unable to endure the suspense any longer, Fletcher blurted out, "You mentioned there was something you wanted to speak with me about. What is it?"

Anna shuffled backward. "Let's sit," she said and

they positioned themselves next to each other on a large boulder overlooking the water. "It's…it's uncomfortable to discuss this."

Fletcher licked his lips and forged ahead. "Whatever it is, it's better that we're open with each other about it."

"I guess I… I was disappointed by your reaction the other night when I told you my memory had begun to return. I thought you would have been happier," Anna confessed. "I thought you would have been thrilled, actually. When you weren't, I wondered why not. I wondered if I'd done something to upset you."

Fletcher closed his eyes as he absorbed the realization that Anna still didn't recall writing her original note. For a split second, he considered not telling her about his concern, but he knew he'd only be prolonging the inevitable. Besides, it had become too big of a burden for him to bear even a second longer.

"You're right, Anna. I probably didn't seem as excited as I should have been," he intoned. "That's because there's something about the past I've wanted to discuss with you, but I couldn't because Dr. Donovan warned us it would be detrimental to your health if you became too upset or if you felt too pressured to recall your memories before your brain had a chance to heal. But it's been weighing heavily on my mind and I can't keep it to myself any longer, especially since it affects our wedding."

Anna gasped and pressed a hand to her mouth before asking, "What is it?"

"It's this," he said, removing the slip of paper from his coat and shoving it into her hand.

She unfolded the note and read it aloud. "'Fletcher, I have a serious concern regarding A. that I must discuss privately with you before the wedding preparations go any further. Please visit me tonight after work. —Anna.'"

Then she read it again to herself. Finally, she said, "It's sloppier than usual, but it's definitely my handwriting. When did I give you this?"

"You sent it with Raymond the morning of your accident."

"Really? I'm sorry, but I have no recollection of what I wanted to talk to you about."

"I believe the A. stands for Aaron."

"Aaron? What does he have to do with our wedding preparations? He hasn't lifted a finger to help as far as I can tell, has he?"

"Neh." Fletcher grimaced. It was clear he was going to have to spell it out for Anna and his stomach lurched as he formed the words. "I believe you meant... You meant you had second thoughts about how you felt about him, so you had second thoughts about marrying me."

Anna hooted, "That's absurd!" She leaped up and twirled to face him with her hands on her hips. "How could you believe such a thing, especially after all the conversations we've had?"

"I don't want to believe it, but it's possible something happened immediately before the accident that caused you to change your mind about how you felt about Aaron and you just can't remember it."

"I might not remember all of what *happened* in the past six months, but I remember how I *felt* ever since breaking up with Aaron," Anna insisted, smacking the back of one hand against the palm of the other. "My *feelings* haven't changed! My *preferences* haven't changed. It's like... It's like lima beans. I didn't like them before my accident and I still don't like them after my accident. I tolerate them because it's rude not to when they're served as part of my family's meal, but do I suddenly like them? Have I changed my mind about loving them? *Neh*, never."

Put in those terms, Fletcher's worries about Aaron suddenly seemed absolutely ridiculous and he felt like the biggest *dummkopf* who ever lived. Yet he still couldn't quite dismiss Anna's note.

"Then how do you explain what you meant by having 'a serious concern regarding A.'?" Fletcher pressed.

Anna sat down beside him again. "Well, I could have meant any number of things," she said, counting on her fingers. "A. could stand for Amos, as in Bishop Amos. Or maybe it was short for April? Perhaps I wanted to change the date from April to March. Or possibly it stood for attendance—the list of people invited. Could I have meant arrangements? Naomi has been fretting over where the *kinner* will sleep. Perhaps I thought—"

"Okay, okay, you can stop now!" Fletcher laughed, holding up his hands. A blush crept over his face as he looked into her eyes. "I clearly let my imagination get the best of me. I don't know what to say except I'm very sorry."

Anna understood: given his history with Joyce, it wasn't any wonder he'd jumped to the wrong conclusions about the context of her note. "You're forgiven," she promised. "I'm just relieved I didn't do anything at the party to offend you."

In response, Fletcher slid his fingers between Anna's as if into a glove, sending a tingle up her arm and dispelling her concern that he wasn't a physically affectionate person.

"Somebody has been using the salve I gave him," she noticed.

"*Jah*. It's working well and it smells *gut*, too."

"You hurt yourself though," she said, indicating his thumbnail. "Poor aim?"

"Poor concentration. I was thinking about a certain *maedel*."

"I've been thinking about you a lot, too, Fletcher. As difficult as it was, I'm glad we had this discussion."

"If the river had no rocks, it would not have a song," he quoted as he picked up a stone and tossed it into the creek.

She crumpled the note into a ball and cast it into the current, as well. "For the birds to make a nest," she said and tugged at his fingers. "Now *kumme*, let's go have dinner before my brothers eat it all."

They dropped hands before entering the kitchen, where Naomi had set a place for Fletcher.

"You're just in time for grace," she remarked warmly.

After thanking the Lord for their food and other blessings, Fletcher said to Naomi, "I hope I'm just in time to help Roy and Raymond with any house repair or yard projects you'd like finished before the wedding, too."

Anna's pulse skittered at his reference to their upcoming wedding. Although she still wasn't positive their pending nuptials would occur as scheduled, with every interaction they shared, she was growing more confident he was the husband God had provided for her.

"*Denki*, that would be appreciated," Naomi said. "There's a fence post in the yard Roy and Raymond are having trouble setting and I'd like your opinion on the window in the attic. It feels drafty up there and I don't want our guests' *kinner* to catch a chill."

"I noticed a loose floorboard in the mudroom, too," Fletcher commented. "The boys and I may also have to take a look at the porch stairs."

The three young men clomped into the mudroom. Eli and Evan were tasked with helping Naomi till the soil for her gardens while Anna focused on scrubbing the floors. In deference to Dr. Donovan's advice, she stopped short of beating the rugs herself, instead hanging them so Melinda could complete the task later that afternoon. The day took on a festive air and by the time the group stopped for supper, they'd accomplished more than they'd set out to.

"If it's alright with you, Anna, I'd like to take you for a ride after supper," Fletcher said over dessert.

"Not so fast." Naomi waved a finger at him, "You still need to address the draft in the attic."

"Of course," Fletcher agreed. "I meant after that."

"Why the disappointed expression? You're being let off easy," his future mother-in-law teased. She turned to her sons. "When your *daed* was keen on me, he volunteered to help your *groossdaadi* build an entire house just for the chance to say hello to me when I came out with a pitcher of water."

Anna fidgeted in her chair and glanced at Fletcher, who was studiously focused on scraping the ice cream from his bowl. Nothing escaped Naomi's notice.

"There's no need to be embarrassed, you two. It would serve most couples well to remember after they're married how eager they were to spend time in each other's company before they wed." Naomi sighed, wiping the corner of her eye. "Time spent with those we love is one of *Gott*'s most precious gifts. We ought to value it more dearly because it passes so quickly."

"Mamm," Evan whined, "the last time Melinda and Aaron mentioned mushy grown-up love talk at the table, you said my ears were too young to hear that kind of thing."

The others joined Naomi in laughter. "That's right," she said, patting his head. "How about if we talk about turtles instead?"

By the time Anna finished washing and putting away the dishes and Fletcher and the boys installed insulation and repaired the window in the attic, it was dusk.

"Why don't we have a cup of tea on the porch instead of going for a ride?" Anna suggested.

They sat side by side on the swing, gently swaying as they chatted. The rhythmic motion lulled Anna into a deep sense of relaxation, and she rested her head against Fletcher's shoulder. Lowering her lids, she imagined the two of them spending evenings like this on the porch of their own house. She could picture their children romping on the front lawn and in her imagination they all had Fletcher's lustrous wavy hair and intense blue eyes.

"Are you tired?" he asked.

"Neh, I'm peaceful," she replied. "In fact, I haven't felt this peaceful in a long time."

"That's too bad," Fletcher said. "Because there's something I want to show you, but you'll have to get up and *kumme* with me."

He took her by the hand, caressing her icy fingers to warm them as they made their way to the expansive maple in the backyard. Its branches appeared black against the ebbing light of the sky, which was beginning to glisten with early stars.

Anna tittered when they stopped beneath its mighty boughs. "Did we argue under this tree, too, as we did when we first met beneath the willow?"

"Hardly," Fletcher replied and his voice sounded gravelly. "You really don't remember what happened here?"

Noticing his impassioned tone, she paused, wishing she could claim every second of their courtship was etched indelibly across her heart. "I'm sorry, Fletcher," she admitted, "but I don't."

Fletcher reached for Anna's shoulders, gently positioning her against the trunk. "Well, you were standing like this. And I was leaning with my hand here, above you. Your hair was dappled with bits of light and your eyes mirrored the greenery all around us."

Fletcher gently touched Anna's cheek with the back of his hand, remembering.

"What happened next?" she whispered.

"May I show you?"

"You may."

He leaned toward her for a soft kiss.

After a quiet pause, he had to know if she experienced the same depth of emotion he felt. "Now do you remember?" he asked.

"I may not remember the first time," Anna spoke slowly, "but I won't forget this time."

Fletcher's heart pranced. It wasn't exactly the answer he'd hoped to hear, but it was the next best thing.

"Evan would be disappointed to hear you couldn't remember the first time," he joked, leading her back toward the house.

"Evan?"

"*Jah.* You and I were sharing our first kiss when you were supposed to be watching Timothy the Turtle. That's how he wandered away."

Anna's laughter rang out through the darkness. "That's terrible!"

Terrible for Timothy, but wunderbaar *for me*, Fletcher thought as he ambled up the steps to accompany Anna to the door. "I suppose it's time to say *gut nacht*."

"Could you please help me find the teacups, first?" Anna requested. "It's gotten dark and I'm not sure I'll be able to see where we set them."

As they cautiously advanced toward the front of the porch, Fletcher abruptly stopped, realizing there was someone sitting in the swing.

"I don't know what Naomi's so upset about," Melinda was saying. "I was only an hour or two late. She's such a worrywart. Besides, if we had arrived in time for supper, she wouldn't have asked you to stay, even though Fletcher was invited."

Fletcher coughed to signal Melinda he could hear her, while from behind, Anna loudly cut her short with, "Is that you, Melinda?"

"*Jah*, and I'm with her," Aaron answered. "Where did the two of you *kumme* from?"

"We were taking a stroll. Enjoying the evening air," Anna responded curtly as she and Fletcher approached the other couple. They were still holding hands and if Fletcher wasn't mistaken, Anna tightened her grasp as she spoke.

"See what I mean?" Melinda continued, unabashed to have been caught complaining about them. "Naomi gives you and Fletcher her blessing to do whatever you want whenever you want. It's not fair."

"*Neh*, what's not fair, Melinda," Anna rebutted, "is that everyone in this household, including Fletcher, has been working all afternoon on house and yard projects that need to be completed before the weddings. Yet you didn't arrive home until after seven o'clock, even though your shift at Schrock's ended at four. If you want Aaron to be included at mealtime, the two of you ought to consider pitching in."

Melinda shifted in her seat and began to protest, but Anna wasn't finished speaking.

"As for Naomi being a worrywart, it's true," she said. "Naomi often frets when the people she *cares* about aren't home when they should be. In part that's because the last time someone other than you didn't return home on time was when I had my accident, and the time before that was when my *daed* died. So you—and Aaron—should think about what goes through Naomi's mind when you decide to amble home several hours after you're expected!"

Anna dropped Fletcher's hand as she stooped to pick up a teacup and saucer near the side of the swing. Fletcher retrieved the other cup and saucer from where Anna left it balanced on the railing and wordlessly followed her to the side door. When she turned to say good-night, Anna's hand was shaking so furiously that the cup rattled against the saucer. Fletcher took the china from her and stacked it with his on the bench beside them. He gingerly ran a finger beneath her chin, tilting her face upward. It was too dark to read the expression in her eyes, but he felt the wetness of a tear moisten his skin.

"Anna," he whispered. "This evening has been too special to allow anything to spoil it."

"I know it has and it still is." She sniffed. "But there

are still many memories about our courtship I hope will
return to me, so I don't want Melinda's rude comments
about your presence here to keep you from visiting me
as often as possible in the next two and a half weeks
before the wedding."

"Are you joking? Wild horses couldn't keep me
away!"

"Do you promise?" Anna asked.

"I promise and I'll even seal it with a kiss," Fletcher
pledged, bending to brush his lips against hers.

On the way home, he marveled over the amount of
time he'd spent anguishing over Anna's note, when he
could have spoken to her about it earlier and allevi-
ated his fears. Even if she still couldn't say for certain
what she meant by her message, her guesses seemed
more likely than the assumption he'd made. He belat-
edly reckoned his experience with Joyce had colored
his perception, but he wasn't going to allow it to cast a
shadow on his relationship with Anna any longer. No,
after their conversation—and their kisses—this evening, Fletcher was thoroughly convinced she carried a
torch for him and him alone.

"*Denki*, Lord!" he prayed aloud as his horse trotted
through the night. "*Denki* for Your grace and good-
ness toward Anna and me, by providing us for each
other and by keeping my foolishness from destroying
our relationship."

In light of his conversation with Anna, any misgivings he'd felt toward his cousin dissolved completely
and soon he was asking God to bless Aaron's marriage
to Melinda, too. *The two of them seem to need all the
prayer and help they can get before becoming husband
and wife*, he mused.

But by the time Fletcher stretched out on his bed, Melinda and Aaron were far from his mind. His only thoughts were of Anna: Anna beneath the willow and Anna under the maple; Anna in sunlight and Anna in starlight; Anna then and Anna now. *Anna, Anna, Anna,* he mumbled drowsily before dozing off. *My bride-to-be.*

Chapter Eight

On Sunday morning, Anna sat bolt upright in bed, unsure whether the vision that just raced through her mind was a memory or a dream. In it, Fletcher had just kissed her and she was filled with repulsion. The images were fuzzy, but the way they made her feel was undeniably clear and Anna shuddered violently.

"What's wrong with you?" Melinda muttered, squinting one eye at her.

"I had a nightmare, that's all," Anna replied.

Melinda rolled over and pulled the quilt up to her ears, but Anna got up, made her bed and dressed and then padded downstairs to begin making breakfast before the family held their home church services. She was cubing potatoes for breakfast when the image of kissing Fletcher crossed her mind again, except this time she recalled his hands gripping her shoulders as well as the breeze lifting his dark, wavy hair when he pulled her toward him for an emphatic kiss.

Disconcerted that the dream played itself out in her waking moments, Anna sat down at the table and covered her eyes with her hand. *I must be overly tired*, she thought. *My mind is playing tricks on me.*

"Are you okay?" Eli cheeped, startling her.

She jumped up and said, "*Guder mariye*, Eli. *Jah*, I'm fine. I was just resting my eyes before I started making breakfast casserole. Look, I'm going to use bacon instead of sausage, the way you like it. I notice you haven't been eating a lot lately."

The boy's eyes brightened. "*Denki*, Anna. I'll go get the eggs from the henhouse."

Naomi was the next person awake. "That smells *gut* already, Anna. But you should allow me to make breakfast. I'll have to get used to cooking all our meals again once you move out."

"Mmm," Anna said noncommittally.

Naomi immediately panicked. "Uh-oh. Is something wrong? Did you and Fletcher decide not to carry through with your wedding? You were getting on so well yesterday."

Anna chuckled. "All I said was 'mmm.'"

"*Jah*, but it was the way you said it," insisted Naomi.

Eli burst into the kitchen with his basket of eggs. "*Guder mariye, Mamm,*" he greeted Naomi. "Anna's putting bacon in the casserole instead of sausage."

"Just the way somebody in this family likes it, but I can't remember who," Naomi teased.

"Me!" Eli cheered.

"I guess your sister has a better memory than I do," Naomi said. "She must have decided to make it specially tailored for you, because you're the first one up. Now please go wake everyone else—without shouting."

After Eli dashed out of the room, Anna replied to her stepmother's earlier question. "Nothing went wrong between Fletcher and me. In fact, yesterday was one of the best days we've had together yet."

"But?" Naomi asked, setting the plates around the table.

Anna sighed; Naomi was so perceptive. "But I guess I'd still like to remember more about our courtship and I'd still like to find my journal," she admitted. "I think that would allay any lingering qualms I might have."

Especially after this morning's nightmare, she thought.

"I can't make your memories return, although I'll continue to pray about that," Naomi offered. "As for your journal, we've practically turned the house inside out with our spring cleaning, so it seems we would have found it by now. Is it possible you stashed it in the stable?"

"I doubt it," Anna said, "although it's worth a look."

"Guder mariye," Roy, Raymond and Evan greeted the women before taking their seats.

"I couldn't get Melinda to wake up," Eli reported, wiggling onto a chair.

"She's probably tired because she was out on the porch late last night with Aaron," Evan commented knowingly.

"Evan, what did *Mamm* tell us about eavesdropping?" Eli chastised his younger brother.

"I wasn't eavesdropping," he insisted innocently. "The window was stuck open."

"Oh! I'm sorry," Anna quickly apologized. "I couldn't get it down again after I washed it. I hope you boys weren't too cold last night. Roy or Raymond, you should take a look at how it sits in the frame."

"See? That wasn't my fault so it doesn't count as

eavesdropping," Evan retorted to Eli. "Besides, I didn't even repeat that I heard Melinda asking Aaron if he was jellies because Fletcher is marrying Anna, not him. And Aaron said if he was jellies, would he do this, then she said to stop that because it tickles and then she kept laughing."

"Melinda didn't ask Aaron if he was jellies, Evan," Eli hotly refuted. "She asked him if he was *jealous*, but you still repeated gossip because you just told everyone."

"Boys!" Naomi squawked, clapping her hands sharply together once. That's all the reprimand they needed to stop talking.

No one else said a word, either, until Melinda sidled into the room. "It's so quiet in here, I thought maybe it wasn't an off-Sunday and you'd all left for church without me," she joked as she heaped casserole onto her plate.

After everyone had eaten their fill, Anna cleared the table, contemplating Evan's disclosure about the conversation he'd overheard. She knew Melinda had come up with some ludicrous theories in her time, but this one took the cake. If Aaron was envious of Fletcher, it was because of Fletcher's inherent character and his superior abilities—it had nothing to do with Fletcher marrying Anna. Still, Anna hoped Melinda and Aaron had resolved the issue; the last thing she wanted was more tension between her and her cousin. Anna felt bad enough about her strong words from the previous night as it was.

Once they finished worshipping together, Evan asked if Anna would accompany him and Eli to the stream.

"Why not?" she asked, eager to lighten the mood after their morning squabble.

"Watch yourselves around the rocks," Naomi cautioned, waving goodbye.

The trio spritely marched through the dewy grass, down the hill and across the meadow. Once they arrived at the creek, Anna alighted on the boulder nearest the willow. Due to the spring rains, the creek's current was moving swiftly and she kept a close eye on the boys as they attempted to chuck stones across to the opposite bank. She was thinking about how the willow's lengthy fringe dancing in the breeze reminded her of a woman's long hair, when she was struck with another memory like the one that had afflicted her earlier that morning.

In the recollection, Fletcher stood not five feet from where Evan was now pitching a rock into the rushing water. He had just kissed her and she was trying to secure her prayer *kapp* over her hair, which had become mussed when she jerked away from him. She recalled that they had argued and she was crying. As the scant details manifested in her mind's eye, Anna's knees trembled and she began to pant, trying to catch her breath.

"Boys," she weakly summoned them. "It's time to go. *Kumme*, take my hands, please. I'm not feeling quite right."

They steadied her up the hill and delivered her into Naomi's care.

"You're as pale as a sheet and shaking like a leaf," Naomi fretted. "I never should have permitted you to do so much last week. I'm sending Raymond to the phone shanty to call Dr. Donovan."

"*Neh*, please don't," Anna argued feebly as her teeth

chattered. "I j-just need to get warm. It was nippy near the creek. Dr. Donovan's office is probably closed for the weekend anyway."

Naomi scrutinized Anna's face. Finally, she allowed, "I'll put on a pot of tea and Melinda will draw you a bath. We'll see how you're doing after that. But if I suspect so much as a hint of a fever, I'll have Raymond bring us to the hospital straightaway."

Although she couldn't stomach the tea and toast Naomi prepared for her, Anna stopped shaking after taking a bath. At her stepmother's insistence, she nestled into Naomi's bed, where Naomi swaddled her in quilts and set a bell at her side to ring if she needed assistance. But Anna only wanted to be alone, and once she was, she wept into her arms, wishing she could forget the very memories she'd been praying so fervently to recall.

When Fletcher arrived at Anna's house on Sunday afternoon, Naomi greeted him at the door. Her skin was wan and her eyes were bloodshot. "*Guder nammidaag*, Fletcher. I'm afraid I can't invite you in. Anna has taken ill and Eli is sick, too. I don't want you to catch whatever is plaguing our household."

Fletcher's heart raced. Anna was ill? But at least it couldn't have been related to her concussion, since Eli was also sick, right? "Is there something I can do to help?" he asked.

"*Neh.* Neither one of them has a fever. And although Eli's had terrible stomach pains, they seem to have subsided. Right now I think rest is the best thing for both of them."

"May I call on Anna this evening?" Fletcher asked.

"*Neh,*" Naomi responded sharply before softening

her tone. "I'm sorry, Fletcher, but I fear it was my fault she overdid it last week, which is why she's sick now, so I have to put my foot down. I'll be sure to tell her you asked after her and wanted to see her, but I wouldn't allow it."

"But—"

"If you don't want her to risk having to return to the hospital, you'll support her recovery by allowing her to rest," Naomi reiterated firmly.

Fletcher couldn't argue with Naomi's logic, so he reluctantly returned home. Once there, he found himself at a loss for things to do. He'd already spent the morning in worship with his uncle's family, and usually Anna and her brothers were the only people he visited during off-Sundays. Since moving to Willow Creek, he'd been befriended by a few of the older men in the district, but he didn't feel comfortable dropping in on them and their families uninvited.

Since it was the Sabbath, all but the most essential work was prohibited. As it was, he'd already completed everything except painting the alcove he'd created for Anna, and he routinely kept up the stable and yard. In regard to the house's interior, it was tidy, but he realized it definitely needed a woman's touch. *Soon enough*, he thought as he sat down in the parlor.

He read Scripture for an hour and then enjoyed a long nap. When he awoke, he decided to write his sisters, as he was long overdue in replying to their letter.

Dear Esther, Leah, Rebekah & Families,
I hope this note finds everyone healthy. Thank you for your good wishes and faithful prayers, as expressed in your last letter. I am sorry for

my delay in responding. I'm afraid I've been distracted because Anna recently suffered a head injury that resulted in substantial memory loss. Rest assured, she is recovering well. Physically, she no longer suffers from the headaches or nausea she endured immediately following her fall, and her recollections are also returning to her. Still, I covet your prayers for her complete healing.

I look forward to hearing all about what has been happening in your lives when we talk in person at the wedding, if not by letter before then.

Until then, may the Lord bless you.
—Fletcher.

After he affixed a stamp to the envelope, Fletcher carried the letter to the mailbox for the carrier to pick up the following day. When he unlatched the door to the box, a flurry of envelopes fluttered to the ground and he snorted to realize it must have been days since he'd retrieved the mail; clearly he valued the notes Raymond delivered much more than those the carrier brought. Most of the spilled items were advertisements and bills, but one was a personal letter written in a hand he didn't immediately recognize. Tearing it open as he walked, he read:

Fletcher,
I've heard the news that you are soon to be wed and I hope you will accept my sincere congratulations. I also hope you will permit me this belated apology for the anguish I caused. Whether you believe me or not, I didn't deliberately intend to deceive you. I honestly didn't know my own heart.

That is, I honestly didn't fully comprehend how
I felt about Frederick until it was almost too late.

For both of our sakes, I'm grateful you and I
didn't marry and I trust you are even more grateful than I. In any case, I pray for you all of the
love and happiness you so richly deserve. May the
Lord bless your marriage abundantly.
Joyce Wittmer.

Fletcher stopped in his tracks and reread the note.
On one hand, he was appalled that Joyce had the nerve
to write him—especially because she said how grateful she was they hadn't gotten married! On the other
hand, she was right: he was even more grateful than she
was. If it hadn't been for Joyce calling off their wedding, Fletcher never would have discovered what true
love was, because he wouldn't have moved to Willow
Creek and met Anna. As for forgiving Joyce, he'd done
that long ago, even if he occasionally battled leftover
feelings related to their breakup. But Fletcher accepted
her apology for what it was: an earnest expression of
contrition.

When he got inside, he crumpled up the note and
threw it in the woodstove. It was a reminder of old
hurts that belonged to the past. He was looking ahead
now, to his future with Anna. As he stirred a pot of
canned soup for supper, he thought about the tender
kisses they'd shared the day before, and he imagined
those they'd exchange in the future; perhaps even as
soon as tomorrow. He ate quickly and, despite having
taken a nap, he turned in to bed early, hoping to hasten
the arrival of a new day.

Instead, he slept fitfully and the night seemed to

stretch on twice as long as usual. As he listlessly twisted this way and that, a single unbidden thought came to mind: *What if* Anna *doesn't know her own heart, either?* He dismissed the idea almost the second he thought it, chalking it up to his thwarted longing to see her again. But his restlessness kept him awake for hours, until he finally decided to dress and go to work, arriving well before the break of dawn.

He was surprised when Roy and Raymond walked in carrying a battery-powered nail gun and drill less than a half an hour after sunrise.

"Guder mariye," Fletcher said. He barely waited for a reply before asking, "How's Anna?"

"I think she's alright," Roy replied. "*Mamm* took her some broth last night and she finished it all."

"But there's no note for you," Raymond said, anticipating Fletcher's question. "She was still sleeping when we left."

Although his hope was deflated, Fletcher responded, "That's okay. I'm sure I'll speak to her tonight. Do you two need a hand carrying in more tools?"

"Neh, there's only one more load. We've got it," Raymond replied as the brothers exited and Aaron entered.

He looked startled to see Fletcher. "What time did you get here?"

"An hour and a half ago," Fletcher replied.

"Why are you always doing that?" Aaron challenged him, setting down the portable table saw with a loud clatter.

"Doing what?" Fletcher had no idea what the problem was.

"You've always got to show me up. Staying later, coming in earlier. What are you trying to prove?"

"Aaron, I'm *helping* you, not *competing* with you," Fletcher argued.

"Well, don't think just because you came in early you're going to leave early. The entire reason I'm here now is because we've got to finish up this floor today. I took another contract that starts tomorrow morning."

Fletcher resisted the urge to ask Aaron why he accepted another simultaneous project when they clearly weren't finished with this one. He could tell his cousin was tense enough as it was, so instead, Fletcher channeled his frustration into performing his work, motivating himself with the fact that the sooner they finished, the sooner he'd get to see Anna again.

On Monday, Anna lingered in bed. After Sunday's long nap and a good night's rest, her quivering had stopped, but she kept her eyes closed, trying to convince herself that yesterday's recurrent unpleasant memory of kissing Fletcher was only a dream. Yet deep down she knew sooner or later, she'd have to ask for Fletcher's help in making sense of the awful image that kept coming to mind. He'd told her he didn't want her to hide anything from him, didn't he? But what would she say? How could she tell him, "I have a vague recollection of kissing you at the creek and being wholly repulsed"? After his vulnerable confession the other day, she didn't want to shake his confidence about her feelings for him.

"Are you still asleep or are you just pretending so you won't have to make breakfast?" Melinda whispered.

"Neither," Anna said, raising her lids. "I'm awake but I'm not deliberately trying to get out of helping with breakfast. That would be irresponsible."

"Oh," Melinda said, seemingly deaf to Anna's reproach. "I was wondering, how far have you progressed with your wedding dress?"

"I've got considerable work to do," Anna responded vaguely, sitting up. Although she was certain she hadn't moved her wedding dress fabric from the other side of the attic, it was no longer there. For fear of being teased about her forgetfulness by her cousin, Anna didn't want to inquire if Melinda had moved it. "Why do you ask?"

"Well, since Naomi will likely confine you to our room today anyway, do you suppose you'd mind making some adjustments to the sleeves and hem on mine? Joseph has asked me to work extra hours at the shop and I don't see how I'll finish my dress unless you help me."

Anna felt like suggesting Melinda might try staying in instead of running around with Aaron every night. But since she knew her suggestion was futile, she reluctantly agreed. "Alright, try it on and let me see what needs to be done."

As her cousin was changing into the violet dress and she was making her bed, Anna asked, "So, Joseph wants you to work extra hours at the shop?"

"*Jah,* he even mentioned keeping me on after you return. Sales are up since I started working there," Melinda boasted as she climbed onto a stool so Anna could examine the hem.

Anna held pins pressed between her lips and she didn't reply.

"I think it's because I have a way with *Englisch* customers," Melinda babbled. "Tessa Fisher barely utters two words to them, so I think they appreciate having a chatty, comely Amish girl like me to approach— Ouch! You pricked me with that pin!"

"Did I?" Anna asked innocently. "Turn toward me, please."

"How do I look?" Melinda hinted.

"Crooked." Anna frowned, smoothing the hem.

"Not the dress—*me*," Melinda emphasized.

Anna took a step backward and tipped her head upward for a better look at the full dress. The color accentuated Melinda's dark hair and eyes, gathering modestly over the curves of her girlish figure. She would make a beautiful bride.

Anna answered honestly, "You look lovely, absolutely lovely." Which was exactly how Anna wanted to feel in her own wedding dress.

It's not fair, she thought in an instant of self-pity. *Why should Melinda get to experience such excitement about her wedding, when I've experienced little but anxiety about mine?*

"*Denki*," Melinda said, hopping down from the stool and twirling in a circle before giving Anna a hug. "*Denki* for everything, Anna. If it weren't for you, I wouldn't be getting married and I wouldn't have a job at the shop. In a way, it's almost a blessing you had a concussion."

Annoyed by Melinda's complete lack of sensitivity, Anna tugged her cousin's arms from around her neck. "Stop that," she snapped. "You're hurting me." *And I've been in pain for long enough as it is.*

After dressing, she made her way into the kitchen where she said good morning to Naomi and then asked, "Are Raymond and Roy out milking?"

"*Neh*, Aaron picked the boys up very early this morning. How do you feel today?"

"As strong as an ox," Anna claimed. She supposed it

was just as well the boys had left before she could send a note with Raymond, since she wasn't sure what to write to Fletcher anyway. She figured he'd come for supper and by then she would have collected her thoughts.

"Oh, am I ever relieved to hear that!" Naomi exclaimed. Then she said, "This morning, I'll be taking Evan to school and dropping Melinda off in town, and then I'm stopping at the phone shanty to make an appointment for Eli at the clinic in Highland Springs."

"The clinic in Highland Springs?" Anna repeated. The *Englisch*-run clinic offered pediatric care exclusively to members of the Amish community. "What's wrong with Eli?"

"He was sick to his stomach shortly after you returned from the creek. His cramps came and went all night, but he doesn't have a fever. I recall his stomach hurting him the other day, too, so I want to be sure there's nothing seriously wrong."

"That's a *gut* idea," Anna agreed. "I'll stay here with him now and then accompany you to his appointment when you get back."

As it turned out, Naomi couldn't schedule an appointment until four o'clock. She sat next to Anna in the front seat, while Eli curled up with a hot water bottle in the back. Once they arrived at the clinic, Naomi was softly reading aloud to her son when the disturbing image again troubled Anna's mind.

"I'm going to stretch my legs," she announced before ambling down the long corridor.

She was examining a colorful mural of barnyard animals when a voice behind her resounded, "Anna! What brings you to the children's clinic?"

She recognized his voice before she angled around

to greet him. "Hello, Dr. Donovan." She couldn't help but smile when speaking to the kind man. "My brother has a stomachache."

"Ah, we get a lot of those around here. I mean, our patients do. I volunteer here once a month," he explained. "Usually, the stomachaches are nothing serious. But what about you, how are you feeling?"

"I'm fine," Anna said, but to her dismay, her eyes unexpectedly spouted fat tears.

Dr. Donovan clasped her elbow, ushering her into an empty office, where he motioned for her to sit. Then he passed a box of tissues across the desk and clasped his hands over his belly while she blew her nose. "I take it your memories haven't returned then, eh?" he asked.

"Actually, they have. Not too many of Fletcher or our courtship, but plenty of other people and events."

"That's a good sign, yet you're not happy?"

"I'm... I'm frustrated. And confused," she confessed. "At first, my recollection of the past six months seemed as blank as a field of snow. Now when the memories come back, some of them remind me of scuffling along a winding path covered with fallen leaves. They're turned every which way and I can't make sense of them. I don't know what's a memory and what's a dream."

Dr. Donovan bobbed his head vigorously. "Those are excellent metaphors for what it feels like to have your memories return. I've never heard a patient describe the process quite like that, but it's very common for them to tell me their recollections are fuzzy, foggy or dreamlike."

"It's common?" Anna raised her eyebrows. "Then how do your patients know what really happened and what didn't?"

"As I've said before, it takes time for the brain to heal. I'd suggest you hold on to your recollections loosely for the time being, because things aren't always as they seem to be. Meanwhile, trust this," Dr. Donovan advised, placing his hand over his heart. "Not this," he added, pointing to his head.

Her mind eased, Anna gushed, "Thank you, Dr. Donovan! Thank you!" as his phone buzzed.

She closed the door behind her and stepped into the hall to find Naomi approaching. Eli was holding her hand and sucking on a lollipop. It occurred to Anna he looked healthier and more energetic than his *mamm* did. After Naomi confirmed the doctor said there was nothing wrong with Eli that two more days of a restricted diet wouldn't cure, they walked to the buggy.

By the time Anna steered them through an especially grueling rush hour traffic jam and up the lane to their house, it was six o'clock. Naomi said she had a blinding headache, so Anna advised her to lie down, even though by then her own head was beginning to pound. Figuring she was probably only peckish, Anna anticipated a good hot meal would revive her and she swiftly stabled the horse before entering the house, where it was clear Melinda hadn't started supper. When she found her cousin in the sitting room with her *kapp* askew and her arms draped around Aaron's neck, Anna clenched her teeth. Couldn't Melinda ever be counted on to perform the most basic tasks without being prompted? Anna's knees felt wobbly and she steadied herself against the doorframe.

"Are you alright, Anna?" Aaron asked and his voice was so sympathetic, for a moment he sounded just like Fletcher. But then he added, "You look as if you've been wrestling a greased pig."

"And she lost," Melinda added, crowing uproariously.

"I'm fine, *denki* for asking," Anna replied in her politest voice to show they hadn't ruffled her feathers. But suddenly, she changed her mind and said. "Actually, Melinda, *you're* the one who looks as if she's been wrestling a greased pig—and he's sitting right there beside you!"

Then she spun around, leaving them to stare at each other in shocked silence.

Fletcher was exhausted. It was nine o'clock and he wasn't nearly finished laying the customer's floor. As he headed for home, he mentally reviewed the dispute he'd had with Aaron earlier that afternoon.

"You know what Anna said about how worried their *mamm* gets when they arrive home later than expected," Aaron argued after announcing he was leaving work at four o'clock and taking Roy and Raymond with him.

"*Jah*, but I can't finish this project on my own. Why don't you just take Roy and leave Raymond here with me? I'll bring him home when we've finished."

"*Jah*," Raymond said. "I'll stay here."

"I can stay, too," Roy volunteered. "I need to learn all the steps of installing flooring. Since you said you arranged to pick up Melinda in town anyway, you can just ask her to relay the message to *Mamm* that we'll be late."

"See what you've done?" Aaron asked Fletcher. "You've trained the apprentice to think his preferences override the foreman's decision."

Fletcher saw the sense in what Raymond and Roy were suggesting and he appreciated their dedication.

But, from his recent heated interaction with Aaron, he also recognized his cousin probably felt his authority was being challenged, so Fletcher tried to show his support.

"They respect the fact that you're in charge," he said. "They were only trying to be helpful."

"If they want to be helpful, fine, they can be helpful, but it will have to be on a volunteer basis. They've been here for over eight hours already today and we've got a busy week in front of us. I can't pay them to stay after hours."

Fletcher again tried to reason with his cousin. "Look at that section there—it hasn't even been stapled yet. Then we've got to take care of the baseboards, the gaps, the puttying—"

"I know the order of layering a floor," Aaron jeered. "Listen, we tried our best to finish it today, but it just wasn't possible. If you feel obligated to keep working on it, that's up to you, but I've made my plans for the evening clear and I'm not changing them."

Fletcher was so frustrated he couldn't speak. He couldn't understand why Aaron didn't pride himself on his work ethic, the way virtually all Amish people did. Yet even as the thought entered his mind, he realized he was guilty of judging another person. Running his hand over his face, he silently prayed, *Dear* Gott, *please forgive me for judging my cousin and enable me to be a help, not a hindrance, to my* onkel*'s business.*

"Fletcher," Raymond suggested, "maybe you should take a break. *Kumme* have supper with us and then we'll all return to put in a few more hours—how's that?"

"Speak for yourself!" Aaron chortled.

"*Neh*, you go ahead," Fletcher told Raymond. "But let me give you a note for Anna."

After finding a scrap of paper, he removed the pencil he kept tucked behind his ear. *Dear Anna*, he wrote. *I hope you are feeling better. I have to work late tonight, but I will see you tomorrow. I haven't forgotten my promise.*

While he paused, deliberating whether to sign the note "your Fletcher," or just plain "Fletcher," Aaron ribbed him, "Hurry up, will you? I'm hungry!" So he simply signed the note "F."

Now, some five hours later, Fletcher decided he'd better let Aaron know he was unable to complete the project and they'd need to return in the early morning. He made a detour toward his uncle's house. There was still a lamp lit in the kitchen, so he gave a quick rap on the door before entering the house, where he found Isaiah sitting at the table, drinking something that appeared to be lemonade.

"It's apple cider vinegar, lemon juice, ginger, honey and everything else except the kitchen sink," his uncle joked, raising the mason jar. "It's supposed to help my arthritis. Want some?"

Fletcher laughed. "*Denki*, but I'll pass. I stopped by to talk to Aaron. Is he still up?"

"Up? He's not home yet," Isaiah said. "I'm waiting for him myself. Is there a message you want me to pass along to him?"

"Well…" Fletcher hesitated. He was concerned he might get Aaron in trouble with his father if Isaiah found out they hadn't completed a project before taking on a new one again.

Isaiah prompted him, "At this time of night, there must be a *gut* reason you came here."

"*Jah*, if you could tell him I'll be installing the floor early tomorrow morning, I'd appreciate it."

"Will do," Isaiah confirmed.

Fletcher was about to board his buggy when he heard the familiar plodding of a horse's hooves, so he waited until his cousin pulled into the yard and explained the situation to him.

Uncharacteristically amenable, Aaron said, "That's fine. I'll join you, if I can pull myself from bed that early. I didn't mean to stay out so late, but you know how it is when you're having fun—you lose track of time. You should have been there. After Anna made supper, we all played Dutch Blitz for hours."

"Anna doesn't like to play Dutch Blitz," Fletcher argued. "She says it makes her head swim."

"That goes to show how well you really know your fiancée," Aaron responded. "She not only suggested the game, she beat us all!"

How could that be? Fletcher wondered, long into the night. *She told me her preferences hadn't changed.* His old worry about what else she might feel differently about plagued his thoughts almost until the sun came up, and by then it was time for him to rise, too.

Chapter Nine

The next morning Anna got up early to fix a tray of coffee, eggs and toast for Naomi before making breakfast for the rest of the family.

"Are you awake, Naomi?" she asked as she slowly pushed open the door to her stepmother's room.

"Oh, *guder mariye*, Anna," Naomi replied, lifting her head from the pillow. "This looks *wunderbaar*, but I feel much better now. I can get up."

"Please don't," Anna pleaded. "I've already checked on Eli and he's sleeping peacefully, so I thought I'd sit here with you and drink my *kaffi* before the boys *kumme* in from milking. I stayed up too late last night."

Naomi held a forkful of eggs midair. "You weren't ill again, were you?"

"*Neh*, I played several games of Dutch Blitz with Melinda, Aaron and the boys. It was nearly nine o'clock when we stopped and then I had to do the dishes."

"But I thought you loathe playing Dutch Blitz?"

"I do…but I was trying to make peace with Melinda and Aaron. Lately I've made a few comments to them I wish I hadn't."

"Whatever you said, I have a hunch they deserved it."

"You wouldn't be saying that if you'd heard the remark I made to them yesterday," Anna hinted before detailing her exchange with them.

"Oh dear," was all Naomi said when Anna was finished.

"I told you it was bad!" Anna lamented. "What I need to do is apologize. Do you suppose I could make a special dinner tonight and invite Aaron, by way of smoothing things over?"

"But you've been ill—"

"I'm all better now," Anna asserted. "In fact, at the clinic yesterday I bumped into Dr. Donovan and we discussed what was ailing me and he said everything I'm experiencing is perfectly normal." Anna didn't clarify that what was ailing her was emotional, not physical.

"Really?" Naomi questioned. "I'm so glad to hear it! In that case, *jah*, we can serve a special dinner tonight. I was invited to Ruth Graber's for supper this evening, but I'll stay home to help you instead—"

"Neh!" Anna butted in. "You deserve a night out with your friends. Please go!"

Naomi hesitated before surrendering. "I'll go under one condition," she stated seriously, holding up her finger for effect. "Whatever you do, don't make ham or pork chops for dinner. Otherwise, Melinda and Aaron might question how sincere you are about apologizing for calling anyone's behavior piggish!"

They burst into laughter as the door swung open. It was Eli, declaring he was starving. While Naomi went to fix breakfast, Anna returned to her room to tell Melinda about the special supper, but her cousin had a pillow covering her head and was snoring softly.

Anna took out a notepad and wrote, *Dear Fletcher, I hope you will be able to come to supper tonight.* Without thinking twice, she signed it, *Your Anna.* Then, she scribbled an invitation to Aaron, too. *Aaron, you're invited to join us for supper tonight. —Anna.*

For their meal, Anna made beef stew and corn bread, with sugar cream pie for dessert, since it was Melinda's and Aaron's favorite treat. After Naomi had left for the evening and the four boys were finishing their evening chores in the stable, Anna approached Melinda and Aaron in the sitting room to apologize before Fletcher arrived.

"I want to apologize to you both for the remark I made the other day," she said, glad the room was dim so they couldn't see the heat rising in her cheeks. "I hope you'll forgive me."

Melinda stuck out her lower lip. "If you must know, I've grown accustomed to your surly disposition since the accident and I've learned to overlook it, but Aaron isn't used to your attitude. He was upset for a long part of the evening, weren't you, Aaron?"

Anna linked her fingers behind her back, squeezing them together as tightly as she could as a reminder to hold her tongue, even though she was thinking that Aaron wasn't so upset he couldn't play several games of cards.

"Jah," he admitted. "I never expected you to make such a churlish remark, Anna."

Please, Lord, she silently prayed, *give me grace.* "I understand how surprising that must have been for you," was as close as she could come to expressing further regret. "I assure you it won't happen again. Now *kumme,* supper is ready."

"Wait!" Aaron leaped to his feet, positioning himself directly in front of Anna and boring into her eyes with his. "I'm sorry, too. I could sense you were in pain or upset and I... I tried joking to make you laugh. I always used to be able to make you feel better, but lately, it's as if... I don't know, as if we're enemies or something."

Anna's feet seemed nailed to the floor and her mouth fell open. She hadn't heard Aaron sound so contrite since before Melinda came to live there. Perhaps she'd been judging him too harshly?

"We're not enemies at all," she said, smiling graciously to prove her point. "In fact, we're about to become family."

"Now there's the dimple I've missed seeing!" Aaron declared, taking a step closer.

"Am I too late?" Fletcher asked from behind Anna.

She twirled, eager to see his toothy grin once more, but she was met with a somber frown. *"Neh,"* she consoled him. "That's the *gut* thing about stew. It can simmer on the stove until we're ready to eat it, which we are! *Kumme."*

"Stew?" Aaron sounded pleased. "Did you make corn bread, too?"

"Jah," Anna replied distractedly, leading them to the table.

"I haven't had your stew and corn bread for ages," he commented. "No one makes it quite the way you do."

During their meal, Eli and Evan recounted the fiasco they'd witnessed that day in school when one of the oldest scholars got wedged between the rungs of the porch stairs during lunch hour and couldn't get free. Then, the men summarized their newest project at work, and afterward, Melinda described her activities assisting customers at the shop.

"It's always so busy there," she remarked to Anna. "I enjoy it, but sometimes I long for the days when I was home and I could have a cup of tea or take a little nap whenever I wanted."

"I'm sure you do," Anna replied, getting up to bring the pie to the table.

"Is that sugar cream pie?" Aaron asked. "My favorite!"

"It's one of Melinda's favorites, too," Anna said. "That's why I made it."

"Will we need forks to eat it or are you going to serve it in cups?" Aaron questioned.

For a split second Anna didn't understand what he was referring to, but then she exclaimed, "Oh! I almost forgot about that! The first time I invited Aaron over for Saturday night supper with *Daed* and Naomi, I made this pie—do you remember, Roy and Raymond? I was so nervous I forgot to put in cornstarch and I doubled the cream. No matter how much I beat it, the mixture wouldn't thicken, but I put it in the oven and hoped for the best."

"It was runnier than that gravy!" Ray chortled, pointing to Evan's half-eaten bowl of stew.

Anna giggled into her napkin. "*Jah*, but if I recall correctly, that didn't stop Aaron from eating his entire serving! He said he wanted a spoon so he could get every last drop."

"I was trying to make a *gut* impression on your *daed* and Naomi," he confessed.

"I have to give you credit for that, especially because

of the stomachache you endured for two days afterward," Anna said, catching her breath.

She remembered how her father's eyes had twinkled when he'd come home from work and confided to her and Naomi that Aaron spent the better part of the following Monday morning locked inside the men's washroom. Picturing her father's amusement as she conveyed the anecdote made Anna smile from ear to ear.

"You've become a much better cook since then," Aaron said through a mouthful of pie.

"Denki," Anna said. "At least, I haven't poisoned anyone lately, have I, Fletcher?"

She reached for his hand beneath the table but he pushed back his chair and dropped his napkin on his plate. "I need some fresh air," he said. "Eli and Evan, do you want to go turtle hunting down at the creek with me?"

The three of them were out the door before Anna had time to put the leftovers away.

Fletcher took such long strides the boys had to run to keep up. He could hear Anna calling him from a distance, but he didn't stop until Evan said, "Fletcher, I think Anna wants to *kumme,* too. We're supposed to wait whenever she calls us."

He stopped abruptly but didn't turn around to watch her approach. When he heard footsteps and the rustle of her skirt behind him, he resumed walking.

She instructed the boys, "I'm going to walk with Fletcher and I'd like the two of you to give us our privacy. You may run up ahead of us, but what's the rule at the creek?"

"We have to stay ten steps back from the edge unless an adult is present," they droned, before sprinting down the hill.

"Are you trying to stay ten steps away from *me*?" she breathlessly called to Fletcher, who slowed his pace slightly.

"Do you want me to?" he asked.

"Of course not! Why would I want that?"

Fletcher didn't mince words. "You seemed to be standing very close to Aaron when I came in. I thought perhaps your *preferences* had changed."

Anna grabbed his wrist, pulling him to a complete stop. Her brows formed a severe line across her forehead as she glowered at him. "Whatever are you talking about, Fletcher?"

"I'm talking about the fact you spent the evening playing cards with him yesterday. You sent him a personal invitation this morning. You were practically standing nose-to-nose with him when I walked in this evening. You made his favorite dessert for supper. And you spent the entire meal reliving your courtship. *That's* what I'm talking about!" he ranted.

Anna didn't so much drop his wrist as flung it at him before she wordlessly tromped down the hill.

"Is that your response?" Fletcher shouted after her. "You have nothing to say?"

Twirling around, she glared at him and shouted back, "Believe me, you wouldn't want to hear the things I might say if I didn't hold my tongue at this moment. Besides, I've lost sight of the boys and I need to make sure they're okay."

Although he was seething, Fletcher followed her at a distance, also concerned about the boys' safety. After cutting through the woods, he spotted them overturning rocks along the upper embankment. Anna was watching from her roost on the boulder. Fletcher picked up a handful of pebbles and tarried midway between Anna and the boys, aimlessly chucking the stones one by one into the water.

"I think if there are any turtles here, they've gone in for the night," Eli hollered.

"*Jah*, probably," Fletcher called back. "They like warm sunshine, not cool evening air. But the frogs might be out. See if you can sneak up on one of them."

While the boys dropped to their knees in the grass, Fletcher ambled over to where Anna was sitting and leaned against the far edge of the same boulder. Her profile was set like concrete as she gazed across the creek and spoke in a controlled monotone.

"The card game, the invitation, the special dinner—it was all because I referred to Aaron as a pig yesterday. I was trying to make amends. When you entered the parlor before dinner, I'd just finished apologizing. You can ask Melinda and Aaron if you don't believe me."

Feeling like a fool, Fletcher said, "That won't be necessary, Anna. I believe you."

"Really?" Her nostrils flared as she faced him. "Because I've told you repeatedly I don't have feelings for Aaron, yet you keep accusing me of—"

"It's not an accusation, Anna," Fletcher interrupted. His throat burned as he admitted, "It's… I don't know. I guess it's some kind of nagging concern on my part."

"But I keep telling you there's no reason for such concern."

Fletcher hesitated. He knew he was in dangerous territory but if he didn't voice his complaint now, it would resurface in his thoughts and affect his relationship with

Anna until he did. "But you really did seem to cherish recalling your courtship with Aaron tonight."

Anna threw her hands into the air and then slapped them against her lap. "What I cherished recalling was a happy memory of my *daed*, not of Aaron!"

Just then one of the boys let out a tremendous shriek. Anna and Fletcher sprang from the boulder and whipped around: the noise had come from behind them.

"He yanked my hand really, really hard!" Evan wailed, purple-faced and sobbing.

"He wouldn't *kumme* when I told him to," Eli tattled.

Anna crouched to examine the mark on the back of Evan's hand where Eli had grabbed it and then she lifted it to her lips and blew on it before giving his skin a kiss. "I know it hurts," she said. "But you'll survive. Why don't you go search that patch of grass over there to see what kinds of creatures you can find?"

Then she took Eli by the shoulders and looked into his eyes. "What has your *mamm* taught you about using your voice instead of your hands to express yourself?"

"But he was spying on you and Fletcher and you said you wanted privacy!" Eli blubbered. "Terrible things happen when you spy and I didn't want you to get hurt again!"

As Anna pulled the sobbing child to her chest and patted his back, she sent Fletcher a quizzical look and he shrugged in return, their own argument momentarily suspended. When Eli was quieted again, Anna took his hands in hers and asked, "What do you mean, you don't want me to get hurt again?"

Eli shook his head. "I can't tell you."

Anna lifted Eli's hands and gave them a small shake for emphasis. "I promise you, no matter what you say, you won't be punished for telling the truth. Do you know something about my accident? Is that what you meant about me getting hurt again?"

The boy nodded and a few more tears bounced off his round cheeks.

"Eli, it's very important you tell me."

Eli sucked his bottom lip in and out as he confessed, "I was spying on you and Aaron at the creek the night before your accident. People can get hurt when other people eavesdrop or repeat gossip, that's what *Mamm* and you always tell me, but I did it anyway and then the next day you got injured. I'm sorry, Anna. I'm really, really sorry."

Fletcher felt as if he'd been walloped in the abdomen with a fifty-pound sack of feed. The night before Anna's accident was a Monday; he remembered because he was personally extending wedding invitations to people outside their church, as was the Amish custom in their district. What were Anna and Aaron doing at the creek together?

"Shh, shh, shh," Anna shushed Eli, enfolding him in her arms. "You were very brave to tell me the truth, but I promise you, Eli, it wasn't your fault I hurt my head."

"Neh," Fletcher confirmed, peeling Eli out of Anna's grasp. "It wasn't your fault at all and this one time, it's okay to repeat what you heard when you were eavesdropping. So I want you to think hard, Eli. What were Anna and Aaron talking about at the creek?"

Anna straightened into a standing position. "Why are you asking him that? He's a *kind*. I'm sure he can't remember what two adults were talking about, much less understand the context—"

"Do you?" Fletcher was squatting on the balls of

his feet next to Eli as he stared into the child's eyes. "Do you remember what Anna and Aaron were talking about?"

"Neh." Eli shook his head. "I wasn't close enough to hear. I only saw them kissing and then *Mamm* called me home from up the hill."

The boy's reply staggered Fletcher and he landed on his backside, too stunned to speak or move.

"It's getting dark." Anna felt light-headed and her voice trembled. "Eli and Evan, I'd like you boys to go directly into the house and tell Melinda or Raymond or Roy that Anna said one of them is to draw a bath for you. Fletcher and I will follow you from a distance."

After the boys scurried into the woods, Anna extended her hand to Fletcher, but he pushed it out of his way. He stood up of his own volition and smacked the dirt from the back of his trousers before striding after the boys.

"Fletcher!" Anna called. Her legs felt as if they were made of pudding and she struggled to keep up. "I don't know what Eli thought he saw, but you can't possibly take it seriously. He's a *kind*. He doesn't know what he's talking about."

Fletcher pivoted and marched back toward her, his eyes ablaze. "You're right, Eli is a *kind*, so I can't trust his interpretation of events. And you have amnesia, so I can't trust yours, either, can I? However, there is *one* person who knows for certain what happened that Monday night and although I've never found him to be entirely reliable, this time I'll have to take him at his word!"

"Neh!" Anna pleaded, tugging on his arm. "You can't ask Aaron that."

"Why not, Anna? Because you don't want me to find out the truth—is that it?"

"Neh, because it's so false as to be *narrish!"* Anna negated the notion, referring to it as crazy. "Besides, you'll upset the *kinner* if you go tearing into the house like a rabid dog! Eli has been bearing the guilt of my accident for weeks. That's probably why he's had such terrible stomachaches. Do you want to upset him further? You know how that will affect Naomi! And what about Melinda? How will she feel if you accuse her fiancé of kissing me?"

Fletcher shook Anna's hand from his forearm. "She'll feel devastated, the same way I feel now—but it's better if she knows the truth before she marries Aaron."

Anna charged up ahead of Fletcher so she could angle to face him as he approached. "It doesn't have to be that way, Fletcher. You don't have to feel devastated and neither does Melinda. The only reason you feel that way is because you've already decided I'm guilty. You're not giving me the benefit of the doubt!"

"I've been giving you the benefit of the doubt since the moment I received the note from you, Anna. I've been hoping and praying and believing it didn't mean what I thought it meant. I convinced myself—*you* convinced me—that there had to be some kind of logical explanation. It had to be some kind of mistake," he sputtered.

For a moment Anna thought he was going to cry, but instead he stopped talking. When he spoke again, his volume was subdued. "I want to believe Eli is mistaken more than I've ever wanted anything in my life.

But until we talk to Aaron about it, I'll always have a doubt in my mind."

"Okay, fine," she conceded. "We'll talk to him—but outside, just the three of us. Not where the *kinner* or Melinda can hear."

When they got within sight of the house, they noticed Roy heading indoors with the milk pail, so they asked him to send Aaron outside to the barn. While they were waiting, Anna lifted her apron to wipe her face, and then smoothed the fabric back into place, unable to look Fletcher in the eye. A second later, she heard the house door slamming, followed by the patter of footfall.

"I have a direct question for you and I expect the absolute truth," Fletcher said frankly when Aaron stood before them near the side of the barn. "Did you and Anna kiss the day before her accident?"

Aaron jerked his head backward and then a bemused smirk snaked across his lips. "You remembered?" he asked Anna, and immediately Fletcher kicked the side of the barn so forcefully the cows inside lowed.

Overcome with disbelief, Anna closed her eyes until the spinning sensation stopped. By the time she opened them, Fletcher had left. Her fists clenched, she snarled at Aaron, "Get out of my way." When he stepped aside, she rushed across the yard to where Fletcher was unhitching his horse from the post.

"Perhaps the kiss didn't mean what you think it means," she said. She was nearly on her knees, pleading for him to consider other possibilities. "Things aren't always as they appear to be—"

"Stop!" Fletcher directed, holding up his hand. "Enough is enough! The kiss means exactly what I think it means and so does your note. I can accept the truth, but now it's time—it's *past* time—for you to admit it."

"And what truth is that?"

Fletcher glanced toward the back door of the house, waiting until Aaron went inside again. "You still love Aaron," he hissed.

Anna's mouth twisted as she cried openly. "But I don't. I'm telling you, Fletcher, I don't love him. May the Lord forgive me, but most of the time I don't even *like* him."

"The facts say otherwise."

"They aren't facts. They're perceptions. Erroneous perceptions," she sobbed. "I don't know how to explain what happened the day before my accident, but I do know what it feels like to be betrayed and I would never, ever do that to anyone, especially you."

"Perhaps not willingly, not consciously, but you don't know your own heart, Joyce."

The slip of his tongue wasn't lost on Anna. "I do, too, know my own heart. I know it far better than you do," she contradicted, "and my name is Anna, not Joyce."

"*Jah*, but you're sure acting a lot like she did."

Anna shook her head sadly, slowly backing away. She choked out the words, "I can't marry a man who doesn't trust me."

"And I can't marry a woman I can't trust," Fletcher retorted as he climbed into his buggy.

Clasping her hands over her mouth, Anna fled to the house. When she got inside, she sailed past the dirty dishes still on the table, avoided the sitting room where Aaron and the older boys were taking out the cards for a game of Dutch Blitz and ignored Melinda's request for assistance above the sound of sloshing water in the washroom. As far as Anna was concerned, the entire household could collapse around her. She was tired of helping them: at this moment, she was the one who needed help. In her bedroom, she threw herself to her knees beside her bed, but found she couldn't say a word to the Lord. Instead, she poured out her heart in the form of rasping sobs, knowing He'd understand.

It was a good thing the horse often traveled the route between Anna's house and his, because Fletcher was so angry he couldn't see straight, and the animal was guided more by habit than by Fletcher's hand. He hardly recalled stabling the horse and walking into the house, but once inside, he paced from room to room, attempting to make sense of the events that had just unfolded. No matter how desperately he tried to allow for the possibility that all was not lost, he kept circling back to the same conclusion: Anna loved Aaron. Or, at the very least, she felt conflicted enough to kiss him only one day after publicly announcing her engagement to Fletcher. In either case, the wedding was off. Their *marriage* was off. Their bond was broken.

Asking himself how this situation could possibly be happening again, he reflected on his early days with Anna. After what he'd been through with Joyce Beiler, he could scarcely believe it when God blessed him with the type of relationship he shared with Anna. She had been trusting, open, good-humored and gracious beyond measure. Until he met her, he hadn't really known what love was—and not just the love he had for her, but the love she reciprocated toward him. The connection they shared grew stronger every day until he was certain it wouldn't just endure throughout their lifetime; it would flourish. But he'd been wrong.

Raking his hand through his hair, he spotted his wedding suit carefully arranged on a hanger that was hooked to a peg on the wall of the parlor. He'd put it there the day after kissing Anna for the first time since her accident. It was meant to remind him to focus on the future. But now the suit's form seemed to mock how lifeless he felt internally and he lunged toward it, swiping it from the peg and hurling it to the floor, where it lay in a crumpled heap like the rest of his dreams.

He kicked it aside and smacked the heel of his hand against the outer wall of the alcove. Then he did the same with the opposite hand. The force of his blows left two cracked dents in the plasterboard, but he was so embittered he swung his foot, putting a third hole in the wall before dropping backward onto the sofa. The damaged wall looked like two eyes and a serious mouth staring disapprovingly at him, so he quickly jumped to his feet and stormed out of the house.

Unaware of where he was going, Fletcher only knew he couldn't sit still. He trekked long into the night, ruminating about what would come next. Unfortunately, he knew from experience that he and Anna would need to meet with the deacon before announcing publicly that they'd called the wedding off. As for the humiliation that would follow, he supposed some might think he'd be better equipped to handle it the second time around, since he knew what to expect. But instead, he felt doubly mortified. Not only would he have to bear the disgrace of his broken engagement in Willow Creek, but word would travel to Green Lake, where he imagined he'd become something of a laughingstock.

Sniggering bitterly, he realized he was running out of places to go to escape the humiliation of being jilted. Nevertheless, he'd have to find somewhere else to live and work. He'd finish up the project they were working on now and give Isaiah and Aaron time to find another crew member to replace him, but then he was going to move on. There was no way he could continue to work for his cousin: it was only by the grace of God he hadn't verbally unleashed his fury on Aaron back at the barn. He knew what the Bible said about forgiveness and anger, yet he also knew what it said about fleeing temptation. Given the option, Fletcher thought it was wise to make himself scarce as soon as possible.

As he ambled up the lane to his own yard again, he realized he'd probably have to forfeit the house to Aaron and Melinda. Or worse, to Aaron and Anna. Crossing the grass, Fletcher tried to convince himself that the tears in his eyes were due to spring allergies and he wiped his face with the back of his sleeve. Still too distraught to sleep, he took out his tools and supplies and began repairing the holes he'd made in the wall. By the time he was finished, the sun was just peeking over the horizon and he was finally exhausted. He laid down on his bed fully dressed and was asleep before he had a chance to remove his shoes.

He woke to a loud banging on the door. Although he had no idea what time it was, he guessed from the sunlight flooding the room that it was after ten or eleven o'clock. *That better not be Aaron coming to lecture me for being late to work*, he thought.

When he tugged open the door, he was surprised to see his uncle. Had Aaron told him about what happened the previous night? Was that why he was here?

"*Onkel* Isaiah, *kumme* in," Fletcher said. "I... I wasn't feeling my best last night so I decided to sleep in. I'm late for work."

"*Jah*, I can see that," he noted. "I'll put on a pot of *kaffi* while you wash up."

After shaving, Fletcher emerged from the washroom. His uncle was in the alcove, examining the built-in bookshelf and opening and closing the built-in drawers on the interior wall. Extending a mug to Fletcher, Isaiah made a sweeping motion with his hand and said, "This is the finest design and craftsmanship I've ever seen from someone your age—your *daed* trained you well. Anna must be delighted."

Fletcher swallowed. So, Aaron hadn't told his father about last evening's debacle after all. Then why was Isaiah calling on him? "She hasn't seen it yet," he replied. "It's supposed to be a surprise."

"How is she doing?" Isaiah inquired cordially.

"She's healing slowly but surely," Fletcher answered. Until Anna and Fletcher met with the deacon, he decided he'd keep the news of the breakup to himself.

"That's *gut*," Isaiah continued. "You've probably been under a lot of financial pressure, what with her injury and medical bills and the work of preparing the house for her to move into it, including making these renovations?"

Fletcher was puzzled by what his uncle was getting at. "*Jah*, I was," he answered without elaborating.

"That must be costly," Isaiah commented, appearing to read Fletcher's reaction.

Fletcher wondered if his uncle had come to discuss his wages. "I try to be a *gut* steward with my resources," he said. "*Gott* always provides."

Isaiah didn't seem to hear him. His uncle's posture was so stiff and his skin so ashen, Fletcher wondered if he was ill. But he reasoned Isaiah would have gone directly home from work if he was sick. Besides, how did his uncle even know he could find Fletcher here instead of at the job site? Had Aaron or Roy or Raymond told him?

Isaiah pulled at his beard, finally stating gravely, "There is no easy way to approach this subject, so I will be direct. I have been looking over our accounts and there are some discrepancies."

"Discrepancies?" Fletcher echoed, confused. "What kind of discrepancies?"

"We have an unexplained deficit of nearly two thousand dollars," his uncle explained.

Fletcher whistled. "That's a lot. Could there be a mistake?"

"I have repeatedly tried to reconcile it myself."

"I see. I'm very sorry to hear that and I'd like to help you, *Onkel*, but aside from using a measuring tape, math and numbers have never been strengths of mine."

"*Neh*, son, I don't want you to look over the account," Isaiah said, his ears purpling. "I—I want to know if you know anything about this matter."

Suddenly the real concern behind Isaiah's comments about medical bills and the expense of making renovations to the house came clear. Fletcher felt as if his uncle had clocked him over the head with a wrench.

"While it's true I've occasionally signed off on the company account—under Aaron's direction—or used the bank card to purchase supplies or withdraw cash for our work projects, I've always provided him the receipts," Fletcher declared. "I don't know anything about this matter."

His uncle took him by the shoulders and looked him in the eye. "I believe you, Fletcher, but it was only fair and right for me to ask. Now drink your *kaffi* and then make yourself some eggs. You look like you could use a little nourishment."

But after the door clicked shut behind Isaiah, Fletcher was too nauseated to eat. He hadn't thought it was possible to feel more betrayed than he'd felt when he confirmed Anna kissed Aaron, but once again, he was wrong. Having his own uncle accuse him of thievery was an indignity greater than he could bear. Setting his hat on his head, he decided then and there that he'd return to work alright—but only long enough to tell Aaron he quit. Then he was packing up his things and leaving immediately. He couldn't get away from Willow Creek fast enough.

Chapter Ten

After her *daed* died, Anna discovered one of the horrible truths about grieving: no matter how many tears she shed, her eyes never ran dry. It was as if her body had an unlimited capacity to mourn. She found this truth returning to her as she soaked her pillow with sadness the morning after her argument with Fletcher, just as she'd done the previous night.

There was a tap on the door and Anna sat up. Her eyelids were so swollen she practically had to pry them open with her fingertips, but since the shades were drawn she hoped her stepmother wouldn't notice she'd been crying. *"Guder mariye,"* she said as Naomi entered with a tray of tea, cheese and fruit.

"You mean *guder nammidaag*," Naomi replied. "How are you feeling?"

"Groggy, but otherwise alright. I'm sorry. I really overslept."

"Neh, I don't mean how are you feeling physically, Anna dear. Clearly something is troubling you and I'd like to help."

Anna was moved by Naomi's expression of compas-

sion. Knowing she could disclose even her deepest heart-
aches to her stepmother, Anna confided what transpired
the evening before and the decision she and Fletcher had
made. She managed to get through most of the details
without weeping, but when she started to sniff, Naomi
moved to wrap an arm around her shoulders.

When Anna finished speaking, Naomi exhaled heavily. "I'm disappointed," she said. "Very, very disappointed."

"I know, Naomi. You've put so much work into preparing the house and—"

"Neh!" She clarified, "I'm not disappointed for my
sake. I'm disappointed for yours. Quite frankly, I'm
disappointed in Fletcher. I thought he was more mature than that."

Anna was surprised to hear herself defending him.
"But, Naomi, as difficult as it is for me to believe it myself, there's very little question that I kissed Aaron. It's
no wonder Fletcher is upset."

"Upset, *jah*. But Fletcher knows your character, just
as I know your character, and I sense a piece of this
puzzle is still missing—especially because Aaron is
involved."

Anna took a napkin from the tray and blew her nose
with it. "It hardly matters anymore. Fletcher and I have
made up our minds. I suppose we'll have to talk to the
deacon before we tell the *leit* from church that the wedding is off. We'll want to notify our out-of-state guests
as soon as possible, too. I guess we'll call them from
the phone shanty, so they can cancel their travel plans.
But I don't know how or what I'm going to tell Melinda. I don't think she has any clue about what happened last night."

Naomi patted Anna's shoulder. "You shouldn't concern yourself with those matters right now. Melinda's wedding is still almost three weeks away. You needn't tell her anything right now. Today, you need all the rest you can get. Your head will be clearer tomorrow."

"*Jah*, since I don't have to keep up with my own wedding preparation schedule anymore, I'll take a leisurely walk down to the creek."

"That sounds like a *gut* idea," Naomi replied as she stood to leave. "It's a beautiful spring day. Just be careful not to slip on any rocks."

By the time Anna finished picking at the plate of food Naomi had brought her, got dressed and journeyed to the creek, she felt so fatigued she wished she were back in bed. Her lethargy was more emotional than physical: every thought she had was of her breakup with Fletcher. Closing her eyes, she reclined on the boulder and tried to concentrate on the warmth of the sun on her skin, the smell of damp earth and the sound of water cascading over the stones. But it was no use: she kept envisioning the shocked look on Fletcher's face when Eli announced he'd seen her and Aaron kissing.

Hearing a rustle coming from the direction of the park, she snapped her eyelids open and pushed herself upright. At first, she could only spy a dark head of hair through an opening of the trees and her breath quickened: it was Fletcher! But then the figure rounded the bend and she realized her mistake. The man's build was stocky and short, not lanky and tall.

"What are you doing here?" she demanded to know.

"*Guder nammidaag* to you, too," Aaron replied. "I've *kumme* to talk to you about what happened when we kissed. I wanted to tell you that you mustn't blame yourself."

Anna shielded her face with her hands to hide her humiliation. Her stomach was turning upside down and she wished Aaron would just vanish, but it sounded as if he was about to apologize and the least she could do was hear him out.

Instead, he patted her shoulder and said, "I know you can't remember it now, but initially you were taken in by Fletcher because you were grieving and he provided a shoulder to cry on."

Anna shook her head. "*Neh*, that's not true," she contradicted.

Aaron persisted, "When he offered to walk out with you, you accepted in order to get back at me for dating Melinda. I confess, I was only feigning interest in her to hasten you to marry me because you'd been putting off the decision for so long. The entire situation had gotten completely out of hand, like a prank that had gone too far. But by the time we came to our senses, you had already agreed to marry Fletcher and I had proposed to Melinda."

"*Neh*." She panted, rising from the rock and spinning to face him. "*Neh*, it wasn't like that. My relationship with Fletcher had nothing to do with you."

"You don't remember, but it did. You as much as told me so yourself, when we discussed the matter under this very tree the day before your accident, the day we kissed," Aaron murmured, inching closer. "You said the charade had gone on long enough. Even though I was conflicted about breaking Melinda's heart, you insisted that I tell her how I really felt. I have to believe that was because you wanted me back."

"Neh," Anna repeated, although some small part of what he was saying struck a chord deep in her memory. Her eyes began to spill and she swiped her cheek against her shoulder. "That's not right. It can't be."

"Jah, it is. But the next morning, you suffered your concussion and since then, you've never been able to recall what we discussed here, have you?"

"I've forgotten, but—"

"After a few weeks, it was clear to me your memory of our conversation would never return, even though I dropped as many hints about how we still felt about each other as I could. Since you were intent on marrying Fletcher, it seemed wrong for me to interfere, especially because Melinda and I had pressed forward with our own wedding plans."

Anna covered her ears to block out Aaron's words but he pulled her hands away and gripped them in his own.

"The other night, playing cards, we had such a *wunderbaar* evening together, like old times. You can't deny it," he insisted. "And now, Fletcher finally knows the truth… I think *Gott* may have brought us back together, Anna. I think it's time we acknowledge we've been His intended for each other all along."

"It was you, not Fletcher!" Anna squawked, suddenly understanding the memory she had of a man kissing her beneath the willow there at the creek. So *that* was why the feelings associated with it were so disturbing to her!

"Exactly, it was me you loved, not Fletcher," Aaron cooed, wrapping his arms around her trembling shoulders and whispering into her ear. "Now you've got it."

"Neh," she threatened. "Now *you're* going to get it if you don't let go of me this instant and get out of my sight."

Aaron stepped back and his mouth dropped open as if he was about to retort, but Anna screwed her face into the most menacing look she could muster and he left without uttering another syllable. Then, she picked up a stone and lobbed it into the current. *I knew I wouldn't have voluntarily kissed Aaron!* she thought. *I knew it!* But her discovery was of little satisfaction: even if she set the record straight by telling Fletcher what happened, he already admitted he didn't trust her. *If he really knew and loved me, he would have trusted me no matter what Aaron had said*, she thought.

She stumbled back to the boulder, where she lay covering her face with her hands and crying until her head began to ache, and she knew if she didn't stop she'd wind up in Dr. Donovan's office again. Squinting, she thought she saw something glinting overhead between the trunk and an arm of the willow. She circled the tree, craning her neck: there was definitely something up there. Like a flash of lightning, the phrase "squirrel it away in a secret place" occurred to her. That's what she'd told Fletcher she did with her journal!

She leaped up and grabbed hold of the bottom branch. However depleted she felt physically, she made up for it in sheer determination, hoisting herself over the limb in a burst of vigor. Once upright, she was an avid climber, ascending the branches as easily as a ladder. She wrenched the tin from its storage place and scampered back to the ground. Scraped raw, her fingers trembled as she pried the rusted tin open.

She removed the journal and pressed the cold leather to her cheek. Using the key from the string she'd worn around her neck ever since she'd learned the journal was missing, she could feel her heart thudding as she unclasped the lock and opened the diary to the first page. *This journal was given to me by Fletcher Chupp, what a heel*, it said.

Her tears were bittersweet as she ran up the hill to the house, clutching all that remained of her relationship with Fletcher to her heart.

When Fletcher arrived at the work site after lunch, he found Roy and Raymond working unsupervised. He didn't want them to hear what he had come to say to his cousin, so he planned to conduct his conversation outdoors. "Where's Aaron?" he asked.

"He was already here this morning when Melinda dropped us off," Roy reported. "But after he talked to her, he left again. It was too early for Melinda to go to the shop—the two of them probably sneaked off for *kaffi* and doughnuts somewhere."

Raymond rolled his eyes over Roy's head. "He also mentioned he had to run an errand," Raymond elaborated. "I wonder if he went with his *daed* to the lumber store to talk about the problem with the accounts."

"What do you know about the problem with the accounts?" Fletcher's ears perked up.

"Nothing," Raymond replied. "Only that Isaiah came here this morning and questioned Roy and me about a discrepancy."

"I told him I didn't know anything about it, either," Roy chimed in.

"We aren't even allowed to sign for anything," Raymond stated. "But Isaiah said as a matter of fairness he was asking each of us on the crew. He said he intended no offense, but he needed to check with us before making a major decision that would affect the responsible party."

"Jah," Roy agreed. "It sounds as if we may be taking our business to another lumber store soon. Either that, or Aaron's really going to get an earful. It all depends on whose fault it was, I guess."

Ach, Fletcher realized, *Onkel wasn't singling me out!* Fletcher was absolutely dumbfounded. He had completely misread the situation. He'd been so indignant about what he deemed was Isaiah's unwarranted insinuation that he'd been ready to quit his job and abandon his family on the spot over the offense. But come to find out, Fletcher was the one in the wrong: Isaiah didn't mean what Fletcher thought he meant. "Things aren't always as they appear to be," Anna said the night before and Fletcher had scoffed at her for it.

Isaiah's words, "I believe you, Fletcher, but it was only fair and right for me to ask," echoed in his mind. Isaiah simply asked the question and accepted Fletcher's response immediately, regardless of how incriminating his financial circumstances may have appeared.

But had Fletcher demonstrated the same level of trust in Anna, the woman he claimed to love? No. On the contrary, he'd badgered her with repeated inquiries and then dismissed her answers anyway. He'd as much as said she was ignorant, if not lying, about her deepest feelings. The realization of how he'd failed her caused his heart to spasm with a searing pain. He had to apologize. He had to beg her forgiveness and keep begging it until she accepted his apology.

"Are you alright?" Raymond asked.

"Neh, I'm not," Fletcher answered. "I have to leave immediately. If Aaron returns, tell him...tell him I'm not coming in for the rest of the day."

Before he could see Anna, there was a present

Fletcher wanted to buy, something he'd seen in the gift shop at the medical center in Highland Springs. He wasted no time journeying there, and when he arrived he hastily hitched the horse in the adjoining lot and hustled toward the building. He made his purchase inside and was about to exit when a familiar form breezed through the door.

"Fletcher!" Dr. Donovan's voice reverberated. "You're not here visiting anyone, are you?"

"*Neh.* Just taking care of a personal matter. Getting a gift for Anna, actually."

"Glad to hear it. After what the two of you have been through, I wouldn't want any more challenges coming your way before the big day." He thrust his arm forward to shake hands with Fletcher. "Congratulations, son—and give that bride of yours my best wishes, too."

"Thank you, I will," Fletcher said. *Provided she's still talking to me.*

Realizing he hadn't changed his clothes since the morning before, Fletcher stopped at home to put on a fresh shirt and pants before calling on Anna. He brushed his teeth and hair and was locking the door behind him when he noticed his uncle sitting on a bench on the porch.

"My knee aches—it must be going to rain tomorrow," Isaiah said by way of greeting.

Clearly his uncle had come back to discuss something more important than the weather, and Fletcher wished he'd let him know what it was because he needed to be on his way to Anna's house.

"I'm getting too old for the kind of work we do," Isaiah confided. "I'm definitely too old to have a son who behaves so irresponsibly. I had hoped by working with you every day, he'd pick up on some of your values and habits, but instead, he's only taken advantage of your scrupulous work ethic."

Fletcher couldn't deny the truth of what Isaiah was saying but neither did he think it prudent to confirm it, so he remained silent.

"What's more, he's made a mess of our orders and our accounts. His sloppiness nearly cost us our relationship with our supplier in the process. But I believe he can improve his abilities if he receives additional training under my tutelage," his uncle proposed. "I'd like him to work with me on our projects in the Highland Springs community."

Fletcher nodded, relieved that Isaiah seemed to have reconciled the deficit in the account. Although he imagined the demotion was disgruntling to his cousin, Fletcher marveled at Isaiah's forbearance toward Aaron. Anna's words, "People change. They grow. With *Gott*'s help, we all do," ran through Fletcher's mind as he realized his uncle still carried that kind of loving hope for his son. Fletcher prayed Anna would see Fletcher's own potential for change and growth, too.

Isaiah continued, "What this means, however, is I'll need a reliable, knowledgeable foreman to handle our *Englisch* clients and to supervise the crew. Raymond is too inexperienced to be a foreman, although he'll get a pay raise. Eventually Roy will, too, if he keeps progressing like he is… Anyway, what do you say? Will you accept the position of foreman?"

Denki, Lord, Fletcher prayed.

"The promotion would mean a raise for you, too, of course," Isaiah offered, prompting Fletcher to his senses.

"*Jah*, of course I will accept the position," he confirmed. "*Denki, Onkel* Isaiah, *denki!*"

"You're the one I should be thanking," Isaiah stated. "You're unfailingly dependable, just like your *daed* always was. But that doesn't mean you don't need a hand yourself. I've been worried about the emotional and financial burden you've been carrying ever since Anna's injury. I understand there were back taxes to pay on the house, too. If you need help, that's what family is for, Fletcher. Just ask."

Fletcher further understood that when his uncle was questioning him about his expenses, it wasn't because Isaiah was accusing him; it was because Isaiah was *concerned* about him.

"*Denki*, I will," Fletcher replied.

Before doddering down the steps, his uncle handed him an envelope. "This is from your *groossdaadi*. I don't know what it says, but he asked me to give it to you in the event your wedding was published in church this spring. Because of the chaos following Anna's accident, I'm sorry to say I forgot all about it until now."

Fletcher waited until he'd embarked his buggy to tear open the envelope. The note read:

To Fletcher J. Chupp,
If you are reading this, it means the lovely Anna Weaver has agreed to become your wife—an answer to my prayers. Although the two of you may have thought you were keeping your courtship a secret, nothing could have been more obvious to me than your mutual fondness, respect and loyalty. It was a delight to spend the last part of my life witnessing the kind of young love that re-

minded me of my own courtship with your grandmother so many years ago.

Although you both suffered painful betrayals,
I'm glad you've decided not to allow past hurts to
rob you of future hopes and present happiness. As
I've discovered this last year in particular, time
passes too quickly, so be sure to keep your heart
open to love.

May you, Anna and your family experience
God's grace and blessings in your new home.
From Elmer J. Chupp.

Fletcher folded the letter and tucked it beneath the
seat. Emboldened by its message, he flicked the reins,
working the horse into a rapid gallop. He didn't have a
minute to spare.

Anna could hear the distant clatter of pots and pans
as Melinda fixed dinner, and she was glad for once she
didn't have to participate in the meal preparation. As
soon as she returned from the creek, Anna had secured
Naomi's promise that her stepmother wouldn't allow
anyone to disturb her, and she sequestered herself in
her attic room, perusing her diary page by page.

As she read, she rediscovered many of the events
Fletcher had already described to her, but many more she
had no idea had ever happened. Whether she'd written
about a picnic by Wheeler's Pond, reuniting with Fletcher
after the tornado struck, or even a small argument over
what time they arranged to meet after church, one theme
consistently ran throughout the entries: she was in love.

Placing the open book on her stomach as she reclined
in bed, Anna realized she didn't need her journal to tell

her that. She knew she'd fallen in love with Fletcher all over again because breaking up with him didn't merely split her heart in two; it smashed it into a million bits. A few tears trickled down her temples before she picked up the journal and turned the page. A folded sheet of paper fell to her chest.

The entry in the journal where the letter was tucked was dated January 12 and it said, *Today Naomi gave me the enclosed letter, which she only just discovered hidden in Dad's Bible on his lamp stand. Although it's nearly a year old, I'm so glad to have received it now. I'll treasure it always.*

Unfolding the paper, Anna gasped at the sight of her father's lopsided penmanship. His letter was dated February 18 of the previous year.

My darling Daughter,
Tonight I stood at the bottom of the attic stairs, as I have every evening this week, listening to you weeping in your room where you thought no one could hear you. I am torn between wanting to comfort you and respecting your privacy (which you have always fiercely guarded, much to your brothers' chagrin!).

As difficult as it is to know you're suffering, I don't believe Aaron is the Lord's intended for you. He has his admirable qualities to be sure, but he lacks the sense of responsibility, selflessness and genuine kindness you deserve. If Aaron possessed those qualities, you would have married him long ago.

Instead, I believe you've continued to allow him to court you in an effort to model the char-

acteristics he ought to have developed by now. I
see you exhibiting the same gentle patience with
Melinda that you've always shown to Aaron. But
ultimately, such growth has to come from inside
them, through the grace of God, as it does for
all of us.

I wish I could take away your heartache, but I
trust God will use it for your good. It is my prayer
He will provide you a husband who brings you joy
instead of grief—perhaps even joy in the midst of
grief. When you meet a man like that, you can be
certain he is God's intended for you.

Your loving Father.

Anna's heart palpitated as she replaced the letter and
turned the page of her journal to the next entry, dated
January 19. It read: *Fletcher asked me to marry him
and I eagerly accepted. He was willing to wait until
wedding season next autumn, but I want to become
his wife as soon as possible, so we will take advantage of the bishop's special spring wedding provision
and marry on the first available date in April. Nothing
would make me more grateful than having him as my
husband by Easter.*

There it was, in black and white, the explanation
she'd been seeking for why she had been certain after
such a brief courtship that Fletcher was God's intended
for her. It was what her father wrote about finding a
man who brought her joy in the midst of grief that must
have helped her to be sure… *But it does me no gut now,*
she lamented.

She knew she could show Fletcher the journal. She
could flip to the last entry, as she'd already done and

insist that he read her words, dated Monday, March 2:

Tonight, Aaron told me he never loved Melinda—he was only courting her to try to make me jealous. Then he kissed me and I was so angry, I would have liked to push him into the creek, may the Lord forgive me! I pleaded with him to confess the charade to Melinda before the wedding preparations went any further, but he refused. I don't know what to do, except to tell Fletcher. He'll know how best to handle it.

But even if Fletcher saw the error in his thinking this time, Anna knew that at some point in the future, an issue or circumstance would arise in which Fletcher would doubt her and she would feel burdened to prove herself again. She meant what she said; she couldn't marry a man who didn't trust her, no matter how much she loved him. The tears flowed freely and she rolled onto her side and burrowed her face into her pillow.

She had nearly cried herself to sleep when she heard a tap at the window. At first she thought it must be the maple tree's branches blowing in the wind, but when suddenly it scraped the pane again, she wondered if it was a bird or a squirrel. She heard it scratch the glass a third time, louder now, as if it were deliberately trying to enter the house. She crossed the room and slid the window open, peering into the maple, which was leafy with new growth.

"Scat," she rebuked the concealed animal. "Go away. Get!"

"Anna, is that you?" a man's voice called softly.

"Who's there?" she questioned, although she realized it had to be Aaron. He hadn't been permitted to visit Melinda at suppertime, so he must have been sneaking to speak with her now.

"It's me, Fletcher," he answered.

"Fletcher?" She was completely bewildered. "What in the world are you doing up here?"

"I'm… I'm going out on a limb for you, Anna," Fletcher chuckled awkwardly. "I've *kumme* to apologize."

Anna laughed. In the midst of her grief, Fletcher was bringing her joy. "But you're afraid of heights," she said.

"Naomi wouldn't let me inside to see you," he explained. "But, uh, I would like to get down now. Would you *kumme* outside?"

"I'll be right there," she agreed. She was so glad to see him that she made it downstairs and outside quicker than he descended the tree's branches, but she stopped short of embracing him when he dropped to the ground. She needed to hear his apology first.

"Hello again, Anna," he said, wiping his hands on the sides of his trousers.

"Hello again, Fletcher," she replied. She started to suggest they go sit on the porch swing, but he gently placed a finger to her lips to silence her.

"Please, what I have to say can't wait another instant," Fletcher insisted. He dropped his hand and continued, "I don't know how to explain the note you sent me, or the kiss you and Aaron shared—"

"But I do," Anna interrupted. "It's all in my journal and I can show—"

"*Neh!*" Fletcher declared urgently. His eyes brimmed and his voice quavered as he explained, "What I wanted to say was I don't know how to explain those things, but I don't have to explain them, because I know *you*. You've always been truthful and trustworthy about your thoughts and feelings, and having amnesia doesn't change that. So when you told me those things didn't mean what I thought they meant, I should have believed you the first time. The fact that I doubted you is a reflection of my character, not yours. My lack of trust— my insecurity—is a weakness I hope *Gott* will change and you will forgive, because I'm very, very sorry."

Upon her hearing the depth of Fletcher's remorse and the intensity of his belief in her trustworthiness, Anna's wounded feelings evaporated and she was consumed by the yearning to be reconciled with him. She hurtled herself into his arms with such force she nearly knocked him over. "Of course I forgive you!" she exclaimed.

After they'd nearly hugged the breath right out of each other, Anna dropped her arms and said, "I need to ask you to forgive me, too. Your suspicion that Aaron still had feelings for me was correct. But because I didn't reciprocate even an ounce of that affection, I was completely blind to his behaviors and I dismissed your concerns. I'm sorry. Perhaps if I had been more aware—"

"I'm not eavesdropping," Evan announced loudly from where he stood by the side of the house. "*Mamm* sent me out here to see if you want any supper before they put the leftovers away, Anna."

Anna laughed. "*Jah*, please. I'll be in in a few minutes and Fletcher would like to join me, as well."

"Alright, if you want to," the boy said to Fletcher, ruefully shaking his head. "But Melinda made ground beef and cabbage skillet and it tastes even worse than it smells. Eli called it ground beef and *skunk cabbage* skillet!"

"Evan!" Anna scolded, but the child had already darted off.

"Are you sure it's okay if I *kumme* in for supper?" Fletcher asked. "Naomi didn't seem too happy to see me earlier."

"She'll be delighted now," Anna insisted. "So will Evan and Eli, since it will mean fewer of Melinda's leftovers for them tomorrow!"

Oh, how Fletcher had missed this kind of easygoing repartee the past few days. "Okay, but just don't tell Naomi I climbed the tree outside your window. She'll lecture me to no end."

"Well, I can't blame her for that—you could have slipped and gotten a concussion," Anna joked. "And I would have been devastated if you didn't remember me."

No sooner had she spoken the words than she clapped her hand over her mouth.

"That's how I injured myself!" she exclaimed. "I fell as I was letting myself down from the tree."

"You climbed the maple tree, too?" Fletcher wondered.

"*Neh*, the willow," Anna expounded. "I was letting myself down from the last branch, but my feet couldn't quite touch the ground. When I released my grip, I sort of floundered and then toppled backward. I remember bouncing onto my backside and thinking 'that wasn't so bad,' and then total darkness."

"You must have hit your head on a rock as you tumbled. But why were you climbing the tree in the first place? You weren't hiding, were you?"

"*Neh*, I wasn't hiding. Rather, I wasn't hiding myself. I was hiding my journal, which contained a terrible secret. You see, the day after our wedding intentions were published, Aaron came to me at the creek and confessed he never really loved Melinda. He'd only been trying to make me jealous, which didn't work, of course. I captured it all in my journal, even the part where he kissed me…" Anna shivered, making an awful face.

Fletcher felt his jaw harden and his temples pulsate, but he silently prayed, *Forgive us our trespasses as we forgive those who trespass against us.* If Anna could forgive Aaron for kissing her, he could, too.

She continued, "So actually, you were partially right when you thought the 'A.' in my note referred to Aaron. I did have serious concerns about him I needed to discuss with you before the wedding preparations went any further. But the wedding preparations I was referring to were Aaron and Melinda's, not ours!"

"Oh, Anna, I'm so sorry," Fletcher said.

"You've already apologized, Fletcher, and it's understandable why you might have thought what you thought, at least initially, so please say no more," Anna replied. "The important thing now is that Melinda needs to know the truth."

"*Jah,* but Aaron is the one who needs to tell her, not us. I'll have a word with him. Something tells me he won't want to risk getting in any more hot water with his *daed.* He'll own up, don't worry. Meanwhile—" Fletcher bent to retrieve the gift bag from where he'd left it propped against the tree "—this is for you."

"*Denki,*" Anna said. She gingerly removed the colorful bouquet of tissue paper to retrieve the bag's contents: a leather-bound journal with a silver lock on the side and a willow tree embossed on the front cover. "It's beautiful!"

"But now that you've found yours, I guess you don't really need a second one."

"But I do!" she protested. "My old journal is nearly full. I can use this to record the next chapter of our lives together."

Fletcher lightly ran his knuckle beneath Anna's chin, tilting her face toward his. "I just hope the next chapter isn't as rocky as the past few weeks have been."

"Oh, but all *gut* love stories have a few rocky patches. That's how they get their beauty," Anna said. "I wouldn't change our story for anything in the world."

"Neither would I," Fletcher agreed as he searched her eyes. They had never appeared so dazzling.

"What is it?" she asked. "Why are you staring at me that way?"

"I haven't seen that look in your eyes for a long, long time," he whispered.

"It's a look of recognition," she whispered back, causing his heart to throb. "I know who you are. No matter what I may remember or forget about the past, I know who you are."

"Who am I?" he asked playfully.

"You're Fletcher Josiah Chupp—*Gott*'s intended for me."

"And you, Anna Catherine Weaver, are *Gott*'s intended for me," Fletcher pledged, pressing his forehead to hers.

"I love you," she murmured.

"And I love you," he echoed.

He could have stayed like that for hours, but when a breeze rustled the leaves overhead, Anna backed away. She smiled, revealing her dimple, and then linked her fingers with his. "*Kumme*, let's go inside. I can't wait to tell Naomi her faithful prayers have been answered!"

Epilogue

Anna expected tears or even an outburst from Melinda the evening Aaron called off their wedding, but instead, the young woman almost seemed relieved.

"I enjoy working in the shop more than anything I've ever done," she told Anna, taking off her prayer *kapp* in preparation for bed. "But I'd have to quit working if I had a *bobbel* after I got married. Besides, once you move out, I'll have this entire room to myself. It will be a little bit like having a home of my own, without all of the work of a house."

"But aren't you sad about...about Aaron?" Anna carefully inquired.

"Why should I be sad? It's not his fault his salary was cut because he's no longer the foreman. His *daed* needs his personal help with their Highland Springs customers—it would be selfish of me to put marrying and building a costly house for me above his obligation to his *daed*." Melinda lowered her voice as if to reveal a great secret. "Isaiah's getting older, you know. He has *arthritis*."

"That's why Aaron told you he wanted to call off the

wedding?" Anna asked, thoroughly astounded by his ability to concoct a tale that actually bore some semblance, however slight, to the truth. She found herself wondering if he ever truly intended to be so disingenuous, or if he simply was so optimistically self-deceived he didn't realize how distorted his perspective was. No matter: as Fletcher reminded her, it wasn't her place to set Aaron's record straight.

"Jah," Melinda said as she ran a brush through her hair. "I told him I understood, but that I didn't know if I wanted to continue to walk out with him."

"Really?" Anna's eyebrows shot up.

"Jah." She leaned forward and whispered. "Don't tell anyone I said this, but I heard that Joseph Schrock's nephew Jesse is coming to visit for the summer. He's about my age and by all counts, he's supposedly very charming."

Even after a year of living with Melinda, Anna still never knew what was going to come out of the young woman's mouth next, but she supposed in this instance, it was a good thing Melinda had such a fickle attention span: it seemed to have saved her from a world of hurt.

Anna slid her feet under her quilt. Soon, it would be too warm for such a heavy bed covering. "By the way, have you seen the fabric for my dress?" she asked. "I left it in the other side of the attic but it's missing and there's only about a week and a half until the wedding."

"Neh. But I thought you were supposed to be cured of amnesia." Melinda yawned.

"I *am* cured. Mostly, anyway. But there's a difference between the fabric being missing and forgetting where I put it. I'm telling you, it's not where I left it!"

"What's not where you left it?" Naomi asked. She'd

crept up the stairs without Anna hearing her and she was standing in the doorway with her arms behind her back.

"My wedding dress fabric. I can't find it and I hardly have any time to sew my dress."

"That's because you spent too much time working on Melinda's dress, even though Dr. Donovan warned you to restrict your sewing activities."

Anna felt her face go warm as Melinda giggled. "I think that's the first time I've ever heard Naomi scold you, Anna!"

Anna playfully tossed a pillow at her cousin. "At least I'm being scolded for doing too much work instead of too little," she responded.

"Now, girls, do I have to separate you two?" Naomi teased, joining their laughter. She entered the room, displaying a deep green dress across one arm, and a dark purple dress on the other. "One for you, one for me, and Melinda's dress makes three."

Melinda and Anna both jumped out of their beds. Melinda darted to the closet while Anna approached Naomi and accepted her dress.

Holding it to her shoulders so it draped along the front of her figure, she looked down admiringly and said, "Oh, *denki*, Naomi. It's beautiful. Look—I can't even see the stitches they're so tiny!"

"Let's try them on, all three of us at once!" Melinda cried, sliding her own dress off its hanger.

"Melinda, you know that vanity is sinful," Naomi chastised.

"*Jah*, but we need to make sure they fit," Anna wheedled. "Please?"

"Not you, too, Anna!" Naomi clucked before agree-

ing it made sense that they should be certain no alterations were needed.

As soon as Melinda had changed, she twirled in a
circle and asked her aunt, "What do you think?"

"It's a perfect fit," Naomi said carefully. "Anna did
a very nice job sewing it for you."

Melinda's shoulders slumped and her lip jutted out.
"But what do you think of how I look?"

Naomi blinked rapidly and wiped away a tear. "I
think you look more and more like your lovely *mamm*—
my sister—each day."

Melinda pranced to the mirror to view her reflection
and Naomi turned toward Anna. In the soft glow of the
lamp's light, Naomi appeared youthful and elegant, the
lines of worry seemingly erased from her skin.

"I knew that color would be striking on you," Anna
whispered. "I wish *Daed* could see you now."

"I wish he could see *you*," Naomi responded. "But
when Fletcher gets a glimpse, you're going to set his
heart aflutter!"

Anna threw her arms around Naomi, half crying,
half laughing. "*Denki*, Naomi. *Denki* for sewing my
dress and for your encouragement and for your prayers.
Denki for everything!"

"There, there, we don't want to wrinkle our dresses,"
Naomi said, but instead of letting go, she squeezed
Anna even tighter.

The wedding ceremony was everything Fletcher
prayed it would be: he'd never been as certain of anything as he was when he answered "yes" to the bishop's
four traditional wedding questions, especially the one
about whether Fletcher was confident that the Lord had

provided Anna as a marriage partner for him. Anna's voice rang out with an equally clear affirmation when the same question was posed to her about Fletcher.

The dinner following the three-hour sermon was especially bountiful, thanks to Naomi and also to his aunt and cousins, who generously shared their supply of celery for the traditional Amish wedding dishes, as well as other ingredients and foods they'd already begun preparing for Aaron's wedding. Tessa and Katie Fisher spent several days baking an excess of pies, cookies and other goodies. And, despite the short notice, Faith Yoder managed to deliver the most unusual wedding cake she said any bride—including Melinda—had ever requested: turtle cake.

To her credit, Melinda was a huge help on the day of the wedding. After the ceremony, she was in high spirits, flitting about the house in her violet dress and engaging the guests in conversation as if she were the bride herself. Although Aaron appeared forlorn at first, Fletcher later noticed him laughing with the young Emma Lamp in the parlor. As afternoon gave way to evening, Naomi and his aunt and cousins spread the tables with supper and more desserts, and the last local guests stayed until after ten o'clock.

Shortly after that, Fletcher readied his own buggy while Anna was inside saying her final goodbyes to Naomi and the rest of the overnight visitors. He'd just provided his faithful horse a carrot when the door swung open and his three sisters, Esther, Leah and Rebekah, emerged.

"You look disappointed. You must have been expecting Anna instead of us," Leah needled him. "She'll be right out."

"Are you getting impatient?" Esther asked.

"Neh," he answered. "I'll wait for Anna as long as it takes."

"Spoken like a man in love," Rebekah noted. "But you don't have to wait any longer, here *kummes* your bride now."

As Anna stepped outside, the light from the kitchen illuminated her silhouette. Although it was too dark to see her face, he could hear the smile in her voice when she said, *"Gut nacht,* everyone, and *denki.* See you tomorrow."

"Are you certain you don't want to spend the night at Naomi's house?" Fletcher asked when she was seated beside him. That was the customary Amish expectation of the bride and groom, because it enabled them to assist with the cleanup first thing in the morning.

"Just this once, I think we ought to do something irresponsible," Anna answered. Then she corrected herself. "Well, not irresponsible, since we'll *kumme* back to help bright and early, but something—"

"Out of character?" he asked.

"Jah. Besides, the house is bursting at the seams with out-of-state guests."

"That's true," Fletcher said. His pulse pounded louder and louder in his ears the closer they got to home. He couldn't wait to show Anna the alcove he'd created for her.

But when he brought the horse to a halt, she said, "Wait, before we step down, I have a gift for you. There wasn't really any way I could wrap it, so you have to take a look at it now. It's in the back seat, under the tarp."

"When did you have a chance to sneak a present back there?"

"I didn't," Anna replied, giggling. "Your *newehockers*, Chandler and Gabriel, put it in the buggy for me while I distracted you. Go ahead—see what it is."

Using the flashlight he kept secured to a hook in the front of his buggy to supply him with light, Fletcher twisted in the seat and lifted the tarp.

"A fishing rod!" he exclaimed. "*Denki*, Anna, it's a really nice one."

"Roy and Raymond told me that yours snapped the other day and I know how you enjoy fishing," she said. "You should be able to bring in a *gut* catch down at the creek using that rod."

"*Denki*," Fletcher repeated. "But *you're* my best catch, Anna."

Her laughter made light work of stabling the horse and soon Fletcher was accompanying her to the house. He kissed her once on the cheek before he unlocked the kitchen door and led her down the hall in the dark.

Before illuminating the room in the alcove, he confessed, "I realize I said I didn't want either of us to feel as if we were hiding anything from each other, but there is one thing I admit I've been keeping a secret."

After Fletcher turned up the gas lamp, Anna blinked several times. Rendered completely speechless, she ran her hands over the shelves and opened each of the drawers before perching on the window seat.

"Fletcher, I don't know what to say," she cried. "I can't believe how beautiful this room is."

"I made it exclusively for you," he said. "So you'll have the space and privacy you need to read or write. There is one condition, however."

"Anything," she said.

"You can't use the room to write, *Fletcher Chupp, what a heel*, in your diary," he said softly into her ear.

"I accept the terms of the agreement," she pledged.

"Not *gut* enough," he replied. "You have to seal your promise with a kiss."

Leaning in, he gave her a firm, meaningful kiss. When he pulled away, he stared into her eyes, which were exquisitely enhanced by the green tint of her dress.

Suddenly, Anna clapped her hands against her cheeks as her eyes widened and her mouth dropped open. "Oh *neh*!" she exclaimed.

"What is it?"

"I think I may be suffering a relapse of amnesia. I can't recall what happened just now between us."

Fletcher threw back his head to laugh. "Don't worry," he consoled her. "I know how to jog your memory."

"With sage tea?" she flirted.

"Neh," he answered. "With this."

He feathered his lips across hers once, twice, three times before asking, "Is what happened coming back to you now?"

"Not quite," she teased. "It's still a bit hazy. But that's alright. As Dr. Donovan said, you and I have a lifetime to make memories together…"

Fletcher chuckled and wrapped his arms around her. A warm breeze wafted through the window: spring was definitely here, a season of hope, a season of renewal, a season of love. He and Anna were married at last.

* * * * *

Get 4 FREE REWARDS!

We'll send you 2 FREE Books plus 2 FREE Mystery Gifts.

FREE
Value Over
$20

Both the **Harlequin® Special Edition** and **Harlequin® Heartwarming™** series feature compelling novels filled with stories of love and strength where the bonds of friendship, family and community unite.

YES! Please send me 2 FREE novels from the Harlequin Special Edition or Harlequin Heartwarming series and my 2 FREE gifts (gifts are worth about $10 retail). After receiving them, if I don't wish to receive any more books, I can return the shipping statement marked "cancel." If I don't cancel, I will receive 6 brand-new Harlequin Special Edition books every month and be billed just $5.49 each in the U.S. or $6.24 each in Canada, a savings of at least 12% off the cover price, or 4 brand-new Harlequin Heartwarming Larger-Print books every month and be billed just $6.24 each in the U.S. or $6.74 each in Canada, a savings of at least 19% off the cover price. It's quite a bargain! Shipping and handling is just 50¢ per book in the U.S. and $1.25 per book in Canada.* I understand that accepting the 2 free books and gifts places me under no obligation to buy anything. I can always return a shipment and cancel at any time by calling the number below. The free books and gifts are mine to keep no matter what I decide.

Choose one: ☐ **Harlequin Special Edition**   ☐ **Harlequin Heartwarming**
(235/335 HDN GRJV)   **Larger-Print**
(161/361 HDN GRJV)

Name (please print)

Address   Apt. #

City   State/Province   Zip/Postal Code

Email: Please check this box ☐ if you would like to receive newsletters and promotional emails from Harlequin Enterprises ULC and its affiliates. You can unsubscribe anytime.

Mail to the **Harlequin Reader Service:**
IN U.S.A.: P.O. Box 1341, Buffalo, NY 14240-8531
IN CANADA: P.O. Box 603, Fort Erie, Ontario L2A 5X3

Want to try 2 free books from another series! Call 1-800-873-8635 or visit www.ReaderService.com.

HSEHW22R3

HARLEQUIN
PLUS

Try the best multimedia subscription service for romance readers like you!

Read, Watch and Play.

Experience the easiest way to get the romance content you crave.

Start your **FREE TRIAL** at
<u>www.harlequinplus.com/freetrial</u>.